9

A Kiss in the Dark

This Large Print Book carries the
Seal of Approval of N.A.V.H.

A Kiss in the Dark

Meryl Sawyer

G.K. Hall & Co.
Thorndike, Maine

Published in 1995 by arrangement with Dell Publishing,
a division of Bantam Doubleday Dell Publishing Group, Inc.

G.K. Hall Large Print Romance Collection.

The text of this Large Print edition is unabridged.
Other aspects of the book may vary from the original edition.

Set in 16 pt. News Plantin by Juanita Macdonald.

Printed in the United States on permanent paper.

Library of Congress Cataloging in Publication Data

Sawyer, Meryl.
    A kiss in the dark / Meryl Sawyer.
      p.   cm.
    ISBN 0-7838-1371-6 (lg. print : hc)
    1. Large type books.   I. Title.
  [PS3569.A866K57 1995]
  813'.54—dc20
                                       95-10841

This book is dedicated to the memory of Judge Rand Schrader, who fought for everyone's rights no matter what the personal cost. And never far from my mind, and always in my heart, are the happy memories Al Singerman gave to all of us who were lucky enough to call him our friend.

The best way to love anything
is as if it might be lost.

G. K. CHESTERTON

CONTENTS

I

Bad Moon Rising

1

The too-real nightmare that soon became Royce Anne Winston's life began very simply, very innocently. With a kiss in the dark.

A forbidden, erotic kiss.

A kiss that changed her life. Forever. It brought her love, the kind of love she'd only dreamed existed. And danger.

But the chain of events set in motion by that passionate kiss didn't become apparent to Royce for a long time. Even when the cell door clanged shut, she didn't suspect a kiss in the dark would result in her arrest for murder.

Now looking back, she saw how naive she'd been not to realize someone she trusted had diabolically set out to deceive her. . . .

"I hope they haven't sat down to dinner," Royce said as her fiancé, Brent Farenholt, escorted her up the steps of the San Francisco mansion on the evening of the fateful party.

"I'll tell my parents we couldn't keep our hands off each other."

"Oh, sure. You'll come up with some excuse,

though. You always do." Royce told herself she didn't give a hoot what Brent's parents thought. Not quite true. Within the year they'd be her in-laws. Try to get along with them.

Dance music drifted out of the French doors, filling the spring air with the sounds of a live band. One more party where the hostess tries to outdo her friends, Royce thought, already dreading the night ahead. What she wouldn't give to spend a quiet evening alone with Brent. Instead she braced herself for another encounter with San Francisco's elite.

Most of them called the city home but actually lived here only a few months a year. The rest of the time they spent at country estates or villas in the South of France. Royce found many of them, especially Brent's parents, to be arrogant. Insulated by their money, they knew no life beyond their closed circle of friends. The real world simply did not exist.

Inside, the foyer's black-and-white, diamond-patterned floor gleamed in the soft light of the chandelier overhead. Royce and Brent greeted Eleanor and Ward Farenholt, then Brent fed his parents some line about the traffic making them so late. Royce doubted he'd fooled the Farenholts.

Being late was merely a symptom of a much greater problem, one she'd diagnosed as terminal Royce Anne Winston. The Farenholts were never going to forgive her for stealing their only son from Miss Perfect — Caroline Rambeau of the

Napa Valley winery Rambeaus, the San Francisco society Rambeaus, their best friends, the Rambeaus.

"Royce, over here," called Talia, one of Royce's closest friends.

She left Brent with his parents. "Wow! Talia, you look terrific."

Beneath bangs the color of bittersweet chocolate, Talia rolled her dark eyes and swayed her slim hips from side to side, fluttering the tiers of her black silk dress. "Not as good as you. If I could wear a strapless sheath like that, Brent would have proposed to me."

"You don't think it's too low cut?"

"There won't be a man here tonight who won't remember you."

The midnight-blue gown accentuated Royce's blond hair and contrasted with her green eyes, making them appear even greener, but the gown was very revealing. She peeked at the prim cocktail dress Eleanor Farenholt wore. One more black mark against Royce. This one she might actually deserve.

What had Daddy always said? *Royce, you're a bit of a Gypsy — all those vibrant prints and bright colors.* She refused to wear black even though Eleanor Farenholt insisted it was the "only color" for evening. Black made Royce feel like one of the herd. And black reminded Royce of funerals — first her mother's, then her father's.

"Don't worry about your dress," Talia assured her. "Everyone adores you. They all read your

13

column. Just be your usual witty self. To hell with the Farenholts."

"Right. To hell with them."

Talia pointed to the small evening bag that fit neatly into the palm of Royce's hand. The bag was a cat of glittering crystal stones — except for the eyes, which were brilliant green. "Where'd you get the money for a Judith Leiber bag?"

"Brent insisted on buying it for me."

"He's going to spoil you rotten."

"I'm loving every minute of it. This bag is very impractical, though. All I can get inside is a lipstick and my keys." She leaned closer and whispered. "Carrying such an expensive purse makes me feel guilty. This would have cost my father a week's salary. Will I ever get used to all Brent's money?" She shook her head, her hair fluttering across her bare shoulders, then she studied Talia, realizing her friend looked distracted. "Are you all right?"

"Fine. I haven't touched a thing. I promise."

Royce slipped her arm around Talia and gave her an affectionate hug. "If you need me — anytime, day or night — call."

"You've been terrific, but don't worry about me." Talia smoothed back her long hair, hooking one dark strand behind her ear. "There's good news and bad news. Which do you want to hear first?"

This was a game she'd played with Talia for years, so Royce answered the way she always did. "The good, then the bad."

14

"You're not sitting with Brent."

"Why on earth not?"

"This hostess throws dinner dances so her friends can meet interesting people — musicians and actors and artists — colorful types who normally wouldn't be included in these circles. Who knows? If you and Brent weren't engaged, she might have invited you anyway — for color."

Suspicious, Royce remembered the hostess was one of Eleanor Farenholt's "oldest and darlingest friends." Was that why she'd been seated elsewhere? "Where *is* Brent sitting?"

"Don't lose your temper, but he's sitting with his parents . . . and Caroline."

"Brent and I picked out a diamond today," Royce said, bridled anger underscoring each word. "The ring will be ready next week. Why's his ex-girlfriend with him?"

"It's a last-ditch effort. Brent and Caroline were practically born in the same crib, that's how close the families are, but he didn't marry her, did he? No. He meets you and three months later you're engaged."

"True, so why does this upset me so much?"

"Because if your parents were alive, they'd disapprove of you marrying a Farenholt."

"You're right," Royce conceded. Her parents had been liberal and literary with lots of "colorful" friends, not arch-conservatives who never ventured beyond their clique and had voted the party line since dirt was brown. "But Papa would have liked Brent. He's nothing like his parents."

"Just be cool. Ignore the Farenholts' pettiness."

"Okay," she said reluctantly, "but they are beginning to get to me. I'm having second thoughts about my relationship with Brent." She sighed, struggling to convince herself the Farenholts would learn to accept her. "Don't tell me that not sitting with Brent is the *good* news."

"Part of it. You're at the Dillinghams' table."

"All right!" Arnold Dillingham owned a local cable television station. Royce was one of two women vying for the hostess position on the *San Francisco Affairs* program. Her first trial show was next Friday night, with the second scheduled the following week.

The downward sweep of Talia's lashes hid her dark eyes, and Royce knew she wasn't going to like this. Talia always faltered before saying something upsetting. "Now for the bad news. Tonight your favorite attorney is seated beside you."

"Obviously not Brent; then someone else in the Farenholt firm."

"No. Mitchell 'I'll Defend You to Your Last Dollar' Durant."

"Sweet Jesus, not that bastard."

"I know how much you hate Mitch, but for once, don't be a hothead."

Every muscle in Royce's body tensed. Mitch Durant. The Farenholts detested him — at least they agreed on something — so why was he seated beside her? They had to be responsible for this fiasco.

"While you were living in Rome, Mitch Durant

16

defended the Dillinghams' grandson on a drunk-driving charge and got him off with community service. Arnold Dillingham thinks Mitchell Durant hung the moon. Don't ruin your chances of becoming the *San Francisco Affairs* hostess by attacking Mitch in front of Dillingham. Be polite even if it kills you."

"Shouldn't I say that if it hadn't been for Mitch Durant in his days as a hotshot in the district attorney's office, my father would still be alive? Shouldn't I?"

"No. Only a few of us make the connection between Mitch Durant and your father's death. If you attack Mitch the way you did at your father's funeral, your career as a television personality is *kaput — fini — over —* before it starts."

A wellspring of grief swept through Royce. *Papa, dear Papa. You won't be here to walk me down the aisle.* This was such a happy time in her life, a time to share with the one person who'd loved her the most — her father. But he was dead. In the ground five long, lonely years now. Thanks to Mitchell Durant.

"You're right," Royce conceded, inwardly cursing Mitch. "I'll be polite."

Brent came up, saying he'd see her to her table, and Royce smiled at Ward and Eleanor Farenholt as if Brent's parents had handed her a ticket to paradise instead of a seat in hell. With Mitchell Durant.

The party's theme was sophisticated black and white. Didn't any of the Farenholts' friends do

17

anything different? Royce wondered as she walked into the ballroom. Floor-length black silk table skirts peeked out from beneath white damask cloths set with gleaming sterling. The centerpieces were clusters of white orchids with deep plum centers arranged with an austere Japanese flair around bent willow twigs.

"Watch out for Durant," Brent said as they approached her table. "I don't want to lose you to him."

No chance, and Brent knew it. He spoke with the nonchalance of a man whose good looks and wealth guaranteed he'd always have whatever he wanted — any woman he wanted. A harmless form of inbred arrogance, Royce acknowledged. Still, there was nothing about Brent she would change, from his blond hair and brown eyes to his engaging smile.

His easygoing charm and love of life had first attracted Royce to him, but later it was his concern for others that made her fall in love. He cared for his family, his friends, but did it with such sincerity and enthusiasm, it was easy to see why fathers approved of him and any mother in San Francisco would give her left arm to have her daughter marry him.

Brent was the complete opposite of Mitchell Durant, Royce decided, remembering the tragic expression on her father's face that last day when he'd kissed her good-bye. Forever.

Brent introduced her to the guests at the table, leaving Mitchell Durant until last, acting as if this were the first time she'd met the prominent criminal defense attorney even though he knew Royce had met Mitch years ago. "Royce, this is Mitchell Durant. Mitch was with me at Stanford Law School."

Mitch had risen when they'd arrived at the table, but now as Brent spoke there was a split second when the men's eyes met. Instantly she sensed the hostility toward Brent that Mitch concealed with a nod. Mitch turned to her, but she made certain she was looking at Brent, smiling happily.

She slid into her chair, hardly hearing Brent say he'd see her later. Why didn't Mitch like Brent? She'd assumed the animosity was one sided. Everyone liked Brent. He had a way of putting people at ease that certainly wasn't hereditary.

She sipped her wine, covertly studying Mitch. In his late thirties, tall, with dark hair, Mitch had a disturbing way of assessing people. His eyes had never left her face, but she'd lay odds he'd noted her stiletto heels and could tell a jury her bra size.

"Your column last week on divining rods was hysterical," Arnold Dillingham told Royce, nodding his gray head enthusiastically.

Mrs. Dillingham agreed with her husband who'd made a fortune in cable television, then added, "I howled, simply howled, at your column about house dust. Why, I had no idea half the dust in my home is actually dead skin. I didn't

19

realize people shed — like dogs."

"Our skin is always flaking off." She kept her eyes on the Dillinghams, but she was disturbingly aware of Mitch looking at her. Why had she worn such a low-cut dress?

"Well, the way you described it was so darn funny," added Mrs. Dillingham.

"That's what I'm counting on," Arnold informed everyone at the table. "Royce has a humorous way of looking at the world. Offbeat. Interesting."

She beamed, justifiably proud of herself. After all, how many columnists her age — thirty-four — were nationally syndicated, producing a byline twice a week and a feature article carried in Sunday editions nationwide?

"But can you carry a television show? And use that wit in discussing important issues?" Arnold asked her.

"I believe I can," Royce said with as much confidence as she could muster. She had no television experience, but she intended to give it her best shot. She was tired of writing a humorous column. She wanted to deal with important issues and this was her chance.

"I'm betting you can, so I personally found someone special for you to interview on your first trial program."

"Great," she said, upset. She'd expected to discuss Women in Crisis with someone from the center. The safe houses for abused women were unique and a subject Royce knew well. Before

Royce's mother had died, she'd helped develop the program. Royce had given hours of volunteer service to the group.

"This guest has a terrific new idea for helping the homeless."

Royce wasn't familiar with programs for the homeless. Rather than appear uninformed, she tried for a light note. "Not Governor Moonbeam. Last I heard, Jerry Brown was trying to work off his campaign debt by waiting tables in a Thai café."

Dillingham chuckled. "Our Mitch has a plan for helping —"

"Mitchell Durant?" she blurted out. She almost cursed out loud. Mercifully the band struck up a waltz and distracted everyone. Except Mitch.

The others rose to dance, but Mitch leaned close. "My name's not a four-letter word, you know."

"You could have fooled me."

Arnold paused by her chair. "Come on, you two, dance."

She opened her mouth to make an excuse, but Mitch was already pulling her chair out while Mrs. Dillingham babbled about how lucky Royce was to have Mitch on her show. She stood, thinking Mitch was notorious for refusing interviews. So, why now? Why me? Lucky, Mrs. Dillingham had said. Okay, remember *luck* is a four-letter word.

Mitch swung her into his arms. She trained her eyes over the shoulder of his expensive dinner jacket, ignoring him. Across the room Caroline danced with Brent. Where was the Italian count his former girlfriend was supposed to be dating?

Don't be jealous, Royce chided herself, thinking what she really resented about Caroline was how easily she fit in with the Farenholts. Except for Brent the group was terrified of rupturing a major artery by really laughing. Instead, they made muted sounds worthy of an aspiring ventriloquist, while Royce admitted she laughed a little too loudly at times. Especially at a good joke.

Royce felt Mitch watching her, subjecting her to a thorough, intimate appraisal. She studied his lapels for a moment, then lifted her head, making eye contact for the first time. Involuntarily she flinched at the intensity of his gaze. She'd almost forgotten how captivating his eyes were — marine blue with flecks of black and rimmed by black bands the same dark color as his hair.

His face was thoroughly masculine with an arresting expression that made it hard to look away. Its angular planes were tempered by two curious scars, small dents like oversized razor nicks. Whatever had caused the scar on the rise of his cheekbone below his eye had narrowly missed blinding him.

The second scar, it, too, bone deep, had etched a hole the size of a nailhead near his hairline. No one could see the third scar, identical to the others, that she knew was hidden by his thick hair.

Mitch had a certain way of holding his head, tilting it ever so slightly to one side as if he were listening intently, anxious to catch every word. Once she'd thought this particular mannerism was endearing. Now it annoyed her. She knew him for what he truly was. An ambitious jerk who'd hounded an innocent man to death.

"We must be in hell," he said, more than a hint of a jeer in his tone.

"What do you mean?" Good work, Royce. You sound indifferent.

"You bastard," he mimicked her voice. "I'll see you in hell before I ever have anything to do with you again."

She recalled her heated words. And a lot more. "You're right, we *are* in hell."

"If memory serves" — now Mitch was smiling, gliding across the dance floor, holding her too securely for comfort — "when I last saw you, you promised . . . now, how did you put it?"

"To hack off your balls with a rusty machete."

"Right. So ladylike."

True, it had hardly been a refined statment. She'd gone nuts when Mitch appeared at her father's funeral. The rusty machete popped into her mind as the best way to kill Mitch — a slow, painful death — the best way to avenge her father.

Mitch leaned closer, his turbulent blue eyes just inches from hers. Boy oh boy she'd love to kill him. But it wouldn't bring back her father. Nothing would. She caught Arnold Dillingham looking at them and managed to come up with a wisp of a smile.

"About my balls" — Mitch's grin bordered on

a smirk — "if you touch my zipper, you'll have to come home with me."

"You know, you're a real bastard."

"You're not the first to bring it to my attention. And you haven't changed, either, except I hear you're engaged." He glanced at her bare left hand. "Love your engagement ring."

"I'll have it next week. A pear-shaped diamond the size of a doorknob. Nine carats."

That stopped him. But she wished she hadn't mentioned the huge diamond Brent had insisted on. The size of the stone wasn't important; Brent was the catch. She still couldn't get used to the idea he'd chosen her when he could have had his pick of all the eligible women in San Francisco.

"How are you getting along with the Farenholts?"

"Fine," she fibbed, "they're delightful."

Mitch stared at her and she felt a taste of what it must be like to be on the witness stand, being cross-examined by him. "Doesn't it piss you off — big time — to have people you don't like reject you because you're not good enough for their son?"

She reined in her temper, reminding herself that Mitch specialized in tricking people into revealing things. "What makes you think they don't like me?"

He grinned — his big-bad-wolf grin — making her wish she hadn't taken the bait. "Lots of things. Let's start with your dress."

"What's wrong with it?" Royce looked down; she hadn't anticipated dancing in the strapless sheath. Her raised arms pulled her breasts upward, dangerously close to exposing the dusky rims of her nipples. She tried dropping her arms, but Mitch wouldn't let her.

His eyes, unusually blue, unusually intense, roamed slowly over her half-exposed breasts. "I can see what you had for lunch."

She would have whacked him except the Dillinghams were dancing too close, smiling approvingly at them.

"Caroline Rambeau, Brent's old girlfriend, would never be caught dead in that dress."

"Of course not. She couldn't possibly hold it up."

Mitch chuckled, a deep, masculine laugh she'd chosen to forget. She cursed herself for having made him laugh.

The Dillinghams stopped beside them. "What's so funny?"

Think of something quick, Royce told herself. A joke came to mind, but she wasn't truly comfortable with it, considering the plight of the homeless in the bay area. But she told it anyway, determined not to let Arnold Dillingham know what really amused Mitch.

"Since Mitch wants to help the homeless, I was telling him about a woman he should date. Instead of carrying a placard saying WILL WORK FOR FOOD, hers reads: WILL WORK FOR SEX."

Arnold hooted. "That's what I like about you,

Royce. You can inject humor into any topic, even a serious one."

Royce didn't think it was the least bit funny. In fact, it was disgusting. Just what did Arnold expect on the show, a tasteless comedienne? She wanted to be serious for a change and get away from the fluff pieces she'd been writing.

But Arnold probably did want someone outrageous. After all, he'd made his fortune with TV stations that played nonstop infomercials that touted ways to become rich, successful, beautiful — or dice an onion in thirty seconds — with a money back guarantee.

Had he lived, what would her father have said? *You're a born writer. Someday you'll be famous.* Well, maybe. Someday. But right now all the newspaper wanted from her was humor. They'd rejected all her serious articles. At least Arnold was giving her a chance.

"Arnie's agreed that during my appearance on the show, your questions will be limited to the homeless," Mitch informed her as the dance ended. "No questions about my practice, my private life . . . my past."

Watching Brent approach, set to rescue her, she recalled Mitch usually avoided the press. "You know what I think?"

"Royce, I'm always afraid to hear what you think."

"I think you have something to hide." She left him standing alone and went to Brent.

"What were you doing with Durant?" Brent

pulled her into his arms as the band began to play another waltz.

She told him about the revised plan for the show. He gave her a reassuring smile; once again she realized how startlingly handsome he was. But unaware of it. Just being with him made her happy. Despite being rich and outrageously good looking Brent was down to earth and so affectionate. He had many of the qualities she had admired in her father.

If only his parents accepted her, everything would be perfect — except for Mitch, of course. How could she conduct a brilliant interview, an interview that would annihilate the competition and win her the show, when she hated Mitch so much, she could hardly speak to him in a civil tone?

"Watch out for Mitch," Brent warned. "He'll do anything to get even with me."

"Why?" She'd assumed the Farenholts disliked Mitch because of his unconventional courtroom tactics, the antithesis of the staid firm headed by Ward Farenholt.

Mitch had successfully defended Zou Zou Maloof who'd been accused of murdering her husband for his insurance. He'd convinced the jury to acquit her using the "Halcion defense," claiming his client had been paranoid from prolonged use of sleeping pills and hadn't known the knife she'd plunged into her husband's heart was *actually* going to kill him.

"Durant has a hair-trigger temper. He can be

violent for no reason." Brent looked at his father, who was dancing nearby with Caroline; obviously the family felt duty bound to entertain the former girlfriend. "He broke my jaw when we were at Stanford, you know."

"Really? Why didn't you tell me?" She ventured a glance at Mitch, who was standing by the table talking with Mrs. Dillingham. There was more than a hint of aggressiveness to him. His stance, legs slightly apart, suggested the readiness of a fighter, creating a compelling quality some women found exciting.

"I didn't mention the fight because I was ashamed." Brent shrugged, his cute one-shoul-dered shrug that had become so familiar. "I wanted to get back at Mitch for being at the top of our class, so I called him a redneck and a cracker. I'd been first in my class at Yale and thought Stanford law would be a piece of cake, but there's always someone smarter, richer —"

"Prettier," she finished for him. "That's what I like about you, Brent, you're unfailingly hon-est." He smiled at her and she couldn't help feel-ing he had the sincerest smile. When Mitch smiled she always wondered what he was really thinking.

Brent glanced over at his father. Ward Faren-holt was laughing at something Caroline had said. "My father gave me hell for not being top gun at Stanford."

She nodded sympathetically, her eyes on Ward as he twirled Caroline Rambeau around the floor,

28

still laughing, which was rare. Hidebound by generations of wealth and tradition, Ward set rigid standards for his only child. Brent had committed the ultimate violation of those standards by not marrying Caroline.

"Do you know what happens when you try to pet a junkyard dog?" Brent asked. "He goes for your throat because he's been trained to attack. Remember that when you deal with Mitchell Durant."

Mitch's beeper went off just as dessert — some pastry with a fancy French name he couldn't pronounce — had been served.

"Damn," he cussed under his breath. All he needed tonight was someone hearing the Miranda and howling for an attorney. He tilted the face of the beeper to the candlelight and caught the number with a sigh of relief. Not someone in jail, but Jason.

Mitch excused himself and everyone smiled at him — except Royce Winston. She didn't even spare him a glance. What did he expect? The five years she'd lived in Italy hadn't changed anything. She was still ready to drive a stake through his heart.

Royce couldn't possibly love Brent, could she? For chrissake, she had to be smarter than that, but the Farenholt money might have done the trick. After all, she'd been quick to tell him about her engagement ring. Okay, so who could blame her? Five minutes at the altar and she'd make more money than he could earn in a lifetime of court appearances.

Screw it. Let her spend the rest of her damn life with that pussy-whipped mama's boy and his snobby family. Mitch hustled upstairs in search of a telephone, his mind still on Royce. He'd thought about her once or twice in the five years since he'd last seen her.

Oooo-kay, a helluva lot more than that. She'd returned this year from living with relatives in Italy, better known than ever thanks to her column in the *San Francisco Examiner*. She'd left right after her father's funeral, but continued to write her column from abroad.

Obviously, she'd needed to get away from the city and its painful memories. To get away from him. He'd tried to convince himself that she was never coming back. Suddenly, she was home again — where she belonged.

But Mitch hadn't counted on her becoming engaged to Brent. He owed the cocky little prick, and he hadn't forgotten it. *Trust me, I never will.* One day, one day soon, he'd pay Brent back.

There was only one man on earth he hated more than that son of a bitch. Damn straight. It was almost a toss-up, but he did hate his own father more than he hated Brent Farenholt. Too bad there was no way in hell he could ever find the bastard. Royce's rusty machete idea would be perfect for his old man.

Mitch found a small study upstairs and dialed Jason's number.

"He's run away," Jason's mother informed him, an hysterical pitch to her voice.

Mitch had expected something like this. In the two years he'd worked with Jason through the Big Brothers program, he'd seen the kid's life change completely. He'd lived with no rules, the son of a single parent struggling to make ends meet. Then his mother remarried a trucker who thought the iron fist was the only way to deal with teenagers. The straitjacket of rules was driving Jason over the edge.

How well Mitch remembered that feeling of being trapped by rules, rules, and more rules. Jason didn't know running away would only get him into worse trouble. But Mitch knew.

"What upset Jason?" Mitch listened while she described Jason's latest fight with his stepfather.

"Oh, thank God, here he is." He heard a muffled noise as her hand covered the receiver but didn't block the sound of her voice. "You're in trouble. You're gonna get it."

"Wait," Mitch yelled to get her attention. "Put Jason on."

"Yeah?" Jason said, and Mitch could almost see the belligerent thrust of his jaw. "She didn't have to bother you. I was jus' kickin' it with my posse."

Kicking it was this year's version of chill out. Mitch still called it hanging out. Posse — his friends. Not quite *Boyz N the Hood* but close. Too close. "I'll pick you up tomorrow at noon. We'll talk about this."

"Forget it. The man says I ain't goin' no-where."

"Let me speak with your mother." Mitch waited, then Jason's mother came on the line. "Please explain to your husband how important it is for Jason to spend time with me and earn Big Brother points so he can go to camp this summer. The baby will be born about then, won't it? You'll need peace and quiet."

She agreed almost too easily, Mitch thought, accustomed to persuading the toughest juries and reveling in the challenge. Mitch hung up and turned off the desk lamp. He peered out the window at the bay and the dancing lights of Sausalito in the distance. Dammit, it was harder than hell to save one kid from the streets. He had the sneaking suspicion Jason wasn't going to make it.

The party was finally breaking up, Royce noticed, but Brent and his father were still at their table in an animated discussion with the Italian count who'd escorted Caroline. After the Dillinghams said good-night, lavishing Royce with compliments and good wishes on her trial run, Royce went to comb her hair, hoping when she returned Brent would be ready to leave.

Halfway up the stairs she met Caroline with Eleanor Farenholt. The two women had been created by the same fairy godmother. Each had the bone structure of a cover girl with an aquiline nose and sculpted cheekbones beneath eyes that could only be described as patrician blue. Naturally, with such perfection both women felt they didn't need to show off their hair, so they cinched their blond tresses into sleek models' chignons.

They were so exquisite that Royce had to remind herself she was thankful for a thick head of wavy dark-blond hair that softened her square-cut jaw and the clan of freckles gathered on the bridge of her nose. Her eyes, though, were her best feature, clear and cool green. Intelligent green, her father used to say.

"You really look terrific tonight," Caroline said. "That dress was made for you."

She spoke with such honesty, looking Royce directly in the eye, that Royce almost believed her, but knew she couldn't be sincere. No woman could like a rival who'd cost her Brent Farenholt.

"Thanks," Royce smiled, noticing Eleanor hadn't seconded Caroline's opinion. Instead she looked at Royce as if she were something she wouldn't want to step on in the dark.

Royce hurried up the stairs, walking as lightly as possible on the parquet floor that magnified every footfall. The first door she came to was closed, but the next was open. The room was dark, but she went in, expecting a bedroom with an attached bathroom. Squinting in the darkness she saw the silhouette of a tall man outlined against the window.

"Can't stay away from me, can you, Royce?"

Why me? Why did she have to keep running into Mitch? And why was he standing in the dark, anyway? He took two steps toward her. He had a disturbingly sensual way of looking at her, or maybe it was just her imagination.

"You're madder than hell at yourself, aren't you?" he asked.

"I can't imagine what you're talking about. I'm speechless."

"For a change." He came another step closer. Then another.

Some primitive instinct fired a warning as she remembered what Brent had said about Mitch's explosive temper. His voice radiated antagonism. And from what she could see of his face in the darkness, he looked positively dangerous. What right did he have to be angry? It wasn't his father rotting six feet under.

"You're damn pissed at yourself for not telling Arnold Dillingham that I'm the biggest son of a bitch on earth."

Mitch was standing so close, she could smell a faint trace of his after-shave, an elusive scent she recalled from the first time she'd kissed him five years ago. The annoying patter of her heart infuriated her. It was an involuntary feminine re-action she'd have to control, or maybe he just intimidated her. There had always been something threatening about Mitch.

"I could kill you."

"You'll have to take a number, Royce."

"What good would come of it? *Nothing* can bring back the dead."

"All night you've been itching to use that scorpion tongue of yours, but you didn't because you know Arnie won't listen. And you're not about to risk your career, are you?"

She automatically swung her arm up, intending to whack him. He caught her wrist, gripping it firmly. The blood pounded in her temples, bringing a wave of shame.

Why, he was right. And she hated him all the more for it. She'd justified her silence by thinking nothing could bring back her father, but on another level she had kept quiet because she wanted that television program.

"Now you know how it feels to be ambitious." He lowered her arm to her side, but kept his hand clamped around her wrist. "When you want success so much, you can taste it. When you're willing to make compromises to get to the top."

"What you did was different."

"Not really. And if you're honest, you'll admit it."

"You're disgusting. Let me go."

Her mouth was open, the last words still suspended in the small space between them, when he twisted her arm behind her back, bringing her against the solid expanse of his chest. His free hand slipped under her chin and held her jaw open. Her brain barely registered what was happening when his lips met hers in a scorching kiss.

Why is he doing this? she asked herself frantically. His kiss was hot and punishing, a primal act of male domination. And he wanted a whole

35

lot more than a kiss. He made that plain by the thrust of his hips against hers.

Infuriated, she tried to knee him in the groin, but he blocked her by twisting his body to the side. Stop fighting him, she told herself. He's too strong. Go limp and he'll quit. She sagged in his arms; if he hadn't been holding her she would have been on the floor. But he kept kissing her with a fierceness that went beyond passion.

The hot gliding of his tongue as it mated with hers brought a ripple of excitement. And the memory of the first time he'd kissed her five years ago. A kiss she'd never quite forgotten, even though she despised herself for remembering. A kiss that unleashed a longing time and distance hadn't altered.

She'd responded then, an instantaneous, instinctive response. And heaven help her, it was happening all over again.

He released her hand, but she didn't realize it until she found her arms around his neck, fingers twining through the soft strands of hair at the base of his head. Past and present merged, driven by a rush of desire. His hands were on her bottom now, boldly cupping it, bringing her up against the firm heat of his lower body. She clutched him, welcoming each thrust of his tongue, knowing in the back of her mind she'd hate herself later, but she couldn't bank the insistent pulse of desire coursing through her as his mind-reeling kiss deadened the heartbreak of the past.

"See?" he whispered, his lips against hers.

"You're still crazy about me. Five years hasn't changed a goddamn thing."

She didn't answer, craving his kiss even though she knew better. When would her body get the message? She hated him.

"Don't bother lying to me, Royce — or yourself."

He pressed himself against her just in case she'd missed the fact that he was fully aroused. He rotated his hips slowly, deliberately forcing her to wonder what it would be like to make love to him. Oh, Lordy, she hadn't moaned, had she? He'd think she liked this. She hated him.

She managed to wrench her lips away, but their bodies were still locked together. "I could kill you."

"You keep telling me that." He nudged her, the heat of his lower body penetrating the gossamer silk of her dress. "Be careful, Royce. I'm armed and dangerous."

She would never be certain how long they stood in the dark. Kissing. It was a raw act of possession. There had always been something untamed, slightly wild, about Mitch. Something she had to admit she found exciting.

A disturbing thought struck her, a deep unsettling premonition. She'd remember this moment, this kiss. Forever.

Her heart was pounding lawlessly when she noticed a strange sound. Oh, please, she hadn't moaned again, had she? Royce jerked her lips away from his.

The look on his face told her that he'd heard something too. The only sound in the room was their breathing, sharp and deep, an echo of desire frustrated too long. The odd sound had to have come from the hall. She turned toward the door but no one was there. Someone must have just walked past.

What if they'd seen her and told Brent? Royce thought, coming to her senses with a jolt of self-loathing. Kissing Mitch Durant. How could she? She didn't have an answer. She couldn't even look at him now for hating him. And herself.

"Ambition," he said, his voice a shade shy of a whisper, "— it's a double-edged sword. It brings out the best in us — and the worst. Think about it."

She looked at him, truly speechless now, but the darkness masked his angular features. He reached into his pocket and yanked out something white. A business card, she realized, wondering what she could possibly say or do to salvage the situation and praying no one had seen her kissing Mitch.

"Call me." Mitch tucked his card into the hollow between her breasts. "Anytime."

2

Monday swept in on a horizon marbled with carbon-colored strafers driven by a rain-scented breeze that promised showers any minute. Royce joined her close friends Talia and Valerie for lunch at Reflections, overlooking the bay and the Golden Gate Bridge.

"Eleanor Farenholt can go to hell," Royce announced. "The wedding coordinator she recommended wants more money to organize our wedding than I make in an entire year writing a column. I'm going to convince Brent to elope."

Talia put down her menu, shaking her dark-brown head. "I doubt Brent will disappoint his mother. She's determined to have a grand wedding, the kind she'd throw if she had a daughter."

Valerie and Royce had grown up in the same neighborhood. They'd met Talia in high school. Rich and rebellious, Talia had been kicked out of several exclusive private schools before entering Sacred Heart Girls' School, where the strict nuns kept the girls in line. Royce and Talia had become close friends, sweeping the shy Valerie along in their wake.

Although Royce trusted both friends to give her their honest opinions, she relied more on Talia when it came to the Farenholts and their circle of friends. She traveled in the same circles — despite the detour to decidedly middle-class Sacred Heart. And Talia had known the Farenholts for years.

"Eleanor Farenholt wants the kind of wedding Caroline Rambeau would have if she'd married Brent," Valerie seconded Talia's opinion, her auburn hair gleaming in the light, her hazel eyes as serious as her tone. "Look on the positive side. At least Brent cares about his mother. They say you can judge a man by the way he treats his mother."

"What about your former mother-in-law?" Talia asked.

The question made Royce cringe, because Valerie was still suffering from her husband's betrayal. Val had always been less sure of herself than Royce or Talia, but since Val's divorce, she'd become withdrawn and bitter. Why upset her?

"The jerk never called his mother. I told her he'd left me."

"See?" Talia said. "He was a schmuck and it showed in his relationship with his mother."

"Have you heard from your parents lately?" Val asked Talia.

"Last I heard they were at a villa in Marbella."

Royce watched Talia closely. It was a shame, but since she'd entered an alcohol rehabilitation program almost a year ago, Talia's parents hadn't been around to give her support. Suddenly the usual lunchtime noises — the buzz of conversation, the soft music coming from the overhead speakers, and the clink of cutlery — seemed deafening. Silence hung between the threesome like a shroud.

What had happened? Royce asked herself. Once they'd all been so happy, so full of hope. Now she was the only one who was happy. Why was she complaining about the Farenholts? Compared to her friends' problems, hers were nonexistent.

"Do you realize none of us have parents, not really," Val broke the silence. "Royce's are dead and ours might as well be."

How true, Royce thought. Talia had been raised by a succession of nannies. Val, though, was a different case. Her family had been close until Val's divorce. Since her husband walked out, Val hadn't spoken to her family.

Royce toyed with her water glass, not wanting to recall her mother's slow, agonizing death from cancer. Or her father's funeral.

The waiter interrupted to take their orders. Then Royce switched the conversation back to a less serious topic with a joke. "I'm going to have to rob a bank to pay for this wedding. What else? My house already has a huge second mortgage that Daddy took when Mama was dying."

"Have you discussed this with Brent?" Talia hooked a strand of sleek brown hair behind one ear. "What does he say?"

"He wants to give me the money, but that's

not right. It's the bride's responsibility —"

"If you ask me," Val cut in as she snapped a breadstick in two, "expensive weddings are a waste of time. Half the marriages in this country end in divorce."

Royce cringed at the bitterness in her friend's tone — so unlike the old Val, who'd been unfailingly upbeat. Until the divorce.

"You'll make a lot of money if you land that TV job," Talia mercifully changed the subject.

"Even if I do get the job, it'll take time to save enough. I want a baby, but my biological clock is quickly becoming a time bomb. Now that I've found the right man, why wait?"

"Speaking of men," Talia said to Val, "Royce found you a date for the auction this Saturday night."

Val wagged her finger at Royce. "Last time you fixed me up with a periodontist. I had to listen all night to how gingivitis is a bigger health threat than AIDS. Then after dinner, know what he did?"

"He flossed — hopefully in the men's room, not at the table." Royce wheedled a smile out of Val, a glimmer of her old self.

"No. He said: 'Your place or mine?' Like sex was a given."

"You'll get back into the swing of dating," Talia said.

Dating was only part of the problem, Royce decided. During the years the three of them had attended Sacred Heart Girls' School, Val rarely dated. She'd met her husband the day they'd arrived at college. Royce doubted Val had ever kissed another man.

A kiss. Heaven help her. Why had she kissed Mitchell Durant like that? She despised him for having forced himself on her, but she hated herself even more for remembering that kiss in such exquisite detail. Even now, in the sobering light of day, she could feel his lips on hers, his masculine body aggressively pressing against hers.

There was no escaping the ugly truth: She'd wanted Mitch in spite of what he'd done to her father. She must need counseling. Clearly, she had some deep-seated psychological problem.

Val expelled a tortured sigh, then asked Royce, "All right, who have you dug up for me this time?"

"Remember that column I wrote: Where Does All the Parsley Go?"

"Uh-huh. Restaurants put parsley on every plate but nobody eats it. That was one of your funnier pieces."

"Well, I received an irate call from the parsley king, the man who supplies the entire West Coast with the stuff, which has made him richer than the Farenholts. I schmoozed him over a cup of coffee, and I really liked the guy. So I called him last night and told him about you."

"Go with him, Val," Talia urged. "Everyone will be there."

"Even the Farenholts are coming," Royce added with an edge to her voice. She waited while

43

the waiter served their salads. "Brent took a table and invited his parents to come with us. Naturally, his mother insisted on including Caroline and that Italian count she's been dating."

"What nerve." Val speared a mushroom with her fork. "I'd come just to give you moral support, but I haven't got a dress suitable for a black tie affair."

"I have the perfect dress. Borrow it." Royce refused to let Val spend another night alone, moping over that heartless jerk. "Go by my place and try on the copper dress in my closet. You know where I keep the key, don't you?"

"Everyone knows. You might as well keep the door unlocked."

Talia added, "You're asking to be robbed."

"I haven't got anything worth taking." Royce winked at her friends and tossed a piece of parsley on Val's plate. "Come on Val. It'll be fun."

They finished their salads and Royce passed on dessert, thinking of Eleanor Farenholt's comment about her weight. Royce didn't aspire to having a stick figure like Brent's former girlfriend, Caroline, but she didn't want condo thighs either. She was only ten pounds or so overweight, but beside Eleanor and Caroline it felt like fifty tons.

"I'm tired of waiting," Talia announced after she was served a chocolate torte that made Royce's mouth water. "When are you going to tell us why you were dancing with Mitchell Durant?"

"Because Arnold Dillingham insisted," Royce said, striving to justify her actions, but having difficulty convincing herself as she informed her friends about the situation with her trial television program.

But she couldn't bring herself to tell them about the kiss in the dark. She simply couldn't explain her actions, even though she'd spent the better part of the weekend thinking about her stupidity.

The noise in the hall. Someone had passed by as she was kissing Mitch. Had that person seen them? Thank heaven it hadn't been Brent. There would have been no way she could have explained to him what she couldn't even explain to herself.

"So," she concluded with false bravado, "I'm spending this week researching the homeless, ready to face Mitchell Durant in front of a camera."

"Don't attack him," warned Val. "While you were living in Rome, one of his trials was televised. The man's a shark. He annihilated every prosecution witness."

"*No one* has to remind me what he's like in court."

Talia touched Royce's hand. "Get it over with and you'll never have to see that dreadful man again."

"I can't just let it go. If I have the chance, I'm going to embarrass that jerk or something. Whatever I do won't pay him back, but I can't live with myself if I don't try."

She didn't add that after the kiss in the dark, she was more determined than ever to get even with Mitch Durant. With any luck it would be

45

Friday night in front of millions of viewers.

"You're positive you want to run away?" Mitch
asked Jason as he drove his Viper into the Ten-
derloin, San Francisco's sinister netherworld, the
side of the city tourists rarely saw. Drug addicts,
pushers, pimps. And worse. Mitch hated being
here, especially at night. Too many memories.
All of them bad.

"I can make it on my own, dude. I'll take
my drums and hook up with a rock band. Or
somethin'. I can't stand that man Mom married
dissin' me. I don't do nothin' right. Nothin'."

How well Mitch remembered thinking the same
thing.

"I'm almost fifteen — old enough to be on
my own."

Yeah, right. The expensive sports car slugged
through the heavy traffic past neon-lit tattoo par-
lors and the latest crop of Thai restaurants. Old
enough? That's what Mitch had thought.

Mitch shot a look at Jason. Short, skinny, with
dusty-brown hair and eyes a shade darker. Tonight he wore his prize possession, the leather
jacket he'd saved for a year to buy, the haute
couture of postpunk chic.

"Tell you what. You want to be on your own?
I'll give you fifty bucks" — Mitch shifted to street
talk — "that's fifty dead presidents, to spend a
couple of hours here."

Jason gazed out the window, seeing the bright
lights, not the walk on the wild side — the living

hell. "You're on," he said as Mitch wheeled to the curb.

"I'll pick you up right here," Mitch yelled to Jason's back, "in two hours." He let the kid saunter into the crowd before he picked up the car phone and dialed. "Paul? You got him?"

"Yo, Mitch, relax." Paul Talbott's mellow voice seemed to fill the car. "We've got a tail on him."

"Great. Now, scare the shit out of him. And while you're at it, snatch his jacket." Mitch hung up and gunned the engine, bullying his way into the heavy traffic. He raised his fist and flipped off a curbside pharmacologist, barely dodging the pimp trying to flag him down by banging on the Viper's hood.

While he drove to his office, he thought about Royce Winston. Son of a bitch. He'd gotten to her. Big time. He chuckled, a low gruff sound that reflected his deep sense of satisfaction. At least on one level nothing had changed between them. Over five years. He hadn't been sure.

Memories could deceive. Lure you. Then betray you. He knew that better than anyone. It had almost gotten him killed.

But this time, unlike the first, he'd been dead-on. Royce Anne Winston could wish him in hell. Still, deep down inside, in that secret window into the soul, an ember of the past remained, more easily fanned to life than he'd expected. Helluva lot of good it would do him, since she was set to marry that wuss.

So, now what? he wondered after he'd parked his car and was unlocking his office. Damned if he knew. But he'd think of something. He always did. Too bad the noise that ended the kiss hadn't been Brent Farenholt. Goddamn, he would have passed on a Supreme Court appointment just to see the look on Farenholt's face if he'd found Royce in his arms.

Brent — the cocky little prick. An intellectual brain trust, he wasn't. He was incapable of an original thought. Proof positive money couldn't buy everything. Too bad he didn't know a woman in love didn't kiss another man with such passion. Especially a man she claimed to hate.

The telephone on Mitch's desk rang before he even sat down.

It was Paul. "The kid's on the corner, waiting for you — already. We've got his jacket. Do you want it?"

"Hell, no. Give it to the first homeless man it'll fit."

"Mitch, it's brand new."

"Screw it. The only lesson Jason will remember is one that hurts."

Mitch let the full two hours expire before even heading down to his car. It was a cold night, typical of early May. Moist fog coiled in from the bay. He heard muffled noises coming from the rear of the subterranean parking structure. A group of homeless men had moved in to avoid the cold. Lost souls, he thought, living in the shadows.

They'd probably found the money and the packets of ketchup from McDonald's that he'd left for them. He caught a whiff of tomato soup they'd brewed from the ketchup by adding hot water. He almost gagged. To this day he couldn't stomach tomato soup.

As he drove up Jason sprang off the curb and yanked open the door. The kid was trembling, his face leached of color.

"Hey, how'd you like it?" Mitch asked, grinning.

"S'okay," Jason said, the threat of tears in his voice.

"You left your jacket somewhere."

"They ripped it off."

"Why'd you let them take it?"

"*Let* them?" Jason cried, swiping at tears with the back of his hand. "A gang of Viets dragged me down an alley."

"Jeezus!" Mitch said, genuine sympathy in his voice now. Yessirree, Paul had outdone himself. Of all the gangs operating in the city — blacks, Chicanos, Koreans, even the Japanese *yakuza* — the Vietnamese were the most deadly. What they'd learned in the jungles of Nam, they'd perfected in the city.

"I guess it's rougher out there than you thought."

Grim faced, Jason nodded. "A man grabbed me" — his eyes shot down to his crotch — "I slugged him."

"Good for you." Mitch tossed him fifty dollars.

"Here, you've earned it. One dead president — Ulysses S. Grant."

"My jacket," Jason muttered, pocketing the bill. "What am I going to tell my mother?"

"That's your problem."

"Wally." Royce kissed her uncle's cheek, then gazed around the Plexiglas cubbyhole that was his office at the *San Francisco Examiner*.

The computer terminal was on and running the international UPI feed. The desk was cluttered with printouts and empty Styrofoam cups partially filled with coffee. The only thing on the stucco wall was the picture of Wally accepting the Pulitzer prize.

He returned her affectionate hug, his green eyes the mirror image of her own. Sixtyish, but trim, with a full head of brindled hair, Wallace Winston was the city's most respected investigative reporter.

"I wasn't expecting to see you before the auction this Saturday night. Did you miss your deadline?"

"No. I'm not here to turn in my column." She sat in the chair beside his desk and explained that the topic of her trial run on television had been changed.

"That's too bad. I know how much the Center for Women in Crisis means to you. That's why I'm going to the auction Saturday night, even though I hate getting trussed up in a monkey suit."

Royce smiled. Uncle Wally would never be a substitute for her father, but he was the next best thing and always had been. Since her father's death they'd become closer, even though she'd spent the last five years with relatives in Italy, unable to face living in San Francisco after her father's death.

She and Wally had written constantly and had spoken on the telephone each week. Now that she was home again, they saw each other more than ever before.

"So, I guess you need some info on the homeless." Wally tapped on his computer to bring up his research files.

"Actually" — she hesitated, knowing her father's death had been every bit as painful for him as it had for her — "I want to know what you have on Mitchell Durant."

He swung around and faced her. "What the hell for?"

"Apparently, Mitch has a plan for the homeless. Arnold Dillingham insisted I interview him."

"Just how important is this program to you?"

"I'd like to branch out from writing a humorous column. I'd like to try more serious issues the way Daddy did. But I'm afraid people think I'm an intellectual lightweight."

"Don't let your father's success bother you. You can be anything you want to be." He patted her shoulder. "But I don't like the idea of you interviewing that bastard Durant."

"Neither do I, but what can I do? Anyway,

Mitch has limited my questions to the homeless. Nothing about his life — at all."

"Not surprising. Durant never gives interviews."

"Doesn't that strike you as strange?"

"No. It's savvy. The more mysterious you are, the more the press pursues you. That'll work to your advantage on the show. There'll be lots of people who'll tune in just to hear Mitch."

"May I look at your file on him?"

"Don't ask for trouble, Royce. A reporter's word has to be reliable. When you're told something is off the record, you must honor that request."

"I plan to stay within the guidelines. No questions not related to the homeless, but I might be able to come up with something if I look into his background."

"I don't see how. Every reporter in the state sifted through the records during his last murder trial when Durant captured the headlines for weeks. Nothing. He enlisted in the Navy when he was eighteen and got his high school degree by passing an equivalency test while he was enlisted."

Royce took out her notepad. "Where did he grow up?"

"Who knows? His birth certificate says he was born in Pugwash Junction, Arkansas. The few shacks that were there were demolished years ago by the Interstate. Checking the neighboring farms, no one found anybody who knew a Mitchell Durant."

"Doesn't that seem unusual?"

"Not really. I know the South pretty well from the civil rights coverage I did in the sixties. I'm going back there soon to do an environmental piece on chicken farming. I'm hoping to retire on top," he confessed, "with another Pulitzer. This could be it."

He shrugged as if it wasn't all that important, but she knew better. The young Turks were baying at his heels. He wasn't getting the choice assignments he once had. And it had been years since his last Pulitzer.

"Anyway, the South is riddled with small towns and itinerant farmers. The fact that Durant didn't have a high school degree when he enlisted in the Navy tells me that he never stayed in one place long enough. It couldn't have been his brains. He sailed through college even though he worked full time. He was top of his class at Stanford Law School."

"Did you discover anything about the scars on his cheek?" She didn't mention the third, which she knew was concealed by his thick hair.

"No, but he was honorably discharged from the Navy before his term was up. They discovered he's deaf in one ear. Apparently they'd missed it when he enlisted."

"Really? That must be why he cocks his head just slightly to one side. He's favoring his good ear."

Deaf in one ear. A pang of sympathy so deep,

she couldn't pinpoint its source surged through her. When she'd first met Mitch, she'd noticed this mannerism and assumed he was just listening attentively to her. She tamped down the ache of sympathy, reminding herself Mitchell Durant wasn't worthy of it. Undoubtedly his pride wouldn't welcome pity — especially hers.

Wally pressed a few keys and information filled the computer screen. "Here's what I have on Durant, including all the cases he's handled. You look. I have to prep for an editorial meeting."

Royce changed chairs with her uncle. She quickly reviewed the cases in Wally's file. "It appears defending insurance companies keeps Mitch's cash cow in clover."

Wally peered at her over the top of the report he was reading. "He works with Paul Talbott, a private investigator who specializes in insurance fraud."

She scanned the files again, more closely this time. "Strange. Mitch has represented a few defendants accused of taking drugs, but no drug lords. I thought they were bread and butter for many criminal attorneys."

"The drug kingpins usually keep the best attorneys on retainer, but Durant has steered clear of them."

"His record's clean. Too clean." She thought a moment, an idea forming. "He's prepping for a political career."

"He's been mentioned frequently for the district attorney's post, which will be vacant next year, but he denies he's interested in politics. Still, I suspect you're right. He's grooming himself for politics, keeping himself lily-white."

"Doesn't surprise me. We both know how ambitious Mitch is." She hesitated, then asked, "What about his personal life?"

"He and Abigail Carnivali were an item for a while, but they split up about a year ago. She's the assistant DA. They don't call her Abigail Carnivorous for nothing. She's set to run for DA when the old goat retires next year."

Royce remembered Abigail: tall, jet-black hair and eyes. She'd sat next to Mitch while he'd crucified Royce's father. She was every bit as ambitious as Mitch. A perfect match. What happened between them? she wondered.

"Of course," Wally continued, "if Mitch ran for DA, he'd beat Carnivorous in a second."

"Nothing else on his personal life?" she asked, telling herself she could care less about his love affairs.

"He's a true lone wolf. His only friend is that private investigator, Paul Talbott. It's anybody's guess how Mitch spends his free time. Other than his work with Catholic Big Brothers, he's kept the lowest profile imaginable. Until now."

"I think he's moving into the political arena."

"We'll find out soon enough, I'm afraid." Wally glanced at the clock. "I'm late for the meeting. Good luck tomorrow night. I'll be watching the TV, rooting for you. Don't let Mitch hog the camera. I want to see my girl get that job."

55

"I won't let him get the best of me," she promised, thinking he hadn't mentioned Brent. Uncle Wally certainly wasn't happy she was marrying a Farenholt, but he loved her enough to let her make her own decisions.

Royce spent the next three hours studying the cases Mitchell Durant had taken since going into private practice. "There has to be a way to pay him back for what he did to Daddy," she whispered to the computer.

It took her another hour, but finally she discovered what she was looking for. No doubt about it, Mitch was grooming himself for a political career. Obviously, he didn't want to announce his intentions — yet.

Well, she'd fix him. She couldn't ruin his political aspirations, but she could expose them. Long before he wanted anyone to know.

3

The powerful klieg lights in the television studio caused a rivulet of perspiration to trickle down between Royce's breasts. Having Mitch staring at her wasn't helping either. The makeup man dusted her forehead and nose with powder again, telling her to relax. Out of the corner of her eye she saw Mitch seated in the guest chair opposite hers, looking cool despite the dark suit he wore.

The jitters she'd had all day had solidified into a hard knot lodged at the base of her throat. Would she be able to utter a single word? Would she remember all she'd learned about the homeless?

Would she have the courage to wait until the final seconds of the program before dealing Mitch a blow, exposing his political aspirations before he was ready? She gulped a calming breath, reminding herself if she played this right she'd land the job as the *San Francisco Affairs* hostess and make life rough for Mitch.

"Two minutes and we're live," yelled the floor director, sending a dozen people scurrying over the skein of cables strewn across the studio.

Someone clipped a tiny microphone on her suit jacket. She followed instructions and said a few words for a mike check, conscious of the glass control booth suspended above the studio floor. Arnold Dillingham was up there, evaluating her performance. She couldn't remember ever being this nervous. Was the job so important, or was it besting Mitch?

Royce stole a glance in Mitch's direction and found him studying her again. For a moment their gazes caught and held. Was he thinking about that kiss?

He suddenly flashed her a knowing grin. He *was* thinking about that passionate kiss. She must have seemed incredibly weak to him. Well, he'd find out.

"Five, four, three, two, one." The director pointed his finger at Royce, mouthing, "We're live."

"Good evening," Royce said, using her high-voltage smile. "I'm Royce Anne Winston. Welcome to *San Francisco Affairs*. This program is dedicated to in-depth discussions of issues that interest our community."

She took a quick breath, justifiably proud of her even voice. "Tonight, we'll be talking about one of the most troublesome problems in our city, the homeless. With me is Mitchell Durant, recently named trial attorney of the year."

The camera zoomed in for a close-up of Mitch, who smiled, an arresting smile worthy of a television evangelist. Trust me, Royce thought, you won't be smiling when this program's over.

"Tell me, Mitch. You're a very busy attorney. Why such interest in the problems of the homeless?"

"The plight of the homeless is everyone's problem," Mitch responded, his tone a convincing mix of authority and concern. "As you know, Royce, San Francisco's city code requires that homeless people who're here thirty-six hours are entitled to register and draw payments from the city."

"That's why our city has become a Mecca for the homeless. Don't you think the law should be changed?"

"It doesn't matter what I think," he replied, true to form. Politicians avoided committing themselves. "We have to deal with the situation as it exists. That's where my plan —"

"Some of the homeless appear to be mentally incapable of holding down a job," she interrupted. She didn't want Mitch to reveal the details of his plan yet. Uncle Wally had warned her not to let him steal the show, to remain in control. "Shouldn't they be in institutions?"

Mitch didn't appear to be the least bit rattled that she'd cut him off. "Under the state law certain mentally troubled individuals who are not a danger to society have a choice. They can remain wards of the state or they can go free. Which would you choose?"

"Freedom," she reluctantly admitted, "but they will never be productive members of society? Add to that number the people who're unwilling to work —"

"How do you know they don't want to work?"

"I have no way of knowing about every person," she backtracked, reminding herself to choose her words with care. Here was a man who interrogated people for a living. She was very sympathetic to the plight of the homeless but if she weren't cautious, he'd make her sound like a heartless shrew instead of a sharp interviewer doing her job by presenting all sides of the issue.

"Some people say the homeless around Union Square station themselves outside the ritzy shops with 'beloved pets' to exploit the situation," she said. "Many believe those homeless people are playing on our sympathy and using animals to get money."

Mercifully, the director signaled for a commercial and she mumbled something about the sponsor. The makeup man reappeared, draping a towel around her neck. She stole a peek at Mitch and found him watching her.

He winked and gave her an intimate look, his gaze scaling down her body and stopping at her thighs where her skirt had ridden up. She tried for a withering glance, but its impact was destroyed by the makeup man blotting the prickles of perspiration off the bridge of her nose and dusting her with powder. Before she could gather her thoughts, they were on the air again.

She said something as the camera zoomed in for a close-up. Out of camera range she saw Mitch wink again. Honest to God, the man had a bulletproof ego.

Mitch leaned forward, talking to the camera as if he were speaking to his most intimate friends. He *was* perfect for politics. "What we as a society need to ask ourselves is how we can walk right past a homeless person with a sign WILL WORK FOR FOOD and ignore him. Yet if that same person has a dog and a sign that says FIDO NEEDS FOOD, we toss him a coin. Can you explain it?"

"Yes," she responded. "People know an animal has no way of feeding itself. They feel responsible for a helpless creature, but they assume the person could — if he wished — help himself."

"That's how most see it, but what if you could assist the person to become a productive member of society again?"

"I have helped. I noticed a woman living in our alley. She was divorced with no job skills. I took her to the Center for Women in Crisis. Now she has a place to stay, and she's enrolled in a training program."

"That's terrific. If everyone pitched in we'd be —"

"Not everyone has the time to help or knows how. It's easier to give money, but a lot of people feel that only encourages begging. So they don't do anything."

The camera was on her, and out of the corner of her eye she saw Mitch smiling, an unspoken challenge in his grin. Now she had no choice except to hear his plan. "What do you suggest?"

"First, tell me what groups you see within the ranks of the homeless."

There. He'd done it. Now he was asking her questions. He'd have her around his finger in a minute, if she weren't careful. "There are the mentally incapacitated and those who find it easier to ask for money than work."

How would she describe the third group? Oh, Lordy, the camera was zooming in for a close-up. She hesitated, seldom at a loss for words, but suddenly unable to express herself.

Her father would have coined a new phrase that would later be repeated by everyone, but she didn't have his intellectual genius. Her gift was pointing out the absurdities of everyday life. But there was nothing remotely funny about the homeless.

"You're validating my point." Mitch filled the uncomfortable pause. "It's hard to classify the homeless. Like most persistent problems its solution isn't simple."

"There but for the grace of God go I." Royce had no idea what made her say that, but the well-known phrase did sum up her feelings. All right, it wasn't an original term, but at least words hadn't failed her entirely.

Mitch gave her an approving nod. "Exactly. A great many of the homeless have fallen through society's cracks. Under the right circumstances anyone could be homeless. The woman you helped is a prime example."

"Just what do you propose?"

"To concentrate on this third group that's fallen through the cracks. We have the best chance of helping them. I've lined up a number of businessmen. We're developing a system using a computer network that will match the skills with jobs."

It was time for another commercial, giving Royce a moment to marshal her thoughts. She braved a glance at Mitch and he grinned. She quickly looked away. Of course, he would smile. He sounded brilliant — the celluloid image of the perfect candidate. Obviously, he was priming the audience for a political career.

How was she doing? Nothing special. No incisive observations. No witty remarks. She'd said nothing that would make Arnold Dillingham choose her to hostess his program.

Well, she had one more shot at this. She had to phrase her final question carefully so that she was within the guidelines Mitch had set. And she had to time it perfectly, making certain Mitch had no chance to answer while they were still on the air.

The next few minutes passed quickly as Mitch explained his plan. Royce asked questions, her eye on the clock, her mind on her final question. She had to admit the plan Mitch outlined sounded innovative. It wouldn't solve the homeless problem entirely, but it would give ordinary citizens a way to become involved.

Her closing question wouldn't sabotage his plan, but it would expose his political ambitions. Mitch wouldn't suffer the way her father had suffered, but it was the best she could do.

The director gave her the "wrap" signal. She took a quick breath, amazed at how the words stalled in her throat despite having rehearsed them countless times. It couldn't have been more than a split second, but it seemed like hours before she heard herself speak.

"I've studied your record, Mitch. When you were in the DA's office you had an impressive conviction rate." She glimpsed his intense blue eyes glaring at her and warning her not to violate the guidelines. "In your private practice you've avoided representing drug dealers. And you've been incredibly sensitive to women's issues. In the DA's office you successfully prosecuted numerous rape cases. Since you've been in private practice you've refused to defend any man accused of rape."

She sensed Mitch's eyes locked on her, anger roiling beneath the facade of composure. "I wonder if your critics aren't right. You've planned your career carefully, avoiding drug and rape cases, grooming yourself for political office."

She hazarded a glimpse at Mitch. He flashed her a look that would have stopped a charging rhino.

"Now you've aligned yourself with animal rights groups by agreeing to defend a vicious cougar the Fish and Game Department wants put to sleep. I'm certain the viewers are asking if this program for the homeless — although not without merit — is just another ploy for media attention in your climb up the political ladder."

The camera switched away from Royce. Mitch shot her a look that bordered on a death threat. He opened his mouth to respond, but her timing was flawless. The theme music began to play.

Paul Talbott knew when Mitch walked into the Liquid Zoo. The bar was darker than Hades, lit only by neon pictures of pink elephants quaffing booze through their trunks, and by a big screen TV. Several of the bar's patrons greeted Mitch, asking if he was running for DA or attorney general.

He couldn't hear Mitch's answer, but Paul figured his blond hair would have a few more gray streaks by morning. He'd never seen Mitch angrier than he'd been in the closing shot of that television program.

Mitch dropped onto the well-worn bar stool beside him and the bartender handed him a Jack Daniel's on the rocks. He took a swig, then asked, "What did you think?"

Paul had known Mitch since they were eighteen-year-old bunkmates aboard a Navy ship. Almost twenty years had passed, and they'd remained close friends by being dead honest. Mitch would forgive anything — except a lie.

"You sounded good, Mitch, until she cold-cocked you with that political angle."

"Yeah, the bitch." Mitch knocked back his drink, then stared at the glass. "Swear to God, I could strangle her."

"You know, I picked up on a subtle bit of antagonism throughout the program. Royce Winston doesn't like you."

"Damn straight. She hates my guts." Mitch shoved his glass forward for a refill. "I'm surprised you saw it, though. I didn't think it was obvious."

"That's my job, remember?" Paul was proud of his ability to read people. He'd zeroed in on Mitch the day he'd met him years ago in Navy boot camp. Lonely, insecure despite his tough appearance.

Paul's years on the police force had honed those instincts. Now his practice as a private investigator demanded he rely on his observations about people. He was seldom wrong.

But it didn't take a sixth sense to know not

to question Mitch. Minutes after meeting him Paul had learned Mitch told you what he wanted you to know. Even after all this time, Paul had no idea about Mitch's life before they met. He doubted he ever would.

"There's a booth free," Mitch said. "Let's order a pizza."

Paul followed Mitch to the booth, his stomach churning at the thought of the Liquid Zoo's pizza. It was like eating melted cheese on an old glove. But Mitch didn't care; he ate a combo pizza — hold the anchovies — seven nights a week.

Paul watched Mitch as .he ordered the pizza and another round of drinks. Why was he so angry? That Winston broad had caught him off-guard, but Mitch had looked damn good.

True, it would be a hassle again squelching rumors that he was running for DA. Mitch had promised his former girlfriend, Abigail Carnivali, he'd stay out of the DA's race so she could run. Good old "Carnivorous" would be screaming for Mitch's blood. What had Mitch seen in her? She was gorgeous, but a ball buster.

"I should have known Royce would pull something like this. Even after all this time she's an ole coon dog nosing down a cold trail."

There was an element of ruthlessness about Mitch that he'd tempered over the years, but never completely concealed. When he was angry, the way he was now, a trace of his southern accent appeared, and he used southern expressions.

"I didn't realize you knew Royce Winston."

Mitch stared across the dark bar for a moment at the fight being shown on television. "I met her a little over five years ago. You were away then, remember?"

"Can't forget being hauled in front of Internal Affairs." Paul had quit the force, his name under a cloud, and had taken off across the country on his Harley for almost a year. By the time he returned, he'd lost his wife and kids. But he still had one friend.

"As usual, I'd let thirty-four out of thirty-six months lapse and still didn't have all of my continuing-ed classes to keep up my license to practice law," Mitch continued. "I'd racked up a few credits going to a Giants game and listening to some bullshit from the team's lawyer on ethics and sports contracts. I spent a week at Club Med, getting laid, improving my tan, and listening to lectures on effectively using paralegals."

The waiter brought their drinks and the pizza with about as much care as a trash collector dumping a can into his truck. Mitch grabbed a piece and took a chunk out of it while Paul watched. What did Mitch see in this place? Didn't he notice the pizza was burnt? Naw. Mitch didn't care what he ate — as long as it was pizza.

"I was still short on the required credits for stress management, so I enrolled in a weekend program at the Self-Awareness Institute in Big Sur," Mitch said. "That was one of those touchy-feely Japanese deals that were so popular before everyone realized we were committing economic suicide kowtowing to Tokyo.

"The first session was held in a mango grove overlooking the ocean. Swear to God, there were meditation pillows on the ground and incense burners. I was looking around for a roster to sign before cutting out when in walked a blond with a clipboard and name tag that read: ROYCE."

"I take it Royce Anne Winston was the leader."

"Yeah," Mitch said, staring into his glass. "I didn't find out her last name until it was too late. The Institute used first names only on our badges so we could 'connect' with each other."

Mitch took a deep breath, not smelling the stale beer or even the overdone pizza he'd hardly eaten. Instead his mind took a detour; the aroma of sandalwood from the incense burner filled his nostrils as he thought about the first time he'd met Royce.

Five years earlier he'd sat on the meditation pillow, his eyes on the blond wearing an oversize sweatshirt splattered with silver metallic paint that couldn't begin to hide a bombshell figure like an old-time movie star's.

He wouldn't have described her as pretty. Her features were a little strong to be conventionally feminine: wide green eyes, a sexy mouth, blond hair styled in a wind tunnel. And cute freckles. She appeared to be several years younger than he was — not yet thirty.

"All right." She clapped her hands for attention. No ring. "I'm Royce, your spiritual guide. Let's begin right away. Everyone find a meditation pillow and sit. Cross your legs like Indians. Put your hands on your knees."

While the group settled on the pillows, Mitch studied Royce. Smart, his sixth sense told him as she glanced around, sizing up the sleepy group who'd never have been here except the legislature had decided to "improve" the quality of attorneys by requiring these classes. What bullshit.

"Close your eyes and take deep, deep, calming breaths of the sandalwood incense. Clear your mind of everything," Royce instructed. "Just let it go. Let it float away on the breeze."

"What a crock," he muttered to himself, his eyes on Royce as she sat cross-legged on her pillow, her hands on her knees, her head slightly bent. She tossed her wayward curls over her shoulder, an unconscious gesture he found very provocative.

She was doing the deep-breathing crap, leading the horde of mostly male attorneys gathered in the early morning sunlight. There was something undeniably sexy about her. She had the type of girl-next-door looks that would fool anyone's mother. But a father would take one look at Royce and haul you behind the woodshed for a lecture on birth control.

She opened her eyes and looked directly at him. Bedroom eyes. "Breathe deeply," she mouthed.

He unleashed the grin that had coaxed more than his share of women out of their panties. She closed her eyes without sparing him a second glance.

"Slowly, ever so slowly, exhale," she instructed, her tone low, hypnotic. Downright sexy.

"Let the air go through your nostrils, taking with it the tension, the stress. Concentrate on what you're letting go of. Imagine that burden floating away. Just let it go."

"They feed more interesting slop to the hogs," Mitch whispered under his breath. She kept talking, but he wasn't listening. He imagined Royce, her hair splayed across a pillow. Her thighs parted. Incense filled his lungs; the possibilities of Royce in his bed filled his mind.

"Mitch. Earth to Mitch," Royce called to him.

Everyone's eyes were on him now. He'd lost track of what she'd been saying. What had he missed? "Sorry. I zoned out for a moment. Too much incense."

She smiled. Nice, even white teeth. "We're sharing what we let go of. What did you let go of, Mitch?"

"I was thinking of something I'd like to get ahold of."

Laughter rumbled through the group. One of the jerks from the Public Defenders office fell off his pillow. Mitch realized the rest of the guys found Royce every bit as sexy as he did.

She ignored his suggestive comment. "Mitch, breathe deeply for me."

He felt like an ass, but he puffed for the hell of it. Okay, because he wanted her attention.

"Now, Mitch," she said, a teasing note in her voice. "Exhale and let go, let go of your obsession

70

with billable hours."

The group howled, slapping their thighs. Too damn much incense. Mitch didn't bother to tell her that he was with the DA's office and didn't bill hours like most attorneys.

The meditation bit went on all morning. Afterward every attorney had questions, swarming all around Royce. Mitch hung back and listened. After a weekend of this she had to hear every line in the book. And she wasn't falling for any of it.

Finally, the last guy was making his pitch. Mitch stood nearby, pretending to admire the ocean view while the creep told Royce how oral sex lifted a couple to a transcendental plane that couldn't be equaled.

"I never engage in oral sex," Royce snapped, losing patience with all the bird-dogging. "That stuff's too fattening."

She walked away before the wiseass could respond. Chuckling to himself, Mitch hurried after her, following her down the trail to the ocean.

"Royce, wait a second."

"Mitch, the Torquemada of torts. You should be at the swimming pool getting aquatic therapy." She still sounded angry.

"They'll never miss me. I'll sign the roster later."

"Go to class." She trotted down the path away from him.

Nice tush, he noted. Great legs. He trailed along behind her, trying to decide what to say next.

He loved a challenge.

She halted abruptly and he seized the opportunity to bump into her. What a chest. Soft. Full. "Sorry," he said, putting his arm around her. She was even cuter at close range. Even sexier.

"Look, Mitch" — she jerked away from him — "I hate lawyers. I believe what my father says. There's no difference between a whore and an attorney. They both screw you for money. And after working around here, I'm convinced he's right."

"So why are you here?"

"I'm a writer. I need the money." She waved her hand. "Go back to class. You're wasting your time."

She scampered down the trail before he could respond. But Mitch went after her. Hell, nothing in this world had been handed to him. Ever. Everything he wanted he'd gone after. And suffered to get.

"I'm a lawyer," he said when he found her sitting on a boulder at the surf's edge, "to make money. But I'm really an inventor."

"You are?" Suspicion fired her green eyes.

"Yeah. I have a drug at the FDA now just waiting for approval. May take years, though. You know bureaucracy."

"Really? What kind of drug?"

He settled himself on the rock beside her, gazing at her with all the sincerity he could muster. "Something no woman should be without."

"A portable bullshit detector?"

He tried to look supremely insulted, gazing out at the parade of foam-capped waves tumbling lazily onto the shore.

She went for it, touching his arm, saying, "Tell me about your invention."

"It's a pill," he said, the picture of seriousness, "a pill to take the calories out of sperm."

She blinked, disbelief firing her expressive eyes. "You creep."

"So, I'm not perfect. But I'm damn close."

She shoved at him, slamming both hands into his chest. But not before he noticed her smile.

He caught her hands in his. "Give me a chance."

They gazed into each other's eyes for a moment, so close their lips almost touched, their breathing swift. He detected a trace of perfume, an alluring scent with a hint of spice. Heated radiated from her body, her soft breasts barely touching his chest. The rolling crash of the waves on the rocks suggested a more sensual rhythm.

"I'm not good company right now," she finally said. "My mother recently died of cancer, and I'm having trouble accepting her loss." Her eyes glistened with unshed tears.

"Tell me what happened."

They spent the next two days together. Mostly she talked about her mother and he listened, his hand in hers or his arm around her. He never let it get any farther than that, sensing she'd had the rush too many times from legal leeches.

He never discussed his job. Why bother? She hated attorneys. It would take time to change her mind. Naturally, he steered the conversation away from his family. Away from his past.

The sensitive male was a new role for him. Usually, he came on strong with women. If they didn't like it, he cut out. But he knew Royce wouldn't fall for locker-room macho.

She intrigued him, sharing with him many of her ideas about life, most of which were thought provoking and decidedly offbeat. He had to admit he found her fascinating.

On the last evening there was a farewell bash around the mud therapy pools where Nolo Contendere Nachos and Subpoena Coladas were served. Mitch waited for Royce, but she didn't come. He found her in the dark parking lot loading her things into a rattletrap Toyota.

"You're not leaving without saying good-bye, are you?" Obviously she was. Cripes, had he been wrong. He'd been positive he was getting somewhere with her.

"My father needs me." She slammed the trunk shut and moved to the driver's door. "I have to get back to San Francisco as quickly as possible."

"Is he ill?"

"He's been . . . depressed since Mama died." It was too dark to see her face clearly, but he heard the touching concern in her voice.

He thrust a cocktail napkin and a pen at her. "Give me your number and I'll call you." He didn't ask if she wanted to see him, afraid of what she might say.

74

She scribbled her number. "I won't be home for a month. I've made enough money to take my father to Italy to visit Mama's people."

"A month?" Sounded like a life sentence. He'd been patient all weekend, goddammit, counting on seeing her in San Francisco. To hell with pussyfooting around. He hauled her into his arms a little more roughly than he intended. "Don't forget me."

Before she could answer, he tilted her chin up and kissed her. He'd meant it to be a sweet kiss, but, hell, what did he know about tenderness? Nothing.

His mouth molded over hers, crushing its soft fullness. She swayed, clutching his shoulders for support, emitting a shocked gasp that parted her lips. His tongue thrust into the moist heat, seeking hers with fierce urgency. Her lips moved hungrily against his, her arms now circling his neck.

She slid her hands into his hair, furrowing her fingers across his scalp. His sex hardened, ramming against his zipper. Why had he waited all weekend?

"Mitch," she whispered, her lips against his. "Another scar from the same fight?"

Aw, hell. Her questing fingers had discovered the third, deepest scar hidden in the thick hair above his ear. She'd asked about the two scars on his face, but he'd dodged the question, saying he'd been in a fight. Not the truth exactly, but close enough for government work.

"Uh-huh," he muttered, then deliberately distracted her by angling his hips against the notch of her thighs.

"Don't," she whispered. Smiling.

If he'd thought — for a second — she meant no, he would have backed off, but her arms were still around him, her lips close to his. Even in the darkness of the moonless night, he saw the passion blazing in her green eyes.

Her lips sought his and he returned her kiss wildly, his hips churning against hers, pinning her against the side of the car. And she loved it. Her fingernails scored the back of his neck; her hips pressed against his.

He looped his hand around her long hair, wrapping most of it around his palm. With a tug he pulled her head back, exposing the soft skin along her neck. Trailing a series of moist kisses, he worked his way downward to the deep V of her blouse. His tongue shot into the tight hollow between her breasts as his hand captured the soft fullness, squeezing slightly.

He tested the shape and texture, teasing the nipple with the pad of his thumb until it was spiraled tightly.

"Oh, Mitch."

He released her hair and took half a step back. She clutched him, burying her head in the crook of his neck. He had her blouse unbuttoned in a second. The bra that greeted him was straight out of a lingerie ad. Half cups. Lacy. It offered Royce's breasts to him like a pagan sacrifice.

"All right, a front-loader." He unhooked the

flimsy bra and cradled her full breasts in his wide-spread palms. He was achingly, painfully hard now.

He felt Royce's heart slamming against his hand. Her breath fluttered against his neck in staccato bursts. He bent and kissed her breasts, sculpting each taut nipple with his tongue.

"The backseat of your Toyota's looking mighty good."

"I hardly know you," she whispered. "It would just be sex."

"Hey, it works for me." He teased one nipple, sucking ruthlessly. He raised his head and grinned his bad-boy grin. "You want me. Don't deny it."

Just then, a car drove into the dark parking lot. Its blaring lights hit them like a gust of arctic air. Mitch blocked Royce from full view. She scrambled to cover herself.

"Jee-sus," Mitch muttered. His timing sucked. The spell had been broken. Royce was inside the car, key in the ignition.

"See you in a month," he yelled as she peeled out of the parking lot.

4

By the light of the pink elephant above their booth in the Liquid Zoo, Paul studied Mitch, who hadn't spoken for several minutes. Obviously, Mitch's mind was still pondering the incident with Royce five years ago.

"What happened after she left?" Paul prompted.

"It was the month from hell," Mitch said. "The DA had been out with a heart attack for weeks, and I had a caseload big enough for ten lawyers. I didn't want to bargain any of them."

Paul noted the disgust in Mitch's voice. Mitch thought plea bargaining undermined the whole judicial system. He was probably right. It certainly made a lot of criminal attorneys rich, defending felons who kept cycling through the system.

"A case came in at the end of the month about the time I thought Royce was due home. A man had been killed in an automobile accident. The survivor claimed the dead man had been driving, but the police suspected the survivor — who'd failed a sobriety test — had actually been at the wheel.

"The evidence was iffy. The question was whether or not to charge Terence Winston, a local celebrity with a column in the *Examiner* and a heavyweight in liberal political circles."

"Didn't you know he was Royce's father?"

"No. We'd been walking along the beach when I'd asked her name. Between the noise of the surf and my bad ear, I didn't pick up what she said exactly. I thought her name was Royce Annston, but she must have said Royce Anne Winston.

"The case was a challenge. Even if we could have proved Winston was driving, a good defense attorney could have gotten the drunk driving charge dropped. The police used a breath analyzer and got a reading that was barely over the legal limit."

"They should have used a blood analysis, particularly since there was a death involved."

"Hell, they were unusually sloppy all the way around. They mopped up the accident scene in an hour."

"Typical," Paul said, then took a sip of his lukewarm beer, thinking. Crime scenes were taped for days, every bit of evidence examined carefully. But on the street *nothing* was more important than maintaining the flow of traffic. Too often those crime scenes were released prematurely.

"I persuaded the filing deputy — a wimp who must have gotten his law degree mail order — to file charges. Winston was a local celebrity. So what? Why should he get away with anything? Still, the charge would have been tough to prove. The car had burst into flames. What evidence wasn't charred was destroyed by water when the fire department arrived."

"Didn't you talk to Royce during all this?"

"I called, but didn't get any answer. The accounts in the paper never mentioned her name, just that he had a daughter and his wife was dead." Mitch shook his head. "At the preliminary hearing I saw Royce again. Only one other person ever looked at me with so much hatred."

The scars on Mitch's cheek were barely visible in the dim light. Paul knew someone hated Mitch a helluva lot more than Royce. But in all the years Paul had known Mitch, he'd never discussed who had tried to kill him. All Paul knew was someone had attacked Mitch. He suspected it was a woman, but he couldn't say why exactly. Just a hunch.

"Winston had an old friend — some probate attorney — represent him. I annihilated him at the prelim hearing without half trying." Mitch shoved the half-eaten pizza out of his way. "Winston was so stricken, Royce had to help him walk out of the courtroom when the judge ruled there was sufficient evidence to go to trial.

"The next morning I picked up the paper. Royce's father had blown his brains out. He'd been depressed since his wife died and couldn't face a trial."

"Christ," Paul said. He'd been away, trying

to put his life back together after leaving the police force. He'd returned shortly after this happened. It had been another six months before he'd rejoined the living. Mitch never burdened him with his own problems during that time.

"Half the city showed up at the funeral. When Royce saw me, she went ballistic."

"I suppose you can't blame her."

"No. I'd insisted on prosecuting out of blind ambition. I admitted it to her at the funeral. It was a spotlight case that would have made my career. Instead the press was in an uproar and every politician in the city wanted blood."

"But the press didn't fry you. I wasn't so out of it that I wouldn't have remembered them attacking you."

"True, the media went after the system and yammered for weeks about evidence ignored in drug cases that are plea-bargained while we'd crucified an upstanding citizen. Back then the media was lobbying for mandatory sentencing, so they ignored me, but it didn't matter. Royce knew what I'd done."

"That's why you left the DA's office, right?" Paul felt more than a little guilty. He'd returned shortly after Mitch had opened his own office, but Paul had been too absorbed with his own problems to ask why Mitch had left.

"Yeah. The DA returned — pissed big-time — and took all my interesting cases and left me with a bunch of crap."

"I guess you can understand why Royce Winston isn't your biggest fan."

"It's been years, dammit. If Royce were honest with herself, she'd admit that ambition does things to people. And even if I'd been overly ambitious, I was only doing my job. How was I to know her father was suicidal?"

Paul could still see Royce's point, but he didn't even try arguing it with Mitch. She'd lost her father and no doubt saw Mitch as the epitome of the conniving lawyers she hated.

"Goddammit. After what she did to me on that talk show, I'm going to be bird-dogged by reporters."

Paul had never heard Mitch this angry. He was one of the most controlled men Paul knew; Mitch seldom lost his temper. Could it be he did intend to run for office, and Royce had exposed his plans?

She'd cleverly picked up on something even Paul hadn't noticed until she brought it up. Mitch refused to defend any man accused of rape. Why?

"Are you defending a cougar? That'll mean more publicity."

"Actually I'm representing the Wildlife Foundation at a Fish and Game hearing. They want to destroy some cougar because he attacked a hunter." Mitch stabbed the air with his finger. "What I want to know is how the hell Royce found out about it. They just hired me."

"Hey, Mitch, you know nothing can be kept secret. How else would I make a living?"

"I don't like anyone meddling in my business. You know that."

Paul nodded, thinking Mitch guarded his privacy — particularly his past — like a pit bull. And he held a grudge like Kohmeni.

"Nobody treats me the way Royce did tonight and gets away with it. She's had it. I swear, I'll screw her."

"Geez, you're a celebrity — already," Brent exclaimed the following evening as they walked into the elegant St. Francis Hotel for the auction to finance the Center for Women in Crisis.

Did she detect a hostile note in his voice? Was her success going to threaten Brent? This was a side of him that she'd never seen until this moment.

A gauntlet of reporters with belted battery packs and klieg-light sets greeted them. Pack journalism, Royce decided. If one station came, they all did. The minicam crews were the harbingers of electronic gossip in the la-la land of TV news — an amalgam of entertainment and journalism. Did she really want to be a part of this?

One reporter lunged in front of her, his bald head sprouting a lonely tuft of red hair like a patch of crabgrass. "Any truth to the rumor you and Durant were lovers?"

"Don't be ridiculous." Butterflies the size of bats flew through her stomach. A kiss in the dark didn't make them lovers. Besides, no one could know — unless Mitch had told.

Would he retaliate for what she'd done to him

last night by making certain Brent found out about that kiss at the party? How could she explain passionately kissing a man she hated? She couldn't even explain it to herself.

"That creep was Tobias Ingeblatt from the *Outrage*," she told Brent.

The *Evening Outlook* was a local tabloid whose stories were financed by supermarket ads touting the lowest prices in diapers and mayo. It was such a joke, everyone called it the *Evening Outrage*, but it was stocked near the registers beside national tabloids. The *Outrage*'s circulation was awesome with its tales of the clandestine clenches of local celebrities.

Tobias Ingeblatt was their star reporter, she thought with disgust. He probably made three times what her uncle earned. Ingeblatt frequently resold his stories to a national tabloid. Usually his pieces featured the exploits of aliens with heads like light bulbs. He'd made the front page of the nation's largest tabloid when he'd come up with a story — complete with a picture — of Bill Clinton getting a preelection endorsement from the aliens. The issue sold out in one day.

Ingeblatt nosing around made her nervous. More than nervous.

"There are my parents." Brent looked across the room. "Let's say hello, then see what they'll be auctioning tonight."

Royce kept her hand on his arm as he negotiated his way around the maze of closely packed tables. The soft light from dozens of chandeliers and the peach-colored damask fabric on the walls cast a mellow glow across the ballroom. The dance floor had been turned into a viewing area for the auction items. She scanned the crowd pre-viewing the auction items for her friends.

"I've ordered wine," Ward Farenholt said as they walked up. "I'm not drinking that inferior cabernet the charity is serving."

"Good idea." Brent kissed his mother's cheek.

Royce had to admit she envied how close Brent was to his mother. There was always a distinct coolness between father and son, but Brent was genuinely fond of his mother. A good sign, she told herself, recalling her discussion with Talia and Val. You could judge a man by the way he treated his mother.

Royce mumbled good evening, thinking nothing ever suited Brent's father. It was a wonder Caroline Rambeau measured up to his standards for a daughter-in-law, but she did. Ward was fond of Caroline — almost affectionate. Evidently, he had a heart, but opened it only to a select few.

"Wasn't Royce terrific last night?" Brent asked his father.

"There's no hope for the homeless. They're a fact of life and have been since the beginning of time."

Ward directed his comments solely to Brent. It was as if Royce weren't present. Ward ignored most people, talking to the chosen few, like Caroline, he didn't consider inferior. He never spoke to Royce unless he couldn't avoid it.

"You're doing another trial program?" Eleanor asked Royce.

"Yes. I'll be interviewing the head of the Center for Women in Crisis. I'd hoped to do it last night to publicize this event, but I guess they don't need my help. The turnout's great."

"On the next show," Eleanor said, a false note of warmth in her voice, "you'll look better if you have the makeup man use more concealer. Your freckles showed. And your hair —"

"Mother," Brent cut in. "Royce didn't want to hide her freckles or change her hair."

Royce challenged Eleanor, staring into the older woman's glacier-blue eyes. Seeking this woman's approval was futile. Never try to please her again. "I don't want to be another blond prime-time clone. God gave me naturally curly hair and freckles. That's what the viewer will get — the real me."

Brent said, "Royce is an original."

Eleanor blessed Royce with the smile she saved for the homeless and liberals. "I see."

Royce turned away before she said something hateful. Was her relationship with Brent doomed? She walked around the table until she found her place card and put her Leiber bag beside her napkin.

The jeweled cat looked more like a piece of art than an evening bag, she decided. It threw off shards of iridescent light like a Fourth of July sparkler. Still, its flashing green eyes looked so real that she imagined the cat was laughing, making fun of her for wasting her time with people who hated her. And always would.

Well, at least she'd have her two favorite men beside her tonight. Brent was on one side of her and Uncle Wally was on the other. Wait. Brent was with her, but the other card had an unfamiliar name. She left her cat bag guarding her plate and marched around the table, remembering the fiasco at the last party when she'd been seated with Mitch. She was positive Eleanor had been responsible.

Naturally, Caroline was at the table between Brent and his parents, seated with the Italian count. The other couples were friends of the Farenholts. Coming to the auction had been Royce's idea. Uncle Wally was supposed to be with her.

Brent walked up. "Let's look at the auction. Mother tells me Cartier's diamond necklace and earrings are spectacular."

"I don't want to look at any jewelry," she snapped.

Eleanor chose that moment to walk up. "Oh, my. What's wrong?"

"Why isn't my uncle beside me?"

"Well, I — that is we —" She turned to her son. "Your father and I thought Wallace Winston would be more comfortable at another table."

"You've got a lot of nerve."

Royce's tone sapped the color from Eleanor's face. She flung a disgusted look at her son, then scurried away.

Brent caught Royce's arm. "Mother was only thinking of your uncle, darling."

She yanked out of his grasp, every slight she'd suffered from the Farenholts surfacing at once. But nothing could top this. Why had she put up with it for so long?

"You're a fool. You know your parents don't approve of Uncle Wally. Never mind that he's one of the city's — this country's — most respected journalists."

"You're right," Brent reluctantly admitted.

"And they hate me too." She took a deep breath, already regretting what she was about to say, but knowing she had no other choice. "I don't want to be engaged to a man whose parents despise me. Uncle Wally is all the family I have, and your parents deliberately hurt him. He bought a ticket tonight to please me. Now he'll have to sit God only knows where."

Brent put his hands on her shoulders. "I'll take care of it."

"Don't bother." She glanced over to where the Farenholts were standing. Caroline and the Italian count had just arrived. Smiles. Hugs. "I'm going to find my uncle and sit with him."

"Royce," Brent said, his brown eyes sad, "I love you. I'll talk to my parents and make them understand."

"I'm calling off our engagement until we work things out."

"No you're not, dammit!" His tone was uncharacteristically angry. "We'll discuss this later"

— he lowered his voice — "when we're alone."

Barely controlling her own temper, she rushed off to find her uncle. The room was too crowded to be comfortable. Too crowded to find anyone quickly. The Dillinghams waved to her, but mercifully they were far enough away to avoid them without appearing rude. She finally found her uncle at the back of the room. Alone.

"I'm so sorry," she said when she found him. "Eleanor Farenholt had your seat changed."

"It doesn't matter," Wally said with his usual smile.

"It matters to me. I can't go on like this. I called off our engagement until we settle the situation with Brent's parents." She linked her arm with his. "Tonight before I dressed I went up to Daddy's office in the attic. I always feel close to him when I'm there. I couldn't help remembering how happy we were as a family. It'll never be that way with the —"

"Honey, don't toss aside a man you love too easily. Above all, don't worry about them accepting me. I've lived with rejection most of my life."

"It doesn't matter. I love you."

"In spite of what I am?"

"Because you're a wonderful person. You know, when I was a little girl I used to tell everyone how lucky I was to have two daddies. Now that Papa's gone, you're my father. And I'm not letting the Farenholts be nasty to you. Come on, forget them." She tugged on his arm. "Let's find Val and Talia."

"You go on. I'll wait right here."

Royce located Val in the auction area. Her friend looked very striking in Royce's copper lamé dress. Val's hair, a unique shade of red somewhere between rich honey and chestnut, was swept upward in clusters of soft curls. Thank heavens, she wasn't spending another night moping over her ex-husband.

"Royce, I've been looking for you." Val's eyes swept over Royce, registering her approval. "That's a great dress."

Royce wore a loose-fitting beaded lavender gown that deepened the green of her eyes. The shower of lavender beads had a high neckline — she'd learned her lesson last weekend — but it glimmered as she moved, making her even more noticeable. Like all of Royce's clothes it had a dramatic flair. This gown had a bare back that plunged to her waist, exposing most of her back, a stark contrast to the demure front.

"So, where's the parsley king?" Royce asked.

"He's inspecting the vintage wine, trying to decide if he should bid or not."

"Here's a tip. The king is into escarole and endive — big time. Tonight, if it's green and it's on your plate, eat it."

"You're too much," Val said with her familiar smile, a smile Royce had rarely seen since her divorce.

"Let's check out the jewels from Cartier." Royce looked at the long table with security guards standing behind the display cases. "Talia is over there."

By the time they'd winnowed their way through the mob, Talia had disappeared into the throng.

"Don't turn around," Val cautioned, her voice low. "Mitch Durant is coming this way."

"What's he doing here? He never attends charity events." Royce turned her back to the aisle, feigning interest in a Frette comforter on display. She kept her head down, determined to avoid Mitch. Although she didn't turn, every muscle tensed, alert to his presence. For a minute he waited behind her, not saying a word, but she could feel the heat of his body.

"Hello, Royce." The tone was thoroughly masculine, undeniably Mitch's voice.

She had no choice but to turn and face him. He stunned her with a smile, not just a casual grin, but an affectionate one. Wasn't he angry? The last time she'd seen Mitch, he'd been furious. Somehow she stumbled through an introduction to Val.

"Excuse me," Val said with a apologetic glance at Royce. "My date is waiting."

Royce could have killed her, except the parsley king was trapped by the mob in the mock vineyard, waving for Val to join him.

"Last night was great, wasn't it?"

Caught off-guard by his friendliness, she managed a nod. Mitch didn't wait for her answer, nor did he attempt to hide his gaze. His eyes roamed down her shoulders to her breasts to the flare of her hips, then up again, lingering on her lips.

The last time she'd been this close to him, she'd been in his arms. She battled the unexpected urge to move closer, sucking in a quick breath and stepping back. For the life of her she couldn't explain her reaction to this man.

"You're clever, Royce. You had everyone in town talking about your show. Arnie loved it."

Arnold Dillingham had liked the show, she thought with pride. He'd sent her five dozen long-stemmed roses this morning. With the flowers was a note saying her Q-factor was unbelievably high. The Q measured name recognition and audience approval. Eleanor Farenholt could go to hell. Freckles, wayward curls, were what the public wanted, not sleek blondes whose only talent was reading the TelePrompTer.

She spun around, pretending to be interested in the comforter, deliberately being rude. Why didn't Mitch just go away? But he moved closer — or maybe it was her imagination. The man to her right had just bumped her. The room was far too crowded.

Mitch's warm hand touched her bare back. Royce froze, shuddering inside. His touch set off a depth charge of excitement. Get away from him, she told herself, but she couldn't move. There were people on either side of her and Mitch stood directly behind her. Or maybe she didn't want to move.

Maybe she wanted to see what Mitch would do next. Every nerve she possessed was on full alert. Mitch had a devastating effect on her. Her mind might hate him, but her body had other ideas.

He hovered near her, his head just behind her ear. For a moment he didn't say anything, letting his warm breath ruffle her hair. When he spoke, his voice was low, smoky. "Did you tell him, Royce?"

"Tell who?" she asked, not daring to turn and face Mitch.

Instead of answering he slid his hand lower and lower . . . and lower yet. The heat in his fingers sent chills across her breasts. And a surge of heat that unfurled in the pit of her stomach. This wasn't really happening, was it?

"Don't!" She elbowed him in the ribs and tried to turn around, but he pressed against her from the rear, his powerful body imprisoning her. There was no chance of getting away without causing a scene.

"Answer my question, Royce."

The ache in her throat was so powerful, she couldn't talk. Lord, what he could do to her without half trying. She hated him, but still found him terribly exciting. Why?

"Answer me." His hand dipped beneath the fabric of her dress, caressing the soft skin on her lower back. Moving still lower with agonizing slowness. Oh, my.

It didn't matter that no one could see what he was doing, she felt it and knew her expression would tell the world how terribly sexy she found him. Her stomach clenched as he stroked the tender flesh at the base of her spine. She wanted to stop him, she honestly did. But excitement, pure sexual excitement, paralyzed her.

"If you don't answer my question," Mitch whispered, his lips brushing her ear, sending a shocking wave of heat to the pit of her stomach, "I'm going to unhook this garter belt and those sexy silk stockings are going to hit the floor."

"You wouldn't." Her words came out in an embarrassing croak. Of course he would. The stinking jerk never played fair. His fingers were now fondling the cleft of her buttocks. And just look at her. She responded with throbbing breasts and a heavy ache in her thighs.

"No, I didn't tell Brent about kissing you."

Her answer should have stopped him, but it didn't; he was still toying with the hook on her garter belt. "Why not?"

She was breathless with anticipation, not knowing what she expected. He wouldn't do anything in a crowd like this, would he? He could get his hand only so far without ripping her dress. But it was far enough.

He explored the flare of her hips where the garter belt rode low, sensuously running very experienced fingers over her sensitive skin. Holding up the comforter in front of her, she sucked in her breath and let his hand edge around to touch her belly button. Even though the people around him couldn't see what he was doing, just knowing they were there made it even more exciting.

"I asked you a question." His voice was low,

rough. A promise and a threat. Every instinct she possessed told her to stop him, but she couldn't.

"What could I tell Brent?" she mumbled.

"The truth."

In that tiny portion of her brain that wasn't sexually obsessed, she knew he was right. She had no business marrying a man — if another man could make her feel like this. But she didn't dwell on the thought, the melting heat between her thighs forced her to concentrate on the moment.

"When are you going to tell him, Royce?"

Before she could answer, a male voice yelled, "Durant . . . Royce." Omigod, not Tobias Ingeblatt.

Mitch swung her around to face the reporter. A flash went off, capturing her startled expression. Mitch was still standing behind her, his hand down the back of her dress. Oh, Lordy, there was another reporter with a minicam.

They couldn't see what Mitch was doing. Thank God. The crowd was too dense, and the way he was standing behind her must look perfectly natural. But it didn't feel that way.

"Is it true you're defending a cougar?" Tobias Ingeblatt asked.

While Mitch explained he was assisting an animal rights group, Royce marshaled her thoughts. Clearly, she needed a psychiatrist. She hadn't come from a dysfunctional family; she had no unresolved childhood issues she knew of; she didn't go in for kinky sex. Then why did she find this so exciting?

Mitch had his fingertips tucked just under her gown's waistband, his thumb tracing erotic circles on her bare skin. In front of millions of viewers — for God's sakes. Her pulse rate soared and moisture built between her thighs. Was she crazy? Absolutely. A screw — or two — loose.

"Ms. Winston, how do you think Mitch is going to defend that cougar?" asked the TV reporter.

Royce prayed she didn't look as flushed as she felt. "I think he's going to get the cougar off pleading self-defense," she answered, justifiably proud of her calm tone. Somehow she found the strength to step forward, forcing Mitch to move his hand.

"That would be an impossible defense," Mitch cut in. "The hunter was attacked from behind. We'll be discussing this — and other issues — on her next *San Francisco Affairs* program, right, Royce?"

"Right," she said, the sensual haze evaporating. What kind of game was Mitch playing? She waited until the reporters left. "What are you talking about?"

"We're such a great team," he said with a go-to-hell grin that implied just what kind of team he had in mind. "Arnie's putting me on again. Didn't he tell you?"

A flash of insight hit her like lightning. His head was slightly canted to one side, exuding a primal sex appeal most women would find irresistible, but she'd learned her lesson. He was deliberately trying to ruin her life. And she was making it easy for him. Stupid, stupid, stupid.

"No, he didn't." A gusher of anger erupted deep inside her, taking with it the fragile hold she'd kept on her temper. "Why are you doing this? You know I hate you."

"I noticed that last weekend. If you'd hated me another few minutes, I'd have had your panties off. And tonight —"

"You bastard." She reminded herself how much she hated him — not that it would do any good to tell him, considering the way she'd just allowed him to touch her.

"Ditch the mama's boy and come home with me. Let's hop in the sack and you can show me how much you hate me."

"Dream on, Mitch." She rushed away from him, elbowing her way through the crowd.

"I promise, you'll never forget your next interview," Mitch called after her.

"Lordy," she said under her breath. As surely as the sun came up, she knew any chance she had at a TV career was finished. Mitch was too clever to let her best him a second time. Worse, he'd be certain to make her look like a fool.

"He's the enemy," she said out loud, but no one heard her. She paused, not certain where she was going. Why? Why did she let him do this to her?

It had to be the result of that summer when she'd met him. She'd been so certain he was THE

ONE. Loving, tender, intelligent. And sexy. All the things she'd wanted in a man.

She'd spent a month in Italy daydreaming about Mitch. Erotic dreams. The way he'd kissed her that night in the parking lot had triggered a profound reaction.

Her body craved him like a potent narcotic. It was as if he'd unleashed something dark and forbidden in her. But now she knew Mitch for the cunning opportunist he was. Tonight's little episode had been part of a plan to show her.

Mitch: one life, so many women — too much testosterone. An ego the size of the Titanic. And she was the one fish that got away. Add to that the fact she'd embarrassed him on TV, and Mitch was determined to humiliate her.

She couldn't let him do this to her. No. Don't blame him, she warned herself. You're letting him do this. There had to be something she could do, but what?

She checked around for her friends, but couldn't find them in the crowd. Even Uncle Wally had vanished. She couldn't bring herself to go back and face the Farenholts. What had begun as a triumphant evening was now a disaster.

Royce scanned the crowd, hoping to find her uncle before they began serving dinner. She didn't want him sitting alone. She glimpsed Wally at the door. Was he leaving? She opened her mouth to call to him, but saw Wally was with Shaun.

Pivoting on one high heel, she turned back before they saw her. They'd split up more than a year ago, but Royce knew Wally still cared. He hadn't been the same since Shaun had left.

"There you are," Talia said, her brown hair tumbling across her cheek, her dark eyes serious. "Your uncle asked me to tell you he was leaving with a friend. He'll call you later in the week."

"Thanks." Over Talia's shoulder Royce saw the blue-white flashes of cameras. The already congested auction area was jammed, people standing shoulder to shoulder looking at someone. "Who's the fuss about?"

"A soap star. She's wearing a dress you can practically see through. I think —"

"Attention! Attention!" A sharp voice came over the loudspeaker. "The diamond earrings belonging to the set from Cartier have been misplaced. Could you check the floor around you? Anyone who finds them please tell a security guard."

"What a mess." Talia looked distracted. "I'd better find my date. See you later."

As Royce made her way toward the table, she noticed security guards hired by the charity had blocked the exits and were searching the auction area, their flashlights combing the plush carpeting.

"Darling, I've been looking for you," Brent said.

He'd been angry earlier, he wasn't now. It suddenly occurred to Royce that she'd never seen him angry until tonight. But even the most laid-back types had their moments, didn't they? Brent couldn't always be happy go lucky, could he?

She stepped into the welcoming curve of his arm. He was a kind, gentle, wonderful man. Mitch could just go to hell.

A rush of guilt made her sad — and angry with herself. Mitch had persecuted her father, knowing he was in a depressed state over his wife's death, knowing he was innocent. But Mitch hadn't cared. He'd been too anxious to capitalize on the publicity. In a moment of weakness at the funeral Mitch had confessed the truth. Her mind knew better than to forgive him, but there'd been something so sensual about that first kiss in the dark that her body couldn't quite forget.

Gus Wolfe wasn't the brightest bulb in the police chandelier, and he knew it. He kept dabbing sweat off his brow as he walked around the ballroom. Shoulda listened to the wife, he thought, and never opened Wolfe Security. But no, he'd wanted to moonlight and make easy money with a private security company. Being a policeman didn't pay squat. And it had been easy pickings — until tonight.

Christ! A roomful of San Francisco's richest citizens. Missing jewels. What should he do? Good question. He couldn't think of a case quite like this whopper.

Private security forces had much broader powers than the police, that much Gus knew. They weren't hamstrung by the same laws. But did they have the right to search this many people?

"What should we do, boss?" asked one of the kids he'd hired at minimum wage for tonight's bash.

"No one left after the jewels disappeared?" Gus hedged.

The kid shook his head and Gus peered across the crowded room. Shit, he didn't know what to say. He wiped off his brow again, running the back of his hand over his receding hairline. Then he spotted Mitchell Durant.

Cocky sonofabitch. Once he'd crucified Gus on the stand. But the bastard was sharp. He'd know what to do. The last thing Gus needed was to screw up now. If he did, his insurance would go through the roof and he'd have to close down. Then all he'd earn would be the crappy salary the police department paid.

Gus made some excuse to the kid and walked over to Mitch. Durant was looking across the crowded room. Gus followed his gaze and recognized Royce Winston from the television program.

Mitch turned to him. "Find the jewels yet?"

"Nah. Boy, it's a tough one."

Mitch nodded, his eyes on Royce again. The bastard wasn't going to volunteer anything. Gus would have to ask. "What do you think?"

Mitch trained his blue eyes on Gus, making him dead certain he never wanted to piss off this prick. "You're going to have to do something fast or people will start wondering why you haven't called the police."

"Yeah, right." He looked across the room. So many people. Rich, influential people. He turned back to Mitch. Was he still looking at Royce Winston? Yup. "Do we have probable cause to search people?"

"You've got cause, but I'd cover my butt or your security service will be up to its eyeballs in lawsuits. Just because you have more freedom than the police doesn't mean you don't have to watch your ass."

"Gotcha. No strip search." He chuckled in spite of the seriousness of the situation. "I was looking forward to pussy-peeping rich broads."

"Get real. Go for voluntary compliance. Ask people to allow you to use a metal detector. They've all been through enough airports to be familiar with the wand detector."

"I don't have any detectors. I've been meaning to invest, but shit . . . you know how it is."

"Ask hotel security if you can borrow theirs."

"Why didn't I think of that?"

"I have no idea." Mitch stared across the room. Royce Winston — again. "My guess is the perp will ditch the earrings, and you'll recover them before the police arrive. The thief is probably expecting you to call the police right away. He has no way of knowing the bond you put up for tonight doesn't begin to cover the loss, and you're desperate to find the earrings."

Arrogant bastard, Gus thought, but he was dead on. "Thanks, Mitch." He choked out the next words. "I owe you one."

"I won't forget."

"They'd better let us go," Ward Farenholt complained to Brent. "This is ridiculous."

Royce studied the lavender beading on her dress rather than look up. Mitch was watching her again with a hot, knowing gleam in his eyes. She could almost feel his hands on her — down the back of her dress. The heat between her thighs said her body remembered too. She couldn't deny she'd played into his hands.

Why? Why? No answer, just a queasy feeling of self-loathing. Clearly, she needed professional help. First thing Monday she'd contact a psychiatrist.

"Attention, please," came the voice over the loudspeaker. "We've searched the auction area and haven't located the earrings. We'd like you to form a line by the fountain and volunteer to have a metal detector scan."

"We might as well do it," Ward said, his eyes on the mass of people moving toward the fountain, "or we'll be here all night."

It took a moment, but Royce finally located her cat bag on a chair. Brent put his arm around her waist, guiding her along behind Caroline and his parents. A funnel-shaped line formed with Royce trapped in the center.

"I'll bet the metallic beads on this dress trigger the alarm," Royce said to Brent.

"It won't matter unless you have the jewels."

The malice in Eleanor's voice astounded Royce.

She had made the right decision. That woman would make life hell if she married Brent.

Royce couldn't resist saying, "I put the earrings in my bra."

Caroline giggled. "Stop it, Royce, or they'll strip-search you. That would be terrible."

"Actually, I have the earrings in my purse." She held out the cat bag, balancing it in the palm of her hand. "It was just big enough to get them in."

"Careful, someone will take you seriously," Brent warned.

The Farenholts were glowering at her as if they really thought her capable of theft, their eyes frighteningly cold. There was a maliciousness there that she hadn't noticed before.

"No one would be stupid enough to have the earrings right where they could be found." Royce snapped open the bag.

For a split second she thought there was a photographer nearby shooting pictures. But the intense flashes of light she saw weren't from a camera. The diamond earrings *were* in her purse.

5

"This is somebody's crazy idea of a joke." Royce turned to Brent, but he'd moved away, joining his parents.

"Royce, how could you?" Brent's voice echoed his disgust.

Fear mushroomed inside her as she appealed to him. "Why would I open my purse, if I'd known —"

"You're under arrest." A muscular hand latched on to her arm.

"This is a mistake," she argued, aware of the crowd crushing closer each moment, straining to see the earrings in the purse the security guard had just grabbed.

"I knew she'd do something like this," Eleanor said to her son.

Ruddy splotches of color mottled Brent's handsome face, his jaw set in a censuring line. Could he actually believe she'd done it? Yes. How could he? He loved her, didn't he? Why didn't he say something?

No one was saying anything. She saw nothing but condemnation in their eyes as she searched the throng for a friendly face. To the rear of the group she spotted Mitch, staring at her, his expression unreadable.

"Why would I do anything so stupid?" she protested.

"Don't say anything." Val suddenly appeared at her side, and Royce saw Talia elbowing her way toward them. "We'll get you help. Don't worry."

Several guards approached, parting the curious crowd. *This is really happening. They're going to take me away.* A white-hot wave of shame surged through her. Her face set in the stubborn, lockjawed expression her father used to tease her about, Royce trained her eyes on the exit, barely conscious of the exploding flashbulbs or the phalanx of minicameras recording her humiliation to boost their late-night ratings.

The ride to the station passed in a blur of images and sensations she was too numb to feel. The staticky squawk of the radio. The wail of the siren. The worn vinyl of the backseat tinged with the odor of stale tobacco. The steel mesh screen that separated her from the front, caging her in like a dangerous animal.

This was no joke, she realized, a juggernaut of debilitating panic hitting her full force. Someone had planted those earrings in her purse. That person intended for her to be arrested. And she'd played into their hands by leaving her bag at the table. It could have been anyone, but the triumphant glow in Eleanor Farenholt's eyes came to mind.

Did she hate me that much? All the little digs, the veiled and not-so-veiled insults paraded through Royce's mind. The signs had been there, but she'd arrogantly ignored them.

"What am I going to do?" she whispered to herself. "Surely, Brent will help me." But even as she said it, she knew it wasn't true. He'd claimed to love her, but he hadn't given her the benefit of the doubt. Somehow that hurt as much as being arrested.

Didn't he love her? The question kept echoing through her mind as she remembered all the times he'd told her how much she'd meant to him. She'd thought he was a sensitive, caring man — like her father. But tonight he'd sided with his parents — against her.

At the station she was taken to a large room filled with women waiting to be officially processed. The steel door to the holding cell clanged shut behind Royce. She stared at the rows of metal benches. All of the seats were filled; the only sound was the droning hum of the fluorescent lights. Some women stared at her suspiciously while others looked openly hostile.

"What's wrong?" she asked herself when no one made a space for her. These women didn't know her, yet they seemed to dislike her. Obviously, they were poor. A hooker in thigh-high boots of worn vinyl. A woman in stained sweats and tennis shoes without laces.

My dress, she decided after a few seconds. It

set her apart as surely as if she'd been wearing a space suit. An expensive gown like hers was as alien to these women as sable coats were to the homeless.

Like the crowd at the auction they were judging her; only, these women were finding her guilty of being rich. *I'm not rich,* she longed to scream. *I bought this dress on sale.*

Finally, a butter-blond with a body like a tombstone slid over, leaving a space the size of a hand for Royce. She wedged herself into the spot as the blond boldly leered at her, a glare that would have backed down a pit bull. The other women stared, too, even more curious now that she'd been offered a seat. The hefty woman was a leader, she realized. Or someone they feared.

Facing forward, Royce was conscious of the muscular woman beside her, studying her, cataloguing everything about her. Then she laid a chunky hand on Royce's thigh, fingering the metallic beads on her gown.

"Stop it." Royce swatted her hand aside, meeting the woman's eyes. They were as black as the roots of her bleached hair, radiating an intense hatred Royce only had imagined existed until this moment.

"Honey," the blond said, her voice blatantly masculine, "you're as good as dead." She yanked off a handful of beads, tearing the dress, and tossed them into the air. "Count on it."

Royce vaulted to her feet and marched to the

door, seeing the matron through the small window. She knocked, but the guard ignored her. Then she pounded on the door, but the guard didn't look up from the comic book in her lap. Beating on the door with both fists, she screamed, "Let me out."

Finally, the guard inched open the door, looking every bit as hostilely at Royce as the women inside. Pointing to the blond Royce said, "That woman's bothering me."

"Settle down, Maisie. I don't want no trouble tonight."

The guard's placating tone told Royce even the guards were afraid of the woman called Maisie. The door slammed shut before Royce could say another word. She turned, her feet aching in her high heels, and forced herself to look directly at Maisie, instinctively knowing not to show her fear.

"I'll be waiting for you . . . inside," Maisie promised.

Royce went to the corner and stood with her back against the wall, her eyes trained on the door, waiting for the matron to call her so she could be formally booked and put into her own cell. But like the wheels of justice it fed, the booking system was so overworked that it had almost collapsed under its own weight. Women poured into the room, but few were taken out.

The women on the benches shifted, making room for new arrivals. An outsider, Royce was as unwanted here as she'd been at the Farenholts'. She had no illusions about what would happen to her if she were convicted.

Time passed. One hour. Two. She lost track, standing alone, her back braced against the cold wall. Her mind, though, was alert, processing the evening's events. Who? Why? Eleanor Farenholt was the only explanation that made sense.

Brent. It hurt so much to think of him, but she couldn't help wondering where he was and what he was doing. Surely, by now he'd realized she hadn't taken those earrings.

She thought of all the good times they'd had together. Long walks in San Franciso's misty fog. Candlelit dinners. Discussions about current events. He'd claimed to love her, but where was he now when she needed him?

"Royce Anne Winston," barked the matron, startling her.

She followed the woman to the processing bay, where her fingertips were pressed against a laser light and a photographer took two shots, full face and profile. The photo gave her a semiembalmed appearance that would have made the Pope look like a serial killer. They confiscated her beaded gown and issued her a Day-Glo orange jumpsuit with the word "prisoner" stenciled on the back.

Remembering Val's warning she refused to speak with the detectives. Did she want to call a lawyer? She nodded, then dialed her uncle's number. It was almost dawn but he didn't answer. She whispered a frantic message to his machine. The only criminal attorney she knew was Mitch. Uncle Wally, though, had spent years covering the city. He'd know who to call.

The rubber slippers she'd been issued flopped against the concrete floor as she was herded down a narrow corridor flanked by cells full of women. The cellblock was more crowded than the holding room; two extra bunks had been shoehorned into cubicles originally designed to hold four. It could have been day or night; in the windowless cavern it was impossible to tell, because they never turned out the lights.

They stopped at a cell with an unoccupied lower bunk. Inside the women were lying down, trying to sleep despite the undertone of noise and blaring overhead lights. The matron nudged Royce forward, then slammed the iron-barred door behind her.

All Royce could think about was sleeping until Uncle Wally arrived with an attorney. She angled her body sideways and edged toward the empty bunk.

"Well, if it ain't the rich bitch."

God, no, not Maisie. The beefy blond swung down from the top bunk, blocking Royce's path. She mumbled a quick Ave Maria.

"No room for you, rich bitch. You'll have to stand."

"That's my bunk." Royce tried to sound tough, but fear was gathering force inside her like a hurricane.

"Fuck you." Maisie hunkered over Royce, an emotion too intense to be merely hate set on each coarse feature.

111

"Guard," Royce yelled. "This woman won't let me in my bunk."

"Quiet. Aaah, shut up," echoed up and down the cellblock.

The two guards huddled around the TV at the far end of the corridor never turned around. Royce had another even more frightening glimpse of what her life would be like if she were convicted.

Forty-eight hours, she thought, gripping the cold steel bars with both hands. The authorities had that much time to formally charge her, then she could post bail and prove her innocence before the preliminary hearing.

The preliminary hearing. How well she remembered her father's hearing. He'd been innocent and yet a fast-talking attorney — Mitchell Durant — had convinced the judge to order a trial. Papa had been terrified of jail. Now she understood his fear, but feeling sorry for herself wouldn't help her.

She turned and faced the snickering Maisie. Royce barreled into her, sledging her thick belly with a punch that carried all her weight. Maisie staggered backward, more surprised than hurt, and Royce scrambled into the bunk, hoping Maisie would leave her alone.

Maisie puffed for a second, then sprang at Royce, hurling herself onto the bunk, landing on Royce like a steel piling. Air whooshed from Royce's lungs and the mattress bowed, threatening to collapse.

Maisie breathed into Royce's face, hot breath rife with a stale pickle odor. She touched Royce's hair, stoking it almost like a lover. "You've had it, rich bitch," she said in a stage whisper designed to carry up and down the cellblock. "You're dead."

Royce started to scream, but Maisie's hand latched over her mouth. Intellectually, Royce knew Maisie didn't hate her. This wasn't personal. Royce was a symbol, a woman who had everything while Maisie had nothing. But this subtle realization did nothing to bank the primal fear surging through her.

"Easy, Maisie," a calm voice came from the aisle between bunks. Strong hands, crowned by a chipped set of false nails, hauled Maisie off Royce, and she looked up at a woman with beet-colored hair and brown eyes ringed with liner like Cleopatra's.

"Thanks," Royce muttered, still trying to get her breath.

"I'm Helen Sykes." The woman plopped down beside Royce. "What brings you to the gray-bar Hilton?"

"Theft. But I didn't do it."

"Mitch Durant's the best mouthpiece — if you can afford him."

Royce told herself there had to be another lawyer as good as Mitch. He was the last person she'd call.

"How'd you get caught?" Helen asked, resting back on her elbows to keep her head from hitting

113

the bunk above them.

"I was framed," Royce insisted, lowering her voice, conscious of the other prisoners listening. Why should any of them know her problems? None of them had come to her rescue. She found herself telling Helen the whole story, concluding with "Would I have opened my purse in front of everyone if I had actually stolen the earrings?"

The clock over the guard's station read seven-thirty when a matron came for Helen. "About time. I got the most worthless pimp in Frisco. I shoulda been outta here hours ago." She gave Royce an affectionate thump on the back and was gone.

Where was Uncle Wally? She'd been in jail for over ten hours. Why hadn't he come? Maybe he'd spent the night with Shaun, but he always went to Sunday Mass. Surely, he'd come home afterward and check his machine.

By noon the sense of alarm she felt when Wally hadn't appeared among the legions of relatives visiting other prisoners became full-blown terror magnified by lack of sleep and a growing awareness that she could spend years behind bars.

Why hadn't Brent come to his senses and realized she was innocent? She recalled the anger in his voice: *How could you, Royce?*

"How could I," she muttered to herself. "How could you desert me? That's the question."

Brent's "undying love" was merely an illusion. She had to accept the fact that she was all alone. He wasn't going to come. He'd never loved her, not the way she'd needed to be loved. With true love came trust. Unconditional trust.

If he'd truly loved her, Brent would have trusted her. He would have known without having to be told that she was innocent.

"I need to use the telephone," Royce told the matron when she finally got her attention.

"You're number sixty-seven," the woman said as she shuffled back to the post where a videotape of last week's soaps was playing.

It was another three hours before her number was called. She dialed Wally, then rested her head against the wall where every inch was covered by graffiti. She listened to her uncle's recorder. The matron was concentrating on the TV, so Royce covertly dialed Val's number only to get her machine too. She tried to keep the frantic tone out of her plea, but heard it anyway.

"I'm still in jail. I don't know what's happened to Uncle Wally. I need your help."

It wasn't until well after dinner, almost twenty-four hours since her arrest, that the matron bawled, "Royce Anne Winston."

She hurried along the visitors' wing, each room the size of a restroom stall with video monitors hanging from the ceiling, electronic sentinels. She stepped into the visitors' cubicle, expecting Uncle Wally and halted.

Not Mitchell Durant. The matron gave her a shove and slammed the steel door behind Royce. Mitch stood at a table hardly bigger than his brief-case.

"Your friends retained me to represent you." He motioned to the chair on her side of the table. "They haven't been able to locate your uncle."

She dropped onto the seat, knowing her situation was worse than she'd imagined. Val and Talia knew how she felt about Mitch. They would never have hired him unless — "How bad is it? Why haven't they formally charged me?"

Mitch took the seat opposite her, his attitude detached, professional, without any hint of compassion. "Abigail Carnivali is milking your arrest to get as much free publicity as possible. She's running for DA next year, you know. She loves headline felonies and isn't going to file charges until your forty-eight hours are up."

Dear Lord, she *was* in hell. It shouldn't be happening, but it was actually comforting to see Mitch Durant. "Then what?"

"You'll be formally charged and bail set. There's already been too much publicity in this case to release you on your own recognizance. I'll need your passport and loan info on your house to meet bail requirements."

"I don't have much equity in the house," she said, her voice surprisingly calm. She hadn't slept in two nights now and found she had trouble concentrating on what he was saying as they settled the details of arranging bail and getting her passport.

"I'm worried about my uncle," she told Mitch as the matron escorted her from the visitor's room. "Please, check on him."

As Mitch had predicted it was almost midnight the following night — just short of forty-eight hours — before she was formally charged with grand theft. Mitch quickly satisfied the bail requirement by surrendering her passport and the deed to her heavily mortgaged home.

Clad in the beaded gown that had once made her so proud, she stood in the release bay, looking for Wally. During the proceedings she hadn't been able to talk to Mitch, but she assumed Wally would be waiting for her. Mitch walked in, his briefcase in one hand. The shadow along his jaw said he hadn't been home since early that morning.

"Did you call Shaun Jamieson? What did he say about Wally?"

"No one's seen your uncle since the auction." His hand on her waist, he guided her down a deserted corridor.

"Where are we going?"

"Out the service entrance. The press is in front."

Wise move. A brief glimpse in the mirror as she'd changed out of her prison jumpsuit had confirmed the worst. Hair hanging in unkempt hanks. Dark circles that had cost Richard Nixon an election. The only reporter she wanted to see was her uncle.

In the back alley a group of homeless men were guarding Mitch's expensive Viper. He gave them money, then helped her into the car. Her dress rode up, exposing more of her thighs than she would have liked, but she was too tired to care.

The last time she'd had a full night's sleep had been the night before the auction — almost seventy-two hours ago.

She settled into the glove-leather seat, the supple curve cradling her like welcoming arms. She closed her eyes and didn't open them until the sports car stopped. Expecting to be home, she was startled to find Mitch had parked in front of Joe Mama's Pizza.

"I'm starving," Mitch announced. "I've been waiting for your release since four." Inside, the aroma of pizza reminded her how terrible prison food had been, and she ordered calzone and black coffee while Mitch had a combination pizza — no anchovies. She sipped her coffee and ate the calzone left over from the Stone Age.

"Get some sleep," Mitch said between bites. "We'll get together tomorrow and decide how to proceed."

She took a head-clearing breath, so groggy she couldn't concentrate. She'd hoped to postpone this discussion until later, but saw it wasn't possible. "You know how little money I have. I can't afford you."

"I'm willing to reduce my usual fee. This case is going to generate a lot of publicity. That's worth more than money" — he gave her an odd look — "to a man planning a political career."

The fires of ambition she'd carelessly overlooked when they'd first met years ago had become a conflagration, but she had no intention of letting him use her to further his career. "I

118

appreciate what you've done, but I don't think it would be a good idea for you to continue to represent me."

"Why not? You won't find anyone better."

"True, but you know how I feel about you."

"You hate me." He flashed his ruthless grin. "We can build on that."

"Very funny, Mitch. You know what I mean."

"Tell the truth. You're afraid of spending time with me, afraid you'll fall in love with me."

"What? Don't be ridiculous. I want a lawyer I'm comfortable with — someone I respect."

The word *respect* detonated on impact. In the frigid depths of his eyes she saw unadulterated anger and maybe even hurt. He had her back in the car without giving her a chance to finish her coffee. They drove toward her home in silence charged with a cross-current of anger.

She half wished she could modify what she'd said. She was grateful for what he'd done — although she was certain her friends had paid him well — but she didn't respect him after what had happened with her father. How could she possibly work with him?

"Let me out here," she said as he drove up in front of her house. "I have a key hidden around back. I can get in." They'd kept her Judith Leiber bag and its contents as evidence.

"I'll make sure you're safe inside."

Too exhausted to argue she led him around to the back and switched on the outside lamp. It flooded the small garden with bright light, revealing clusters of cheery pansies and a weeping willow.

Below the tree was an empty rabbit hutch. It was wobbly with age, but she couldn't bear to throw it out. Like all of her father's woodworking projects it was far from perfect, but they'd made it together years ago. Then Papa had taken her to select a lop-eared bunny she'd named Rabbit E. Lee.

The pet store had failed to mention how long rabbits live, and Lee had been frisky the day she'd kissed him good-bye and left for college, entrusting his care to her father. Older, slower, but just as loving, Lee was still alive after college when she'd lived in her own apartment. By then, though, he was her father's pet. Papa would sit under the tree writing his column in longhand, feeding Lee carrots.

But the gunshot that killed her father might as well have pierced Lee's heart too. It was almost as if the bunny knew Papa had killed himself. From the moment that shot had rung out, nothing could persaude Lee to eat. Royce had tried; God knows she'd sat by the cage, tears in her eyes, begging Lee to take a carrot for her father's sake. But he kept staring up at the attic where Papa had taken his life.

A week later Rabbit E. Lee died, his eyes still open, still staring at the attic window. The vet claimed it was old age, but Royce knew better. He'd died of a broken heart. She'd closed up the house and left for Italy the next day.

She gazed out into the darkness. Somewhere in the city was another little girl standing by her daddy's side "helping" him build a bunny hutch. Her young heart was swelling with love that would last a lifetime as she made herself a promise: Someday she'd marry a man just as wonderful as her daddy.

Something snapped inside Royce's chest. Brent. The man she'd thought was so much like her daddy had been nothing more than a cheap imitation. How could he have deceived her? Why hadn't she seen how shallow he was, how much he wanted to please his parents?

"The key?" Mitch prompted, reminding her that he was standing beside her, waiting.

He'd killed her father as surely as if he'd pulled the trigger. She wanted to hit him, or scream, but she was overwhelmed with sadness. Nothing could bring back Papa just as nothing could change Mitchell Durant.

"It's under here." She lifted a planter her father had made so the key could fit underneath. Nothing. "Did you have Val get my passport?" He nodded. "She must have been so upset, she forgot to put the key back."

"Perhaps she put it under one of the other pots."

"No. It was on a special Zodiac key ring that had my sign —"

"Scorpio. It figures."

She was bone weary, too tired to be baited by his sarcasm. "My father made the key ring to fit

121

under this planter." She took off her shoes; her toes were screaming for mercy. "I'll climb —"

A thunderous crash and the sound of splintering glass was followed by shouts of "Police" as the lights inside her house came on.

"My God," she cried, "they've broken down the front door."

"Get your hands up! Now!" Mitch's hands shot into the air.

Common sense told her to reach high, her shoes in one hand. God knows, she didn't want to be mistaken for a criminal and be shot in her own backyard. "They had no right to break into my home."

"This isn't a social call. It must be the Narcotics Unit with a no-knock warrant. If they knock, the stash goes down the toilet."

"I don't" — she started to protest, but the back door flew open and guns were leveled at them. She'd watched similar scenes on TV, but that didn't keep her knees from turning to putty.

"Durant? That you?" called an officer, obviously surprised.

"Yeah, and this is Royce Winston. You better have a warrant and an affidavit to back it up." Mitch reached out his hand, but Royce waited until the guns were holstered before lowering her shaky arms and clasping her shoes to her chest.

Mitch read the warrant, then turned to her. "It's valid."

She sank down on the back step. Dear God, what now? Inside, glass shattered and along with it her eggshell composure. She rested her head on her knees, hugging her legs to keep from screaming. This couldn't be happening to her. But it was.

Mitch sat beside her. "They're looking for drugs."

She lifted her head. "I don't have any drugs."

"The judicial system sucks the big one. I'm the first to admit it, and the first to exploit it. But one thing that's still sacred is our right to privacy. Hell, every cop in the city knows where the drug lords have their caches, but they can't troop in without a search order. When they get one, it's because they're dead nuts certain to find what they're looking for.

"This search warrant's affidavit says it was issued on the word of an unnamed informant whose reputation is good enough to convince a judge to allow the search."

"Unnamed? Anyone could make up anything —"

"Judges don't take the word of an unreliable informant and they have to protect them by not revealing their names." He took out a business card and scribbled on the back of it. "Here's the name of a lawyer. You don't have to worry about him. All he chases is ambulances. Call him as soon as they take you to the station. You're so exhausted, you're liable to confess."

Mitch hustled down the path toward the front of the house where he'd parked the car. "Okay, buddy," he muttered to himself. "You're long on hormones and short on common sense."

She didn't "respect" him — whatever that meant. Yessir, she'd won. Award her a black belt in verbal karate. He was so blasted mad, he could strangle her. Even if he'd been a bastard — hey, he wasn't admitting anything — she should at least respect his ability.

But Royce hadn't a clue how much trouble she was in. Like most yuppies her idea of a felony was a dent in her BMW. Just wait, sweet cakes.

What did he expect? Gratitude? Ha! No way. If anything, Royce hated him more for seeing her so vulnerable. Not that he cared. The world was full of women.

"So why does she have you running in circles like a crazed possum? She's a heartbreaker. A ball buster. Why can't you forget her?"

The answer hit him like a straight shot of Kentucky moonshine. Five years hadn't changed a damn thing. He still wanted her.

"Goddammit!" He was royally pissed. That stunt she'd pulled on TV still had him fried.

The pictures in today's edition of that rag, the *Evening Outlook*, had sent his blood pressure into the stratosphere. They showed Royce in dental floss that passed for a bikini, lolling on the beach with Lover-Boy Farenholt. Tobias Ingeblatt's headline shrieked: SEXPOT COLUMNIST HEISTS JEWELS.

"Get the hell out of here," he told himself.

But leaving her was the hardest damn thing he'd ever done. A grim reminder of the past.

124

His mother. She'd refused his help too. Swear to God, you never knew what a woman would pull. She could love you one minute and try to kill you the next.

Ahead, Mitch saw the flashing lights from the armada of police cars had attracted a crowd of neighbors clad in robes and curlers. No sign of the media barracudas. Yet.

The K-9 unit pulled up and four German shepherds leapt out just as the police video crew arrived. There you go. The narcs did expect a big find.

"Mitch . . . Mitch." He turned and saw Royce hurrying toward him, streamers of blond hair billowing over her shoulders, her shoes in her hand.

"Well, I'll be jiggered." He couldn't keep the undertone of bitterness out of his voice.

She stopped a few feet from him, hesitated, taking a frantic look at the legions of narcs swarming around her home. Then she came closer, a step at a time. Her soulful green eyes glassy with unshed tears.

"I want you to be my attorney," she said, heartfelt emotion breaking in her voice, but the earnest plea came as much from her eyes as her voice. "Don't . . . leave me."

Despite her stricken expression she squared her shoulders. He'd bet his life those were the hardest words she'd ever spoken. She was scared to death, and he didn't blame her. Someone wanted to make dead certain she went to prison for years.

Every instinct he possessed, instincts that had

never failed him, told him to turn his back and get the hell out of there. But she looked so forlorn, standing clutching her high heels, the flashing strobes from the police cars washing her face red-then-white-then-red.

"I'll represent you, Royce, but I have several conditions."

"What?" She was shaking. Obviously she needed a good night's sleep to pull herself together.

He shucked his jacket and put it over her shoulders, then lifted her long hair free. His hand lingered, testing the softness of her hair, the spring in the curl. "I want you — and your uncle — to promise that you'll never write or reveal anything you find out about me during the course of this case. Not one word about me. None of that shit you pulled on the TV program, understand?"

"I promise. I'll never write — or say — one word about you. Ever. I swear."

"Absolutely no questions about my past."

"All right, Mitch, I understand."

"And you'll have to agree to do whatever I tell you." He arranged the silky length of her hair over the lapel of his jacket as it hung from her like a choir robe.

"That's fine with me. I don't know what to do. I'm on the ropes here."

"No, babe. You're down for the count." He tilted her chin up and looked directly into her eyes. She had the damnedest eyes. "It's going to be hard for you, Royce, but you're going to have to trust me."

She gazed at him, her eloquent eyes expressing her deepest emotions. Fear. Anger. Guilt over accepting his help. And overwhelming vulnerability. She didn't want to put her life in his hands, but she had no choice.

He resisted the urge to cradle her in his arms. She'd allowed him to help out of sheer panic. Anything more would have to wait.

From inside the house someone yelled, "We've got a thousand smackers here."

"Recount it," yelled another cop. "Tell 'em to dust it for coke."

"That's my earthquake money," Royce explained to Mitch. "After the earthquake the credit lines were cut off. No one could use charge cards or cash checks. I wrote a humorous column about it, saying along with quake supplies everyone should keep some cash. They aren't going to find cocaine on it."

"Tell that to the FBI. Their stats show eighty percent of all the money in this country shows traces of coke. That's how much cash goes through drug dealers' hands, then to the bank."

"Kill the baby," yelled someone inside the house.

Royce clutched his arm. "What baby?"

"Just cop talk. It means they found what they came for."

"They couldn't have. I don't . . . it's impossible."

A sergeant rushed over to them, pulling a laminated index card from his pocket. "Royce Ann Winston. You're under arrest for possession of cocaine." He looked down at the card. "You have the right —"

"Can it," Mitch said. Jesus, you'd think the guy could memorize the Miranda. "She knows her rights. She isn't saying a damn thing until we're in court."

A screech of tires announced the arrival of the press corps. You could almost hear their collective sigh of relief: They hadn't missed *all* the fun. The sergeant unsnapped handcuffs from the side of his belt.

"Cuff her and I'll nail you for harassment. You jerk-offs let every two-bit drug dealer walk into the station with their attorneys. You're not dragging my client off in cuffs for some media circus. I'm riding in with her."

The sergeant backed off. Lately every lawyer who wasn't chasing an ambulance was suing the police department — the newest legal boondoggle. Sometimes they deserved it; sometimes they didn't. But the thought scared the piss out of them. It meant suspensions, appearances before Internal Affairs, a black mark on your record. And that's if everything went in your favor.

They marched over to the cruiser with Mitch shielding her from the cameras with his body, his arm protectively locked around her. He got in the back with Royce while the police had their moment of glory giving the media maggots their nightly dose of mayhem. Royce had stopped shaking, but her eyes had a distracted look. The same look he'd seen at her father's funeral.

The cops jumped into the car and pulled out, leaving the special operations units to go over the house. Interesting, Mitch thought, they're throwing everything they have at this. Why?

He pulled Royce close, angling his head so his good ear was closest to her, then whispered, "Listen to me."

Her expressive green eyes were inches from his. She seemed more angry than frightened. A good sign. "Yes?"

He put his lips so close to her ear that when he spoke, he brushed it. "You're going to be in there another two days."

"I can't. Please, help me."

"You're tough. You can gut it out," he said, more to bolster her confidence than anything else. Life in jail was as alien to the middle class as life on Pluto. Stephen King couldn't invent some of the people inside prison walls.

She nodded bravely. "I can handle it."

He gave her a reassuring squeeze, whispering, "Don't discuss this case with anyone. There are snitches everywhere who'll invent anything. They'd roll over on their own mothers just to get their sentences reduced."

"I talked about the case already. But I'm certain Helen Sykes isn't a snitch. There was this horrible woman, Maisie Something, she threatened to hurt me. Helen came to my rescue."

Aw shit! Mitch cursed to himself. He liked to think of himself as the meanest son of a bitch in the valley. But even he couldn't muster the gall to tell Royce she'd put another nail in her own coffin.

6

After Mitch left Royce at the police station, he found a pay phone and dialed Paul's number. "What did they get?" Mitch asked. Although Paul no longer was on the force, he kept a radio that monitored transmissions from the police station.

"They got half a kilo."

"Christ." Mitch hadn't known exactly how much dope they'd found at Royce's. Possession for personal use was one thing, but for every gram more the mandatory sentence escalated, the assumption being the person was a serious drug dealer.

"Mitch, are you sorry you pushed for mandatory sentences?"

"No way. There was too much bargaining for lighter sentences, but, hell, the law should have been written so judges would have some leeway in sentencing first time offenders. If Royce is convicted, she'll be sentenced to five years."

"I talked to her friends. Talia Beckett had already given a statement to the police."

Mitch frowned. "If this were a mass murder, the cops wouldn't take secondary statements for weeks. Damn suspicious."

"Sounds like pressure, right? The Farenholts?"

"Or the DA's office. Go on, what's Talia like?"

"A knockout, black hair, dark brown eyes. She's a recovering alcoholic who's into every variety of therapy known to mankind."

"Any chance she put the earrings in Royce's purse?"

"Don't rule it out. Talia's the type that likes to chat, and she told me an interesting story. It seems that she's known Brent Farenholt for years. After Royce moved to Italy, Talia began dating Brent. He had a party just after Royce returned and Talia brought Royce and Val. Shortly after, Brent asked out Royce. It's possible Talia's upset with Royce for stealing Brent."

"What about Valerie Thompson?" Mitch vaguely recalled the redhead Royce had introduced him to. She and Talia had come up to him after Royce had been arrested, but Talia had done all the talking.

"Val refused to talk to the police without a lawyer."

"My kind of woman."

Mine, too, Paul thought, but didn't say so. He hesitated, listening to Mitch as he drove into his garage. Paul still felt the heat surging through him the way it had when Valerie Thompson had answered his knock earlier that day.

Val. Honey-brown eyes. Thick auburn hair. Long, slim legs. He had flashed his ID, but she'd glared at it. Most women had a glorified vision of private investigators, honed from too many television programs. Not Val.

"I work for Mitchell Durant," Paul had said. "I'm here to help your friend, Royce Winston. May I come in?"

She admitted him to a small apartment that overlooked a back alley. A mouth-watering aroma wafted from the kitchen into the living room furnished in garage-sale rejects. "I need to ask you a few questions."

"Just a minute. I have to turn off the oven."

He smelled lasagna and his stomach contracted, but not as much as it did looking at the provocative sway of Val's rear.

She returned and sat just near enough that he could see the gold flecks in her eyes. "How can I help?"

"Was Royce near the earrings?"

"Everyone was near them."

Smart-ass. "A witness says you were with Royce examining the earrings." He didn't add their friend, Talia, had volunteered the incriminating information.

She looked down, revealing the gold tips of her lashes. "We passed by them, talking, not really looking. I left Royce with Mitchell Durant — near the earrings."

There was a cutting undertone to her voice. He didn't pursue it. Mitch had told him how

Royce felt about him. Obviously, Val shared her opinion. "Do I smell lasagna?"

"Yes. I was just sitting down to dinner."

He gazed at her shamelessly. If she invited him for dinner, he'd have an excuse to draw out the interview.

"It's tofu lasagna."

"Love it. I've given up red meat."

"Really?" She looked genuinely pleased. "I took third place at the Tofu Sculpting Contest in Golden Gate Park."

Tofu sculpting? S'okay. It takes all kinds. "Amazing. What did you make?"

"An eagle. A peacock took first." She led him into the kitchen and gave him a hearty portion of lasagna, then poured him a cup of coffee.

"Did Brent Farenholt ask you out?"

"Why?"

She sounded on guard, more than just defensive. Was she hiding something? "Background info."

"I didn't go, so he took Royce."

Interesting, Brent had asked out all three friends. And Royce had landed him. Had one of the others been jealous enough to frame Royce? "What do you think of Brent?"

"I don't like him. He's too . . . too smooth."

Paul had never formally met Brent, but he knew him by sight and reputation. San Francisco was widely regarded as a big city, although less than a million people lived there. Everyone in legal circles knew each other. Brent was well liked; Mitch's in-your-face personality won him few friends. But he was respected for his ability and for having built a powerhouse firm. Brent was a legal lightweight who'd be nothing without his father's law practice.

"Why'd you get a divorce?" Paul asked.

"That's none of your business."

Obviously the wound was still fresh. He hoped that accounted for Val's defensiveness. He didn't want her to be the one responsible for Royce's troubles.

"Val, do you have any idea how a defense attorney builds a case? Mitch will have to persuade the jury that there's a reasonable doubt Royce is guilty. He does that by casting suspicion elsewhere. He's going to have to put witnesses on the stand who support his case. Very likely, he'll call you."

"My divorce has nothing to do with this case."

"The prosecution could come up with an angle. That's why I'm here doing a thorough background analysis. You refused a substantial settlement when your husband divorced you. Why?"

She gave him more lasagna, clearly considering whether or not to answer. "My husband left me for someone else. They'd been seeing each other — behind my back — for years. I was angry. I had no intention of taking money so he wouldn't feel guilty."

"You'd rather live like this than accept what was rightfully yours?"

"He can keep his damn money. I don't need it or him."

Wow, Paul thought as he took another bite of lasagna. She's carrying a mule load of emotional baggage. He changed the subject. "What do you do for Global Research?"

"Global is a fancy name for the Tomaine Tommy's burger chain. I'm a spy. I visit the various franchises to make sure there's TP in the restrooms, the fries aren't soggy, the help smiles — that sort of thing."

Paul was familiar with her job. All the major chains had people checking on their franchises. And if a problem was found the spy would return day after day to determine the extent of the trouble. That took someone who was extremely deceptive and skilled at disguises.

"I've been a PI for years. I've learned people have great instincts. I've saved a lot of time by pursuing those leads first. What's your gut feeling about who took the jewels?"

"Wade Farenholt. He'd selected Caroline for his son. Royce — though I love her like a sister — is hardly a demure, classy lady like Caroline. And Royce was a threat. She would have encouraged Brent to resist his father's demands."

"Great," Mitch said, as he stood in the cramped phone booth and listened to Paul finish telling him about his interview with Valerie Thompson. "No one can agree who put the jewels in the purse."

"A crime of opportunity," Paul responded. "Who could predict Royce would leave her purse at the table? But this drug deal took planning and cash. I doubt Royce's friends have the money."

"But don't rule it out. Get as many people on this as it takes, and keep me posted."

Mitch hung up, then called information for Gus Wolfe's number. It was well after midnight, so the phone rang several times before the policeman answered.

"It's Mitch Durant. You owe me one. Remember?"

"Yeah . . . I remember." Wolfe sounded pissed.

"A search warrant was issued for Royce Winston's home. The informant's name on the affidavit is confidential. I want that name."

"Well, hell . . . you know I don't work in Narcotics."

"You've been on the force for years. You must have a Narc buddy who'll tell you the informant's name."

Mitch hung up without giving Gus a chance to argue, then he walked through the swinging doors into the prison offices.

Jewel Brown looked up from the duty roster she was scheduling and saw Mitch Durant coming her way. She wasn't surprised. He often dropped by and left cigarettes or candy.

The other attorneys oiled the boys out front to be certain they were given the first available visiting room, or to get hustled through the jail's metal detectors, but Mitch was smarter than the rest. He made certain the gang in the back got their share.

136

Mitch sat on the edge of her desk next to her computer terminal. "Here are two tickets to the Giants game. I can't go, but maybe someone around here can use them."

"Thanks." Jewel pushed the tickets aside as if seats behind home plate weren't pure gold. She hated baseball, but her son and one of his no-account friends would be in pig-shit heaven. He might even help her with the laundry.

"I need some information," Mitch said. That's what Jewel liked about Mitchell Durant. Another attorney would jive you to sleep, then ask for help. "What can you tell me about a prisoner named Maisie? I don't know her last name but —"

"Shit, everyone knows Maisie Cross. That bull dyke's been in an' outta here two dozen times for clockin' 'caine. Cain't never raise bail, so we're always stuck with her until her trial."

Mitch frowned. If Maisie was a veteran of a cruel prison jungle, Royce was no match for her. "I need a favor."

"Shoot." Jewel was pleased to be able to help. Mitch had never asked her for anything. Not that she felt guilty for taking so much from him. Everyone knew lawyers were rollin' in dead presidents.

"I don't want Royce Winston assigned to Maisie's cell."

"Sure 'nuf. When she's booked, the computer will find her a bunk on B level. It has windows."

"Great." Mitch smiled, looking relieved. "One

more thing — what can you tell me about Helen Sykes?"

Jewel punched a few keys. "She's outta here. Yesterday morning." She saw Mitch expected her to say more. "She's a hubba." The lowest of whores, hubbas screwed — anytime, anywhere — not for money but for coke.

He rubbed his forehead. "Then she's a snitch."

Jewel rocked back, all three hundred pounds balanced on the chair's back legs, and hooted. "Course. She'll say whatever the DA tells her. Two witnesses saw her whackin' a john under a streetlight. But the charges were dropped. Any fool knows she musta cut a deal. She ratted on some poor sucker."

"How could the cops know to plant a snitch so fast?" Mitch asked Paul the following morning. "Unless they were tipped."

Mitch stared out the plate-glass window of his seventeenth floor office at the expanse of the bay. Clouds draped the Golden Gate Bridge, leaving only the tips of the tall pillars visible above a bank of pewter-colored clouds swollen with rain.

"Sounds like someone called the DA's office from the St. Francis," Paul offered.

Mitch had kept in contact with a clerk in the DA's office since he'd left years ago. Insurance. Mitch reached her and explained what he wanted. She agreed to get the information and call him back.

Mitch hung up, dead certain the DA's referral

service would have the answer. To insure their safety attorneys in the DA's office never listed their numbers or addresses. The office referral service handled after-hours messages. The clerk returned his call just minutes later, and Mitch switched on the speaker phone.

"Ward Farenholt called at eight minutes after eleven the night of the auction. Abigail Carnivali took the call."

"Carnivorous," Paul said after Mitch had thanked his source and made a note to send her a gift certificate from Saks. "But why the snitch if Carnivorous was going for a search warrant?"

"Abigail thought Royce could talk her way out of the charges. Why would she have deliberately opened her purse? She sent in a snitch to make her case. Then the informant surfaced and implicated Royce in a drug deal."

"Makes sense. Got a line on the informant?"

"I should hear soon."

The day passed slowly, but not as slowly as it must be passing for Royce, Mitch realized. Gus Wolfe didn't call with the informant's name. Late that night — Royce had been in jail for another twenty-four hours — Mitch waited for Royce in a prison visiting room.

She dropped into the chair opposite him, her face leached of color. Even her green eyes looked paler, almost sunken behind dark circles. "Any word on my uncle?"

He took a paper out of his briefcase. "No. Here's a missing persons report. Has to be signed by the next of kin." He gave her his pen. Her hand trembled as she signed her name. "I don't think anything's happened to your uncle. Paul got into his house. Wally had returned from the auction and changed his clothes. Shortly after midnight he withdrew three hundred dollars from the instant teller. His car's missing. Looks like he's taken a trip except that the paper expected him in on Monday, and he didn't show."

"That isn't like Uncle Wally. He's steadfast, someone you can count on. That job is his life. He wouldn't not show up without calling. I'm certain something's wrong."

"Paul's looking for him and now the police will be looking too." He put the paper back in his briefcase. "How are you doing?"

She lifted her eyes from the table to meet his; for once they weren't filled with hate. "It's better this time. I'm allowed visitors, and the matron comes to get me to use the telephone even when I haven't asked."

"Don't discuss the case with Talia or Val," Mitch cautioned.

"I haven't, but it's difficult. They're my friends."

He put his hand over hers, touching her lightly, looking directly into her eyes. "You've got to learn not to trust anyone — except me."

The next morning Mitch called the DA's office and asked to speak to Abigail Carnivali. It was a courtesy call. In most cases attorneys discussed bail. It cut down on the time spent in court, where everything was already backlogged.

"Mitch, how've you been?" Abigail crooned as if this were a social call, but he knew she hated him and had since the moment he'd declared he'd never marry her. Damn straight, she'd do her best to fry Royce just so she could make a fool out of him.

"I'm great. How are things with you?"

He let her rattle on about her trip to the Cayman Islands with her current lover — another notch on her bedpost. The eternal search for justice made everyone in the DA's office hornier than hell. Okay, anything made lawyers horny. He hadn't been any exception.

He'd resisted for several years, then let Abigail seduce him. He'd assumed it was her power trip, because she'd dropped one hotshot lawyer after another. But then she'd wanted to get married. Why me? For damn sure his luck sucked the big one.

She came up for air and he said, "I have no intention of running for DA."

Silence, then, "I wasn't worried. Anyway, after the Winston trial no one will be able to beat me."

"Actually, I was calling about Royce Winston's bail."

Another silence. She loved them. "Let 'em squirm," she used to tell Mitch. "Bail?" she said, as if it were some foreign word.

Mitch checked his watch. "Your forty-eight

hours will be up soon. Between photo ops and TV interviews about the case, I suggest you think about bail."

"I'll get around to it . . . sometime."

A pit bull litigator, but on an intellectual plane all Abigail appreciated was trendy restaurants and designer clothes. When she wasn't in the office, she haunted Saks. Honest to God, what had he ever seen in her? Ambition. A career. But not a real life. A reflection of himself. And he hated it.

"While you're getting around to a bail request, shit can Helen Sykes's statement. If you make me waste my time tearing that hubba snitch apart in court, I promise you, I will run for DA." A bullshit bluff, but she didn't know it. Mitch had no intention of running for any office. Ever. How could he? His past would be front page news.

"Mitchell Durant, don't you dare threaten me. As it happens, I don't need her statement, but if I did —"

"Don't piss me off. Pull out a bail schedule and let's work on this now." Mitch was worried they wouldn't locate Royce's uncle. With the new charges she'd need Wally's help to post bail. Abigail confirmed his suspicions.

"What?" he yelled. "That's way too high for bail in this case and you damn well know it."

"She's a threat, Mitch," Abigail's voice was all sugar. "What can I do? It's my responsibility to protect society."

"You bitch." He slammed down the receiver.

When was the last time he'd lost his temper? But he could see it coming: Abigail would ask for the moon and Royce wouldn't be able to raise it. Nothing looked worse than a defendant who couldn't make bail. The media would love it. Abigail could get more free publicity for her political campaign.

And Royce would rot in jail. Or worse. Royce seemed to have the inner strength she'd need to get through this. But never forget her father committed suicide. She might, too, if things got bad enough.

7

Royce lay in her bunk, awake but hardly conscious of where she was. Even the woman sitting beside the cell's toilet, flushing it for the hundredth time and staring into it as if it were a crystal ball, didn't quite register. It was as if she'd retreated to some distant part of her body. Or better yet, had moved out of it to another place. Sleep deprivation, she told herself, finding it hard to hold even that thought for more than a moment.

Her mind wandered through a labyrinth of disjointed thoughts. Cocaine. In her home? Mitch. Hell. *Don't talk to anyone about the case.* The nerve shattering sound of her front door splin-

143

tering, destroying the stained-glass panel her father had so lovingly made.

Who? Who would frame her like this? Who hated her this much?

She curled on her side, facing the wall, praying for sleep that would revive her. And bring an answer.

"Winston," yelled the matron, "you've got a visitor."

Royce opened her eyes, at first not remembering where she was. She staggered to her feet. A glance at the wall clock confirmed she'd slept for over an hour. She hurried down the hall to a visitor's room, hoping for Wally but finding Talia.

"Omigod, Royce. Are you all right?"

Royce dropped into the chair. "Sure. I'm just tired. I've hardly had any sleep. I was napping."

"I didn't mean to wake you, but Mitch said to keep visiting you to keep your spirits up. I — I —"

"It's okay. What's happening? What are the papers saying?"

Talia swept her dark hair behind one ear. "That Tobias Ingeblatt is the worst. He's . . ."

"Go ahead tell me. I can take it."

"Ingeblatt has interviewed all the Farenholts' friends. The consensus is you're a fortune hunter that —"

"What did Brent say?" Some part of her still couldn't believe he'd deserted her. Why hadn't she foreseen this? But she hadn't. Nothing she'd known about him could have predicted this reaction. "Didn't he deny that I'm a fortune hunter?"

"Brent hasn't given a statement." Talia hesitated and Royce knew she was hiding something. Talia had a newborn sensitivity honed by months of introspection, thanks to an outrageously expensive psychotherapist, and bolstered by encounter groups. Now Talia was obsessed with finding the true meaning of life.

"Talia, don't keep anything from me."

"There have been pictures of Brent — and Caroline at posh restaurants like Postrois."

Not Postrois. Not "their" restaurant. She put her head in her hands. In some hidden corridor of her mind she'd expected Brent to love her enough to come to her rescue. Each passing minute confirmed what her brain already knew, but her heart refused to accept. Brent had never really loved her.

Then she felt it again, the odd sensation of her spirit leaving her body. The fight was going out of her; she couldn't muster her usual biting comment at Brent's betrayal. If she didn't get out of here soon, the Farenholts would get what they wanted. They'd destroy her. Completely.

"I think Caroline did it," Talia insisted. "She wanted to marry Brent and had to get rid of you."

Don't talk about the case.

"Val insists she put the key back after she picked up your passport. But didn't you say Caroline had been with the Farenholts once when they'd dropped you off and you'd mentioned the key?"

Had she told Talia that? Royce's mind was too foggy to remember, but she did recall the incident. All the Farenholts and Caroline knew she had a key hidden under a flowerpot. It wouldn't have taken Sherlock Holmes to find it.

"I've been cooperating with the authorities," Talia confessed, a little more shamefaced than necessary. "The truth will set you free, don't you think?"

Judge Clarence Sidle gazed over the rims of his half-moon glasses and cursed his bad luck. Night court — the judicial pits. But a newly appointed judge could expect no better: drug addicts, prostitutes, and a stream of homeless who committed petty crimes so they could spend the night in jail out of the cold.

Clarence thought of his father, who'd called in every favor to get him appointed to the bench before his legal practice failed entirely. "A judge is only a lawyer who knows someone," his father had reminded him a thousand times. "They're no smarter than you are."

Really? His father wasn't sitting in night court packed with reporters, facing two of the best legal minds in San Francisco, Abigail Carnivali and Mitchell Durant. Attorneys this important didn't appear in night court, and the media didn't turn out in force, unless something big was up. Beneath his black robe and the white shirt his wife had so carelessly pressed, Clarence began to sweat. Shit, he didn't want to screw up. Not now, not during his first month on the bench.

Abigail Carnivali rose and Clarence suppressed a shudder. What a ball buster. It didn't take long for Abigail to enumerate the state's charges against the sexy blond.

"Royce Anne Winston," Clarence said, angling his head down so he could peer over the tops of his glasses and get a better look at her.

Royce Winston was standing, appearing stunned, not nearly as sexy as in those bikini photos in yesterday's paper. Still, Clarence shifted in his chair, his cock responding to the attractive blond and reminding him that his wife was holding out for a mink. He hadn't been laid in over a month.

"Royce Anne Winston," he began again, striving to sound stern, "you are charged by a complaint filed herein with a felony, to wit, a violation of section forty-three of the Penal Code in that you did, in the City and County of San Francisco, willfully and unlawfully commit grand theft. Further, you are charged with violating section one thirty-seven of the Penal Code, in that you had in your possession a controlled substance, eight ounces of cocaine, for the purpose of sale. How do you plead?"

The press corps leaned forward, straining to hear the soft voice. "Not guilty."

Immediately Durant stood, taking Clarence by

surprise. The prosecution was supposed to suggest bail now.

"Your Honor," Durant said, and Clarence almost looked over his shoulder to see if there was someone else in the room. But no, it was just the power of the title. "I would like to request the court order participants in this case to refrain from discussing it with anyone from the media."

"Unfair," and a lot of other complaints, rose from the Fourth Estate.

Clarence rapped his gavel. Silence. He swallowed a smile. Power. He could get used to it. "Continue."

"The biased press coverage" — Durant looked at the DA's table — "and blatant attempts by the assistant district attorney to grab headlines to further her political career are jeopardizing my client's right to a fair trial."

"Objection!" Abigail Carnivali shot out of her chair as if spring loaded. "Your Honor, I have merely answered media questions without impinging on Miss Winston's right to a fair trial."

Sweat sealed Clarence's shirt to his chest. Oh, boy, a legal shoot-out at the OK Corral. What should he do? He rapped his gavel several times although the room was silent. Royce Winston suddenly appeared less dazed, truly alarmed, her eyes fastened on him.

The pack of slavering dogs from the local media glared at him. He recognized Tobias Ingeblatt, who was seated directly behind Royce Winston. Clarence's wife believed every word the man wrote, unashamed that her vision of the world was shaped by what she read in supermarket checkout lines. Clarence couldn't stifle a smile, imagining the headlines: JUDGE SIDLE INVOKES GAG ORDER.

Power. He could spend a whole year in night court, bored shitless with a litany of drug charges and stoned hookers. This was his chance to become a name overnight.

"I agree with the defense council. I refuse to allow any defendant's rights to be jeopardized. All parties in this case are hereby ordered to refrain from discussing it." He wasn't positive he had the wording right, but close enough.

Durant looked over his shoulder at the disgruntled press and Clarence hesitated. Was he supposed to toss them out now? The only person he'd ejected so far had been a drunk who'd thrown up just as he'd pled not guilty.

Clarence whacked the scarred top of his desk with the gavel. "Bailiff, clear the court. The prosecution may continue."

Abigail Carnivali rose, obviously caught off balance. "Your Honor, in view of the enormous amount of cocaine found in the defendant's home and the threat she poses to society, the state is requesting bail be set at one million dollars."

"Jesus," Clarence muttered under his breath. He had the suggested bail chart right under his elbow. This was excessive.

"Your Honor," Abigail continued, "we have reason to believe Miss Winston may leave the country. After all, she has lived abroad before and has relatives in Italy."

Royce needed sleep so badly, she felt drugged, all her energy now consumed by the effort to stay awake. She struggled to concentrate as Abigail gave the court the reasons for the astronomical bail. Why, she'd never be able to raise that. Even if she found Uncle Wally, he didn't have that much money. She gazed at Mitch; his remarkable profile gave no clue to what he was thinking. Why hadn't he told her there would be a bail problem? *Trust me.* Who did he think he was kidding?

"Your Honor." Mitch rose, papers in his hand. "May I approach the bench?"

Judge Sidle peered over his half-glasses, uncertain for a moment. "Yes."

"I've prepared a list of defendants charged with possession of narcotics for sale arraigned within the last year. Not one of them received this steep a bail despite the fact that many of them are repeat offenders and known drug lords. Many are foreign nationals who could return to South America in an instant."

Royce tensed, anticipating Abigail's response. How could any woman be that beautiful, that confident, that cold? She reminded Royce of a black widow. Mitch walked toward Abigail and handed her a sheaf of papers. Their eyes met and Royce found it difficult to believe they'd once been lovers. They seemed more like prizefighters squaring off before the opening bell.

Had they loved each other? Royce refused to dwell on it; not now, not with so much at stake. Instead, she studied Judge Sidle, whose Adam's apple was bobbing like a yo-yo, thinking he seemed far less confident than either attorney. Had he ever been inside a jail? Did he know what he'd be doing to her if he insisted on a bail she couldn't raise?

"Since when," Mitch continued, his voice cool, forceful, "do known drug dealers get a break and citizens never before charged with any crime get more than the maximum?" He glanced pointedly at Abigail. "Your Honor, I'm grateful you had the wisdom to eject the press. What would they say about the assistant DA's favoritism to drug interests?"

Royce bit back a smile as the polished Abigail Carnivali turned the color of an eggplant. Don't get excited. This wasn't over yet. They haggled until Judge Sidle decided on a modest increase over the existing bail.

"I've got a bail bondsman standing by," Mitch told her after Judge Sidle had retreated into his chambers. "We're using your BMW for collateral."

"Why didn't you tell me there'd be a problem with bail?"

"Were you afraid, Royce?" His blue eyes flashed a challenge. "Didn't I tell you to trust me?"

"I have a right to know when there's a problem."

"If there'd been a problem, I would have told you."

Royce was still fuming as she changed out of her prison jumpsuit and into her beaded dress. But she had to admit, Mitch was good. He'd outmaneuvered Abigail, playing on her ambition to maintain a good image with the press to further her political career.

She conceded it was a relief to have Mitch representing her. Normally, she wasn't the insecure type, and Mitch would have been her last choice. But these weren't normal circumstances.

Exhausted, emotionally stripped — frightened, she was being pummeled by an unknown adversary. She needed Mitch. Still, jerk that he was, he infuriated her, harping on trust, throwing it in her face. He'd let her sweat it out on purpose.

Mitch was waiting when she emerged, and he hustled her down the back stairs rather than make her face the hordes of reporters waiting in the halls. She expected his Viper to be parked out back, but instead Mitch helped her into a van. The graphics on its side read GODZILLA'S PIZZA — BUY TWO GET ONE FREE.

The van's interior looked like a space station, with more electronic gear than she'd ever seen. "What is this?"

"A surveillance van," Mitch explained as he touched the driver's shoulder. "Meet Paul Talbott. He's heading the investigation for your defense."

Royce remembered the name from her research

on Mitch. "Hello." She assessed him quickly before he said, "Hi," and turned away to gun the idling engine. Sandy hair, friendly blue eyes, body like a linebacker's.

Mitch sat beside her. "Pizza vans, phone company trucks — common sights in every neighborhood. No one suspects when Paul's conducting an investigation. If Paul tells you to do something, do it. Paul speaks for me. Sometimes I'll be away on a case."

"I'm willing to cooperate with both of you, but I insist on knowing what's going on." She leveled what she hoped was a furious glare at Mitch, but the surge of adrenaline she'd experienced in court was beginning to wear off. She felt punchy, weak. "This is my future — not some game."

Mitch put his hand on her shoulder, and she had to admit it felt warm, reassuring. "Okay, let me explain what's going to happen. Paul is driving us to an apartment where you'll stay —"

"I want to go home." Heaven — her own bed. There was a mystery here, she knew, but she was beyond exhaustion, intellectually incapable of solving the puzzle or even lending a coherent thought to the process. But with just a little sleep she'd be herself again. If only she could sleep.

"You can't go home. The police are still inventorying it as a crime scene. Even if you could go there, reporters would be on you like locusts. They're a pack of self-anointed moral mascots led by that ass, Tobias Ingeblatt."

"Part of our job is going to be to reverse the tide of negative publicity," Paul said over his shoulder. "Contrary to what you may think, the public perception of a defendant often affects the jury's verdict."

"Until your trial the media isn't going to see you. No one is except the defense team," Mitch added.

"I have to see my friends and" — she sucked in a head-clearing breath of air. How could she have forgotten? — "Uncle Wally. Have you learned anything?"

"Looks like he took a trip to me," Paul responded. "Any ideas where he might have gone?"

"No. I can't imagine him taking a trip without telling the editor at the *Examiner*."

She worried about her uncle as the van left the brightly lit streets for elegant Presidio Heights with its classical Beaux Arts homes nestled between immaculate Victorians. They drove down a back alley and used a remote control to open a single-car garage typical of the area.

Inside, Mitch helped her out as Paul said, "I'll pick up Gerte and come back for you."

They're a good team, she realized, smooth, efficient. Mitch put his hand on the back of her waist and guided her up a narrow flight of stairs to an apartment over the garage that had obviously once been servants' quarters for the main house she glimpsed on the other side of a small garden. Beyond it she saw the bay and knew the main house would have a million-dollar view.

"We've stocked the kitchen and have what you'll need in the bathroom. The clothes will have to do until I get the police to release yours." Mitch opened the door and flicked on the light, revealing a small living room and kitchenette. The furniture, in muted shades of aqua, looked brand new but feminine. Mitch tossed his briefcase on the dainty coffee table. "The bedroom's in there. Get some sleep and I'll wait for Paul to bring Gerte."

"Who's Gerte?"

"She'll stay here and make sure no one bothers you."

She was still a prisoner, Royce decided, almost opening her mouth to argue, but decided Mitch was right. She was so exhausted, she couldn't concentrate. She didn't have the strength to fight off tenacious reporters like Tobias Ingeblatt. "I need to take a bath. The showers in the jail don't have hot water — unless you're first in line."

Mitch flopped down on the sofa. "Go ahead."

The small bedroom had a double bed with an eyelet dust ruffle and an antique nightstand. Again everything looked and smelled new. It was even more feminine than the living room. A dozen downy toss pillows in various shades of aqua were arranged against the scalloped headboard shaped like a seashell. The aqua towels in the adjacent bathroom were new, too, but the old fashioned ball-foot tub reminded her that this was one of the city's oldest neighborhoods as well as one of its most prestigious.

The cabinets held more than she'd need for a short stay. "How long did Mitch say I'd be here?" she asked out loud, hoping the noise would clear her muzzy brain. But her groggy mind couldn't formulate an answer. She turned on the taps and poured a stream of bath salts into the deep tub. She undressed and tossed the beaded gown into the wastebasket. "Talk about bad memories."

There was a terry robe on the hook on the back of the door. She had faith that she'd find suitable clothes in the bedroom closet. Obviously, someone had gone to a great deal of trouble.

She was in the tub, neck resting against the rim, her hair tossed over the side to keep it dry, when she thought about locking the door. She wasn't comfortable being naked in the tub with Mitch just outside. Her mind finally registered what her eyes must have seen when she'd noticed the robe. The lock had been removed, leaving small holes and a mark.

Several disjointed thoughts occurred to her before her exhausted brain settled on the obvious. "Mitch thinks I'm going to kill myself," she said to the bank of bubbles tickling her chin. "That's why Gerte's staying with me." She put her hands on the rim of the tub, set to get out and tell Mitch that she'd never do such a thing. But all her energy had been sapped. "It isn't worth the effort."

Bone weary, she closed her eyes, glorying in the luxury of the privacy of a hot bath — and the quiet. It was never quiet in the county jail. Someone was always talking or crying. It was never dark, either, she recalled, seeking refuge in the darkness behind her lids. Heaven.

Her mind drifted and she went into a dreamlike trance. She pretended to be at home again, standing in the living room she'd known all her life. So very real, she mused, comforted by familiar surroundings. Home.

But why was it dark? So very dark. Pitch-black, shapes were discernible only by varying degrees of darkness. Why wasn't the light on? She reached for the switch, feeling the cool plaster of the wall beneath her fingers. Nothing.

Something disturbed her, making her wary. The concealing darkness hid an evil presence she could almost feel. Something evil. No. Someone evil.

Someone else was in the room with her. Breathing heavily. Like a wild animal she sensed mortal danger and reacted instinctively. She spun around, charging toward the door, her mind screaming, "Escape or die!"

A glint of light shot at her, a reflection of the streetlight through the hexagonal window in the front door. A knife. Its blade gleamed a pure, hateful silver in the eerie light of the full moon. A deadly knife.

This was no ordinary knife, she realized, debilitating fear overwhelming her. Before she could escape, the cold steel blade found her jugular. Her only chance was to scream loud enough to attract the neighbors' attention.

The keening cry made her flinch. Her eyes snapped open, the shrill wail still echoing in the tiled bathroom. She wasn't at home.

She was — where was she? For a moment her brain stalled. Oh, yes, at some apartment Mitch had found. Safe.

"A dream." She gasped. "Thank God."

"But you're not safe," she said to herself. "This is a premonition." Someone would try to kill her.

Mitch burst through the door. "What the hell's going on?"

She put her hand to her throat where the knife had been, dead certain she could feel blood, but there was nothing on her fingers. Still, she'd been warned.

"Royce, why did you scream? The neighbors will call the cops."

She sagged back, head against the rim of the tub, unaware the bubbles didn't quite conceal her breasts. "It's the only way."

Mitch studied her a moment, and she vaguely noticed he'd taken off his tie and unbuttoned his shirt. His cuffs were rolled back to the elbow, revealing strong forearms. He flipped the lever on the tub. "Get out."

It took several seconds to comprehend the tub was quickly draining. She'd be sitting stark naked in bubbles. "I dreamed someone was trying to kill me."

Mitch handed her the terry robe, then turned away for a moment. She stood, up to her shins in bubbles. Before she could tie the belt, he lifted her out of the tub. Her feet hit the cold tile and she almost collapsed, fear and exhaustion overwhelming her.

A thought nagged at her. There was something strange — different — about the house, something didn't fit. She was so weary that she was intellectually incapable of solving the mystery.

"Mitch, I'm serious" — he was rubbing her briskly now, drying her off with the robe, the oddest expression on his face — "someone is trying to kill me."

He stopped and looked into her eyes. The intensity of his gaze was enough to take most women's breath away. He freed her long hair trapped beneath the robe's shawl collar and fanned the damp strands across her shoulders. "Angel, listen to me."

The intimate tone of his voice brought her up short. Angel? We're in hell, aren't we?

"You haven't slept much in almost a week, have you?"

Angel. The word kept ringing through her mind. "No."

"Without sleep the mind plays tricks and induces paranoia. It's the best way to brainwash a person. Always has been."

"But it wasn't a dream exactly, it was a premonition."

"Do you get them often?"

"No. This was the first time."

"It was just a nightmare, Royce. That's all."

"No, it was a warning," she protested as he

guided her into the bedroom. There was something very strange about the dream. Something was wrong. Still, her mind couldn't focus on what it was.

"They've killed Uncle Wally." She had no idea what made her say it, but she knew it was true. Just as she knew she'd face a psychopath with a knife.

Mitch didn't answer, instead he yanked back the covers, then eased her down on the bed. "We'll talk about it tomorrow."

"You don't believe me." She had the feeling he was concentrating more on the deep V of her robe than what she was saying. "Someone's after me."

Mitch sat on the bed beside her and touched her cheek with the pad of his thumb. "Only Paul and I know where you are. Gerte, the woman staying with you, is tough. Her family invented the SS. She comes with a black belt — and a Magnum."

He put his arm around her, bringing her against the solid strength of his chest. She was astonished at how safe he made her feel, even though she knew he was wrong. Someone had killed Uncle Wally. She'd be next.

But for now it was comforting to have someone strong, someone who'd thought about her protection — even before she knew she was in danger. She tested the idea. "I'm safe." Safe with Mitch. This had to be hell.

His lips brushed her forehead; she was too

groggy to decide if it had been an accident or if he'd kissed her.

He started to rise, but she grabbed his hand. "Get some sleep. I'll be nearby preparing for court tomorrow."

She couldn't stop herself from reaching for him, his broad form silhouetted against the light from the living room. He leaned toward her, and her hands grasped his muscled shoulders, slid around his neck, and clung.

"Don't leave me." Her words were muttered against the curve of his neck. "I'm afraid."

His arms circled her waist. "I won't let anyone hurt you." His hands caressed her tangled hair, then gently kneaded the base of her neck. "I promise."

"Mitch." His name was really a sigh, an exhausted expression of her relief and growing sense of security. As she said his name, her lips brushed the hollow of his neck. His hands froze, no longer soothing her. "Hold me," she whispered against his warm skin.

"Royce." He pulled back a fraction of an inch.

But she refused to let him go. The grip of mind-numbing fear had eased. Still, being in his arms felt right, safe. Affectionate by nature, she'd always enjoyed cuddling. He held her snugly, rocking ever so slightly. She allowed one hand to slide down to the opening of his shirt and touch the whisk of chest hair, brushing the skin beneath. Before she knew it, she was sensuously stroking the wall of his chest and the strong muscles that greeted her fingertips.

"Royce," he repeated, his intake of breath sharp.

Exhausted, frightened by her dream, she still sensed he wanted her as much as she needed him. A fair trade, she bargained, unwilling to face the night alone. She tilted her head back and offered him her lips, vaguely aware the robe had opened, revealing even more of her breasts.

He cupped her head between his hands as his lips met hers in a searing kiss. A kiss that made her toes itch. Itch for more. She angled her head to the side, her tongue dancing with his. Now her breasts itched, especially her nipples. She sensed there was a reason she shouldn't be doing this, but for the life of her couldn't think what it was.

She took his hand and edged it under the robe. He didn't need any more encouragement. In an instant his hand found one taut nipple, his fingers circling the tip. She furrowed into his thick hair, stroking his scalp. Before she realized it, Mitch had her stretched out on the bed and he was beside her, the robe fully undone, revealing damp skin still pink from the bath and scented with lavender.

"Don't stop." Did she say that?

Warm and firm, his hand closed over one breast, squeezing ever so slightly, reshaping it to fit his palm, then easing it back and forth against his shirt.

"Royce, you're so goddamned sexy."

Emboldened by his words, by his passion, she slipped her hand down to the waistband of his trousers. Then dipped underneath. Here his skin was hot, so much hotter to the touch. The tips of her fingers edged into the thatch of curly hair, knowing what she wanted, what she needed. Her mind might be groggy, still confused by lack of sleep, but her instincts were flawless.

She circled his shaft, squeezing, caressing the smooth tip. Mitch groaned and muttered, "Aw, hell, do you know what you're doing?"

"Uh-huh." She traced her thumb down the ridge, then cradled the full weight of his sex. "Why am I not surprised, Mitch? I knew you'd have big balls."

"Damn right." His hand shot between her thighs as his head bent to kiss an erect nipple. He sculpted the breast with an aggressive tongue while his fingers eased between the soft folds, testing the taut nub, then teasing it with expert precision.

Her stomach fluttered, then dropped in one long freefall. The strokes of his tongue matched his finger. Impossible to resist. She parted her thighs, her hand gliding up the hard length of his sex, squeezing, stroking.

"You're so hot, Royce. So damn wet." He muttered something else but she didn't understand. He lifted his head and cocked it to one side.

His good ear, she thought, suddenly wanting to kiss it.

He jerked upright. "Goddammit. Paul's back."

163

Dimly she realized he'd heard the van pull into the garage beneath the bedroom. He had the covers over her and was out of the room before she could utter another word.

8

Mitch stared out his office window the following morning, thinking of what Paul had said to him last night. "A lawyer who screws his client fucks himself." An old saying, but true, Mitch decided. He'd tried to resist her, he honestly had, but she'd been so insistent. He heard the sharp knock on his door, but kept looking at the carbon-colored clouds skulking on the horizon as he told Paul to come in.

"I have a copy of the *Outrage*," Paul said. "Tobias Ingeblatt has another article about Royce. Helen Sykes was with her in jail —"

"Aw, shit!" Mitch spun around. "What does it say?"

"This Sykes woman claims Royce confessed she'd taken the jewels."

"Just what I expected." Mitch sank into his chair. Sure enough, not only was Royce getting tried in the press, she was being convicted. And he couldn't do a damn thing about it.

The gag order only covered the attorneys and

witnesses. It gave the press carte blanche to cull info leaked by questionable sources. The classic nonstory. And the ultimate power because it allowed the press to make up their own version of events.

"I've got background on that informant whose word was good enough to get a search warrant for Royce's home," Paul said.

Gus Wolfe had called with the name late last night after Mitch had left Royce. A consummate professional, Paul had tracked down the woman's record within hours.

"Linda Allen is a new informant. This is the first time she's ever given the police a name."

"Unfuckingbelievable! A judge issued a warrant on the word of an untried informant? Next thing we know pathological liars will be getting exempt status to 'confidentially' rat on people."

"I know this search warrant violates standards, but Linda was working with the police on a Peruvian connection. They have total faith in her. That's why the warrant was issued."

Mitch nodded; with all the heat on the Colombians the drug kings were using Peru now. "I want to talk to this Linda Allen."

"She's undercover until this drug deal she's doing with the feds comes down."

"How convenient. Find her, goddammit."

"I've already got men on it," Paul assured him, then hesitated. "Do you have any idea how much this is costing?"

"You'll get paid. Send me the bills."

"I wasn't worried," Paul responded, and Mitch believed him. Paul didn't give a damn about money; he loved his work. He'd have been the best detective in the city if things hadn't gone wrong. "I mentioned money because I have the prelims ready on the case. A check into all the suspects' bank accounts doesn't show any unusual activity. It's going to cost a bundle to get a forensic accountant to go over all their financial records."

"The money to buy the coke planted in Royce's home had to have come from somewhere. The dealers don't take American Express. Get the accountant on it."

"Right. I also have the results of the supermarket poll."

Like many criminal attorneys Mitch used a polling service to monitor public opinion. It helped him gauge which jurors might be sympathetic to the defendant.

"Ninety-three percent of those polled think Royce is guilty."

"Christ! That's higher than Zou-Zou Maloof, and she was caught with the murder weapon in her hand. It's fight-back time."

"You plan to leak info to get around the gag order?"

"Damn right. That's exactly what Carnivorous is doing. I knew all the gag order would do was keep her off television. But she can't be held responsible for leaks or snitches like Helen Sykes selling their stories to the press, can she?"

"No, and neither can you," Paul reminded him.

"As soon as Royce has rested I want her to take a drug test. Then you find someone to leak the results to the media. I also want her to take a lie detector test. Again, I can't be involved in this, so you'll need to find a way to get the results to the press."

"No problem."

"I want Royce to take that laser lie-detector test."

"Jesus, Mitch. That's expensive."

"But totally accurate." Mitch grinned. "And revolutionary. The media will lap it up with a flavor straw. Front page news."

"You'll want another poll after the results are leaked, right?"

"Yeah. Schedule a series of polls. I want to know right through the trial how the public sees Royce."

Royce awoke, smiling; she'd been dreaming about going on a picnic with her mother and father. A memory that translated into a sweet dream, but the reality was quite different. Her parents were dead, her uncle had disappeared, and — she gasped at the thought — she'd almost made love to Mitch. She opened her eyes and saw the woman who'd introduced herself as Gerte last night.

"You are sleeping these thirty-six hours," Gerte informed her.

Had it been that long? Royce was still drowsy, still shocked at the memory of what had happened with Mitch. What was wrong with her?

"I have made soup. You will eat now."

Sitting at the table overlooking the peaceful garden between her quarters and the main house, Royce ate, wondering if lack of sleep had induced acute paranoia. The dream that had seemed so real last night haunted her now even in the light of day. It was hard to believe someone was trying to kill her. Still, her uncle was missing and she'd been framed. It wasn't too farfetched to think she might be murdered, was it?

The nightmare had seemed so real. Even so, something had been wrong, something about the house she'd lived in all her life hadn't, in the dream, been quite right. What was it? She gazed down into the garden where a frisky golden retriever romped with the largest tabby she'd ever seen and tried to think what about her house wasn't the way it was supposed to be.

All she could remember clearly was darkness and an overwhelming, mind-numbing sense of fear.

A knock at the door interrupted her thoughts. Gerte motioned for her to go into the bedroom. She hid behind the door, listening. She wasn't easily frightened, but so much had gone wrong lately. What next? She recognized the familiar voice and rushed out.

"Uncle Wally," she cried, a sob stalled in her throat. "You're all right. Thank God."

He bear-hugged her, and she squeezed tight. "Royce, I'm so sorry I wasn't here. I had no idea." Tears shone in his eyes.

"Where were you? I was so worried."

Wally guided her over to the sofa. "I needed some time to think, so I went up the coast and rented a cottage overlooking the ocean. I didn't pick up a paper or watch TV."

"Shaun," she guessed. "You're not getting back together." For years they'd had an on-again-off-again relationship. The night of the accident that had killed her father's friend, they'd been going to see Wally after one of his fights with Shaun.

"No, this time it's really over. Shaun and I are finished." Sadness etched every line in his face. "That doesn't matter right now. You're what's important."

She didn't know how to tell him she'd hired Mitch. If Wally had been around, she never would have turned to Mitch, but she'd been desperate when she'd seen the police ransacking her house.

"Mitch told me what he's —"

"You've seen Mitch already? Do you think I made a mistake hiring him?"

"If I'd been here, I would have called him immediately."

"Even after what he did to Daddy? If it weren't for Mitch, he'd still be alive." Guilt washed over her in suffocating waves. Hadn't she betrayed her father's memory by almost making love to Mitch? She couldn't meet Wally's steady gaze for fear he'd guess what she'd done.

"True. If Mitch hadn't insisted on prosecuting your father, he might still be alive." He gave her a reassuring hug. "But there's no denying Mitchell Durant is one of the finest legal minds — ever. He made his name overnight as a defense attorney."

"I was in Italy then, but I read something about DNA."

"Right. Everyone assumed a DNA match was as good as a fingerprint in identifying a criminal. But Mitch proved that some DNA matches are blurry like smudged fingerprints. They match only on certain points and aren't conclusive proof. He's got a kid on death row from a small town where everyone's related. Mitch discovered the DNA match that convicted him could have convicted half the town. The Supreme Court has agreed to review the case."

"Now a lot of DNA matches are being challenged."

"Exactly." Wally smiled encouragingly. "I spent several hours talking to him this morning about your defense while you were sleeping. I'm impressed."

"It's going to cost a fortune, isn't it?"

Wally's eyes, the color of her own, were weary pools of experience. None of it encouraging. "You'll have to sell your house and car. I'll have to sell my home —"

"No. I can't let you. You'll need the money to retire."

"I'll have to get by on Social Security. Millions do." He brushed back a tear she didn't know was dribbling down her cheek. "You're more important to me than that house."

"But, Uncle Wally —"

"Hush. You have no idea what my life was like when I was growing up. I didn't know I was a homosexual. I just knew I was different, and I was miserable. Who was the only person who loved me? My brother. When he married your mother, she was just as kind. That's more than I can say for my own parents."

She knew it was true; her grandparents were dead now, but they'd shunned Wally.

"It's a tragedy too many gays still face. Our families reject us, but I had my brother. I miss him to this day. And I'm going to take care of you just the way he took care of me. With him gone you're all I have left. I couldn't bear losing you."

A sob caught in her throat at the love in his eyes and the timeless wisdom in his voice. "If I'm convicted I'll be an old lady before I get out. My career will be over. I'll be too old to have children." An even worse thought occurred to her. "You might get sick and I couldn't be with you. You might even die before I'm free again."

Wally put his arm around her, and she indulged her tears for a few minutes, reminding herself things could be worse. Her paranoia was just prolonged lack of sleep. No one had killed Wally. No one was going to kill her.

Wally stroked her hair, soothing her the way he had when she'd been a child and had come to him with a cut or bruise, but now he talked to her like an adult.

"I want you to do exactly what Mitch says."

She listened while Wally told her Mitch's plans. It sounded complicated and frighteningly expensive. "How does the average person afford a trial?"

His world-weary expression intensified. "They can't. They get a public defender and pray. Think of it as getting cancer without health insurance."

"No wonder they call him Mitchell 'I'll Defend You to Your Last Dollar' Durant."

"Don't be hard on him. There are plenty of expenses we'll have to pay even though Mitch is skipping his fee."

"He is?" Her shame resurfaced, even more intense now, and along with it confusion. How could she accept Mitch's charity? Why was he helping her? Did he feel guilty about her father?

"Don't worry," Wally said, attempting to reassure her.

"I can't help it. Someone's behind this. Who?"

Wally shrugged. "Paul Talbott asked me the same thing. I told him, ah . . . well, it's my gut feeling that it's Valerie Thompson."

"Val?" She sat bolt upright. "Never."

"Maybe not, but she's always seemed jealous of you."

"Perhaps Val was a little envious when we were younger, but she grew out of it. Don't you think it's more likely Eleanor or Caroline did it?"

He paced across the small living room.

"Something's fishy about this whole deal. Tell you what, I'm doing some sleuthing on my own. Being an investigative reporter has its perks."

"Don't you think you should coordinate with Paul Talbott?"

"He won't tell me much. I'm on the suspect list, you know."

"Why? That's crazy."

"It's sound technique. Anyone who had the opportunity to put those jewels in your purse has to be a suspect until they can be eliminated."

"Of all people, you wouldn't have had any reason to do it."

"True." He chuckled derisively. "But I would have a good motive for killing you. I'd inherit your house."

"With its huge mortgage?"

Wally chuckled and gave her a reassuring hug.

How could anyone be so lucky? She had an uncle willing to give up everything to help her.

II

Rabbit E. Lee

9

The following evening Paul Talbott drove into a less than fashionable area of Seacliff. He'd warned Mitch about getting involved with Royce, and Mitch had left without a word, a stick of dynamite in his pants.

It wasn't like Mitch to get involved with a client. He knew better; it was against the bar's code of ethics. True, many attorneys' ethics were like bringing coals to the devil's hearth, but Mitch set high standards for himself. Except for Royce Winston. From the night Mitch had told him about Royce, Paul had known she wasn't just another sexy blonde.

"Don't get personally involved in your cases," Paul reminded himself as he parked in front of Valerie's apartment. "You don't have to see Val to find out why she called."

But he didn't take his own advice. Instead he rang the bell and waited, adjusting the knot in his tie. The door swung open. Hair in pink rollers, Val glared at him, her face covered with a brownish masque that looked like a curbside deposit by one of the neighborhood mutts.

"You left a message that you needed to talk to me."

Val closed the door and left him standing under a yellow bug light. Minutes later she let him in, her face scrubbed pink and her russet hair softly tumbled around her face. Paul's groin tightened; he knew exactly why Mitch was involved with a client. It was mighty tempting. Eyes on her slim hips sheathed in leggings and almost concealed by an oversized sweater, he followed her inside.

"Sister Rosemary from the Center for Women in Crisis made this videotape of the auction." Val handed him a tape.

"The police haven't seen it?"

"No." There was something strange about the way Val was looking at him as she spoke. "They haven't interviewed the sisters yet."

Paul knew they wouldn't. With an airtight case, why waste manpower? Why was Val studying him so intently? "I want to run this through the equipment at the office, but I'll need help identifying all the people. Can you spare an hour?"

"Sure," she said, but she still had an odd expression.

No question about it. Val was gorgeous but weird. He didn't want to think she was guilty. Still, his instincts told him she was hiding something. He recalled Wally's suspicions. He was an ace reporter. Was he onto something?

Paul drove to the office with Val riding beside him in silence. He supposed she'd be friendlier if he was driving his own Porsche instead of the battered Chevy he used for surveillance. Beautiful women had plenty of rich boyfriends. They didn't encourage gumshoes with overdrawn bank accounts.

Not that Paul was poor; he had more money than he'd ever imagined having. He'd bet Valerie would be a lot sweeter if she knew he owned Intel Corp. Why tell her? Women who were after your money were nothing but trouble.

"Intel Corp occupies two floors," he said when they were in the building, waiting for the elevator. "We're going to the sixteenth floor where we have video analysis equipment."

Val surveyed the building's roster. "I see Mitchell Durant's office is here too."

"He has the floor above us." On the way up he added, "Intel has technical units to investigate credit card fraud and cellular scams."

"What do you do?" She sounded genuinely interested.

"I'm not much for punching a computer to track fraud operations," he hedged. "I'd rather be out on the street."

"I love computers. I've taken several classes. I hope to change jobs soon and work with computers."

Inside the video room he put the tape in the machine and sat beside Val at a monitor. "We'll be able to enlarge and freeze frame — the works." He didn't mention that the sophisticated equipment would also tell him if anyone had tampered with the tape. "Here it goes. Point out all the people you know."

She had a soft, melodic voice. He listened as he watched, occasionally hitting the freeze frame button to take a better look at someone. "That's me in the lamé dress," Val told him.

He punched the freeze frame, then pressed the enlarger. "Wow!" She had her hair piled high in a loose cluster of curls. With a single caress the mass would fall into some lucky devil's hands. Before he could stop himself Paul said, "Nice, but I like your hair down and no makeup."

"You do?" She actually smiled.

He didn't know what to say. When was the last time he'd felt so off balance with a woman? He opted for the truth. "I like the natural look. That's why I came over to your place to get the tape. I wanted to see you again."

"I've *never* been more embarrassed," she confessed. "I could have taken the tape to your office, but I wanted to see you too. I wanted to look good so I put on the masque and curled my hair. I never thought you'd show up without calling."

"You wanted to see me? I'll be damned. I didn't think you were the least bit interested."

"I'm not very good at this." Her voice dwindled to a whisper; he had to lean toward her to hear better. "You're easy to talk to. Besides, you ate two helpings of my tofu lasagna."

The narcotic effect of her tentative smile shook him.

"I planned to ask you over for dinner. I made

zucchini enchiladas."

"How about tomorrow?" He tried to keep his tone light.

"Sorry." She zinged him with another smile. "I'm on the night shift, checking out reports of soggy fries in Milpitas."

Paul chuckled. Val had a sense of humor, but she was insecure. "How about Saturday night? I'll take you to —"

"No. I want to make you dinner."

"Okay." He leaned toward her and gave her a peck on the cheek. She turned her head, parting her lips, obviously expecting a real kiss. How could he say no? He pressed his lips against hers and she put her arms around his neck and kissed him back. Her eagerness shocked him for a second, but he quickly took advantage of the situation until she pulled away.

"Who were you with that night?" he asked, then listened to how Royce got Val a date with the parsley king. Honest-to-Pete, it was hard to believe the lady didn't have a steady boyfriend.

"There are the Farenholts" — Val pointed at the screen — "and there's Royce's bag next to the napkin and place card."

"Good. Let's check subsequent frames to see when it was moved. Royce told Mitch she put her bag by her napkin but later found it on a chair."

There was a lot of footage of sweet-looking women wearing gowns from the fifties. They turned out to be nuns who were friends of Sister

Rosemary, who was doing the filming. Finally, there was a shot of Mitch. Paul was fascinated by Mitch's intent expression. The camera followed his gaze. He was staring at Royce Winston.

He pondered the screen a moment, then asked, "How did Royce feel about Mitch when they met — what was it? Five years ago?"

"Yes. It was a little over five years ago. Royce was crazy about him. She called me the night before she left for Italy to tell me she'd met the 'right' man. She even came back from vacation early just so she could see him. But then her father was in the accident that killed his best friend. The next time she saw Mitch, he was prosecuting her father."

Paul tried to imagine what would have happened if Royce and Mitch had dated. Yeah, it might have worked. Mitch was a true lone wolf, an insular man who valued his privacy above all else, but Royce might have changed him. She had an Italian flair, an animated zest for life. Just what workaholic Mitch needed.

"It wouldn't have worked, anyway." Val seemed to read his mind. "Royce will never find the right man because no man will ever be as good as her father." The tape was continuing to run, and Val added, "There's Talia looking at the jewels."

"And Caroline Rambeau. Who's the guy with her?"

"Some Italian count. I don't remember his name."

Paul thought the count looked slick, that polished, processed appearance that was supposed to be Continental.

"Royce thought his accent was phony," Val offered.

"She spent years in Italy. I'll check on him."

"Hold it," Val said and he hit the freeze frame. "There's Eleanor and Ward alone at the table with the purse. Does it look like it's been moved?"

"Watch this. I stored the earlier shot of the bag. Let's superimpose the two." On a separate monitor the shots merged. "It hasn't been moved." He advanced the tape, thinking the special instruments showed the tape hadn't been altered. In the next shot the Farenholts were talking with friends, but Ward's eyes never left Caroline.

"You know what strikes me odd?" Val pressed the freeze button.

Paul shook his head, thinking of the way she'd kissed him. He was ready to wind this up and take her home.

"Caroline Rambeau is beautiful. Next year when she's thirty-five she'll inherit millions. Why would she stick around waiting for Brent?"

He shifted in his chair and his thigh touched hers. Uhh-ohh. "She must love him," Paul said. "They're dating again. That creep Ingeblatt has them plastered all over his rag."

"I don't buy it," Val said. "Most women hit their mid-thirties and their biological clock — as Royce would say — becomes a time bomb. Caroline should have married by now."

"Maybe she's different. After all, her parents died when she was in her late teens. The Rambeaus and the Farenholts were best friends for years. Maybe they're all the family she has."

Val shook her head, her glorious hair shimmering in the blue-white glow of the TV monitor. "I still think it's odd that she would hang around even when Brent announced he planned to marry Royce."

"Sounds like you think she's the one who framed Royce."

"No. I went with Royce and Brent one night to the Farenholts' and Caroline was there. Caroline truly seemed to like Royce. But the Farenholts — particularly Ward — were cold. I was surprised. It wasn't like Royce to let anyone treat her that way."

"Brent's money might have —"

"No. Royce told me all Brent has is a small trust. The money is Eleanor's," Val said. "Brent won't inherit it until she dies. Anyway, money has never meant much to Royce. But it has kept Brent tied to his mother's purse strings. Ward, too, I guess, since it's Eleanor's money in a separate trust even Ward can't touch without Eleanor's approval."

"Don't hold any charity benefits for Ward and Brent."

"No, but in their circles they're nothing without Eleanor's money. I guess she loved Brent enough not to oppose his marriage to Royce, even though she preferred Caroline." Val gazed at him, her beautiful eyes serious. "Something doesn't make sense."

"True." He wished he could discuss the case with her; she was sharp, homing in on the complexity of the relationships the way he had and sensing something wasn't right. But he couldn't talk to her until he'd ruled her out as a suspect. Still, just sitting beside her knowing she was interested in him without realizing who he really was tightened the knot in his groin.

Val pressed the button and the video advanced. This time the camera focused on Talia. She was hovering near the jewels.

"Any chance Talia is the guilty one?" he asked as the tape kept running, showing Royce introducing Val to Mitch.

Val hesitated a fraction of a second. "No."

"Tell me what you're really thinking." He took off his sport coat and tie, then dropped them in his lap. If she looked down he'd be embarrassed.

"Do we ever *really* know anyone? You think you know someone until something happens," she said, and he knew she was referring to her divorce. "Talia was so thrilled to be dating Brent. Suddenly, Brent dropped her. Royce wouldn't go out with Brent until Talia insisted. I don't think Talia would do anything to hurt Royce. After all, when she needed help, Royce was there — a true friend."

Paul had his doubts but said, "Let's see what else is on this tape. Isn't that the actress coming into the ballroom?"

"Yes. It was really overcrowded by then. They must have been violating the fire code at this point."

"Absolutely. It's getting hard for the camera to focus on just one person. Tomorrow, I'll freeze frame this and jot down the names of everyone near the jewels." Right now, he wanted to take her home, and get back to kissing. Or whatever.

"Look." Val stopped the camera, then pressed the enlarger. "In the corner of this shot, isn't that Wally? Isn't he standing in front of the Farenholt table?"

"It's him. He must have been looking for Royce before he left," Paul said, but he was thinking he ought to check on the uncle. "Enlarge the shot."

The enlargement showed Mitch in the corner of the frame walking toward the table. Suddenly, the camera turned away.

"Could Mitch have done it?" she asked.

"No," he said emphatically. There was a dark undertow to Mitch's personality, enhanced by his mysteriousness about his past, but he'd never do something like this.

"He came up to Talia and me just after Royce was arrested and volunteered to help her. He said he knew she wasn't guilty. How could he know that?"

"Val, there are two factors behind every crime: motive and opportunity. The number-one reason crimes are committed is for money. Mitch has plenty of money."

"He planted the jewels so she'd need a lawyer and come to him. Someone else is behind this drug thing."

Not only was Val beautiful but she was smart. His original suspicion was that these were two separate crimes, one well planned, the other a spur-of-the-moment opportunity.

"You know," he blurted out, "there's a job here in the credit card fraud unit working with computers. Why don't you fill out an application?"

She fired him a smile that turned up the heat in his pants yet another notch. "Thanks for the tip. I'll call tomorrow."

He didn't want her to know he owned Intel Corp just yet. He wanted to know how she felt about Paul Talbott the man, not Paul Talbott owner of Intel. Hiring her wasn't his best idea when she was still a suspect, but he'd be damned if he wanted her running around Milpitas — at night, for God's sakes — checking out greasy French fries at Tomaine Tommy's.

She touched his arm. "Mitch is in love with Royce."

In lust might be a better term, Paul thought, feeling slightly sheepish because he wished he were in bed with Val.

"Rewind the tape, Paul. You missed something earlier."

If he missed something, it was her fault. He hadn't earned his reputation botching cases, but then, he'd never been this distracted. He rewound the tape, stopping where she told him at the footage of Mitch coming up behind Royce and putting his hand on the small of her bare back.

"Freeze it," Val said.

Wow! He'd never seen a sexier shot. Royce's back was to Mitch and her unguarded expression revealed the thrill of his touch. Mitch looked as if he was going to rip off her clothes, throw her down on the table, and make wild, passionate love to her in front of everyone.

Paul turned to see what Val thought and saw she found the frame every bit as erotic as he did. Her lips were parted, ready to yield even before he kissed her. This time he wasn't as gentle, the heat pulsing in his groin, getting the best of him.

His tongue eased between her lips and her mouth opened more as she leaned against him, her soft breasts pillowed against his chest. How lucky could he get? No bra.

The thrusts of his tongue took on a purely sexual rhythm. A low, feminine moan urged him on. She was as hot for him as he was for her.

She pulled back, her eyes glistening in the light of the TV screen, her sensuous lips moist. "I knew you'd kiss like that."

"Like what?"

"Like you want me — really want me."

He heard the anguish in her voice and professionally sized up the situation. She needed to feel loved, desired. Most people were mentally divorced long before they were legally divorced. She probably hadn't felt loved in years. What a waste.

He took her small hand in both his big ones, then kissed her soft palm, never taking his eyes from hers. He guided her hand to his crotch and pressed it against his erection, encouraging her to close her fingers over the thick shaft.

"Of course I want you. It took you exactly one kiss."

"Oh, Paul." She rubbed his sex through his trousers. Her pupils were dilated, and her mouth slightly open, the pink tip of her tongue skimming over her lower lip. "I love your body."

He dipped under her sweater, finding her soft, warm skin. He explored with the tips of his fingers until he reached her full breasts. He brushed her tightly spiraled nipples with the rough pad of his thumb, and she moaned again, a low, satisfied sound. She had his trousers undone before he came to his senses.

"Val, I'm not prepared for this. I don't have a condom."

"I have some in my purse." A rush of pink heightened the color in her already flushed cheeks. "I was hoping you'd have dinner and stay. *Cosmo* says women should take responsibility."

"God bless *Cosmo*."

While she took out a condom, he thought about leading her to his office where he had a soft leather couch, but she was kissing him again, her hands in his pants. He switched off the TV.

Who needed Mitch and Royce?

"I can't believe I'm doing this," she whispered.

He couldn't either; she didn't seem to be the type to make love in a chair. But years of experience told him people were capable of anything. It was always a serious mistake to underestimate.

He worked her leggings and panties down her slim thighs and she kicked them aside. "Come, here." He pulled her onto his lap, his erection nestled against her bare bottom.

He kissed the sensitive curve of her neck, telling himself to make this good. He didn't have a lot of experience in chairs, so he planned quickly as he stroked her inner thighs. He eased slowly upward, his fingers finding the moist curls. Hot, slick, she was more than ready, but he refused to rush. He stroked her, reveling in her soft moans, then he inserted one finger deep inside her, his thumb still fondling her.

"Hurry, hurry," she pleaded.

"I'm not ready." A fib. He was more than ready, grinding his pulsing erection against her as she wiggled on his lap. He withdrew his finger just enough to tease her before entering her again, this time with two fingers. With smooth, sure strokes, he made certain she was totally aroused.

He lifted her to her feet and positioned her in front of him, standing, straddling his legs. One firm hand on her buttocks, he pulled her down until the tip of his shaft was probing her.

"I knew it. I knew it," she moaned.

Paul didn't bother to ask what she knew; he

needed all his self-control now. He lowered her slightly, entering her just a little. "Take off your sweater." Both hands on her hips, he held her in place as she tossed the sweater aside.

The room was dark, lit only by moonlight. Her skin was pale, delicate looking with high, full breasts and taut nipples. "How could any man give you up, Val? How?"

He didn't wait for an answer. He thrust upward just as he pulled her down, penetrating her to the hilt.

She grasped his shoulders with both hands. "Oh, Paul," she moaned against his lips, "I knew it."

Knew what? He took possession of one hard nipple, sucking slightly while his tongue swirled around the delicate tip.

"Ride me, Val. Hard. Put everything you've got into it."

She moved against him, pulling away, then coming down over and over. He was imbedded deep inside her when he felt her contract and slow her pace. He let himself go, clutching her, thrusting fiercely. He held her for some time after he'd climaxed, gasping for breath. Where had she been his whole life?

10

Royce sat in the chair, allowing the technician to adjust the headset for the lie detector test. It was an odd contraption that fit over her head, with special lenses trained on her eyes. Off to one side she could see Mitch and Paul talking with the doctor who'd administer the test.

Mitch and Paul had taken her for a drug test before coming here, and Mitch had been totally professional. It was almost as if she'd imagined being in bed with him the way she'd dreamed someone had tried to kill her. Almost.

But she knew better. There was no excuse for the way she'd thrown herself at Mitch. What had happened had been her fault.

Oh, go ahead. Admit it. She found Mitch physically attractive. Never mind what he'd done; her body didn't care. The talk she'd had with Wally had sobered her, though. When the chips were down — and, boy, were they down now — you could count on your family. Her father had loved her. She refused to betray his memory.

"We're ready," the doctor told her. "I'm going to switch on the laser." The blue-white beam of light could have shot through the eye of a needle with room to spare. It hit her, causing her to blink several times before she adjusted to it. "The laser records minute changes in the pupil's size."

"If I lie, it'll contract," she said. Paul had explained the process on the way over; Mitch hadn't talked much.

"Yes," the doctor answered, "and the laser will detect the change. Mitch and Paul are at monitors. They'll be asking questions too."

"This session will give us background info," Paul put in from the table nearby. Out of the corner of her eye she could see Mitch next to Paul, studying her.

"I'm ready," she said, anxious to get this over with. The idea of conducting a publicity campaign was foreign to her, but Mitch insisted most cases were won or lost with jury selection. Going into the trial Mitch wanted prospective jurors already to be doubting her guilt, and the only way to influence them was to alter public opinion.

The doctor began with a series of questions about her background, then said, "Tell me why you believe Eleanor Farenholt committed this crime."

"She never liked me. When I opened my purse and found the jewels, I swear, she was gloating."

"And you believe she planted the drugs."

"Yes. Everyone knew where I'd hidden a key. I doubt she planted the drugs herself, but she must have paid someone to do it."

"And the informant?" This from Mitch.

"Somehow she managed that. I don't know how, but Eleanor has boodles of money. It wouldn't have been hard for her."

"Give us an example of something Eleanor did before the crime."

"She always said nasty little things like giving me the name of her seamstress so I could get my clothes better fitted, or suggesting a book I might read to improve my mind, things like that. But mostly, she threw Caroline in my face. Caroline was perfect, and Eleanor never failed to remind me of it." Royce hesitated. Should she tell them?

"We've got a blip here," the doctor said.

Criminy! Just how sophisticated was this machine? "Eleanor invited me to join one of her charity groups. It was really just an excuse for the women to get together and gossip, but once a year they threw a luncheon to raise funds for blind children. They make all the food themselves, which is a joke because all of those women have cooks on staff.

"Eleanor headed the salad committee. Every year someone donates lettuce straight from the field. It was my job to wash it. The ladies had developed a system for cleaning the dirty lettuce. Boy — this sounds stupid — they put the leaves in a pillowcase and put it in the washing machine on rinse.

"They swore they'd done this with total success for years. The trick is to stop the machine before the spin cycle. So there I am in the basement of some mansion, washing lettuce. I was dicing celery nearby while I waited for the lettuce. Eleanor was the only other person with me. When I looked up, the machine was on the spin cycle."

Silence filled the room. Out of the corner of her eye she saw Paul battling a grin. "I know it's silly, but Eleanor turned that dial. The woman is an out-and-out sneak."

More silence. She didn't add that she'd felt totally humiliated. "Eleanor convinced her friends it was my fault the luncheon had been ruined."

"Describe your relationship with Ward Farenholt."

"There wasn't one," she answered the doctor. "He spent hours chatting with Caroline, but he never spoke to me unless he couldn't avoid it."

"How did he treat Brent?" asked Mitch.

"Ward doesn't like many people and he's terribly hard on Brent. He expects too much. He's cruel."

"Did you like Caroline?" the doctor asked.

"Actually, she was always very nice, but if someone's waved in your face too often, it's hard to like them."

"How was Brent with Caroline?" Paul asked.

"He loved her like a sister. He was always kind to her. Eleanor dotes on her like Caroline is her daughter. Even Ward, who finds fault with everyone, loves her. He spends as much time — or more — with her than Eleanor does."

"Did you ever have any reason to think any

of them used drugs?"

"No. Never."

"Have you ever used drugs?" asked the doctor.

"Once I tried marijuana in college. That's all."

"Did you know there was cocaine in your house?"

"Absolutely not."

"Have you ever met a woman named Linda Allen?"

"Never." She'd heard the name today for the first time when Mitch asked if she knew the informant.

"Did you take the jewels?"

"No, I did not. I never touched them."

"Let's talk about Brent Farenholt," Mitch said.

Let's not, she thought. Somehow, she'd stupidly harbored a flicker of hope that he'd contact her. But when time passed and he hadn't even bothered to call and see how she was doing, hurt became anger. Most of it directed at herself. Why hadn't she seen this side of Brent?

"How did you meet?" Mitch asked and she told him. "Did Talia give you any reason to think you dating Brent upset her?"

"No, but I always felt a little guilty about it. She'd flipped for him, then he suddenly lost interest. I would never have gone out with him, but Talia insisted."

"What did you see in Brent Farenholt?" Mitch asked.

Royce hesitated, not wanting Mitch to ask these questions. Her feelings were raw; Brent had let

196

her down when she'd needed him the most. How could she explain loving him? "Brent's fun. He makes a woman feel . . . well, you know, like a queen. He's thoughtful. He's —" She stopped herself from saying: loyal.

"When did he tell you he loved you?"

She wasn't comfortable having Mitch ask her these questions. Did her anxiety show on the monitors? "The third date."

"When did you tell him you loved him?"

Really, what did this have to do with her case? "I told him the night of our three-month anniversary."

She could have predicted Mitch's next question. "When did you go to bed with him?"

"The night I told him I loved him." So there. He probably thought she was lying, but one look at the monitor would verify her words.

"Do you?"

"Do I what, Mitch?" She could barely see him out of the corner of her eye. But she could feel his implacable determination filling the room. What did he want from her?

"Do you love him?"

Did she love Brent? Part of her did despite the way he'd humiliated her. It was crazy; she could passionately kiss Mitch, but there was that side of her that wanted the security, the feeling of being cherished, Brent had once given her.

"Yes. I loved him. I wanted to be his wife and have his children."

There was an uncomfortably long pause. She

197

saw Mitch studying his notes. The silence lengthened until the doctor finally asked, "Why did you put up with the way the Farenholts treated you?"

"Lots of wives don't like their in-laws. Mother barely tolerated Daddy's parents. Despite it their relationship worked perfectly. But as time went on, I realized it wasn't going to be the same for me. On the night of the auction I called off our engagement until we could work out the situation."

Mitch looked up but didn't say anything. She went ahead and told them what Eleanor had done to Wally. When she finished no one commented; she sensed they were waiting for Mitch.

Finally, Paul spoke up. "Eleanor Farenholt controls the money in that family. If she wanted to get rid of you, why didn't she cut off Brent? It would have been easier."

"True. But she loves Brent. Ward's such a cold man that I think she's actually closer to her son than her husband. That's why she was so sneaky. She wanted to get rid of me without alienating Brent."

"What drugs has Talia taken?" Paul asked.

"She's a recovering alcoholic, but I'm sure she's experimented with many drugs over the years."

"What about Valerie Thompson?" Paul sounded intense.

"She barely drinks wine. Drugs — never."

Another silence, broken only by the hum of the laser monitors. Mitch hadn't said one word since she'd admitted she loved Brent. What did he expect? She would never have married a man she didn't love. Right now Mitch was staring out the window. She doubted he was even listening.

"Did you know Wally loaned Shaun Jamieson money?" Paul asked.

"No, but I'm not surprised."

What did this have to do with the case?

Paul asked, "Mitch, anything else?"

"Nope." He was still looking out the window.

"I have a question I'd like to ask for my research work," the doctor said. "What do you find the *most* difficult thing about this ordeal?"

Before any of this happened, she would have said working with Mitch, or she might have said the threat of a prison term ruining her life was the worst. Having her reputation — and career — destroyed would have ranked right up there too.

She tried to ignore the irritating laser beam, thinking back to happier times. Hours spent with her uncle putting together puzzles as a child. Her first date — she'd doubled with Talia. They'd spend all day trying on outfits, experimenting with makeup. Learning to bake bread with Val, then eating the loaf hot from Mama's oven. The night Brent had told her he loved her.

Wonderful memories. Memories of a happy life surrounded by friends, loved ones. Above all, laughter. She'd been happy. Yes, she'd suffered tragedy, losing both parents. But she'd still been able to count on her uncle, her friends. Brent.

She'd had everything that was truly important in life, but hadn't realized it until this moment. Why did someone hate her enough to take away what she valued most — her friends and family?

"Nothing is worse than not knowing who's doing this to me, suspecting everyone — even lifelong friends . . . my uncle. Now I don't know who to trust. Not even when I stood over my father's grave, did I feel so totally alone."

Sonofabitch! Royce actually loved that cocky little prick, Brent Farenholt. Mitch wanted to wring her neck; she was riding beside him on the way back to his office. He was close enough to do it. Put your hands around that soft throat and squeeze. Until she changed her mind about Brent.

Women! Trust me, you never know what they're thinking. He glanced at the rearview mirror as he changed lanes. The scar below his eye was highlighted in the mirror. For damn sure you couldn't trust women. You never knew when they'd turn on you.

"Mitch, you're not listening." Paul tapped him on the shoulder. "I asked who do you think wants Royce in prison?"

"Brent," he said, just to piss off Royce. Actually, he thought it more likely Ward Farenholt was trying to frame Royce.

"That's ridiculous," Royce snapped. "Why would Brent do this to me? All he had to do was tell me he didn't love me and he'd be rid of me."

"True," Paul agreed. "And I've checked all the Farenholt bank accounts looking for a cash withdrawal that matched the value of the coke planted at Royce's. Brent's living on a shoestring. His mother pays most of his charge accounts."

"Figures. A mama's boy." He stole a peek at Royce, but she was staring straight ahead, her jaw clamped shut.

"Royce," Paul said, "we're not ruling out anyone who was near those jewels and near your table, regardless of whether or not they have a motive."

"Assuming one person is responsible for both crimes," Royce said, and Mitch gave her credit for zeroing in on the problem.

"Mitch and I discussed it," Paul responded. "This whole thing was too well timed to be two separate incidents, but it could be two people working together. Remember, there's no perfect crime. There's a key somewhere — usually in the records. Phone records, charge receipts, bank accounts."

Paul let the two of them stew in angry silence for the rest of the ride. I'll be damned, he thought. Val might be right. Mitch cared a lot more about Royce than Paul had suspected. He'd been livid since she'd said she loved Brent, so angry he couldn't conceal his fury, which wasn't like Mitch.

For years he'd thought Mitch was like an iceberg, two-thirds hidden beneath the surface. Paul suspected Mitch suffered from a deep psychological wound that he kept hidden beneath a veneer of cynicism. Somehow Royce had exposed a chink in his emotional shield.

Inside the building Paul went up to his office, promising to join Royce and Mitch in a few minutes. Paul rifled through his messages, stopping when he saw Val had called. She was on the late shift again tonight, checking out stale buns in Oakland. She'd been hired yesterday in the computer department, but she wouldn't begin for two weeks.

He closed the door to his office, wishing he could see Val tonight instead of having to wait until tomorrow. She'd been on his mind constantly these last two days. Mitch would have a coronary when he found out Paul had hired a suspect, but he didn't give a damn.

"It's Paul," he said when Val answered. Just hearing her voice sent a ripple of heat through him.

"Guess what?" She sounded breathless, excited. "When I gave notice, the old geezer fired me on the spot. So I called the computer department and they said to report on Monday. Isn't that great?"

Not really. He'd planned on giving their relationship two weeks before he told her who he was. "Fantastic."

"That means" — her voice was low now, intimate — "I don't have to work tonight. I'll make you dinner."

"Let me take you out." He hated her spending money she didn't have when he could well afford to take her out to the best place in town. "Let's celebrate."

"No. I want to make you dinner. You were so sweet to suggest I apply for that job. I want to show you how grateful I am."

If she were any more grateful than she'd been the other night, he might not live to tell about it. He'd taken her home and they'd spent the night in each other's arms.

Thinking about Val, Paul battled an erection as he went downstairs into Mitch's office. The frigid air hanging over Royce and Mitch like a subzero shroud took care of Paul's problem.

"How long will I have to stay in hiding?" Royce was asking.

Mitch rocked back in his chair and gazed out the window at the Bay Bridge. "I'll tell you when you can leave."

Mitch could be a real hard-ass sometimes, Paul thought, particularly when you crossed him. "Tobias Ingeblatt is hovering around," Paul told her. "If he gets a picture of you, he'll make up his own story. Until the preliminary hearing late next week you're a POP — a prisoner of the press."

Mitch swung his chair around and stared hard at Royce. Paul perched himself on the edge of Mitch's huge mahogany desk, waiting for the bomb to drop. "We've got to fix your image."

Royce bristled at Mitch's tone, but controlled

her voice. "What is wrong with my image?"

"Your hair always looks like you've just been laid." Mitch turned to Paul. "Get the image consultant we use to change it."

Royce's jaw snapped shut as if spring loaded.

"Find her a conservative navy suit." Mitch went on. "All she owns are outfits that would give the Pope an erection."

Paul wondered if Mitch knew he'd just admitted how incredibly sexy he found Royce. She didn't have a clue, for sure. She seared Mitch with a glance that could have fried bacon.

Mitch pointed at Royce. "Lose ten pounds — at least — before the trial."

"What?" She vaulted out of her chair. "I'm size eight."

An incredibly sexy size eight, Paul decided, not beautiful like Val, but very sexy, the kind of figure too full for a model, but every man's wet dream. Obviously, Mitch's.

"Royce" — Paul used his soothing tone — "weight is tricky. Statistics show more fat people are convicted than thin. I don't know why, but the public equates being fat with some moral shortcoming. Overweight people are seldom elected as jury foremen unless they have superior credentials like being a doctor or a scientist. We're dealing with psychology here, and we want you to have the edge."

She dropped into her chair, only slightly subdued. Mitch looked like he'd been chewing tin foil. If Paul lit a match the room would explode.

This was getting mighty interesting.

Royce's eyes narrowed. "I want to see my friends."

"No way," Mitch shot back. "Just your uncle."

"I have an idea." Paul ignored Mitch's warning glance. "There's no phone in that apartment. I'll lend her one of my portables. She can keep it in her purse. That way no one can trace the calls and find out where she is. She can call her friends all she wants."

"Okay," Mitch conceded. "Not one word about the case."

"Thanks," Royce said to Paul, ignoring Mitch. "Tell me what I can do to help."

"I'm going to get you a couple of wigs. Wear them when you go out. Watch for anyone following you. Double back, stop and look in shop windows, cross the street — that sort of thing.

"*Don't* develop a routine. Most people are creatures of habit. They leave by the same door every day, use the same bus, return home at the same time. Vary your schedule."

Royce nodded, pointedly facing away from Mitch. "What I meant was: What can I do to help with my defense?"

"Stay the hell out of my way," Mitch fired at her.

"You can't help Mitch," Paul said, "but you can help me. I could use someone to go over the suspects' telephone records. It'll be boring, but there's got to be a clue somewhere."

Her grateful smile twisted Paul's heart. Mitch

didn't look thrilled, but Paul knew he wouldn't object. The way costs were escalating, free help was a godsend.

"I could work at night, too, since I'm all alone," Royce said.

"You'll need a computer." Paul hesitated, then plunged on, trusting his instincts. Enough of this verbal dog-fighting, strafing each other constantly. Most obsessions were unhealthy, but Royce was exactly what Mitch needed. Either they would fall in love — or kill each other. "You can use Mitch's home computer. Right, Mitch?"

It took a second before she got it. "Mitch lives in the main house? I'm in *his* apartment?"

"Keep your mouth shut about it," Mitch ordered.

"I can't stand this," Royce said to herself as she looked out the window of her apartment at the lights in Mitch's house. She was fighting for her life with this case, yet every time she tried to talk to Mitch he was angry, his words calculated to hurt her.

It was bad enough that she was isolated like this, alone for the first time ever. But not to be able to discuss the case rationally with the attorney defending you was ridiculous, infantile. Should she change attorneys?

How could she? Even with Wally's help she didn't have enough money to hire someone as talented as Mitch. As tenacious as Mitch. She had no choice but to work with him.

She mustered her courage, tromped out of the apartment, and charged across the dark garden. She banged on his door like a narc ready to bust in, and the door swung open.

Mitch frowned at her, standing in well-worn sweatpants that gloved his muscular thighs and rode low on his hips. He wasn't wearing a shirt to conceal the captivating network of dark hair that fanned across his chest and funneled down beneath the waistband of his sweats. It struck her that this was the first time she'd seen his chest. Of course, he'd seen hers.

She barged in saying, "I need to talk to you."

"I'm on the phone."

She jammed past Mitch into the brightly lit kitchen, conscious of him following her. A golden retriever bounded up to her. She couldn't resist bending down to pat the friendly dog.

"Jason, call me tomorrow and let me know how you did on that test. I'll see you this week-end." Mitch hung up and turned to her. "That's Jenny," Mitch said, nodding to the dog. "The cat's Oliver." The tubby tabby was doing a face-plant in his bowl. "Want some pizza?"

"I've eaten . . . thanks." Someone had told Gerte about Royce's diet. The fridge was stocked with Lean Cuisine. The enticing smell of pizza almost made her sigh, but she refused to give in to her craving for high-calorie food.

He leaned back against the counter, his arms belligerently crossed over his bare chest and gave her a slow once-over. Twice. "Okay, pork chop. Shoot."

She ignored his barb about her weight and his attempt to sexually intimidate her. That tactic wasn't going to work anymore. Too much was at stake. "Let's be completely honest with each other."

"Go on. This should be fascinating."

"You've been angry with me since I said I loved Brent." Mitch remained stubbornly silent. "I would never have agreed to marry a man I didn't love."

"Is this supposed to interest me?"

"Don't be such a wiseguy. It's childish." She'd raised her voice enough so the tabby cocked his head to one side to peek at her but kept chewing. "I know you hate Brent. He told me all about what went on at Stanford."

"He did? Just what did he tell you?"

"I know you were" — she chose her words carefully. He'd been deliberately cruel, but she wouldn't make a bad situation worse by calling him a redneck — "poor, not as polished as Brent. He had lots of friends and you found it difficult to make friends. You became so angry with him, you hit him when he called you a hick."

"That's it? That's what Farenholt told you?"

"Well, Brent also admitted he resented you because you won the National Moot Court competition that Wade Farenholt expected Brent to win. That's why he teased you about being a hick."

"Really? That's what he said? That's all?"

"Yes." The subtle change in his voice warned her something wasn't right, but what? "Brent feels terrible now. It was immature, but you have to realize what pressure Ward had put him under, and to lose out to a man who . . . ah, ah —"

"Was a redneck from Arkansas."

"You had the grades, but Brent had the class, the friends, the social standing. So you spent the next years polishing yourself to be more like Brent."

"That's crap! I worked on my accent because studies show juries equate southern accents with uneducated people. I bought a sports car, a nice home, and great clothes — not to be like Brent — but because I could finally afford them."

"All right," she conceded, secretly glad he hadn't wanted to be like Brent. Mitch should be proud of what he was, what he'd made of himself. "But you're being nasty to me because I said I loved Brent, aren't you?"

He pierced her with a look that forced her to suck in a calming breath. "Hell, no. I'm pissed because you have shit for brains. I was there, Royce. I saw it all. The minute you were in trouble that pantywaist turned tail, didn't he? Yet you'd go right back to Brent if you got the chance."

She didn't want to give Mitch the satisfaction of knowing how many times she'd thought just that. Brent hadn't loved her enough to stand by her. She would never go back to him. Never.

"Brent Farenholt doesn't know how to fight for anything," Mitch insisted. "His *mommy* has to give it to him."

She understood that nothing had been handed to Mitch. He'd fought for everything he had. He was a born fighter; that's why he was so valuable to her now. But she hated his censuring look, knowing she'd disappointed him with Brent.

"When I agreed to marry Brent, I thought I loved him. During the test I said I loved him — past tense. I loved the idea of the stability a home and a family represents. Brent seemed so right." She smiled, attempting to lighten the mood with a dose of humor. "Who would refuse a rich heterosexual — a rare commodity in this city — who declares his undying love for you?"

Mitch didn't respond. Instead he leveled an unwavering stare at her.

"In retrospect I see marrying Brent would never have worked. Never."

The silence that followed felt as wide as the Pacific. She needed him on her side, completely. "It'll take a miracle to keep me out of prison. I have to be able to talk to you civilly. I can't go on like this."

He silently glared at her, his eyes so compelling, there was nothing she could do but gaze back at him. And wonder what he was thinking. His head was canted ever so slightly to one side, unconsciously favoring his good ear. What had happened? she wondered with a deep pang of compassion.

"Okay, so I've been shitty. I'll shape up." He picked up a slice of pizza and fed it to Jenny. "As long as we're being honest, let's talk about us."

"Us?" An unwelcome tightening in her throat made the word sound funny. Us? After the way she'd thrown herself at him, what must he think? Be honest; your future is at stake. "I'm sorry about the other night. You were right. I was so exhausted, I was paranoid, convinced Wally had been killed. I would never have clung to you like that except my mind was playing tricks on me. Now my head's on straight. It won't happen again."

With one swift stride he closed the gap between them. His hand came up under her chin and tilted her head upward so she had no choice but to look into eyes that were unusually blue, unusually turbulent. Eyes that were staring at her parted lips. "Wanna bet it won't happen again?"

Her heart didn't flutter too much as she took a step back. "My whole future's on the line. Your reputation could be ruined if you were involved with me. Don't you carry malpractice insurance to protect you against situations like this?"

That got him. He retreated toward the refrigerator.

"Let's behave professionally," she said, knowing Mitch was a man who targeted a weakness and exploited it ruthlessly. Fine. His career, his unbridled ambition, was his Achilles' heel.

"Okay, but don't deny you're attracted to me."

"It's ridiculous," she conceded, "but it's true. I find you very" — she stopped herself from saying *sexy* — "interesting. But I promise not to come on to you. We've got a monumental task ahead of us. Getting involved is out of the question."

Uncomfortable seconds ticked by. Why was he looking at her like that? Finally, her patience gave out. "Right? Right." She mustered a weak smile. "So now we agree."

He subjected her to a thorough, intimate appraisal meant to shock her. But this time she wasn't letting him get to her.

"I admit you turn me on." He shook his head. "It doesn't make any sense, but it's a fact."

A secret thrill shot through the barrier of her control, but she tamped it down. "Then it's settled. We can work together if we ignore this — this attraction. No more hateful jibes, no more" — she didn't know quite how to put this — "physical contact. We're a team now."

He gazed at her, his look so intense that she almost flinched.

"You know, Royce, I've never met anyone like you. With luck I never will again."

11

Still busy? Who could Val be talking to? Royce hated telephones, but this was the only way she could keep in contact with her friends. She dialed Talia's number on the portable telephone Paul had given her.

"Royce," Talia cried, "you're home. I've been so-o-o worried about you."

"I'm not home. I'm in a safe house." She stared at the blinking cursor on Mitch's computer as she sat in the office he had on the second floor of his home.

"Safe house? You mean you're hiding? Why?"

"There's been too much bad publicity. I don't need more, so I'm keeping out of sight. But I have a phone. You can call me anytime."

Talia took down the number then asked, "Do they know who framed you yet?"

"I can't talk about the case — at all."

"Why not? They don't suspect me, do they?"

"It's just the way Mitch operates." She side-stepped the truth. They suspected everyone, but didn't have a substantial lead.

"Really? When are we going to see each other?"

"Not for a while. But call me. I'm a little lonely."

A little lonely didn't come close to describing how she felt. Mitch had left town on a case, and she was living in his apartment, spending her days — and nights — using his computer to check phone records for Paul. Each day she battled the frightening, suffocating feeling of being trapped in a situation beyond her control with no one she could truly trust.

"So, what's been happening with you, Talia?"

"The usual. AA meetings. Work." Talia paused and Royce imagined her hooking one long strand of dark hair behind her ear the way she always did when she was nervous. Royce closed her eyes. Lord help her; she was developing a sixth sense about bad news.

"The police have been interviewing me, Royce. I know you can't talk about the case, but just listen. They asked me if you were having financial problems with the wedding. I told them the truth."

Royce kept herself from groaning. What had she told Val and Talia that day at lunch? "I'll have to rob a bank." The police were bound to find out about the fancy wedding she couldn't afford, but did Talia have to be the one to give them the details?

"Val told me to refuse to talk to the police. That's what she did, but my therapist says I avoid telling the truth if I think it's going to cause trouble. Chronic Avoidance Syndrome. That's my problem. My therapist says the truth will set me free."

The therapist was right; Talia avoided confrontation. She needed support to make changes that would keep her away from alcohol, but right now Royce didn't have the strength to give it. She hung up with the disturbing thought that Talia, one of her oldest and most trusted friends, was going to be a witness for the prosecution.

She wandered downstairs into Mitch's living room and gazed out at the bay. She was uncomfortable having to work in Mitch's house, but she had no choice. The police still had her home impounded as a crime scene. If she wanted to help with her case she had to use Mitch's computer, which was fine now. But what would happen when he returned?

Their confrontation had cleared the air. In his own cynical way he'd admitted to being as attracted to her as she was to him. And he wasn't any happier about it than she was. *I've never met anyone like you. With luck I never will again.* Could she work in his office every evening if he were home?

It was more than his sexual attraction that disturbed her. Each day her curiosity about Mitch grew, magnified by spending so much time where he lived. What about his past? she wondered. There wasn't a clue in his home. There were no personal photographs, diplomas, or awards anywhere. Didn't Mitch have a life beyond his job?

She turned away from the window with its panoramic view of the bay. Mitch's home left few clues about him, yet there was something strange about the place. Paul had told her Mitch had bought the run-down mansion and remodeled it. The exterior was a tasteful example of Beaux Arts design: a narrow lot with a hidden garden and servants' quarters over the garage in the rear.

Mitch had restored a classic mansion, but why had he restructured the interior? He'd taken the linen closet, butler's pantry, breakfast area, and kitchen and bashed out the walls to create one huge kitchen. The dining room wall had been sacrificed to make a living room the size of Golden Gate Park. He'd taken down the wall between two bedrooms to create one enormous master bedroom suite with an awesome view of the bay. Obviously Mitch had a fixation about big rooms. He needed space with a capital *S*.

Something cold touched her hand and she jumped sideways. "Oh, Jenny, for heaven's sakes. You frightened me." She patted the golden retriever's head. Jenny tugged at the leg of Royce's pants. "What are you trying to tell me, girl? You've already eaten."

The dog sprinted toward the kitchen, barking and turning, urging Royce to follow. In the kitchen Jenny stopped in front of a drawer and bumped the handle several times with her nose. Royce couldn't imagine what Jenny wanted. Royce had agreed to care for Jenny and the porked-out tabby, Oliver, while Mitch was away, but their food wasn't in this drawer.

Jenny barked at the drawer until Royce opened it. Inside was a jumble of paraphernalia for pets: flea spray, brushes, chew toys, a choke chain.

"What a mess!" Royce looked around the kitchen. It was every bit as Spartan as the rest of the house and just as spotless. "Mitch's cleaning lady must love him. He's an anal retentive treasure, but what happened here?"

Jenny nosed into the hodgepodge and grabbed a leash. She sat back on her haunches, leash in her mouth, wagging her tail.

"A walk? Is that it? I'm not supposed to leave the house." She thought about the wigs Paul had given her. In the dark, wearing a wig, who would recognize her?

She set the burglar alarm and led Jenny, who still had the leash in her mouth, across the garden to her apartment. Before she could put on a wig, the portable phone in her purse rang.

"Royce, how are you?" Val sounded more like her old self, the predivorce Val. "Talia gave me your number."

"I'm fine. Tell me what's happening with you."

"I have a new job." There was no mistaking the excitement in Val's voice. "I'm working with computers at Intel Corp."

"Intel Corp?" Warning sensors fired in Royce's brain. What was Val doing there? Would she be working on the case even though she was a suspect?

"I'm in the credit card fraud division. I . . .

ah, really like it there."

The unnerved feeling heightened. Royce knew Val and Talia so well that she sensed withheld information immediately. She cradled the receiver against her shoulder, wondering what next.

After a few awkward seconds Val continued, "I've been seeing someone — someone special."

Relieved that Val's hesitancy had nothing to do with the case, Royce said, "Tell me about him."

"There's not much to tell," Val hedged, and Royce decided Val didn't quite trust this man yet. Who could blame her after that disaster of a marriage? "We'll see what happens."

"I'm glad," said Royce, truly happy for her friend. She shouldn't be so concerned about Val working at Intel Corp. "How did you know about the job?"

"From one of the detectives who interviewed me about your case. Paul told me to —"

"Paul," Royce cried. She slumped down in the sofa; Jenny licked her hand sympathetically. "Not Paul Talbott."

"Yes. Do you know Paul?"

"Of course. He owns Intel Corp. Paul's personally conducting the defense investigation." Why would he hire a suspect?

"He owns Intel Corp? He never told me."

Royce heard a knock on the door and knew it was Wally. She promised to call Val later, then answered the door with Jenny at her heels. She gave her uncle a bear hug.

"Wait for me to put on a wig. Then let's go for a walk. I have to get out of here."

Wally talked about things at work as they strolled through the quiet neighborhood. She knew he was trying to take her mind off her desperate situation. Finally he stopped under a streetlight haloed by the condensing fog creeping in from the bay.

"What's the matter, Royce?"

"I hate not knowing who's behind this mess. I'm beginning to be suspicious of everyone — even my closest friends." Without commenting Wally listened while she told him about Val and Talia. "Be honest, do you think I'm paranoid? We've been friends for over twenty years and suddenly I'm riddled with suspicion."

"No, you're not being paranoid. You're being realistic."

"Are you implying Val or Talia might be responsible?"

Wally stopped and Royce reined in Jenny. His expression was troubled, hardly the reassurance she was seeking. "I've been conducting my own investigation. So far, I can't even establish a motive. It simply doesn't make sense."

"Eleanor wanted to get rid of me."

"I'm not certain I buy that. There are easier ways of dumping a fiancée."

"You didn't see the look on her face when I was arrested. She was elated — believe me — elated."

"I don't doubt it," Wally conceded, "but that

219

doesn't mean she framed you."

"Surely you must have some theory about my case."

"I wish I did." They rounded the corner and found the fog thicker, spiraling up from the bay as sullen as the ominous clouds lurking beyond Golden Gate Bridge. "I had a very interesting call . . . from Val."

"Really? She didn't mention it." Royce saw an odd expression on her uncle's face. "You've never liked Val, have you?"

"I thought you two had an unhealthy relationship. She was always hanging around the house when you were growing up. She imitated you, wearing her hair the same way, choosing the same clothes. It wasn't healthy."

"Val was just unhappy. You know how cruel her family was. And you know what happened with that jerk she married. Her mother and father knew about his affair, but no one bothered to tell Val."

"Two troubled friends," he responded. "You're just like your mother. Misfits clung to her — me included."

"You're not a misfit and neither is Val." By her omission she'd silently conceded that Talia was, and always had been, a misfit. "If Val hadn't married that creep, she'd be well adjusted, happy."

"Mmmmm." Wally did not sound convinced.

"So tell me, what did Val call you about?"

Wally motioned for her to turn around; the

fog was so dense now that she could barely see Jenny at the end of the leash. "Val called because she's worried about you. She thinks Mitchell Durant is too interested in you."

Royce was aware of her uncle's eyes examining her. Did he suspect how attracted she was to Mitch — in spite of everything? Wally had been so upset after her father's suicide that she'd been terrified he would kill himself too.

He'd taken a leave of absence from his job and came to Italy with Royce. It was almost a year before Wally returned to the newspaper. And his reporting had never been quite the same.

Her life had never been quite the same either. She'd lived in Italy, continuing to write her column for the *San Francisco Examiner*. But staying in Italy hadn't changed a thing. She still felt guilty about her father's death. And so did Wally.

Wally might admire Mitch professionally, but he would never understand if their relationship became physical. "I think Mitch feels guilty about what happened to Daddy. That's all."

"Val asked me to investigate him."

Royce stopped, jerking Jenny to a halt. "You can't do that. He made us promise —"

"Not to print anything, not to go public. I don't plan to." Wally put his hands on her shoulders. "There's something mysterious about Mitch. If it has anything to do with you, I want to find out about it before you're sent to prison."

She didn't need this, not now, not with her life in turmoil. She had to be able to trust Mitch, if not on a personal level, at least professionally.

"Already I've discovered something that makes me even more suspicious. I compared a photocopy of his birth certificate to an official certificate. Mitch's certificate is a forgery — not a good one either."

"But why would he have a phony?"

"Maybe he was in trouble with the law."

"Well, he used that certificate to get into the Navy," she said. "He must have been running away from something, or someone."

"Exactly, and I intend to find out what."

"Do you think I ought to change attorneys?"

"God, no. Wait until I find out more. Mitch is still the best. This might have no bearing on your case. And, frankly, we can't afford an attorney of his caliber."

There was a dark, forbidding side to Mitch that frightened her. If he discovered they were investigating him, what would he do? "Don't let Mitch find out —"

"Don't worry. I won the Pulitzer for investigating the Chinese mafia. They never suspected a thing."

She had the distinct impression Mitch guarded his back a whole lot more closely than the local Chinese gangs.

"Trust me, Royce. Have I ever let you down?"

12

Paul walked into Beyond Lascaux, the expensive men's shop just off Union Square where Shaun Jamieson worked. Next to London's Savile Row, San Francisco had the most fashionable men's clothes in the world, Paul thought, and this shop was no exception. No tacky racks here. Instead there were mannequins modeling the latest in men's suits and tables with artful displays of ties and shirts.

Paul introduced himself to the attractive man who'd been Wallace Winston's on-again, off-again companion for years. Slender, with striking brown eyes and darker brown hair, Shaun gave Paul a quick once-over.

That's life in San Francisco, Paul thought. Men sized each other up as soon as they were introduced. Paul knew Shaun recognized with a glance that he wasn't a homosexual.

"How can I help?" Shaun asked, eager, charming.

It was easy to see why Wally was attracted to Shaun. He was one of those people that others instantly liked. In Paul's experience those people were the least likable in the long run. He chatted with Shaun for a few minutes, saying Wally had sent him, before asking, "How well do you know Royce Winston?"

"I've known her for years. I watched her grow up, you know."

"What's your opinion of her?" Paul had no idea why he'd sought out Shaun — just gut instinct. Shaun had been at the auction. And he owed Wally a lot of money.

"Wel-l-l . . ." Shaun appeared reluctant to give his opinion, but Paul had interviewed enough people to know better.

Paul waited, knowing people felt obligated to fill voids.

"Royce thinks she's better than everyone. I never cared for her."

Interesting, Paul thought. No one else felt that way about Royce. And he'd never gotten that impression of her.

"I understand Wally lent you some money," Paul began cautiously.

"He *gave* me the money." Shaun's veneer of charm evaporated.

"I see. You recently asked for more?"

Now, this was a wild guess based on the periodic loans Wally had made to Shaun over a number of years. According to the forensic accountant's report Wally hadn't lent him anything in over a year.

"Yes. I had an opportunity to invest in a surefire winner, a metaphysical shop, but Wally claimed he was tapped out. I knew better. That bitch was back from Italy. Royce convinced Wally not to loan me any more money."

Mitch leaned against the wall of the old-fashioned wood telephone booth outside the Sacramento courtroom and called Paul. Honest to God, most of the time he hated being a lawyer. Take this case — pleeeze somebody take this case. Talk about boring. Talk about needless delays.

Typical, though. A white collar crime that called for high-priced lawyers in a legal face-off. Armadas of expert witnesses were set to testify for each side.

He had struggled to keep his mind on the case, but odd things triggered images of Royce. The gleam of the bailiff's holstered gun reminded Mitch of the shimmery dress Royce had worn the night of the auction. His hand down her back stroking her soft skin. Christ, he could get an erection just thinking about her.

Where was she now? He'd been tempted to call her last night, but resisted. He wanted her to get accustomed to being in his house. Being with him. Mitch conceded he should move Royce out of his home before someone found out and accused him of conflict of interest. But he couldn't.

Was he crazy? Damn straight. Who could blame him? Craziness ran in his family. That was a fact. Even so, he'd worked hard to maintain a sterling reputation in a profession famous for sleaze-balls.

But he was crazy — too crazy about Royce to let her go.

The phone in Mitch's hand rang until Paul's secretary answered and put him through. "Hey, Mitch, how's it going?"

"Same old crap. It looks like a short trial, though. I shouldn't be here long. How's Royce's case coming?"

Mitch listened while Paul told him about interviewing Shaun. "Royce didn't know Shaun had asked Wally for money the night of the auction."

"True," Paul agreed. "I checked with Wally. Christ, is he ever touchy about Shaun, but Wally did say he'd never mentioned it to Royce. He refused to make the loan because he was sick of Shaun's wild schemes."

"Is Shaun crazy enough to try to get rid of Royce?"

"Nah. Shaun is hot and heavy with someone else — someone very rich. Looks like a dead end."

"How's Royce doing?" Mitch hoped he sounded casual.

"I have her checking on Farenholt, Weintraub and Gilbert's phone records. I doubt if we'll find anything at the law firm, but who knows? I've been taking a closer look at the Farenholts' finances. Eleanor doles out money to Brent and Ward — a dollar at a time. They have to go to her several times each month."

Brent was a wuss, a mama's boy. It gave Mitch a perverse sense of satisfaction to know how much money he'd made — on his own. When his clients could afford it, he charged outrageous fees. If he liked a case, and a client couldn't afford him, Mitch waived the fee. No matter. He'd still gotten rich — all by himself.

"Caroline is coming into an enormous trust next year. If I were Brent, I'd marry her for her money and get away from Eleanor." Paul laughed. "Still no leads on that informant, Linda Allen, but I'm working on it just as hard as Royce is working on your computer."

Mitch tried to envision Royce at his computer, spending every day in his home, but he couldn't. He liked the idea, though. Hell, he loved it. She belonged with him and by the time he got her off, she'd understand that the past was behind them. He'd been wrong to prosecute her father, but she'd forgive him once she'd been acquitted.

Paul announced, "I've hired Valerie Thompson in the credit card fraud department."

It took a second for the name to register. Oh, yeah, Royce's friend. "You what? She's a suspect."

"She's in a totally different department. Val doesn't have access to computer codes. She can't possibly find out anything about this case. Besides, I need competent help in that section. It's the fastest-growing segment of my company."

Mitch recognized that tone — a mule digging in, burrowing his legs in sand. Mitch didn't like it; he remembered Wally thought Val had framed

Royce. But what could he say? Paul ran his own business; he didn't take orders from Mitch. Even more important, Paul was his only close friend. And the most honorable man he'd ever met.

Paul let out an audible sigh. One hurdle over. Mitch was pissed, but he accepted Paul's authority. The one friendship Paul valued most was Mitch's, not because it was the hardest won or the longest in duration, but because when Paul needed Mitch, he'd been there.

He'd quit the force and his marriage — already in trouble — had failed. All he had was a friend. Not that Mitch was the sentimental I'm-your-buddy type. No way. Mitch had kicked butt, saying: "Know where you can find sympathy? It's in the dictionary between *shit* and *syphilis*. Now get off your ass and go for that PI firm you've been yacking about."

Paul had taken Mitch's advice. And the result? A lucrative private-investigation firm unrivaled in the country. Mitch had believed in him when he hadn't had faith in himself. It took a lot of nerve to cross Mitch. But Val was worth it. Paul believed in her as much as Mitch had believed in him.

Paul's secretary announced Valerie Thompson. He heard her come in, his stomach clenching. She must know he wasn't a lowly detective or she couldn't have found his office.

Val walked with the quick, graceful stride he found so alluring. She halted in front of his desk, her dark eyes serious. "Why didn't you tell me you owned Intel Corp?"

He came around the desk to stand beside her. "I was testing you," he admitted sheepishly. "I've met too many women who come on to me because they think I'm rich or powerful."

She gazed at him with the most serious eyes he'd ever seen. "I had plenty of money when I was married. In the end it won't make you happy." She leveled an even more intent look at him. "The only thing that matters is how we are together."

He had the uncomfortable feeling she meant sex. They talked, sure, a lot, but Val needed constant physical contact. She wanted to cuddle and make love twice a night — at least.

"Why did you offer me a job?" she asked.

"You're too talented to waste time inspecting rest rooms in fast food dives. And I don't want you out at night. It's dangerous."

Her bottom lip dropped and she stared at him for a moment. Then she moved closer, a smile on her face. He was half sitting on the desk now, one hip resting on the top. She touched his knee and bent forward to kiss his cheek.

"Oh, Paul, that's the sweetest thing anyone ever said." Her hand traced its way up his inner thigh. "No man ever cared about me. Ever."

Her hand reached his crotch the same time as his jaw fell open. She kissed him, a long, lingering open-mouthed kiss, while her small hand cradled his shaft. She squeezed gently as her tongue plied his, stroking, until he gasped.

"Paul," she whispered, her lips against his, "I'll never let you down. I promise."

Royce had already been in Mitch's office fifteen hours when the phone attached to the answering machine rang. Mitch seldom received messages on his private line. Since she'd been using the computer the only message that had come in had been from some kid named Jason. She was curious about this call because it was so late at night.

She heard Mitch say, "Pork chop, if you're there —"

She grabbed the receiver. "Mitch, you creep. I'm not a pork chop. I'll have you know I've lost four pounds."

He laughed and she had to remind herself that fate, not choice, had thrown her together with this man. A surge of the old anger swept through her — thank heavens — she didn't want to soften toward him. It was too dangerous. Despite her wariness his laughter rang in her ears, bringing with it the comfort of human contact. The days were unbearably long. And lonely.

"I put Oliver on a diet too. He's the fattest cat I've ever seen. I figured if I had to suffer, so should he."

"Aw, Christ, you didn't." Mitch laughed again. "Ollie gets pissed and kicks gravel from his litter box to kingdom come if he's hungry."

Royce stifled a giggle, remembering finding the near-empty litter box. "He already did."

"Next he'll steal Jenny's food."

"He tried, but I stood beside her with a broom while she ate."

"Give Ollie a break. The vet cut off his balls. All he has to enjoy in life is food," Mitch said, his tone teasing. "Did I mention I'm gaining weight? Right now I'm lying on my bed pinching my spare tire."

Usually a witty comeback would have sprung to her lips. Instead she saw a mental image of Mitch stretched out across a bed. The telephone was cradled against his right ear, his good ear, and his lips . . . his lips were close to the receiver. His hand was toying with the phone cord, long tapered fingers twining through the coils. The same fingers that had covertly dipped down the back of her dress. She shifted in her seat, aware of a subtle, unwilling change in her body.

Why had he used a phony birth certificate? she asked herself, trying to recapture the suspicious feeling she'd had earlier, trying to escape Mitch's sensual lure. Her intuition told her there was probably a reasonable explanation. After all, back then he'd been a boy. It had nothing to do with the present.

"Still there?" Mitch asked, a husky pitch to his voice.

"Yes. I was just wondering if it's all right to take Jenny for a walk at night. I'll wear a wig."

"Sure. Stay in the neighborhood where it's safe. Starting next Monday you'll be spending the afternoons at the office. We'll be prepping you to go on the witness stand using a videotape. That way you can see what you look like, and you'll be prepared for the prosecution's cut throat questioning."

Royce shuddered, imagining Abigail Carnivali questioning her. It had been frightening enough at the preliminary hearing when Carnivorous convinced the court to try Royce on one count of grand theft and three narcotics violations that carried mandatory sentences if she were found guilty. The prelim had come just four days after her bail hearing before Judge Sidle. Abigail had been so convincing that Royce had almost believed she had committed the crimes.

"Will you be here to help?"

"No. This trial won't go to the jury for several days. Just remember to look directly at the camera while you're practicing. At the trial look right at the jury. Have they shown you the tape of the William Kennedy Smith rape trial yet?"

"I have it, but I haven't watched it yet."

"Do it before Monday. Notice how Smith didn't let the prosecution rattle him. Then read the report on Kim Basinger's breach of contract trial. Jurors said she didn't seem sure of herself and she kept looking down. It cost her almost ten million dollars."

She closed her eyes, dreading the trial and frightened that the investigation hadn't turned up any solid leads. "I'd rather give up ten million than ten years of my life."

After a short pause Mitch said, "Stop worrying.

Didn't I tell you to trust me?"

The next day Royce walked up the path to her house with Paul Talbott. Ahead she saw the boards nailed over the front door — what there was left of it — and the yards of black and yellow crime scene tape. Even at this distance she saw her father's beautiful stained-glass door was damaged beyond repair.

"Wait till you see the inside."

Paul was right; the interior looked like the aftermath of a tornado: every drawer emptied, every book tossed on the floor. Stuffing ripped out of the furniture.

"Why?" she gasped.

"They were looking for drugs and an address book with the names of your clients, your connections."

"Where's my computer?"

"The police are examining it." He withdrew a huge computer printout from his briefcase. "It's listed here along with several other items."

"Why?" She looked around at the attic room that had been her father's office, the room where he'd shot himself, the room she'd so carefully restored and made into her own office when she'd returned from Italy.

"The police figure you have records in your computer."

"Great. What next?"

"I'll get a crew in here to straighten things."

"No. That'll be expensive." She pointed to the

daybed in the corner that was no more than a pile of ticking peeking out from beneath shredded chintz. "I'll order a new mattress and sleep here in the attic. I can straighten the house a little at a time between breaks from the computer."

"Aren't you forgetting something? The computer's at Mitch's. Anyway, you'll have to ask Mitch to let you come home."

"He won't mind. The media has forgotten me. I've had my fifteen minutes of fame."

Royce returned to the apartment with Paul, determined to take up the matter with Mitch. Late every night he called, and she waited until "Are you there, pork chop?" came through the answering machine. Pork chop, really. Just wait until he saw her. Now she'd lost five pounds thanks to a liquid diet that tasted like chocolate sawdust in nonfat milk.

Paul stopped in the alley behind her apartment. He handed her the thick computer printout, saying, "Give this to Mitch. Bring it back to me Monday."

"Mitch? He's here?"

"Back for the weekend recess."

She climbed out of the car with a sense of dread. She'd expected Mitch to be gone at least two weeks. She liked him at a distance. Talking to him on the phone was far easier than seeing him in person. Less tempting by half.

Well, there was nothing she could do about it. She'd have to face him. Should she tell him what she'd found on the phone calls from the

Farenholt law firm? No. It was probably nothing, probably just coincidence. She need to check a little more before she mentioned anything to Mitch.

13

Mitch answered the knock at his back door, nudging Jenny aside with his knee. The dog was beating the wall with her tail, obviously as anxious to see Royce as Mitch was. The porch light shone down on Royce, making her blond hair seem even more golden. The consultant had restyled her hair with a sleek cut that tamed her rowdy curls, and it hung just below her chin, curving in slightly to frame her jaw. Sexy as hell.

She handed him a computer printout as thick as a Bible. "Paul said to give you this. It's the police inventory of the contents of my house."

He moved aside and motioned for her to come in. "Let's go over it together."

"Why?" Her tone was guarded. "The evidence list is on top. We can see what they're using."

He tossed the printout on the kitchen table where she'd have to sit next to him to examine it. "We can tell what they were looking for by the way the inventory is arranged." He pulled out a chair for her. "First, I'm ordering a pizza. Want some?"

"And give you a reason to call me 'pork chop'?" She flashed him an insolent smile. "I'll have a salad with the dressing on the side . . . please." She slid into the chair and began thumbing through the printout.

He ordered the pizza, joking with Ernie, the owner of the pizza parlor that Mitch called almost every night. While he talked, he studied Royce. He'd decided to take a different tack with her — a more subtle approach.

"What do you see?" he asked as he hung up.

"My God, they listed every single thing I own. No wonder it took them so long. I never knew I had this much stuff."

"Typical in drug cases. They're looking for stolen goods that people gave you instead of money."

"You're right. Everything of value comes first. The earthquake money, which they've kept for evidence. The good luck piggy bank my father gave me when I was eight. It had thirty-one dollars and twenty-six cents in it. Jewelry . . ." She ran her finger down the short list.

Mitch sat beside her, deliberately not sitting too close. As always, Jenny moved to his side and put her head on his knee. He stroked her silky fur, his eyes on Royce. She was so absorbed by the list that she failed to notice him studying her.

"Hmmmmm." She stopped and checked the

236

evidence list, then looked at him with those matchless green eyes. "I don't see my mother's gold charm bracelet. I wear it almost every day. I'm very sentimental about it."

Mitch seized the opportunity to scoot a bit closer as he reached across the Lucite table for the printout. "It's probably listed under another category."

But it wasn't. It took them over an hour to check the lists. By that time the pizza and salad had been delivered, and they were eating as they worked.

Mitch never thought he could be this close to Royce without touching her. Not that he wasn't tempted. But she seemed to be relaxing with him. Don't push your luck. "Where did you keep the bracelet?"

"I usually wore it, but it didn't go with that beaded cocktail dress. I must have taken it off in my bedroom. Maybe the bathroom. I'm not sure."

Mitch reached for the last piece of pizza. "Someone on one of the special teams might have tucked it in his pocket. They're usually above reproach, but it's happened. That's what got Paul into trouble."

"Really? Jewelry was missing?"

"No. Money. It was a drug bust. Paul was there with another homicide detective because they'd gotten a tip there was a body in the basement. They found several suitcases of money. Some of it disappeared. Paul was under suspicion because he'd been down there by himself for a minute, but they couldn't prove a thing. Still, the Internal Affairs guys were merciless. Paul resigned."

"That's terrible. Poor man." Royce sighed and he battled the urge to take her into his arms.

"It was the city's loss. He's the best detective I've ever seen. That's why he's on your case."

"Val's working for him, you know."

"In the credit card fraud department. That's upstairs away from the unit working on your case." He tried to sound reassuring, but he was concerned. He didn't like having a suspect so close to case files.

"About the bracelet," Royce said, "it's possible they missed it. My place is such a mess that it's hard to tell what's there."

"We're going to report it. If it turns up, we can cancel the report. That way you'll get insurance money if it doesn't." Mitch got up and tossed the pizza box in the trash compactor.

"Will I bother you if I use the computer tonight?" she asked.

"No, I'm going to be in the office too," he said, making this up as he went. "Doing research."

Now he could picture it, he thought, after they'd gone up to the office and were working. When he was away, he'd been unable to imagine her in his office: Royce tapping softly on the computer keys, her head bent, sending a fall of blond hair over her shoulder. She was so damned cute, he could kiss her. And even though his back was killing him, nothing could have budged Mitch, not even faithful Jenny gazing up at him, silently pleading to be taken for a walk.

Later Mitch looked up, ready to suggest walking Jenny. Royce was staring at the computer screen. Her profile was to him, so he couldn't exactly see her expression, but she seemed upset. He gazed at her a few more minutes but she didn't move. He rattled some papers. Nothing.

He walked over, turned a chair around backward and sat down, straddling the chair. Jenny followed him, nudging her head under his hand so he could pet her. Royce's eyes were fired with a light he'd seen too often. She was pissed big time.

Aw, hell, not tonight. The last thing he wanted to do was fight with her. He wanted to take her into his bed with soft music crooning from the stereo, slowly undress her, and make love all night.

"You're right, Mitch. I have shit for brains. Look at this."

He let out a sigh of relief. There was a God. Royce wasn't angry with him. For once. He scooted so close that he caught the fresh scent of her shampoo.

She was too preoccupied with the computer to care how close he was. "The entire time I was dating Brent, he kept calling Caroline from the office." She scrolled down the screen, saying, "The average call was over half an hour. He wasn't really over Caroline. No wonder he's dating her again. Did he ever love me?"

"Caroline is still dating that Italian count. She may never have been out with Brent after your arrest. Tobias Ingeblatt probably dug up an old photo. You know he fabricates his stories." Jeezus, why was he defending that prick Farenholt?

Royce scowled, unconvinced. "Well, phone records don't lie. He called her every day from the conference room phone."

"Sneaky bastard. He's smarter than I thought he was."

"What do you mean?"

"Ward Farenholt is executor of Caroline's trust, so she's a client. Secretaries keep logs of billable hours. If Brent called from his own phone, Caroline would have been charged. But he called from the conference room, where he had privacy and no one would bill Caroline."

Now Royce looked hurt. Part of him was glad, but another, nobler side felt for her. Women were fools for Brent. Hadn't he learned that lesson once?

"Come on," he said. "That's enough for tonight. Let's take Jenny for a walk."

Outside the bracing night was heavy with the scent of the sea and night-blooming jasmine, a welcome change from the winter months when wispy fog crept in from the bay. In the distance iridescent stars of light danced on the water. Royce had run up to her apartment and put on a red wig that made her look like a stranger.

240

A sexy stranger. Hot, swift currents of arousal surged through him, but he controlled himself. Tonight he had a game plan.

"You don't have to hold the leash," he told Royce as Jenny marched ahead, the leash between her teeth. "Just hook it to her collar and let Jenny hold the other end in her mouth. That way if a cop stops you for violating the leash law, you just say: 'But, officer, my dog *is* on a leash. The law doesn't say a person has to be holding the leash.' "

She laughed, a warm laugh that reminded him of the night he'd met her. She'd joked with him then, happy, relaxed.

"Leave it to a lawyer to find a way around the law."

"Hey, Jenny loves running free. Just call to her when she gets to the corner. Sometimes she sprints ahead. I'm afraid she'll get run over."

"Don't worry, Mitch," Royce said in her familiar sassy tone. "I know the *intent* of the law. When I walk Jenny, I'll hold on to the leash."

There was something subtle in the air between them now. Umm-hmmm. It wasn't just his imagination. She cocked her head to one side and offered him a shy smile charged with sexual chemistry. Ooo-kay. Now what?

They walked several blocks, then stopped to admire the lovers' moon suspended above the Golden Gate Bridge. It was perfectly round and as soft white as a magnolia against the night sky. But Royce's mind wasn't on the panoramic view.

He could tell she was still worrying about Brent.

Her self-esteem had to be zero right about now, and he wasn't sure what to say to make her feel better. He was great with words, all right. He'd persuaded countless juries to let guilty men go free, but he'd be damned if he knew what to say in this situation.

He believed Royce when she said she no longer loved Brent. But, dammit, she *had* loved him. Not that he could blame her. He'd seen it all before. And it hurt just as much now as it had then.

Brent Farenholt was handsome in an unfair way. Women couldn't take their eyes off him. Mitch never got that kind of attention until a woman realized he was *the* Mitchell Durant. Add money and charm to Brent's looks and it was no wonder that so many women fell for him. Had anyone ever said no?

Had any woman ever turned her back on Brent Farenholt?

They headed home, walking in comfortable silence with Jenny strutting ahead, her leash in her mouth. Mitch called to Jenny to stop on every corner, but his awareness focused entirely on Royce, excluding everything except the erotic signals her body sent to him. He'd bet the farm she wanted him, but she wasn't about to let him know it. The past stood between them like a wound that refused to heal.

He followed her up the stairs to her apartment. She said good-night and turned to open the door.

"Royce," he said, touching her arm.

She swung around, whipping the red hair around her cheeks. It resettled in rippling waves across her shoulders as her eyes met his. He'd be damned if he'd let her go to bed tonight heartsick over that mama's boy.

He caught a strand of hair between his fingers. Not nearly as soft as her own hair, not nearly as sexy. He slowly brushed the curl over her lips. Her eyes were luminous in the moonlight; the pupils had reduced the vibrant green to narrow hoops. How could one woman be so astonishingly appealing?

"Good night," she repeated, a seductive undertone to her voice.

Hey, Mitch, don't give her a choice. When you do, she runs. He pulled her to him — Uhhooh — more roughly than he'd intended. Her body conformed to his, the soft fullness of her breasts flattening against his chest as his mouth found her sensuous lips.

Her mouth was already parted, the tip of her tongue waiting for his. Heat spiraled through him, faster and hotter than ever before, becoming a tight knot in his groin.

"Don't," she whispered against his lips, but he felt the physical pull emanating from her body.

His sixth sense told him not to give her a choice. Make certain you're the one she dreams about tonight, not that prick. He moved his mouth over hers, devouring its softness. Instantly her lips responded. Her whole body did.

243

He felt her surrender deep in his gut. She was indisputably under his control. That savage satisfaction was heady and every bit as arousing as her kiss. She didn't have the power to resist him because she didn't want to — no matter what she said.

Her tongue flirted with his, enticing him to delve deeper. Her hips were tilted upward, flush against his turgid sex, challenging him to take this kiss a step farther.

Should he? No way. Hell, he was tempted, but he had a point to make. So he lingered, kissing her. It was a hot, yearning kiss calculated to let her become accustomed to his arms around her, his tongue caressing hers, his hardness pressed against the notch of her thighs.

Somehow he wedged his hand between them and touched her breast. Even through the sweater he could feel the erect nipple. It had been five long years — dammit — but he remembered exactly what her breasts were like. Soft, full. Taut nipples flushed with desire. There was nothing he'd like better than to lower his lips and sculpt those nipples with his tongue, but he couldn't allow himself to be sidetracked.

He used sheer willpower to pull away. "You hate me, don't you, Royce?"

She stared at the toes of her running shoes. "Why are you doing this?"

"You hate me, but you want me. There are some things between people that just can't be explained, right? Right. That's how it must be with Caroline and Brent. He's been close to her for years. So he talked to her even when he knew he loved you and was going to marry you. No big deal."

"I wish I could believe that."

So did Mitch — for her sake — but he didn't say a word. Instead, he just walked away. Who knew what that cocky little shit was thinking? But he'd be damned if he'd let Brent destroy her self-confidence. When he reached the bottom of the stairs, he turned. She stood transfixed, watching him.

"Think about us, Royce. Can you explain it?"

14

Paul found it surprisingly easy to obtain an interview with Eleanor Farenholt. His disguise as a reporter for *Town and Country* doing advance work for an upcoming layout worked perfectly. He sat in the living room of the Farenholts' Nob Hill mansion, watching the bay sparkling in the distance. Bright sunlight reflected off the Louis XIV furniture in a blaze of gilt.

So far, Paul had managed to balance the dainty tea cup and saucer and keep up a steady stream of inane conversation. Boy, he hated prissy rooms like this. Pretentious museum-like rooms that left him cold. Pretending to love the furnishings and find them "smashing" for an upcoming issue wasn't easy, but he decided that he'd finally gained Eleanor's trust enough to broach the subject of Royce Winston.

"Nasty bit of business with those jewels taken at the auction, wasn't it?" he asked, keeping his intonation eastern and his attitude officious.

"Terrible," Eleanor agreed, "most embarrassing."

"Wasn't your son" — he paused as if he couldn't quite bring himself to insult the lady by saying her son was engaged to a criminal — "friendly with the suspect?"

"Royce Winston chased my son. She was after his money."

Paul pretended to sip his tea. Eleanor Farenholt was a classic beauty: fine features, a model's cheekbones, and bright blue eyes. She wasn't the cold woman he'd expected; actually, she was quite pleasant. But then, she wanted to impress him.

"I had hoped my son would marry Caroline Rambeau," Eleanor informed him. "You remember her, don't you? *T and C* featured her at Tiffany's last year."

"Of course." Paul smiled, hoping he sounded convincing. "I was thinking of inquiring about her home for this same piece we're doing with you, but I wasn't quite certain it was up to snuff."

"Caroline's home would be perfect," Eleanor assured him.

"Well, I hadn't contacted her from New York,"

he hedged, giving Eleanor the opportunity to help him.

"I'll call her for you. Caroline's just like a daughter, you know. My husband and I love her as much as if she were our own child." Eleanor laughed, a giggle that sounded odd for such a mature woman. "Ward might just love Caroline more than Brent. He expects so much from his son."

"It's harder to be a man," Paul sympathized. "Expectations are a lot higher."

An hour later he was on his way to see Caroline Rambeau. He wasn't sure he'd learned anything helpful from his discussion with Eleanor, or that he'd get much from Caroline, but he liked to have a feel for his cases. Sometimes his sixth sense kicked in to help him solve a crime.

Caroline Rambeau's home was within walking distance of the Farenholts', causing Paul to speculate on just how close — geographically and emotionally — they all were. There was a certain inbred feeling in the upper echelons of society, a type of protectiveness, an insular attitude toward those with less that Paul had noted from his earliest days on the police force. But the Farenholts' relationship with Caroline seemed to go beyond anything he'd previously encountered.

Caroline answered the door herself, clad in a silk jumpsuit. She was even more beautiful in person than she was on the videotape he'd seen. She bore a startling resemblance to Eleanor Farenholt. But then she smiled and invited him

247

in. Paul instantly knew the engaging smile and the cheerful attitude weren't a facade. Beauty, money, and a winning personality. A dynamite combination.

"Eleanor tells me you're doing an article on San Francisco's homes with views."

Paul wrinkled his nose, doing his best imitation of New York smugness. "Not just any view — only the spectacular ones" — he looked around the room approvingly — "with appropriate furniture to showcase the scenery."

Now, here was a classically beautiful room, he thought. None of that ornate gilt crap that Eleanor loved. Caroline's home was decorated in soft shades of white that complemented the warm wood tones of the antiques.

"I see," Caroline responded, but she didn't sound nearly as enthusiastic as Eleanor had. Paul had the feeling that she wasn't as snobbish as the older woman.

"Did you work with the decorator?" Paul asked to fill the uncomfortable silence.

"My mother worked with Gaston Norville — years ago."

"Well" — Paul smiled brightly — "good taste always survives the test of time."

"What do you need from me?" Caroline asked.

"I'm just doing background. The legal department will send releases for you to sign before we can photograph your home." Paul hesitated, mentally rolling the dice. "I might have to delay this article a bit. There's been so much negative publicity about those stolen jewels. You were right there, weren't you?"

"Yes," Caroline admitted, "but I don't see —"

"We want our readers concentrating on the story, not wondering how that odious Winston woman infiltrated one of the best families —"

"She didn't infiltrate. Brent brought her to meet his family." Caroline sounded angry, almost as if he'd accused a close friend — not a rival. "I like Royce. I thought she was good for Brent. He lets Ward bully him too much."

"Were you surprised she stole the jewels?"

Caroline looked him directly in the eye. "Royce didn't take the jewels. She isn't that kind of person."

"Well," Paul said, taken aback by Caroline's attitude. "Who do you think did?"

"I have absolutely no idea."

"Watch the video monitor," Brian Jensen told Royce as they sat before the video camera in the jury-preparation room of Mitch's office. "See how you're waving your arms? It makes you look agitated, nervous."

"I'm half Italian. I can't talk without my hands."

"Oh, yes, you can." Brian was Mitch's in-house expert on juries. "You'll do better next time."

Next time Royce groaned inwardly. They'd been at this for hours, but she knew days of preparation stretched ahead of her before she'd be ready to face a jury.

"Try to sound as sincere and unrehearsed as possible," Brian instructed. "A jury likes to think they're hearing everything for the first time."

"Even though everyone from the arresting officer to the star witness for the prosecution has been prepped for hours," put in the young associate who'd been doing the questioning, pretending she was Abigail Carnivali.

The two laughed, but Royce couldn't even force a grin. To them it was a game. They'd seen it all before, and they'd see it again. For her, though, it was dead serious. If she were found guilty she'd spend the next ten years of her life behind bars without possibility of parole, the mandatory sentence for the drug charges.

"Get more cameras in here tomorrow," Brian said. "We need more angles."

"What for?" Royce asked. "I can see perfectly well what I'm doing wrong."

Brian averted his eyes and the associate busied herself shuffling papers. Something was up.

"One of you tell me what's happening." Why was she shouting? Because she had lost control of her life and was being bounced around like a tennis ball. She hated it. Any second she was going to . . . to what? There was nothing she could do, and that was doubly frustrating.

"A local TV station has petitioned the court to allow cameras to cover your trial," Brian told her. "Mitch will fight it, of course."

But she wondered if that was true. Part of his payoff for taking her case without a fee was publicity. She'd been with him all weekend and he hadn't mentioned the petition. He hadn't told her Abigail Carnivali was going to ask for a higher bail than she could possibly raise either. What was wrong with him? She had every right to know these things.

By the time the phone rang late that night, she was more than ready for Mitch. She rushed across his office, faithful Jenny dogging every step. Royce yanked the receiver out of its cradle.

"You know, you're a real bastard, Mitch. You never told me there's a petition to televise my trial. I don't want to be on TV, you understand? This is not some media circus. This is my life."

There was dead silence at his end but that didn't stop her. "Mitch, listen to me. No television."

"You don't have any choice. It's up to the judge." There was a weariness, a note of resignation, in his voice that brought her up short. "I'm totally against cameras in courtrooms, but it's the judge's decision."

"Why didn't you tell me about the petition?" she asked, backing down a little. He sounded exhausted.

"I got the fax this morning. I was in court all day."

"Oh," was all she could say, but she felt bitchy for losing her temper. A silent scream of frustration ripped through her.

"Judge Ramirez is aiming for the appeals court bench. No matter what I say, she's going to allow cameras."

She remembered Superior Court Judge Gloria Ramirez from the preliminary hearing when it had taken the judge less than three minutes to decide the state had enough evidence to try her. Uncle Wally had covered numerous trials and assured Royce that Judge Ramirez was one of the best — but ambitious. "It's not fair to televise my trial."

"The judicial system tries to be fair, but it doesn't always succeed. Cameras make everyone nervous. The whole proceeding will be stilted, but what can we do about it? Prepare for it. And thank God the state's nearly bankrupt. They don't have the money to prep their witnesses the way we do."

The fight went out of her as surely as if she'd been knocked to the mat — out cold. What could she say? The judge had the final decision. For a moment she wished Mitch were beside her so she could look into his eyes. Oh, go on, Royce, be honest with yourself. You want Mitch to hold you.

Mitch had a kiss that could make her forget anything — even the fact that Brent had called Caroline every day when he was supposed to be in love with her. And Mitch could make her think and question her deepest feelings. After he'd so passionately kissed her, then left, she'd spent a sleepless night. Thinking.

But no answer came to the question of how to explain her reaction to Mitch except an upsurge of guilt when she thought about her father. Where had Mitch's compassion been then? Still, she couldn't help admitting how hard Mitch was trying to help her when no one else could. She felt confused, torn between past and present, between loyalty and desire.

She realized Mitch had kissed her to make a point. He'd agreed to behave professionally, and so far he had. Just talking with him each night gave her a sense of confidence and optimism she desperately needed. She wanted to keep their relationship at this level, friendly yet professional.

"How's your trial going?" she asked.

"It went to the jury this morning. This is the roughest time. Waiting. Trying to guess the verdict."

She took a deep breath and held it, knowing Mitch was preparing her for her own ordeal. "I'm going to ask for a postponement of your trial."

"Why?" A jolt of panic rocketed through her. "What's wrong?"

"Things aren't going the way I expected. Paul hasn't found any evidence — no matter how flimsy — that anyone framed you. I can't sidetrack a jury without something, anything." He paused and she heard him sip a drink. "Don't worry. Defense attorneys have three rules: delay, fight, appeal. This is stage one of the game plan — delay.

"A postponement will help you. People have already forgotten the details of the crime. Our latest survey shows only sixty-seven percent of those polled think you're guilty. As time goes on the percentage will drop. You'll get a better jury."

"You're saying justice has been sacrificed on the altar of strategy and tactics. I suppose that's the system and I have to live with it, like it or not."

Mitch didn't respond to her outburst. There was a moment of silence before he spoke again. "Royce" — Mitch's voice had that low, intimate pitch that never failed to send an electric charge through her body. But this was no sexy come-on. She braced herself for more bad news — "Paul's taking a closer look at your friends and Wally."

Once she would have angrily denied any of them could be guilty, but now, after hours of lying awake at night, mulling over the situation, she wasn't sure. Could she trust anyone? Not when her future — her hopes, her dreams — were at stake. She had to know the truth. Who hated her enough to destroy her?

"Mitch," she said, thinking he'd soon be home. Obviously she had no self-control where he was concerned. The only solution was to put space between them — "I want to go home."

There was a long, awkward silence before Mitch said, "Okay. Wait until Friday when your new mattress has been delivered."

"Let's keep our relationship quiet until after the trial," Paul told Val as they sat on the sofa in his house. He didn't add Mitch had cautioned him several times about employing a suspect. He knew Mitch was right, but he couldn't help himself.

"Okay." Val snuggled closer, smiling seductively.

Not again? They'd made love twice tonight. He'd like to spend time here in front of the fire, sipping wine and talking. He needed to find out what was behind Val's insatiable appetite for sex. Undoubtedly, it was rooted in her troubled marriage. He'd waited for Val to talk about it, but now he could see he was going to have to force the issue.

"I was married for ten years," he began. Perhaps if he told her more about himself, she'd be more comfortable sharing her problems with him.

"What happened?" Her dark eyes examined him intently.

"Our marriage had been dead for several years. Even if I hadn't been brought up before Internal Affairs, it wouldn't have lasted. And it was my fault. My job was my life back then — until I found out how easily I could lose everything." He gave her a blow-by-blow account of the drug bust that had gotten him into trouble.

"Who took the missing money?" she asked.

"One of the other officers took it. He had a kid with leukemia and was strapped for cash. You have no idea how tempting it is seeing bundles of bills bound for the evidence locker when you make diddly-squat. You think: Who'll miss one bundle?"

"Didn't you tell anyone?"

"Nah. I felt sorry for the guy. If my kid was dying and my insurance ran out, I might have taken the money. Anyway, I couldn't prove anything, so why drag a guy before IA when he already had enough troubles?" He gazed at her, encouraged by her compassionate expression. She really cared about him. It wasn't just sex.

"Darling, I'm so sorry," she said, genuine emotion in her eyes.

"Tell me what happened to you, Val," he said, but she hesitated and he could see the pain was still great. "Don't you know I love you? I can't make you happy unless I know what you need." He hadn't meant to blurt it out like that, but it worked.

She smiled fondly at him. "My father was a cold, domineering man, and my mother never wanted children, but I was always close to my brother, David. Very, very close. I was stunned when I found out my parents — and David — had kept Trevor's affair a secret . . . for years."

"You didn't suspect your husband had a lover?"

"No. I was pretty naive when I got married. The only marriages I could use to compare were my parents', which was a cold relationship, and then Royce's parents — just the opposite. No one could miss how much they loved each other. I used to hang around because they all were so happy. My marriage was somewhere in between my parents' and Royce's.

"You see, I was so happy having my own home

256

that I didn't question our relationship. I confess I lorded my marriage over Royce and Talia. They were so competitive. Always searching for Mr. Right, but I'd found him."

Mmmm, Paul thought, not the first time someone's mentioned how competitive Talia and Royce were. He'd checked out Talia and found nothing. Maybe he should take another look.

"Then Royce moved to Italy, and Talia began dating some questionable characters. I spent my time with Trevor, and my brother was around constantly, which was great because we'd always been close.

"It didn't dawn on me that there was someone else until the last year we were married and I realized how seldom we were making love." She studied the wine glass in her hand, running her fingertip along the rim in endless circles. She gave him a shy smile. "Sex with Trevor was never like it is with you. You want to hear something funny? I knew it the moment I met you."

He recalled the first night they'd made love. More than once she'd said: "I knew it."

"The next time Trevor claimed he was working late, I followed him." Her words came slowly, almost against her will. "I caught him in the act."

Paul put his arm around her and drew her close. "It happens. Put it behind you."

She gazed at him as if she had more to say but couldn't bear to say it. Her lashes were dewed with unshed tears, and Paul was astonished at the rush of jealousy that hit him. Did she still love her husband, or was it just the lingering hurt?

"Trevor's lover was my brother David."

In the uneasy silence that followed the bombshell, they couldn't meet each other's eyes. Jesus Christ, what a mess! Did he have what it would take to bring her out of this? He loved her, but would that be enough?

"I can't forgive David. I haven't seen my brother since the night I caught him with Trevor. And I'll never speak to David again."

Wally escorted Royce up to Mitch's back door. Jenny had sprinted ahead and stood, leash in her mouth, on the steps. These late-night walks had been comforting to Royce, a break in the lonely hours when she saw no one except Jenny. But now Wally was leaving on a special assignment and she'd be alone.

"I found out more about Mitch," Wally said quietly. "Every year he puts a lot of his income into a bank in the Cayman Islands."

"Really? Why would he do that?"

"I'm not sure. He's been doing it since he began working."

"There must be a fortune in there by now."

"That's the interesting part. I had a buddy at Bay Area Savings make a call to check funds."

"You didn't. If the bank calls Mitch, he'll go ballistic."

"Don't worry. I had my friend cover by saying he'd made a mistake with the account number.

The Caymans are like Switzerland — no names, just numbers. Anyway, I found out there's less than a hundred dollars in Mitch's account."

"Where did the money go?" she asked.

"Somewhere Mitch doesn't want anyone to know about. It's going to be hard to find out, but I have a contact who'll help me."

"Don't bother. What could this possibly have to do with me?"

"It took thousands of dollars to buy the coke they found in your apartment. All the other suspects' money is accounted for — with the exception of Mitch's."

"He wouldn't stoop this low," she protested. Mitch was direct, honest, and often cruelly sarcastic, but he'd never lied to her. Even at her father's funeral when Mitch had apologized, he'd admitted he was the sole reason the DA's office had gone ahead. He could have blamed someone else, but he hadn't.

"Remember, he's using a phony birth certificate," Wally reminded her.

"Something happened when he was young. He's a runaway . . . or something." She didn't add that she'd tried to question Mitch about his past over the weekend. But he'd cut her off.

With mixed emotions she said good-night and went into Mitch's house to work on the computer. Her purse was sitting on the kitchen table and the portable telephone inside it was ringing. She dashed to answer it; the phone was her only connection to her friends.

"How's tricks?" It was Talia.

"The same." What could she say? She couldn't talk about the trial. She never saw anyone. Then she remembered some good news. "I talked to my editor-in-chief today. He's had lots of mail protesting because I'd stopped writing my column."

"Are you going to be writing again?"

"No. I don't feel the least bit funny these days." When had she last laughed? The night of the auction. The night her whole life had changed. "So, what's new with you?"

"Nothing, really," Talia said, and Royce could almost see her: midnight-brown hair as sleek as mink and the withdrawn expression in her dark eyes. This wasn't going to be good news. "I have to learn to confront things, to tell the truth — no matter how painful."

Royce eased herself into a chair. What now?

"I'm going out with Brent tomorrow night." Talia's words came out in a breathless rush. "He called and said he's lonely."

That jerk doesn't know thing one about lonely. How well she remembered sitting in jail — waiting. Afraid. Hoping to hear from Brent. What had she ever seen in him? She thought about Mitch and wondered if he'd called while she was out. He always called around midnight when she was loneliest.

"Royce, are you there?" Talia asked. "Don't be angry with me. I'm going out with him only to convince him not to testify against you."

"I'm not angry." Surprisingly, she wasn't, but she did wonder about Talia's motives. Did she love Brent? Had she loved him all along?

"I've got to do what I can to help you, Royce. I can't live with myself if I don't do something," Talia said, but Royce couldn't help wonder if she was sincere.

After Royce hung up, she heard a knock at the back door and answered it, expecting Paul or Gerte. Instead she saw a teenage boy dressed in clothes so baggy that a dozen of his friends could have gotten into them with him. His Giants cap was on backward, revealing dusty-brown hair and a smattering of pimples on his forehead.

"Where's Mitch at?" the kid asked, his tone insolent.

He obviously knew Mitch, so she motioned for him to come in. If Oliver got out again, she'd spend half the night hunting for the blasted cat. "He's away on a case. I'm house-sitting for a few days."

She didn't quite know how to explain her presence, but a warning bell cautioned her. Mitch didn't want *anyone* to know where she was. "Are you Jason?" She remembered his voice from the calls on the answering machine.

"Yeah." His eyes narrowed. "You stole those diamonds."

"I was framed." Why was she defending herself?

"That's ba-a-ad, man."

They stood staring at each other until she realized how late it was. "It's late. Don't you have school tomorrow?"

"Nah. It's some conference day. I was jus' in the hood and saw the light. I thought Mitch came home."

In the neighborhood? She didn't challenge him. This wasn't a neighborhood you cruised. And he couldn't have seen the light unless he'd come up the back alley, which was the closest route to the corner bus stop. She motioned for him to follow her into the kitchen.

"I wanted to talk to Mitch. He's my big brother, ya' know."

She was familiar with the Catholic Big Brothers. Underprivileged kids. Perhaps Jason was in trouble. "Can I help?" She forced a joking note into her voice. "I know a lot about trouble."

He shrugged, seeming ill at ease.

"Want a Coke?" she asked, anxious to make friends. All she needed was for Jason to tell someone she was staying at Mitch's. She could just imagine what Tobias Ingeblatt would make of that tidbit.

He nodded and she opened the refrigerator, thinking, not for the first time, how odd of Mitch to keep little else inside except Cokes and jars of hot salsa. The freezer was even more of a mystery — bags of frozen spinach and two pizzas.

They sat at the table and she got him to talk, sort of. His mother was expecting a baby. "The man," who turned out to be his stepfather, was happy. And so was Jason, even though he wouldn't admit it. He hated school but was "zoning out" there every day so he could go to Big Brothers' camp.

"I'm gonna ride a horse and learn to water-ski," Jason informed her. "Mitch can't ski, and he's never been on a horse. Hell, he can't even ride a bike."

"Really?" It suddenly occurred to her this kid with a chip on his shoulder the size of Alcatraz knew Mitch better than most people.

"He don't even skate." Jason drained the can. "That's what happens when you're a runaway, you miss out on the good stuff."

Well, well. Her intuition had been correct. That's why Mitch had a phony birth certificate. She tried to imagine his parents. They must have abused him. Otherwise he would have asked them for his real birth certificate. What about the scars and his deaf ear? What had happened to Mitch?

She fished for more information. "It couldn't have been too much fun wandering around Arkansas."

"Alabama."

"That's right. I get all those states mixed up." So he'd grown up in Alabama, not Arkansas. And he'd joined the Navy in some small town in Tennessee. Had he run away and wandered through the South until he was old enough to join the Navy? Did his commitment to the homeless have something to do with his past? She pumped Jason, but didn't find out anything else.

"You know about girls, don't you?" Jason flushed and she suspected this was what he'd come to talk to Mitch about.

"Sure. I was one once. Why?"

"I jus' wondering what it means when a girl keeps walkin' by your locker but never says nothin'."

"It means she likes you but she's too shy to say hello. She probably thinks you won't talk to her."

Jason digested her observation in silence.

"Is she cute?" Royce prodded.

He shrugged. "Sorta."

Royce was tempted to remind him that he was no movie star. "Try saying hello first." How was it today's kids thought they were all grown up when in truth they were as insecure as teenagers had always been?

"If she turns out to be interesting you could ask her to go to *Rocky Horror Picture Show*. That's always a kick." The weird movie had become a cult phenomenon. All that audience participation, the dancing in the aisles. The crazies. Two shy kids wouldn't need to fumble around for conversation.

"Really?" He smiled for the first time.

"Yeah. Remember to bring lots of rice to throw."

The word *throw* brought a devilish gleam to Jason's eyes. "Great. Thanks a lot."

She got Jason out the door before the buses stopped running. "Mitch would appreciate it if you don't tell anyone — not even your mother — that you saw me here."

Jason trotted down the path and tossed "Okay" over his skinny shoulder.

Royce headed upstairs to Mitch's office, followed by Jenny, and heard the telephone ring and transfer to the answering machine. Mitch's voice came over the line.

"Royce, where in hell are you? If you're there, pick up." Mitch sounded frantic.

Royce sprinted into the office and grabbed the phone. "I'm right here. What's wrong?"

"Goddammit, where have you been?"

"I was walking Jenny." She decided to tell him about Jason later. He was in no mood to hear someone knew where she was.

"I want you to do *exactly* what I tell you. Exactly."

"All right." Her antennae had detected more than just another bit of bad news. Mitch wasn't easily rattled.

"Turn on the burglar alarm. Spend the night right there. And don't let anyone in."

"Why?"

"I'll explain it to you when I get home. The jury has reached a verdict. Gotta go."

"Just tell me —" Damn him! He'd hung up. What was wrong? Was she in danger?

15

"What a jerk," Royce complained to Jenny as she trudged downstairs to set the burglar alarm. "Mitch never tells me anything."

At the sound of her master's name Jenny wagged her tail and licked Royce's hand. It was her way of reminding Royce to pet her. She stopped and rubbed Jenny's chest the way she'd seen Mitch do. Having a dog was great. The only pet she'd ever had was her bunny, Rabbit E. Lee. If she ever got out of this mess, she'd get a dog.

A noise came from the back of the house. "What was that?" she whispered to Jenny, but the retriever had gone still, her nose pointed toward the dark kitchen.

Had she turned out the light? Royce didn't remember, but she had no trouble recalling Mitch's warning. *Don't let anyone in.*

The feeling she was in danger returned. It was the same panicky feeling she'd had that night in the bathtub. Someone *was* trying to kill her.

She tiptoed to the fireplace and grabbed a poker, thinking how frequently she was able to predict something was wrong. She'd told Mitch she didn't have premonitions, but now she wondered. Certainly she didn't make the sensational predictions that the tabloids loved, but she often sensed things before they happened. Especially lately.

With Jenny at her heels Royce silently moved across the huge kitchen. The dog growled, a low warning deep in her throat. Royce stopped, clutching the poker. The moonlight from the window revealed the pantry door was ajar. It hadn't been that way when she'd said good-night to Jason.

Royce hesitated. Should she dial 911? What if it was nothing and the police found her at Mitch's? He'd be furious. Damn him. He should have told her more. Then she'd know what she was up against.

Jenny charged past Royce into the pantry. Frenzied barking echoed from the small room. Royce raised the poker with one hand and switched on the light with the other. Jenny was standing inside the pantry barking at Oliver.

Royce dropped the poker, cursing her nerves. "You stupid cat. Look what you've done."

Oliver had clawed his way into a fifty pound bag of dog kibble. The bag had fallen over, which must have made the noise she'd heard. Kibble was strewn across the pantry.

It wasn't enough that the beast kicked kitty litter to Chinatown twice a day. Now this. The damn cat had eaten so much kibble that his already bloated tummy looked like the *Hindenburg*.

She went to the back door and armed the so-phisticated alarm system. It took a lot of sweeping, but she finally cleaned up the mess. This time when she shut the pantry door, she made certain it was secure.

"I have an overactive imagination," she told Jenny on the way upstairs.

Thanks to Mitch's obsession with space the second floor was an office and a huge master suite the size of a polo field. She'd ventured into the bedroom one time — just for a peek. Now she flipped on the light and studied the room.

Beige carpeting so thick she couldn't see her toes surrounded a king size bed with a headboard of rich mahogany that matched the nightstand and chest of drawers. The only picture in the room was an oil of a bayou.

Was there a bayou in Alabama? She didn't think so. Had Mitch spent time in Louisiana too?

Her curiosity got the best of her and she opened his walk-in closet. "I'm betting it's a mess," she said to Jenny, and the retriever wagged her tail in agreement as the door swung open and revealed a before shot for California Closets.

Really! How did you account for a man who appeared to be frozen in the anal stage, yet in reality was alarmingly disorganized? To look at his home or office you'd think Mitch was com-pulsively neat. Everything had its place, but just open a drawer or closet.

Jenny nosed through the pile of dirty clothes on the closet floor and found sweatpants. She dragged them to the edge of the bed and plopped down on them. No question about it, Jenny loved Mitch. And he was crazy about her. He would sit at his desk, pen in one hand, the other stroking Jenny.

Royce took a T-shirt that didn't look too dirty off the closet floor to sleep in. Nestled down in the bed she inhaled deeply and smelled Mitch's spicy after-shave on the pillow. Or was it coming from the shirt? It didn't matter. She found the scent oddly comforting and slightly arousing. She hugged the pillow, anticipating another sleepless night, another night of wondering who and why.

She came awake with a start, not certain if hours or just minutes had passed. Someone was standing beside the bed. This time it wasn't her imagination. The dark shape was hovering over her. She unleashed a scream that could have been heard across the bay. He jumped back, caught off-guard, and Royce vaulted out of bed.

The lights flipped on. "Shut up, Royce."

She spun around and saw Mitch. Relief and anger waged a war. Anger won. "You sneaky bastard. You scared me."

"A bastard, huh? I'd never deny it." He smiled, doing a slow pan of her from head to toe. A tide of heat washed over her as she realized Mitch had targeted her breasts. She didn't have to look to know how well she filled out his T-shirt. Or that her nipples were erect.

She crossed her arms in front of her chest. "Why are you here?"

"Verdict's in. I said I was coming home." His eyes scorched a trail down her bare thighs to her toes and up again, coming to rest on her lips. "Get back in bed."

"With you here? No way."

"I've been holding my client's hand for the last forty-eight hours straight. I just drove from Sacramento. I couldn't get it up if I tried."

She didn't believe him for one minute. Look at him. He was mentally taking off what little she wore. Still, there were deep shadows under his eyes and lines etched into his brow. How well she remembered that bone-deep fatigue. What was so important that he hadn't stayed the night and rested?

"Remember, you promised to do exactly what I said. Now, get in bed and I'll explain what's happening."

Reluctantly she climbed between the sheets and sat up, making certain the comforter covered her. Mitch stretched out on top of the bed. Uhh-ooh. She didn't trust him — or herself, for that matter.

"We located Linda Allen."

"The informant. Thank God," she said with a sigh of relief. Finally, something had gone right. "Now we can find out the truth."

Mitch looked down and traced the herringbone pattern on the comforter with his fingertip. "She's been murdered."

For a second Royce was tongue tied. How could something like this happen? She'd been hoping and praying. And believing that the truth would save her. "I was counting on her to lead us to the person behind this. Do you know who killed Linda?"

"The police don't have any suspects."

Oh, God, could things get any worse?

"Paul and I think Linda was killed to keep her from telling the truth about you." He touched the pillow behind her head. "It's possible your life may be in danger."

"Why? I'm as good as dead already."

But the premonition she'd had earlier hung over her: Someone *was* trying to kill her. Maybe she wished they would kill her. Turning the screws like this was mental torture. The little time she'd spent in jail was a glimpse of her future — a bleak, ugly future with creeps like Maisie Cross hounding her.

He moved nearer, closing the small space between them, and gazed intently at her, his face now just inches from hers. She was uncomfortably aware of how much bigger he was than she. Normally, her body would have had its usual shameless physical reaction, but she was too shell shocked by his news.

"Royce, I won't tell you this isn't a setback, but we can overcome it."

"How?" She knew she sounded like a petulant child, but couldn't help herself.

"By continuing the investigation." He adjusted his pillow and she had to admit he looked bone weary. "Remember, there's no perfect crime.

Every perp screws up sooner or later."

His confidence boosted her spirits a bit. "You're right. But do you really think I'm in danger?"

His eyes skimmed down her body, barely concealed by the lightweight comforter. She was in danger, all right.

"It's possible. This is such a weird case that it's hard to tell what's going on. There may be a bigger picture here — a hidden agenda — that we haven't discovered yet. But let's not worry about it tonight," he said, clearly indicating his mind was on her, not the killer. "Paul is having a security system installed in the apartment. And you're not to go out alone."

Prison. She was already in prison. Her nightly walks had been so special. Suddenly she thought of her beloved pet, Rabbit E. Lee. Often she took the bunny out of his cage and he hopped with glee, kicking up his heels. How Lee must have cherished those moments of freedom. How trapped he must have felt in his cage.

Trapped and lonely. Thank heavens her father spent time with him. No wonder Lee had simply given up when her father had died. He hadn't responded to her pleas for him to eat because Royce had never understood him. His frustration, his loneliness. Oh, Lee, I'm so sorry.

A silent scream ripped through her. It was all she could do not to cry. Someone had extinguished the small hope she'd harbored that Linda Allen had the key to this puzzle. And her freedom, her chance for a happy life.

Mitch brushed a strand of her hair off her shoulder. The defeated expression on his face mirrored her thoughts. He'd been counting on Linda Allen, too, hadn't he?

Her sense of despair went beyond tears. But why was he so upset? Maybe his case had gone badly. Immediately contrite for her selfishness, she asked, "Did you win your case?"

"Yeah. They found the sonofabitch not guilty.

"I charged him five times the going rate just to put up with him and what he did."

"Was he guilty?"

Mitch laughed, but he wasn't really amused. "Yup. Only four percent of the felony arrests in this state go to trial. The government only prosecutes slam dunks. Virtually everyone I defend is guilty."

"How do you win so many cases?"

"Depends." Mitch's eyelids were at half-mast now. "This time it was the battle of the expert witnesses. My client stole someone's patent. Our experts said it was different from the original. Their experts argued it wasn't. The jury was confused. That's when reasonable doubt kicks in to save asses like this guy."

"How do you live with yourself?" she blurted out.

"By taking certain cases for nothing."

"Innocent people like me."

He tried to smile. "Not always innocent — but deserving."

"Like the cougar they want to put down."

"Uh-huh." His insolent smile said he had his doubts.

"What about Zou-Zou Maloof? Was she paranoid from Halcion when she stabbed her husband to death?"

He seemed more interested in the way the blanket molded her body than the subject. "She had a prescription for Halcion," he responded, an intimate pitch to his voice.

She tried to throttle the sexual current surging through her. This was serious business. Her future depended on this man and his ability to manipulate the system. But what did she really know about him? Not nearly as much as she should.

"You have your own standards," she said with a flash of insight into this complex man. "That's why no drug lord has you on retainer. That's why you don't touch rape cases."

He edged closer; his legs, still above the covers, brushed hers. The gleam of desire in his eyes couldn't be disguised. Why didn't she turn away? Or say no?

But his hands . . . Oh, Lordy, his hands were already threading through her hair, caressing her scalp. Then his lips touched hers, soft but firm. Demanding. Of course, she opened her mouth.

Thick and heavy, her blood pounded in her temples. She should get up this second. Mercy, what he could do to her without even half trying. There was a dreamy intimacy to their kiss and the way his body, separated by the covers, still managed to mold against hers. It wasn't as blatantly carnal as some of Mitch's kisses, but it was a kiss for a frightened soul to melt into.

A soul kiss. Most definitely. It annihilated her defenses, her better judgment. She lost the will to resist, with an inward sigh, as she succumbed to the seductive kiss, his tongue burrowing a little deeper into her mouth with each thrust.

Her breasts swelled with pleasure and a depth charge of excitement exploded in the pit of her stomach. Though buffered by the thin covers, she savored the muscular planes of his torso and the heavy thud of his heart against her soft breasts. Oh, my, he was simply too good at this.

Unexpectedly, Mitch drew back and gazed at her. "Remember, Royce. We're in hell. And the pact you made with the devil was never to dig into my past or ask questions about my business."

Those lone wolf eyes flashed a warning that would have terrified most people. Why, he'd kissed her to shut her up. He didn't want to explain why he didn't defend men accused of rape. And fool that she was, she'd leapt at the chance to kiss him.

"Sorry," she mumbled as he rolled onto his back, but she wasn't one damn bit sorry she'd asked about his business. She wanted to know more about him.

Why was he so protective of every facet of his life? Perhaps there *was* some kind of link between how he practiced law and his past. She waited a few minutes for him to say something and fill the awkward silence.

Finally, she whispered, "Mitch."

He didn't respond. His chest was moving evenly; he'd fallen asleep. She propped herself up on one elbow and studied him.

Whiskers bristled across his jaw, making him look even more masculine and a little dangerous. He shifted restlessly to one side so his good ear was now against the pillow. If she whispered his name, he wouldn't hear her. If she said, "I love you," he'd never know.

She fought an overwhelming urge to gather him to her breast and tell him how sorry she was about whatever had happened to his hearing. Instead she reminded herself that he was the enemy. It didn't quite ring true, the way it once had, but it did keep her from touching him, from caressing his bad ear.

What had cost him his hearing? It must have happened in those lost years of his youth when he'd been desperate enough to forge a birth certificate to get into the Navy. How old could he have been? He had to be eighteen to enlist, so his troubles had begun before then.

But what about the present? Why an account in the Cayman Islands? What was Mitch hiding?

She turned out the light and was surprised at how easily she fell asleep. True, haunting thoughts of someone stalking Linda Allen paraded through her mind along with the usual array of vignettes about people she suspected one minute — and trusted completely the next. Even so, having someone nearby, someone she could rely on, comforted her more than she could have imagined.

The hazy light of early dawn filled the room when she awoke and found the covers were down around her waist. Mitch's head was on her pillow and his arm was draped across her midriff, her breasts resting on his forearm.

She was still under the covers and he was on top, but she was disturbingly aware of the intimate — almost natural — way their bodies were entwined. How long had they been that way? All night, most likely.

Anyone walking into Mitch's bedroom would assume they were lovers. She scooted away an inch at a time, but she only got so far before Mitch hauled her back against the solid wall of his chest.

He didn't awaken, but just snuggled closer, his face now buried in her hair. She had to concede it felt comforting to be cradled in his arms, the firm length of his body curved securely around hers. Drowsy, she drifted back to sleep, feeling protected.

How could her life be in danger?

"You remember what to say?" Mitch asked Royce. "Just those two sound bites. Nothing more. It'll be perfect for the evening news. Then Wally takes over for a full interview."

"Yo, Mitch. She's got it," Paul said from the driver's seat. "You've been over it fifty times."

Royce and Wally were riding in Paul's car to the courthouse, where Judge Ramirez would listen to their request to postpone the trial. Before the hearing Royce would give her first interview, part of Mitch's strategy to change the public's opinion of her.

Since staying the night with Mitch, she'd seen little of him. He had spent the weekend going over the details of Linda Allen's murder with Paul while she watched the workmen install a security system in the apartment.

Mitch and Paul believed that there was something going on that they didn't understand. They were convinced that she could be in danger. Personally, she had her doubts, but they insisted she keep the alarm on even in the daytime. Walks, of course, were out of the question.

Paul and Mitch left her in the car with Wally, outside the courthouse. In the distance she saw the legions of reporters, the mobile news units, and even a helicopter circling overhead. Her mind was congested with doubts. She wished she were as confident about pulling this off as Mitch was.

"My friend was able to check into that Cayman account," Wally said interrupting her thoughts.

She smoothed the skirt of the suit Mitch's consultant insisted she wear, a conservative gray skirt with a long jacket and a demure white blouse. This was the first time she'd been alone with Wally since Mitch had arranged for the interview.

"Mitch's money is going to a private clinic in Alabama — a very expensive private clinic," Wally added.

Royce wondered if Wally heard her sigh of

relief. "What kind of patients are there?"

"They treat everything from schizophrenia to mental retardation. It's a first class place."

She saw Mitch talking to the reporters. The breeze ruffled his hair, making him look slightly boyish despite his intense expression. "Obviously, it's someone in his family. Drop it. He has a right to his privacy."

"True. If I snoop around the clinic, someone's bound to report it to Mitch, but I'm going to the South to do an article on chicken ranching's negative impact on the environment. I'm going to try another angle and see what I can find out about him."

She put her hand on Wally's arm. "Please, don't."

"Oh, shit."

Royce flinched; Wally never cursed.

"What the hell are Ward and Brent doing here?"

Her gaze swung to the top of the courthouse steps, where Brent and Ward were talking and looking down at the crush of reporters. She stifled a gasp. Why were they here? Of course, they might have business, but now? Or was it merely Ward's perverse way of humiliating his son, showing him that he'd almost married a common criminal?

It took her a few seconds to realize she was staring at Brent. Handsome, charming Brent. And feeling nothing but disgust. A fine sheen of perspiration covered her — pure nerves generated by the thought of facing the media. Once she would have sworn Brent would have stood by her side throughout an ordeal like this. Now she knew better.

"You know," Wally said quietly, and she turned to meet his earnest green eyes, eyes that were so like her own, "I just had a wild thought. Could it be that this is a huge conspiracy involving Brent, his parents, and Caroline?"

Royce would have laughed if Wally hadn't looked so serious. "Like the Agatha Christie novel where everyone was guilty? I doubt it. I can understand the Farenholts and Caroline, but why Brent?"

Wally shrugged. "You're probably right. I'm just frustrated that I can't find anything. I hope Paul Talbott's having better luck."

Royce didn't answer. Her uncle was too savvy to honestly believe Paul had found anything. If he had, they wouldn't be asking for a continuance. Mitch had opted for the delay after the informant's murder. Without Linda Allen the defense had a weak case. No case, actually.

The car door swung open and Paul said, "They're ready for you." He gave Royce an encouraging smile.

Royce and Wally walked up to the bank of microphones just as Mitch had instructed. Think of Marie Antoinette stepping up to the guillotine, he'd said. Look noble, but tragic. She wasn't much of an actress, but she'd rehearsed, and watched herself on the video playback, enough to know just how to hold her head, how to keep her eyes open wide as if fighting back tears.

She looked over the reporters elbowing each other, jockeying for position, and the dozens of cameras, and froze, seeing Tobias Ingeblatt. Why did that man make her so nervous? she wondered, staring at him. His bald head glistened in the sun, the bristly tuft of red hair shot up from his crown and fluttered in the breeze. No question about it; he gave her the willies.

She was aware of the crowd's expectant glare. Could she do this? Mitch touched the small of her back, and beside her — the way he'd always been throughout her life — stood Wally. For some reason Royce thought of her father. He always told her: "You'll never walk alone." Papa was here with her — in spirit.

Royce looked into the cameras. "Please help me."

Before Royce could deliver the second, well-rehearsed line, she heard, "Royce is innocent. Royce is innocent. We want justice."

It took her a minute to locate the female voices that were shouting their support for her. Talia and Val stood off to the side with several other friends. Royce couldn't bank the tears that came to her eyes.

"I've been framed," she said, struggling to keep her voice level and blessing her friends for coming out to help her.

The reporters waited, expecting more than two quick sound bites, but she stepped back as planned and Wally took over.

"Great," Mitch whispered in her ear as he took one arm and Paul took the other, leading her into the court.

The plan was to let Wally, the veteran reporter, known and respected in the media, field questions. The evening news, if everything went as expected, would feature Royce's simple statement designed to be remembered in a world bombarded with media hype. Instead of being painted the conniving bimbo, she'd become the victim, the underdog.

Out of the corner of her eye Royce saw Brent and his father go into the building. She wondered if Mitch had seen them. Before she could ask, Val and Talia broke through the crowd. Tears again welled up, threatening her composure. How could she have suspected them?

"Mitch, I need to talk to my friends." For a moment she didn't think he was going to let her go, but he stepped aside.

Talia hugged Royce, openly crying. "I've been so worried."

Val was more subdued, but every bit as sincere. "We're with you, Royce, all the way."

"Thank you," Royce said. "I don't know what I'd do without you two. I love you both."

Mitch put his arm around her and guided Royce into the building. Behind them she heard Wally still answering questions. How could she have ever doubted those closest to her?

"Listen," Mitch whispered in her ear as they

passed through the metal detector, "Judge Ramirez's name and the word *delay* are rarely mentioned in the same sentence. Don't be upset if she refuses the continuance."

Royce walked into the already packed courtroom and braced herself. What else could go wrong?

The courthouse had been built after the Depression and it had been that long since the room had been painted. For the walls, once a government-issue green, the nonsmoking ban had come too late. They'd become a wash of mustard green that did nothing to take the edge off the straight-backed oak benches, giving Royce the feeling that she was indeed in prison.

None of the courtrooms had windows, enhancing the trapped feeling that gripped her more each moment. How would she be able to get through a trial? What if she were convicted?

Royce took her seat at the counsel table in the defendant's chair and looked down at the table where gang members had etched their signs into the wood. Out of the corner of her eye she saw Abigail Carnivali — in a red suit the color of a fire hydrant — take her seat at the state's table. Abigail shot a smug smile at Mitch. This was a lost cause and she loved it.

A clerk rushed up to the bailiff to let him know the judge was ready. "All rise," he said, his voice coming from a barrel chest that became a loose slab of flesh that hung over his belt and partially hid his holster.

"Hear ye, hear ye! Department seven of the Superior Court of the city and county of San Francisco is now in session. The Honorable Judge Gloria Ramirez presiding."

Judge Gloria Ramirez had flown into the judicial nest on the wings of affirmative action. Her appointment clobbered three birds with one stone. She was a woman with an Hispanic surname, and best of all — in San Francisco — a lesbian.

If anyone had bothered to check her background, they would have discovered she had nothing in common with the millions of Hispanics in the state. She was the product of an age of Aquarius marriage that lasted less than a year.

As for her sexual preference it was her private business. She wasn't active in the gay movement, but she liked the political clout it packed. After all, gays could be counted on to vote in a state where less than half the eligible voters ever made it to the polls in any election.

Gloria was proud of her reputation as a tough judge. Never let it be said that she tolerated senseless delays. No, sir. Her court didn't add to the legal logjam that threatened to bring down the whole system.

She had to admit, though, she was a little embarrassed about her decision to allow television cameras to cover Royce Winston's trial. She hated to see any trial become a media event, but pressure from her superiors colored her decision. She was positive they'd been influenced by the Farenholts' money. After all, judges had to run for election.

"Your Honor," Mitchell Durant began his motion for a delay of Royce Anne Winston's trial. "The defense requests a postponement of the defendant's trial. The death of an important witness has created a highly prejudicial situation for the defendant if she goes on trial as scheduled."

"Highly prejudicial." Ha! Gloria knew the tinkling of the appeals bell when she heard it. But Durant didn't have a leg to stand on.

Gloria leveled him with her this-is-bullshit look. She knew Mitch was stalling because he didn't have his defense strategy worked out.

She listened to his argument, which was weak, but brilliantly delivered, and made the proper notation in the trial notebook. What Durant didn't win, he appealed — with amazing success. Gloria would never make it up the next rung of the judicial ladder, the appeals court, if Durant tricked her and was granted an appeal on what promised to be a surefire conviction.

"Your Honor." Abigail Carnivali rose for the prosecution. "The State believes the defense's request is merely a delaying tactic. There's no valid reason this case shouldn't go to trial as scheduled."

Gloria couldn't have agreed more, but she despised Abigail. The nickname "Carnivorous" didn't convey the contempt Gloria had for the legal nymphomaniac.

Durant was another case entirely. He never tried to flirt with Gloria in the typical macho belief she wouldn't be a lesbian if she had slept with him. Mitch gave her what she wanted —

respect. She gave him what he deserved — respect.

"What should I do?" Gloria asked herself as she made another note in her log. If the trial proceeded as scheduled, Royce would be convicted — not that Gloria cared.

She'd watched the interview outside the courthouse on the small television she kept in her chambers. Royce's plea would play well on the six o'clock news, but Gloria wasn't fooled.

Still, Wallace Winston's interview had been inspired. Now, here was a man that she liked. He'd covered several of her cases, being extremely complimentary, which, coming from a Pulitzer-winning reporter, never hurt a prospective appeals court judge.

"Where is Wallace Winston?" Gloria asked herself, looking across the standing room only courtroom. She spotted him directly behind Royce, his hand on the rail that separated the gallery from the court. Obviously, he loved his niece and he'd been close to his brother, the respected columnist, Terence Winston.

How lucky. Gloria experienced a pang of unadulterated envy. Gloria's family had disowned her as soon as she announced she was a lesbian.

Her family's attitude was typical of what all gays faced. Gloria had long since accepted it, but she had to admit she missed her family. Could she really deprive Wally of his family, when another senseless delay — in a parade of delays that plagued the court — could possibly save a family member he loved? And who, more importantly, loved him.

"The motion to postpone this trial is" — she looked out across the blur of faces, conscious only of one kindred spirit, Wallace Winston — "granted."

Gloria ignored the astonished rumble that swept the court, and she didn't really notice the shocked look on Mitchell Durant's face. Even Abigail Carnivali's angry scowl almost escaped her. Gloria focused on the tears of relief in Wally's eyes.

16

Royce practically skipped up the steps to Mitch's back door. She should have been exhausted after a full day of being bullied by Mitch's crew in a mock trial, but she wasn't. They'd taken a break midafternoon to watch Mitch on a local cable station that had televised the Fish and Game Department hearing on the fate of the cougar who'd attacked a hunter. Seeing Mitch had given her a much-needed boost of confidence.

She opened the back door. Had she forgotten to set the alarm after feeding Jenny and Oliver this morning? Obviously. The alarm wasn't on. Setting the security system was so new to her that she sometimes forgot to do it. "Jenny, where are you?"

The retriever usually met Royce at the door. She called again and checked Oliver's litter box. For once there wasn't gravel all over the floor. When Mitch was out of town like this, Oliver tormented her by kicking kitty litter, and he was getting really good at it.

"Jenny," she called again, and the retriever came bounding into the kitchen, her tail whipping through the air. Royce sat on the floor and hugged Jenny.

"You should have seen Mitch defend that cougar." My God, was she actually talking to a dog — like a friend? Once she would have felt silly, but she spent so much time alone that talking to Jenny had become a habit.

"First, the Fish and Game warden showed these gruesome pictures of the turkey hunter's back where the cougar had mauled him. Believe me, it's a miracle the guy lived." Jenny wagged her tail as if she understood. "The warden kept referring to the hunter as 'the victim' and saying how 'vicious' the cougar was. Then it was Mitch's turn.

"You wouldn't believe how great Mitch looks on TV. Tall, handsome — really sexy." It was true; the females in his office steamed up the conference-room television set watching the hearing. "Incredibly sexy."

Jenny wagged her tail and Royce decided Jenny knew all about sex. Undoubtedly, she'd seen plenty of it in that huge bed or the adjacent bath with its sunken tub. Inside the nightstand drawer

Royce had found enough condoms for an army. Yup, Jenny understood sex.

"Not only did Mitch look sexy, but he projects supreme confidence. He whips out these charts that show 'the hunter' — notice Mitch didn't call him 'the victim' — was smack in the middle of cougar terrain hunting wild turkeys.

"Then he calls a game warden to testify that the wind was blowing the other way so the cougar couldn't smell the hunter. Next Mitch produces an expert witness, a vet who claims the cougar is nearsighted."

Jenny nuzzled her. "Can't figure out what his plea will be, can you? Well, don't worry, neither could the hotshots Mitch has working for him. Obviously, Mitch isn't going for self-defense. Finally, he shows pictures of the hunter in camouflage gear and he demonstrates how the man was squatting in tall grass blowing a turkey whistle to lure a turkey close enough to shoot."

Royce leaned back against the cabinet. She could still feel the excitement of watching a stellar performance. Mitch was the best. If he couldn't get her off, no one could.

"His summation was brilliant. Mitch said: Put yourself in the cougar's place. You're wandering through your own land, looking for dinner. You spot something in the tall grass.

"Looks just like a turkey. Sounds like a turkey. You sniff the wind. Nothing. So, you figure here's din-din." Royce smiled, recalling Mitch's final comment. "This is clearly a case of mistaken identity. The cougar thought the guy was a turkey."

Royce slapped the floor and laughed the way everyone in the office had burst into astonished laughter earlier that afternoon. "It was so simple, so obvious, but no one thought of it. Mistaken identity."

Jenny cocked her head to one side and Royce caught a movement out of the corner of her eye. She whipped around and saw Mitch. The contours of his bare chest, feathered with dark hair, dipped and curved, tapering to narrow hips clad in sweatpants faded from countless washings. Didn't he ever wear a shirt around the house? And look at him! Obviously he was naked beneath the snug-fitting sweats, his sex a full bulge.

"You creep, you're always sneaking up on me."

He smiled, a grin that would have convinced the toughest jury that he'd just received a supreme compliment. "I live here, remember?"

"How long have you been there?"

"I came in at the sexy part." He had the audacity to wink. "Mighty interesting."

That's what she'd been afraid of. Fine. He already knew she was attracted to him. They'd even spent the night in the same bed — although nothing had happened. "What are you doing back here so soon?"

"The Nature Nazis gave me a lift in their jet."

"You mean the Ecological Society? Jeeez, you're cynical."

"I'm realistic. They wield a lot of power, and

290

because they've convinced everyone they have the moral high ground, they can stop development or cost people jobs to save an endangered gnat."

"But, Mitch, they do a lot of good. Remember —"

"I don't want to argue. Let's celebrate. Find the champagne glasses." He pointed to a cabinet.

He should celebrate, she thought. He'd done the impossible. Again.

While she found the glasses, he trotted upstairs and returned wearing a T-shirt. Thank God. The Big-Dog shirt had a huge dog on it and said: IF YOU CAN'T RUN WITH THE BIG DOGS, STAY ON THE PORCH.

Outside in the small garden lingering shadows melded into each other, softening the angles of the building, signaling day was yielding to a cool summer evening. The light breeze stirred the leaves on the thick robe of ivy cloaking the high stone wall around the yard. Mitch dropped to the ground under the chestnut tree, Jenny at his side. Royce carefully positioned herself near him, but not too close, as he popped the cork.

Mitch filled the two flutes with champagne and handed her one. Royce touched her glass to Mitch's, edging just a little nearer to do it. At this range she could see each individual eyelash, thick and spiked. "To you — and the cougar."

"We're toasting you, Royce."

"Me!" She almost spilled the champagne. "What on earth for?"

He brushed her cheek with his knuckles, his

eyes resting on her lips for an uncomfortably long time. "For holding up through pure hell until we saw the light."

"What light?"

"Sometimes things get so bad in your life, so terrible, that you think it's hopeless. But if you have the tenacity to hang on, you'll spot the light at the end of the tunnel."

Recalling his troubled youth, she wondered if he weren't talking about himself as much as her. True, things were better. The interview had been a tremendous success. Her brief statement had been played hundreds of times.

The latest poll showed far fewer people believed her guilty thanks to a media consultant who'd dished out info about her to the press, who embellished every word. Was the public so gullible that they'd now believe she wasn't a fortune hunter but a hardworking intellectual who watched nature documentaries when she wasn't writing poetry or reading philosophy?

Well, maybe. Miracles did happen. Judge Ramirez had granted a delay, something even Mitch had sworn was a long shot.

"When did you see the light, Mitch?"

"The day I joined the Navy, I —" He stopped, obviously caught off-guard. "I'm talking you, not me. Guess what Paul found on the property inventory of Linda Allen's room?"

By the triumphant gleam in his eyes something important had been discovered in the informant's room, but what?

"The missing key to your house." He clinked his glass against hers. "To the light."

There is a God, Royce thought, realizing just how important this was. "Her sworn statement said she met me at a party, and I told her to come to my home. She claimed I opened the door and let her in."

"Obviously, someone gave her the key or told her where it was hidden. I didn't have a prayer of tearing her statement apart until now." He leaned closer and cupped her chin with his warm hand. "Not a word of this to anyone — not even Wally."

"But if you're going to use the key as evidence, don't you have to let the DA's office know?"

"True. But we've already exchanged documents." He sipped his champagne. "Christ! That's a paper blizzard. Now, there's a project for the Nature Nazis — the mountains of paper generated by depositions, discovery, witness lists. Forget the spotted owl. Entire forests vanish every year in the so-called pursuit of justice. Hell, there's one hundred and thirty-seven pages on your friend Talia. The testimony she'll give boils down to a couple of sentences: You didn't have any money and threatened to rob a bank to pay for your wedding."

Talia's name evoked a feeling of sadness and disappointment. Sure, Talia had come to see her at the courthouse and she called — faithfully — every evening. But she was still dating Brent, claiming to be trying to help her.

"Won't Abigail see my key on the property inventory?"

"Yes, but no one described the special key ring your father made. When I send her the additions to the evidence list, I'm going to conceal the key among several other items." He poured himself more champagne and motioned for her to finish her glass. "Abigail will miss it because she'll be concentrating on the addition to our witness list — our star witness."

"Who's that?" she asked, smiling. His excitement was contagious.

"The FBI's top perp pro. You know, an expert who puts together a profile of the perpetrator. They've been amazingly accurate, especially about serial killers. This case was giving me so much trouble," Mitch confessed, "that I flew him out even before we received the inventory."

Royce gazed into her champagne glass, the tiny bubbles bursting against the rim. Her preconceived ideas about Mitch were being destroyed like the bubbles floating to the surface. Obviously, he'd been extremely worried about how to defend her. How could she hate him when he was doing so much to help her? She was touched — and frustrated. Nothing on earth was worse than not being able to help yourself.

"What did the perp pro say?"

"Just what Paul already figured. The killer tried to make Linda Allen's murder look like a drug hit by using a Mac-10 semiautomatic, but she was shot at close range, a mistake a pro wouldn't make. A Mac bullet fragments on impact. There wasn't enough of Linda's head left to put in a Baggie. The killer had to be covered with her brains."

Royce gagged, but Mitch had seen enough violence to make him immune. He went right on talking.

"She was hiding in a one-room dive in Chinatown's worst area. If anyone saw the killer in bloody clothes, they aren't talking, but we know she let him in."

Her glass was empty even though she didn't remember drinking it. "Him. So it's a man?"

"The perp pro isn't sure. More women have been committing crimes. If they kill, they usually do it with a gun."

A woman, Royce silently reflected. She couldn't imagine Eleanor or Caroline or even Talia shooting Linda at point-blank range. But then, she hadn't been able to imagine herself in prison either — until now. Anything was possible.

Mitch moved closer as he poured her more champagne, his thigh now touching hers. She struggled to ignore the pulse of sexual tension that suddenly surfaced. She had to keep her mind on her problems.

"Paul discovered Ward Farenholt has a mistress," Mitch said.

"Really? Brent never mentioned it, but maybe he doesn't know. He's not as close to his father as he is to his mother." She took a sip of champagne, mulling over this new information. "In a way I'm not surprised. Ward is polite to Eleanor, but he's cold."

"Since the money is hers, he's taken extreme care to hide the fact that he's having an affair. Only an expert like Paul picked up the subtle clues."

Royce was intrigued and elated. She had two of the best in her corner. She'd fight her way out of this mess yet. "What clues?"

Mitch chuckled. "Paul's a big believer in sifting through the trash. He found several cash receipts for items that Ward purchased from Victoria's Secret."

"Really?" Royce giggled. "I can't imagine stodgy old Ward in Victoria's Secret. Well, Paul must be right. Ward certainly wasn't buying anything for Eleanor in that shop."

"Right. We figure his mistress is a younger woman."

"Didn't Linda Allen work for an elite escort service?" Royce asked, and Mitch nodded. "She claimed to have met me at a society party, right? Well, couldn't she have met Ward at a party? If she traveled in those circles, it's certainly possible."

"True," Mitch agreed. "But nothing in her hideout links her to Ward."

"Didn't you tell me the place had been ransacked? Maybe Ward removed any incriminating evidence."

"Possibly. I've always thought Ward was behind this. I had the perp pro take a look at the whole case. He says the crime was well planned over months, maybe years. The work of a diabolical mind. He said find the motive and we'll solve the case."

She should be able to solve this. She'd always been the top of her class. She'd been a Phi Beta Kappa, for God's sake. But the too familiar feeling of frustration and helplessness returned. She didn't have a clue. But there was a killer out there. Who knew why he was doing this to her or what he might do next?

Mitch seemed to have reached the same conclusion. "I don't want you to move home. You may be in danger if the killer can find you."

"Forget the murderer. He isn't going to kill me. Just make sure I don't go to jail. That's death to me."

"You're not going to prison." There was such confidence in his voice, so much authority that she almost believed him. Mitch stood and held his hand out to her. She instinctively realized without knowing the details of his past that he'd been through hell. He'd endured. He'd survived. And triumphed.

"Forget about prison for now." Mitch smiled. "Let's get some dinner. Put on a wig and we'll go to North Beach. No one will notice you there."

Mitch was right. San Francisco had defined the sixties and had never forgotten its roots. Nowhere was this more apparent than in North Beach with its leather boutiques, head shops, and ethnic cafés and coffeehouses. Now that tie-dye and bell bottoms had staged a return, it was like being caught in a time warp where past and present merged, creating a new reality.

No heads even turned when they walked into Vaffanculo. The Italian café had clouds of fake ivy hanging from the ceiling and walls plastered with Roman street signs. In the middle of the room lit only by candles planted in bottles of Ruffino was a fountain that sent a trickle of water over its rocks and sounded, not like a soothing stream, but like someone gargling.

"Know what *vaffanculo* means?" Royce whispered as they sat down at a small table in the darkest corner of the café.

"Nope. I thought it was the owner's name — or a place in Italy."

Royce loved knowing more than Mitch. It was hard to get one up on him. "It means go screw yourself."

Mitch chuckled, then said, "Great. I'll have to remember that."

"Don't tell me you're going to have pizza," she said after Mitch ordered a carafe of Chianti. He nodded and she couldn't help thinking how adorable he was. Don't soften, she warned herself. "Tell me, when do you eat all that spinach you keep in the freezer?"

"I mix it with salsa and have it for breakfast."

"Yuck! It's a wonder you're so healthy." There was no denying he was in prime shape. She'd never been quite as aware of a man's body as she was of his.

"I might try something else if you'd fix me breakfast every morning." He gave her a smoky look that would have sent most women into a core meltdown.

"I'm on a diet, remember? Just Slim Fast for me."

"It isn't working."

"I'll have you know I've lost thirteen pounds."

His eyes dropped to her breasts and she cursed herself for wearing the halter-top sundress. "We have to be careful how we dress you. Suits like the one you wore to court won't make you look so top heavy." He still hadn't taken his eyes off her chest. Why did he always do this to her when they were discussing something important? "The jury will see you sitting down most of the time. We don't want you to look fat to them."

"I didn't realize so much went into image," she said, and he lifted his eyes to meet hers. About time.

"Most experts would have dressed Amy Fisher in a school girl dress with a wide white collar to play up her youth, her innocence, not the grown-up power suit she wore. Your case is the reverse. We want you to look professional, so when you're on the stand, the jury will believe you."

"That's why they're drilling me so hard — to make sure the jury believes me. Wouldn't it be better if I just told the truth in my own words?"

The waiter arrived with the Chianti and took their order. Royce had a salad again. Naturally,

Mitch wanted pizza — hold the anchovies.

"What do you think most cases come down to?" Mitch asked.

She shook her head. Her perception of justice had changed dramatically since her arrest. Was there justice in America?

"The battle of the expert witnesses. Hell, if you look hard enough and are willing to pay enough, you will find an 'expert' to testify to anything. How do you think I found that vet? I told the Nature Nazis if they wanted to spring the cougar to find a vet sympathetic to their cause. I needed a nearsighted cougar."

He's a realist, she thought. But was this justice? What if you couldn't afford someone like Mitch, who swam so well with the sharks because he was one?

He leaned closer, radiating a virility that she was powerless to ignore. "It's the system, Royce. If I don't defend these people, someone will. If you want to be angry, be angry with the courts. Judges allowed these 'experts' to testify. No one else can waltz into a courtroom and draw conclusions. They can only state the facts — what they saw or heard.

"Eleanor Farenholt can't say she *thinks* you're paranoid from too much cocaine because you had a hissy-fit over the lettuce in the washer. She can only say what happened — no conclusions. But trust me, Abigail will haul in experts to say that type of behavior is symptomatic of heavy drug use."

"You're forgetting the drug test I passed."

"No, I'm not. Their expert will challenge the way the lab processed the sample or some other bullshit."

Their food arrived and Royce gazed at her bowl of lettuce, downhearted.

"Don't worry. We'll have impressive experts. In the end the jury will be judging you. Your job is to convince them you're telling the truth."

17

Royce knew she shouldn't have come to the night-club with Mitch. Being alone with him in a pitch-black club filled with snuggling couples wasn't her brightest idea. But she honestly couldn't face another evening by herself.

"Want a drink?" Mitch asked.

"Champagne and Chianti — I'm beyond my limit."

Mitch looked around. "I don't see a table and there's no place at the bar either. Guess we should dance."

The dance floor was a semicircle hardly bigger than a bath mat. Directly in front of it was a stage with its crimson velvet curtains drawn. A quartet stood off to one side playing a waltz.

What on earth are you doing? Royce asked herself as she stepped into Mitch's arms. He didn't pull her any closer than was proper, but his warm hand planted squarely on her bare back felt too good, his powerful body too comforting. As he danced his thighs brushed hers through the cotton skirt. Uh-oh.

"I'm driving Jason to camp tomorrow." Mitch couldn't think of what else to say. Royce felt like a tombstone in his arms. Would she ever relax? Would she ever trust him?

"How long will he be there?" She wished she hadn't noticed the intriguing whisk of dark hair visible beneath his partially unbuttoned shirt.

"The whole summer. He'll be back just before the trial."

"You don't think Jason will tell anyone he saw me, do you?" She'd told Mitch about Jason and he'd spoken with the boy.

"He won't say a word." Mitch silently wondered why Royce wouldn't relax. He'd done his best all evening to make her feel better.

Had the nice guy routine worked five years ago? Hell, no. And it wasn't getting him anywhere now either. The sensitive male might work for some guys, but he obviously hadn't received an instruction manual.

What did work with Royce? Don't let her think too much. She says no because of what happened to her father, but deep down, she wants you. And he was tired of pussyfooting around. Tonight was the night.

But first, he was going to set her straight. He

changed his stance so she was forced to look at him. "Welcome to the real world, babe. I'm no white knight. I'm the meanest son of a bitch in the valley. Five years ago you found what a bastard I can be. Remember, only the strong survive. You need me."

Royce sucked in her breath. What had brought on that comment? She didn't know what was more unnerving, the fierce look in his eyes or his caustic tone. She was almost afraid of him. "I know I need your help."

Royce understood — she hoped — what he was really saying. Her perception of the world had been shaped by her father, who was an intellectual and an idealist. But Mitch represented reality, the cold, ugly world as it existed, not her idealized view.

From everything she knew about him, Mitch had faced the brutal world since . . . since when? How young had he been when he'd left home? Fifteen, sixteen? Or younger. Was it any wonder he was so cynical? He was well equipped to deal with adversity.

Her father, though she loved him dearly and missed him even more as time went on, had been quite the opposite. He'd emotionally collapsed when her mother had been diagnosed with cancer. Royce had moved home to keep him from breaking down just when her mother needed him most.

Oh, yes. She got the message. Justice in America was an ideal distorted by grim reality, but Mitch had the key to the system. She needed him in a way that she'd never needed anyone before. He was the last person in the world she wanted to need, but she had no choice.

"While you were prissing around some girls' school, I was on the street. Hell, I was usually in some dark alley — the school of hard knocks. I educated myself in the Navy when I finally had food and a place to stay so I could study."

"What happened to your parents?"

The dance ended and everyone clapped. Mitch didn't let Royce go. As disconcerting as it was to hold her, it was even more disturbing to be this close to her lips. The only light on the dance floor was a faint glow from the lone spotlight trained on the singer, who was again belting out a torch song. Mitch tightened his hold, eliminating what little space had been between them.

Royce knew she should pull away, but when he looked at her in that special, intimate way, her willpower evaporated. Besides, she was thoroughly discouraged by her situation and profoundly disillusioned with the legal system. What would become of her? She longed to be comforted and allowed herself to enjoy the reassuring strength of his arms.

"Remember your promise, Royce?" There it was again, that threatening glint in his eyes. "My past is off limits. If I catch you snooping, you'll have to find another lawyer."

"I'm not snooping." She prayed he would never find out what Wally had done. "I know so little about you, but you know everything about me."

"Not everything." His thumb casually stroked the inside of her finger. Somehow that subtle movement caused her body to react shamelessly. "You haven't told me how lousy Brent was in bed."

"What makes you think he was lousy?" She could have kicked herself for stepping into another of Mitch's verbal minefields.

"You were engaged, but you were dying to get into my pants."

She was tempted to slap that smirk off his face. "Brent was wonderful in bed." Not quite true, but she wasn't about to give Mitch satisfaction. "I admitted I was attracted to you. That explains everything."

"Does it?"

"Of course. What do you want out of my life?"

"You know what I want."

She pretended she'd stolen her Phi Beta Kappa key and was so dumb that she'd missed his arousal. He couldn't do anything on the dance floor, could he? She didn't want to think of how she'd put him off later, but she'd have to.

Mitch swayed to the music, the full curves of Royce's body molded against his. He let his hand drift across her bare back. He savored her involuntary shiver. Damn straight. They communicated much better physically than verbally. Tonight was one night he'd be damned if he'd let the past come between them.

How was she going to get out of this? Royce

asked herself. There was no mistaking Mitch's desire — or her own reaction. Her chest was so tight, she could barely breathe. Insistent currents of excitement warmed her inner thighs. The only sensible thing to do was talk.

"Who's singing next?" Too late she realized she'd whispered into his deaf ear. He thought she was being provocative, because he lowered his lips to her neck and flicked his tongue across the sensitive curve. Goose bumps waltzed up her spine.

Mitch's voice was filled with soft urgency. "There's only one thing that beats slow dancing."

She knew *exactly* what he meant. His sex, hot and hard, pressed against her. She couldn't resist putting both arms around his neck and snuggling against him. Stop, she told herself, but she honestly couldn't. Being in his arms was so erotic, and yet comforting. Through this whole ordeal she'd yearned for someone to hold her, to reassure her things would be all right. A weak, childish reaction to be sure, but she couldn't help herself.

His strong hands were caressing the small of her back. Then a hand roamed lower, fondling her bottom. They weren't moving now; this was only a parody of a dance. Not that anyone around them cared. There was so much kissing going on that this could have been a high school prom. Royce couldn't stifle a low moan as he held her against his rigid arousal. And then he was kissing her, his tongue moving with the same slow, evocative rhythm of the music — and his hips.

"Let's get out of here."

Mitch didn't give her a chance to protest; Royce didn't want to leave. Being cuddled felt too good. And now she'd have to find the words to tell him no. How could she, after giving him every reason to think she wanted to make love to him?

The rush of night air outside the club cooled her flushed cheeks and brought another thought. Her father. She'd forgiven Mitch for what he'd done — almost. He was trying so hard to help her. Even so, a thought niggled at the back of her mind. Sex with Mitch would betray a lifetime of her father's love.

Royce braved a glance at Mitch as he drove the Viper through the steep streets as if he were on a Le Mans course. *Royce, boy oh boy, you've really done it this time. Shamelessly arousing a man, knowing you weren't going to make good on the implied promise, was inviting rape. Less honorable men wouldn't take no for an answer.* But Mitch was honorable, she assured herself. Despite his cynical nature he placed a high value on his reputation. His word.

He parked the Viper in the garage under her apartment and guided her out the side door, his arm anchored around her. *Why doesn't he say something?* She stopped at the stairs leading up to the apartment behind his home.

"Good night, Mitch. Thanks for dinner." She moved away from him and put her foot on the first step.

His strong hand clamped over her arm. He swung her around, his hands now on her upper arms, and walked her backward until the force of his weight thrust her up against the building. His legs straddled hers, permitting no chance for escape. His lips were dangerously close to hers.

"Angel, you started something. You're going to finish it."

"I'm sorry. I didn't realize."

"Like hell you didn't." He pushed the brunt of his arousal, hot and blatantly aggressive, against her. "You want it bad."

A frantic need to remember she hated him swept over her. Where was the memory of her father? I hate Mitch, she whispered to herself. It wasn't quite true, but it did give her courage. I hate him, she repeated to convince herself. "What you're doing is unethical. You could get in trouble with the bar association."

"Now you've got me scared."

"Let me go, Mitch."

"We're way past the talking stage."

He tried to kiss her, but she was too quick for him. She kept her teeth locked, her lips squeezed shut. She never knew a man could move so fast. Before she could stop him, he had her halter top undone and his hands were greedily exploring her bare breasts. The pad of his thumb grazed a nipple once. Twice. Oh, Lordy.

Mitch pulled back and wantonly gazed at her exposed breasts, following every sensitive curve with his eyes. The moon would have to choose that moment to peek from behind a cloud to reveal her full breasts and raised nipples.

"Five years. A helluva long time to wait. You better be worth it, Royce."

That did it. Now she did hate him. Was she the prize in the One-That-Got-Away Sweepstakes? "I'll hate you for this."

"Uh-huh. I love the way you hate."

"Go to hell."

His hands were on her breasts again, erotic hands molding her sensitive flesh and toying with her nipples. "Remember, angel, we're already in hell."

What did you expect, Royce? Mitch is as contemptuous of sex as he is of life. Still, his attitude infuriated her. She wanted him to . . . to what? Be sweet? Be loving? Dream on, Royce. This is hell, remember?

Mitch's mouth covered hers, commanding her lips to open with an assertive thrust of his tongue. His kiss was hot and rough — and thoroughly arousing. He used his hand under her derrière to bring her up on her toes. He pressed his arousal into the notch of her thighs until it fit snugly into the cleft. She couldn't resist moving against it — just a little — cuddling him, savoring the heat and the hardness for a moment.

"You don't just want to get screwed, angel. You need it."

The words hit home. Screwed? "You cocky jerk, don't do me any favors." Both hands on his chest, she shoved him hard.

He grabbed her wrists in one hand and pinned them over her head. "I love charity cases."

She swapped hostile stares with him. She had half a mind to scream. It would serve him right if the neighbors called the police. His eyes roved leisurely over her exposed breasts as they lifted with each angry breath. Almost of their own volition her nipples tightened even more, offering themselves to him.

He dropped her arms and they fell to her sides. He nudged her chin upward and forced her to look into his eyes. "I'm not crazy about screwing alfresco, Royce, but I don't know if you can make it up to my bedroom."

She opened her mouth to curse him, but his hand was under her skirt. Between her thighs. She'd felt the throbbing moisture building all evening, heightening these last few minutes.

He actually laughed, a low, smoky sound that was unspeakably erotic. His talented fingers burrowed inside her panties, stroking her where she needed it most. Exquisite sensations overpowered her, rendering her incapable of protest. Guilt and common sense were swept away in a rush of desire while his questing hand took even more liberties.

Unexpectedly, he stopped, his hand intimately cradling her, not moving but caressing her softness with an erotic touch. She bit the inside of her lip to keep from begging him to finish what he'd started.

"Last chance, angel," he said with an insolent grin. "Tell me no and I'll stop." He took her hand and pressed it against his fly, forcing her fingers to curl around his erection. "Otherwise, I'm going to let you hate me until I get you out of my system."

18

Son of a bitch, Mitch cursed under his breath. Royce had him nervous there for a second. He thought she might actually tell him no. Jee-sus, he would have had blue balls for a week, but he would have backed off. Instead he'd gotten to her. She hadn't said a damn thing.

Close enough for government work. In seconds he had her out of what clothes weren't already half off. She was even sexier than he'd ever imagined, standing in the silvery moonlight filtering through the branches of the chestnut tree, her blond hair tumbled across her bare shoulders, her breasts rising and falling with each breath.

She could destroy him in a second if she realized how much power she had over him. He'd be damned before he'd let her find out. He'd been down that course once. What had it gotten him?

Get you out of my system. Those words changed Royce's mind. Why fight him? Denying she wanted him was futile. And getting harder each day. Admit it, Royce, at least be honest with yourself. You're obsessed with him. Mitch knew what a devastating effect he had on her and exploited it ruthlessly.

Making love to him might be for the best. She desperately needed to get him out of her system too. It would ease the sexual tension between them, Royce decided.

If they'd made love five years ago, it wouldn't have been an issue now. But frustrated desire often intensified — fueled by the imagination. Reality always destroyed these illusions.

Royce shivered and reached for Mitch, but he backed away, quickly unbuttoning his shirt. His eyes traveled down her flushed breasts, across the peaked nipples, then moved lower to the crown of curls between her thighs. Finally, he gazed at her legs, inspecting every inch right down to her toes, which were curled into the plush grass beneath her bare feet. She didn't remember kicking off her sandals, but she must have.

He tossed his shirt into the air, and it landed on the grass at the base of the tree. Mitch's eyes were tracking along her thighs while Royce watched his fingers on his belt buckle and the noticeable bulge below it. He yanked the belt free.

Royce tried to swallow as he jerked open his trousers, but couldn't. How many dreams had she had about him? How many times had she imagined him naked?

Nothing compared to reality. His shoulders were more powerful, the funnel of hair on his chest was denser, darker. Her eyes were drawn lower across his taut belly to the nest of hair cradling the proudest erection she'd ever imagined.

"See something you like, Royce?" He took a step forward and nudged her down onto the cool grass, the scent of the damp earth and night-blooming jasmine filling her nostrils.

He loomed over her, mysterious, menacing. Huge. And everything she ever wanted in a man. His eyes never left hers as he joined her on the ground. He angled himself across her, gradually letting her absorb his weight. His arousal nestled against her thigh, hot and shockingly hard.

With the pads of his fingers he explored the soft curve where her breasts rested against her rib cage. She sucked in her breath and held it. Why hadn't someone told her how sensitive that area was?

A shudder stirred deep within her, heightened by his lips purling over her breasts, leaving a damp, hot trail. With the point of his tongue he teased the sensitive nipple and drew it into the moist heat of his mouth with a touch of suction. The sensation was so utterly arousing, she dug her nails into his back.

"Oh, Mitch."

He blew across the taut bud. She felt the cool puff of air deep inside her body. She grabbed his head in a futile attempt to coax him to continue kissing her breasts. Instead he guided his shaft into the moistness between her thighs, homing

313

in on her most sensitive area.

"When I kiss you here's where you feel it, don't you, Royce?"

The tip of his sex nuzzled her. Once. Twice. It was the most intimate, the most seductive caress she'd ever experienced. There was no way she could have responded, she was concentrating on not begging him for more.

"Answer me."

"Yes," she whispered, and then squeezed her eyes shut. Any second she was going to explode. Criminy, would that be embarrassing.

He'd obviously given up his amateur status years ago and knew how to arouse a woman like a consummate professional. Why was she surprised? Everything Mitch did, he did exceptionally well.

She opened her eyes when she felt the weight of his body leave hers. He grabbed his trousers, which were in a heap nearby, and fumbled in the pocket. It took a second for her to realize he had a condom in his hand.

"You bastard. You had this planned all along, didn't you?"

"Damn straight." His voice was husky and his eyes swept up her bare legs, lingering at the crest of her thighs, then moving upward more slowly across her breasts. Finally, his gaze met hers. "Tonight was the night, Royce."

What could she say? Tonight was the night. Somehow she'd sensed it from the moment she'd looked up and seen him standing at the kitchen door. Still, it irritated her that he'd known it all along — and planned for it.

"Sweet cheeks, you're damn lucky I didn't haul you into the storeroom at the club and take you — standing up — right there." He caught the edge of the wrapper between his teeth. A shaft of light from the moon glinted off the foil as he ripped it open.

"Hell, I even considered pulling the car into some dark alley on the way home."

She tried to joke. "The Viper's too small to —"

"The hood's perfect."

She gasped in utter astonishment, realizing he wasn't joking. He was completely serious. He would have taken her — anywhere — tonight. She'd known he desired her, but the undertone of passion in his voice frightened her. She was totally out of her league here.

He handed the unwrapped condom to her. "You do the honors."

Royce scooted to an upright position. She was eye level with his navel and a very intimidating erection, which she managed to ignore. Just below his belly button was an area of smooth skin the size of a half dollar. Beneath it a thin strip of hair unfurled into a dense thicket surrounding his sex.

She brushed his erection aside, not knowing what possessed her, and kissed the bare spot. She flicked her tongue over the smooth area, savoring the baby-soft skin and the thoroughly arousing intimacy of kissing him in a secret place no one else knew about.

How long had she wanted to taste him, really taste him? Years. His skin had a trace of salt and smelled erotically masculine. Mitch. This was truly Mitch.

Aw, hell. Mitch wound his fingers through her hair, sucking in a steadying breath. Her golden curls tickled his cock and brushed against his thighs as her lips caressed his belly, her tongue tracing a lazy circle.

A-mazing! He expelled his breath in a sigh that rippled through his body like a shudder.

How had Royce zeroed in that area on the first try? The smooth skin beneath his navel had always been extremely sensitive. Other women had touched him there — accidentally. Not Royce, she'd homed in on the spot immediately. Face it, buddy. She has your number.

She moved lower, her soft lips teasing him mercilessly, nibbling a little, tracing seductive circles with the moist tip of her tongue. Her hand cupped his balls, testing their weight. He sucked in his breath and shifted restlessly, as her inquisitive fingertips discovered the sensitive spot at the base.

He knew what she was going to do, but he couldn't let her. He'd lose it before he was even inside her. Gritting his teeth, determined to remain in control, Mitch snatched the condom from her hand and put it on with one quick stroke.

He eased her onto her back and nudged her legs apart, positioning himself between her thighs. His gaze locked with hers, he guided himself into her. She was wet, more than ready, but unexpectedly tight. She shuddered, clutching his bare shoulders, her nails digging into his skin.

"Easy, angel, easy," he soothed, pushing his thick shaft deeper.

She writhed beneath him, moaning slightly and raking her nails across his back, unable to completely accept his girth. Mitch pulled back, then slowly, excruciatingly slowly, edged forward again, squeezing deeper and deeper, his body quaking with pleasure.

Had he ever been quite this aroused, this close to a climax without being completely inside a woman?

He pulled back again, feeling her body grow even more moist, more accepting. Close to an orgasm, he surged forward and buried himself to the hilt. He wasn't sure if he gasped with pure pleasure, or she did. Hell, maybe they both did.

Fighting to control himself, he drew back, edging out of her until only the tip of his shaft was still inside. Then he lunged forward again, using more power than necessary — just to experience the overwhelming thrill of possessing her, making her undeniably his.

She lifted her hips to meet him, her silky legs wrapped around him. Welcoming him. She tucked her head into the curve of his neck, her breath moist and hot and unbelievably erotic against his bare skin.

He lowered his lips to hers and thrust his tongue

deep inside her mouth in a kiss as hot and carnal as his possession of her body. Her heart throbbed in her ears and she couldn't quite catch her breath.

For a moment the force of his embrace, its overwhelming power, frightened her. It seemed to come from some deep, hidden part of him that she had never imagined existed. The experience was utterly sensual, almost primitive, suggesting that nothing but complete surrender would satisfy him.

She'd never dreamed anyone would make love to her with such all-consuming passion. She braced herself and welcomed the powerful thrusts, her face now buried against the curve of his neck, her arms wrapped around his shoulders. Each jolt swept her a little farther, a little deeper into a new world. His world. Each surge brought a heightened sense of . . . belonging to someone else.

Suddenly, he went rigid in her arms and threw his head back, breathing from between parted lips, his teeth clenched. He lunged forward one final time. Hard. Deep. Totally satisfying. His release racked through her body with erotic power and something snapped inside her, tearing her from everything she'd ever known — except him.

Seconds later he collapsed on top of her, his head nuzzling the crook of her neck, his breath hot and harsh against her skin. She loved his weight, the uncompromising possession of her body, his sex still embedded so deep that they were one.

She stroked the back of his neck and found raised welts. Had she done that? Obviously. It didn't really surprise her. No one had ever made love to her with such abandon.

She reveled in these strange new sensations. She'd been lost, but now she was found, discovered. She couldn't worry about the past or the future. For now, for this night, there was only the blissful present.

It took a few minutes for their breathing to approach normal as they lay cradled in each other's arms. Mitch raised himself up, bracing his weight on his forearms. He flashed her the cockiest grin she'd ever seen.

"Angel, I love the way you hate me."

A blast of hot sunlight awoke Royce and she groggily opened her eyes. The digital alarm clock read almost noon. She sat bolt upright, remembering she was in Mitch's bed. Last night hadn't been another erotic dream; it had really happened. She'd made love to Mitch over and over and over.

What had possessed her to act so wantonly? She sank back to the pillow, thankful that Mitch must have left hours ago to take Jason to camp. At least she didn't have to face him yet.

What must he think? Had she really done all those things? Royce, face it. You loved every minute. So true. Despite instincts that warned her against Mitch, he'd fulfilled every fantasy — and some she'd never known existed.

She rolled over and buried her face in his pillow. Breathing deeply she inhaled his scent, conceding she'd made love to Mitch because she'd wanted him for years. She hated admitting she was so weak, but there was no denying it. She'd disappointed herself, and she couldn't even think about her father. But her regrets didn't change anything!

She hugged the pillow and wished it were Mitch. How did he feel about last night? Had he gotten her out of his system? *The cocky jerk had dared to mock her. I love the way you hate me.*

He could be a real bastard when he wanted, but she thought he was teasing. He'd kept after her all night, not giving her a chance to leave him. He cared about her, didn't he? She wasn't positive; you never knew exactly what Mitch was thinking.

She wandered through his house, hoping to find a note. Nothing. Dream on, Royce. Mitch isn't the romantic type. The most she could expect was a telephone call, she thought, remembering he was going to drive Jason to camp, then go to L.A. for a case.

She returned to the garage apartment with Jenny at her heels. The portable phone on the coffee table was ringing, and she answered. It wasn't Mitch; it was Val. Like Talia, she called her each day, usually in the evening.

"Is everything okay? I tried to get you last night."

"I went for a walk." Royce hated lying, but she could hardly say she'd let Mitch seduce her and spent the night with him.

"You sound upset."

Royce slumped down on the sofa. She tried to picture Val with her deep auburn hair and serious eyes, but couldn't. Somehow she kept seeing a lonely young girl tagging along after Royce. "I'm okay. A little lonely, that's all."

"I know how you feel. After Trevor left I was totally alone."

Was Val criticizing her? She'd done all she could to help, hadn't she? Did Val harbor some deep-seated resentment?

"You always had your family, Royce. I thought I had my brother. Friends are great, but there's nothing like your family."

"True." Royce breathed a sigh of relief. Val hadn't been finding fault.

"At least you have your uncle. Does Mitch let him see you?"

"Yes, but he's down South doing an exposé on how chicken factories pollute the environment." She hadn't heard from Wally in days. Was he all right?

"Royce, I've never asked but" — again Val hesitated — "did you ever blame Wally for what happened to your father?"

"No," she responded, then amended it to, "not really."

Her father had been sipping brandy with his closest friend the night Wally had called. Shaun was being abusive again and Wally had asked her father to come for him. The fatal accident had occurred a block from Wally's house. Wally had arrived on the scene just as the police drove up.

"It was fate, bad luck, whatever. Wally was devastated. When he called me from the police station, he sounded drunk himself, but, of course, he wasn't. It's been years now and he's never fallen off the wagon."

"I hope Talia does as well," Val said softly. "I'm helping her."

"Do you still get together every Monday for lunch?" Royce asked, not adding, *without me.* Their Monday luncheons had been a long-standing tradition. It hurt to think of being excluded, but everything had changed. Val was giving Talia the support she needed. Once that had been Royce's role.

"Can't you meet us? We promise not to talk about the case."

Royce almost smiled. "I'll ask Mitch." She paused, thinking Val sounded strange. "How's the new guy?"

"Fine."

It wasn't like Val to hide things from Royce, but now they were playing by new rules. Instead of being the friend everyone leaned on, she needed them and she couldn't help wondering if they really cared. Or if one of them was behind this.

"Come on," Royce said to Jenny after she hung up. "To hell with Mitch's security fetish. I'm taking you for a walk."

Outside the bright sunshine and the soft breeze off the bay brought the uplifting cheerfulness of spring. Granted, it was midsummer, but San Francisco's summer weather usually came in the fall — after the tourists went home. July felt more like April with a hint of honeysuckle on the sea breeze and a lazy sun that chased away morning fog for the warm afternoons.

Without meaning to go there Royce found herself at the Golden Gate Cemetery, standing under the majestic oak looking at her parents' tombstones. Jenny flopped to the ground in the tree's shade and Royce sat beside her.

After she'd returned from Italy, she used to visit their graves with fresh flowers every Sunday, but this was the first time she'd come since her arrest. It was silly, but she hadn't wanted her father to know how much trouble she was in.

What would Papa say if he were alive? He would insist justice would prevail. Once she would have believed him, but now she prayed and found it hard to truly have faith — considering everything that had happened.

And she couldn't shake the feeling the worst was yet to come.

"Here," she said to Jenny as she put her hand on the soft mound of grass just above her father's grave. "This is Rabbit E. Lee. I knew he wanted to be with Papa, so I secretly buried him here. You know, he was a prisoner in that horrible cage all those years with only Papa to love him.

And when Papa loved someone, you knew it. He always had time for you.

"Mama wasn't like that. She loved me, but she was very busy, translating for the embassy or cooking or being with Papa. They loved each other so much, I sometimes felt like a third wheel."

Jenny licked her hand sympathetically. These days the retriever seemed to be her best friend — the only friend she could truly trust. Talking to Jenny had become second nature to Royce. Of course, she was really talking to herself, but Jenny was so intelligent that she actually seemed to understand. And she always listened.

"I guess I shouldn't complain. Think of what Mitch must have suffered. I don't believe anyone's ever really loved him. And I doubt if he'd know what to do if someone loved him now." She fondled Jenny's silky ear. "Except you. He's crazy about you."

He brushed Jenny every night and kept her at his side whenever he was at home. Come to think of it, Mitch was great with animals. He indulged that beastly Oliver, slipping him food despite his diet so he wouldn't kick kitty litter all over the kitchen. Under the right circumstances there might be hope for Mitch.

Honestly, Royce, what on earth are you thinking? Forget about Mitch. Loving him is out of the question.

She leaned back against the tree and concentrated on the regatta sailing across the bay, their white sails a brilliant contrast to the deep blue water and the lighter blue sky. Enjoy this while you can. The view from inside a cell won't be so spectacular.

She placed her hand on her father's tombstone. It was warm from the late-afternoon sun. She stared out at the wind-ruffled water, but saw instead her father on the morning he'd killed himself.

She could almost feel his arm around her — the way it had been on that fateful day — as he'd said, "I'm going upstairs to my office." He'd kissed her cheek, his lips lingering longer than usual. "Always know I love you and you'll never walk alone."

She hadn't been able to answer the odd comment because her mind had been on Mitchell Durant. At the preliminary hearing the previous day he'd annihilated her father's attorney. The judge had ordered Papa to stand trial.

She'd never forget the look on her father's face. He hadn't said it but she knew he was thinking: This is the man you came home early to see? This is the man you thought was so kind, so caring? She was sorry she'd ever met Mitch, and even sorrier she'd told her father about him.

Papa walked out of the kitchen, his once proud shoulders stooped. She almost followed him, but decided to let him do some thinking. She'd tried to persuade him to hire a better attorney and fight, but he'd been too depressed to discuss it.

He'd been despondent since Mama died, saying

he had no reason to live. The ache in her heart almost reduced Royce to tears. She loved him more than anyone in the world, but she wasn't enough. Mama had been his strength, his inspiration.

Would anyone ever love her that much? Royce wondered.

She was feeding Rabbit E. Lee when a loud noise like a car backfiring rang out from the attic. Lee dropped the carrot, his eyes riveted on the upstairs window. No one had to tell them anything, they both knew Papa had killed himself.

Upstairs in the attic office Royce covered her father with the comforter from the daybed before reaching for the envelope with her name on it. Inside were two notes, one for Wally and one for her, and a picture. She'd never seen this photograph of her mother, but she instantly recognized her mother's expression. She was smiling at the camera, her eyes alight with love. Obviously, Papa had taken the picture. On the back was her mother's graceful script.

"You're all the world to me. There isn't anything else."

Royce stared at the picture and felt her father's presence as if his spirit still filled the room and she could talk to him. "You couldn't live without her, could you, Papa?"

For one heart-stopping moment she thought she heard him answer, "No. There's nothing more precious than her love."

Royce slowly unfolded the note, with the uncanny feeling that her father's spirit was still present, lovingly guiding her, treasuring these last moments before his spirit crossed over to another, far better world.

Dearest Royce,

Please try to understand. I can't face this trial without your mother. I'm only part of a person without Sophia. When she died, I died too. I've looked down life's road and what do I see? Profound, all-consuming loneliness.

I'm sorry to leave you and sad to miss the treasured moments I planned to share with you. Oh, how I'd looked forward to walking you down the aisle, to toasting everyone at your wedding, to holding my first grandchild.

There are memories I won't have, but I cherish those memories you gave to me. You took your first step, toddling forward and yelling, "Dada! Dada!" I'll never forget the Christmas pageant when you played the elf in the third row. You kept waving to me all night.

Most of all I remember how you looked the night of your first prom. That's when I realized that one day I'd lose you to another man. One day you wouldn't be Daddy's little girl any longer. And I hated that man even though I never met him.

This isn't about you. It's about me. Darling, go on with your life. You have Wally and your career. And one day that special man will appear and you'll fall in love with him just as I fell in love with your mother.

Remember, I will always be with you in spirit. I'll be in the flowers we love, in the midsummer sky, in the song of our robin who comes to our garden each spring. Look for me there — in the things we loved — in your heart. And you'll never walk alone.

Forgive me. I love you, but I can't go on without your mother. One day, when you find your special man, you'll know how I feel. That person becomes so much a part of you that existing without them becomes unimaginable.

Good bye, my darling.

Royce stood and gazed at the blanket covering her father. She could feel his spirit reluctantly leaving her. Across every childhood memory she saw his loving smile and heard his encouraging words. What would she do without him?

"I forgive you, Daddy." She knelt and touched his chest where the bullet had pierced his heart. "I'll never stop loving you."

She came to her feet slowly. "When you get to heaven and find Mama, give her my love."

Until that moment she hadn't realized how fortunate she'd been. Truly blessed. She'd had two devoted, loving parents. And her father had taken special care to spend time with Royce. She'd lost something precious, unique. And nothing would ever be the same again. Nothing.

Royce sat in the deserted cemetery with her memories, Jenny at her side, until the sun slipped below the horizon, leaving shards of golden light dancing on the water and a backwash of mauve to herald the night sky. She rose and walked along the cobbled path toward the exit. At the gate she turned and looked back at the matching headstones beneath the sheltering canopy of the noble oak tree.

"Mama and Papa together the way they always wanted . . . for eternity." Tears pooled in Royce's eyes. "And Rabbit E. Lee — free at last."

19

"What are you reading?" Val asked.

Paul looked up from the criminology bulletin, surprised to see Val standing there. She'd been moody all weekend, but she'd become even more withdrawn since talking with Royce a few hours ago. He patted the space on the sofa beside him. "I'm reading about soft lasers. The FBI has developed a technique for lifting fingerprints from fabric using laser light. Makes it harder for perps to get away with a crime."

"I see," Val said as she sat beside him, but she didn't sound really interested.

"Are you upset about Royce?"

"Yes. She sounds — I don't know — distant. I wanted to talk to her about something, but I wasn't comfortable. I think she suspects I did this to her."

"Right now, Royce must feel like a rabbit cornered by a pack of wolves, but I'm certain she doesn't suspect you." He excused his lie, thinking he didn't want to upset Val. Until this weekend she'd been so upbeat that he'd hoped she was finally getting over her brother's betrayal.

"You're going to find out who's doing this to her, aren't you?"

Now he couldn't lie. This was the damnedest case. Whoever the perp was, he — or she — had thoroughly covered his tracks. Despite an intensive investigation only one new development had been uncovered, and he doubted it had any bearing on the case. "We're going to have to count on Mitch to convince a jury that Royce was framed."

"Oh, no. Poor Royce." She shook her head. "Now I'm glad I didn't bother her with my troubles."

"Can't I help?"

She leaned over and kissed him — just a peck, not her usual provocative kiss that led to sex. "I'm always crying on your shoulder. I didn't want to bother you. I thought Royce would understand because she felt as close to her father as I did to my brother."

Trying not to be hurt because she hadn't confided in him, he put his arm around her and gave her a reassuring hug. "I love you. Let me help you. Talk to me."

Val heaved a sigh, her eyes intense, filled with pain. "Friday, Mother called to tell me" — she looked away — "my brother has an inoperable brain tumor. It's just a matter of time . . . but he's going to die."

Paul stared bleakly at her. Val had been through too much already. Not this too. He gathered her in his arms and held her snugly. "Oh, Val, I'm so sorry."

Tears trembled on her lashes and finally broke free, leaving a moist path down her cheeks. "I don't want him to die. What am I going to do?"

"David will want his family around him in his final days, won't he?"

"Yes, of course, but how can I face him? My ex-husband, Trevor, will be there. And Mother. They all lied and deceived me. I'm still so angry. I don't know what I might say or do."

He handed her his handkerchief and let her wipe away her tears. "Val, nothing is more final than death. When David's coffin is lowered into the ground, you'll never be able to turn back the clock. He'll be gone — forever. How will you feel then?

"There'll be a thousand things you wish you'd said, a thousand memories you'll wish you'd shared, a thousand times you'll wished you'd laughed together . . . a thousand times you'll wish you told him you'd forgiven him. But you won't have the

331

chance. This is it, darling. If you don't go to him now, you'll never have another opportunity."

The next day when Royce arrived at Mitch's office to work with the defense team while Mitch was in L.A. on another case, Paul was waiting for her. "Did you find out anything new?"

"You were right about the Italian count that Caroline is dating," Paul answered.

Royce thought what a nice man he seemed to be, but it still struck her as unusual that he would have hired Val without being totally certain she wasn't the one behind this.

"The count is really an actor from Texas. He filmed a few spaghetti Westerns in Italy. That's where he picked up his accent. I've gone over him with white gloves. He looks clean."

Royce thought about Mitch. He'd reinvented himself. Why not the Italian count? It was his entrée into society. He might even marry an heiress. "Does Caroline know?"

"No, and it's not my place to tell her."

"Any luck finding Ward Farenholt's mistress?"

"None. Ward is sticking close to home these days. Caroline and the count are over a lot, but that's it."

"Brent's there too?"

"No. He's spending time with Talia."

Royce didn't let the stab of betrayal she felt show. What could it possibly matter? Anyway, her mind was on Mitch — not Brent. Last night she'd checked the phone a dozen times, certain it was out of order. It wasn't. Mitch just didn't bother to call. Obviously, he'd gotten her out of his system.

She told herself it didn't matter. She wasn't in love with Mitch. They'd simply reached a point where their physical attraction had to be resolved. Now it was. Come on, Royce, concentrate on what's important. You want your life back, don't you?

"I haven't been able to discover who murdered the informant either," Paul admitted with a shake of his head. "I want you to be careful. I'm not sure what's going on with this case. My gut instinct says you could be in danger."

"All right," Royce promised, but she doubted she was in danger. Why would anyone want to kill her? Torturing her like a turtle on its back in the desert sun had to be more satisfying than a bullet, which would mercifully end her life in a second.

By the end of the week Royce's emotions were fluctuating dangerously between anger and hurt. Mitch hadn't called once. The defense team was working her hard now, conducting a mock trial for a focus group of participants paid to pretend they were real jurors evaluating her case.

This was supposed to give the defense team a chance to try out their arguments and prepare Royce, but facing twelve sets of accusing eyes was wearing on her. When evening came she was alone with too much time to think. She honestly didn't know what she'd do when she saw Mitch.

A sharp spasm of guilt hit her. Hadn't she learned anything from her father's experience with Mitch? Remember, Mitch is a man whose ambition overrides anything else. Don't fall for him. It'll only compound your problems.

A knock at the door startled Royce. It couldn't be Mitch; he wasn't due back for a few days. She cautiously peered out the window. Even if she didn't share Paul's opinion that the informant's killer might target her next, she was cautious. But it wasn't a killer at the door; it was Wally.

She greeted him with an affectionate hug. "I've been worried about you. Why didn't you call?"

"Sorry," he said, with a half-smile that lit up the green eyes that were so like her own. "I had to go underground to get the scoop on the chicken farm. No phone."

She smiled. Now, this was the Wally she remembered. A master of disguises, he often went underground to get a story. But he looked tired, worried. Was he still concerned about Shaun? Or was she causing him to lose sleep?

He put both hands on her shoulders and peered into her eyes. "How's it going?"

"Preparing for the trial is grueling." Although she usually shared her problems with Wally how could she possibly explain to him that she'd made love to the man who'd persecuted his brother, causing him to commit suicide?

A gnawing emptiness, almost an emotional paralysis, enveloped her. Isolated, she couldn't share her feelings with anyone. Her despair must have shown in her face.

"Let's get you out of here," Wally said. "Put on a wig and let's go down to Fisherman's Wharf and have dinner. You love to watch the sea lions."

Wally was right. They sat on the pier, sharing a jumbo basket of fresh crab legs and watching the horde of sea lions basking in the last rays of a waning sun. Royce felt much better than she had all week.

She told herself that it didn't matter if Mitch called. Making love to him had been inevitable, but she had to get on with life, with the upcoming trial. She couldn't afford to mope over him like some teenager with more hormones than common sense.

"How's Mitch?" Wally asked casually. Too casually.

"He's away on a case." Did he suspect?

"While I was in Alabama, I did a little checking on him."

"You didn't! I thought we agreed to drop it." What would happen if Mitch found out? Dear God, she didn't need anything else to go wrong.

"I was just passing through Gilroy Junction and saw the recruiting office. Know what? The officer who signed up Mitch was still there and he remembered him." Wally paused and tossed a piece of crab to a sea lion who kept barking at them. "The officer knew Mitch had been accused of stealing a carton of milk."

"He must have been hungry. Maybe he was a homeless runaway." Royce tried to imagine Mitch as a boy forced to steal to survive. No wonder he's so tough, so cynical. Who knew what private hell he'd emerged from?

"You're right. Mitch was homeless. The officer felt sorry for him because he'd been sleeping in the alley behind Pizza Hut. He thought Mitch would be better off in the Navy, so he ignored the bogus birth certificate and called someone who'd vouch for Mitch. A nun named Sister Mary Agnes at St. Ignatius Academy in Waycross Springs verified the facts on the phony certificate."

A wave of shame washed over Royce. How can you feel sorry for yourself? Why, she was surrounded by people trying to help her. Not Mitch. Back then he'd been totally alone, sleeping in the cold, eating anchovies people had picked off their pizzas, forced to steal milk to survive.

A living hell. But he'd survived — and triumphed. That knowledge gave her courage. Somehow she'd get through this.

"For some reason the nun lied," Wally insisted. "Why would she do such a thing? I'm going back South next week. I'll see if I can find out the truth."

"Please don't. This has nothing to do with my case. Don't make Mitch angry."

"There's something strange about this case, something even a pro like Paul Talbott can't uncover. There's a missing link somewhere, and I'll

336

be damned if I let you go to jail if there's something I can do to prevent it."

Royce couldn't argue with him. Too much had happened — including murder. Even the most farfetched possibilities had to be considered. "Please be careful. I don't want Mitch to drop my case."

Later that night Royce's portable telephone rang. It couldn't be Val or Talia. They'd called as they usually did earlier in the evening.

"Hello?" Was it Mitch?

"Royce?" The deep voice sent a shock wave of raw anger through her. Brent. The disloyal jerk. "Talia gave me your number. I hope you don't mind."

Royce forced herself to be calm. Once she would have told him what a bastard she thought he was — just the way she'd attacked Mitch at her father's funeral — but too much was at stake to alienate Brent. This was her chance to persuade him not to testify against her.

"I'm sorry about all that's happened, Royce. I want to talk to you."

"I'm listening," she said, her tone not betraying her anger.

"I think we should meet somewhere."

Mitch would go ballistic if he found out she was even talking to the star witness for the prosecution. Meeting Brent would be pure insanity.

"Please, Royce, it's important. I need to talk to you."

She almost said no, but a wrenching pain, an amalgam of hopelessness and a deep anger borne of frustration, kept her quiet. Everyone ordered her around, taking charge of the case that was just another case to them, but one that would decide her future. This was her chance to do something to help herself by persuading Brent not to testify.

An hour later she rushed into a North Beach coffeehouse. They'd agreed no one would recognize either of them in the dark café. She hadn't worn a wig, but she was wearing huge tortoiseshell glasses that disguised her face. Brent was waiting at a booth in the dimly lit rear section. He rose when he saw her approaching.

Designer clothes had been intended for bodies like Brent's. Lanky. Lean. An inbred air of understated elegance. Mitch was a shade too tall, a bit too muscular, but he was infinitely more masculine. And he was mentally and emotionally tougher than Brent.

For a second she wondered what Mitch would have been like had he grown up in a life of wealth and privilege. He'd never have been as easygoing as Brent, as comfortable with himself and the world. No. There was a subterranean undercurrent to Mitch's personality that would have shaped him into a dynamic man no matter what the circumstances of his birth.

Still, she couldn't help asking herself just what had happened to Mitch. Why had he run away from home? How had he lost the hearing in one ear? Who was the nun who loved him so much she'd broken her vows and lied for him, verifying a phony birth certificate? There had to have been a good reason for a nun to take a risk like that.

"You look terrific," Brent said as she slipped into the booth, taking care to keep her back to the room so she wouldn't be recognized.

She removed the glasses and asked herself what she'd seen in Brent. True, he was outrageously handsome and charming. But something was missing, she realized. Or maybe this ordeal had simply changed her so much that she was no longer the same person. Brent was probably *exactly* what he'd always been — an endearing boy who had grown older, but never quite grown up. He simply didn't have Mitch's depth and power.

Had she ever really been in love with this man? Of course not. She'd wanted a home. A family. Losing both parents had taken its toll on her emotionally, leaving her more vulnerable than she'd realized until now.

Could she trust Brent? No. He'd proven how unreliable he could be the night she'd been arrested. Could she trust anyone? Not really. Bewildered, she prayed nightly — not for revenge, but for deliverance.

Somehow she had to save herself. She had to focus on that and nothing else. What did it matter if she had once deceived herself into thinking she loved Brent? Did it even matter that she was slowly — against her will — falling hopelessly in love with Mitch?

No, Royce. Nothing is more important than saving yourself.

"Royce," Brent began, and she could hear the nervousness in his voice that she'd only noticed before when Ward was angry with him. "I'm really sorry about this mess, you know. Are you all right?"

She managed a nod. All right? How could she be all right when faced with a trial that could cost her the best years of her life? Calm down. Now isn't the time to lose your temper. "You wanted to talk to me?"

Brent tried the smile that could melt the ice cap, but it didn't work. She gazed at him, barely able to keep from telling him what she really thought of him.

"I'm ashamed of myself, you know," Brent confessed. "I should have come to your rescue the second they found those diamonds in your purse."

"It certainly would have helped if you'd insisted it was a joke. If it had been Caroline, you and your parents would have jumped to her defense."

"Yes, Father would have protected Caroline," Brent admitted. "But I was too blown away to react. I'm not used to scandals . . . or anything."

How true, Royce thought. Life had been smooth sailing for Brent. Money and good looks meant untroubled waters. No one would expect his girlfriend to be arrested. Without giving it a second thought she knew Mitch would have stood by her.

"I know you're not guilty. You'd never steal or take drugs."

"Who do you think did it?" She assured herself this wasn't actually discussing the case, but maybe she could learn something that Paul hadn't.

Brent shrugged, his one-shouldered shrug she'd once thought so cute. Now it annoyed her as much as his habit of adding *you know* to his sentences. "That Italian count Caroline's been dating is probably behind all your problems."

"Why would he have a grudge against me?" Royce remembered the count was really an actor from Texas, but didn't share the confidential information with Brent.

"You know, there's something funny about the guy, but he wouldn't have any reason to hurt you, would he?"

She wasn't surprised that Brent had detected something odd about the count. Brent loved to play the good ole rich boy to the hilt. He put people at ease by never emphasizing his wealth or his intelligence, but he had a very incisive mind. He was a lot more intelligent — and shrewder — than most people thought.

"Did you meet the count in Italy when you were living with your cousins?"

Mitch and Paul had asked the same question. "No. The first time I met him was when he came to dinner at your parents' with Caroline." There had been something strange about that evening. Eleanor, easily impressed by titles, fawned over the count, but Ward and Brent had been unusually silent.

Brent paused for the waiter to take their orders, then said, "I wouldn't be surprised if Mitch was behind this." There was an edge to Brent's voice that she'd never heard before, and a solemn look in his eyes that said he actually believed Mitch had done it.

For a second her protective instincts flared — not that Mitch had ever needed her protection — and she experienced an annoying surge of affection for him. "Mitch, why? It doesn't make sense."

Brent ran his slim fingers over the demitasse spoon the waiter had given him, his highly buffed nails catching the dim light. "He wanted to make certain you didn't marry me. We've been rivals since Stanford, you know."

"Did your father throw Mitch's success at you?" This was a wild guess. She'd never heard Ward compare his son to Mitch. Brent had never mentioned it either.

After an uncomfortable pause Brent admitted, "Yes. Father calls him a hillbilly, but he never loses an opportunity to remind me how successful Mitch is."

This certainly sounded more like Brent's problem than Mitch's, but she refrained from saying so. She wanted to persuade Brent not to take the stand.

"Of course, Mitch always wanted to be a part of our crowd, but even when he became successful, he still had that crude edge."

Royce conceded Mitch could be abrasive, but she doubted he aspired to the Farenholt circle with their limited interests and bored arrogance. Actually, Mitch was the most solitary man she'd ever known. He guarded his privacy like Fort Knox and seemed content to spend his free time by himself.

Brent was entirely different. He spent most of his evenings socializing with friends. When they'd been together, they'd spent very few evenings by themselves. Looking back, she realized Brent needed a court around him. Mitch didn't need anyone.

Brent gazed at her speculatively. "I bet Mitch is spending a lot of time alone with you, isn't he? No one else knows where you are. No one is allowed to see you."

She took care not to react to his insinuation about Mitch, even though it disturbed her that he'd hit the mark. Yes, Brent was a whole lot sharper than he appeared. "We're trying to counter my negative image with the media. That's why I'm keeping out of sight."

"Don't tell me he hasn't hit on you." There it was again, that disturbing edge to his voice that Brent tried to temper with the full force of his smile.

Instinct told her not to give a hint of credence to this accusation. "I rarely see Mitch. He's usually away on a case. I work with the defense team. He won't join us until closer to the trial." She was surprised how easily the lie came. The next one came even easier. "I live like a Gypsy, moving from safe house to safe house."

She looked directly into his eyes. This time the words came from her heart. "It's terribly lonely, so lonely sometimes, I just want to cry."

Brent took the bait. He eased his arm around her just as the waiter arrived with their cappuccinos. Neither of them moved to pick up the mugs topped by a cloud of cream and a swizzle stick of cinnamon bark. He pulled her closer and she let her head rest against his shoulder with an anguished sigh that would have made Sarah Bernhardt proud.

"You know, I've never stopped loving you," Brent whispered. "I want to help you."

"Then why are you testifying against me?"

He looked genuinely shocked. "I'm just verifying the diamonds were in your purse, that's all."

Could he really be this naive? Maybe. He was an odd amalgam of intelligence and . . . and what? Indifference, she suspected. When Brent chose to analyze a situation, no one could best him — but most of the time he was too busy or too bored to bother. Obviously he didn't care enough about her to realize what testifying against her would do.

She pulled away from him. "Don't you know the psychological impact your testimony will have? Abigail Carnivali will persuade the jury that I used you for your money. They'll feel sorry for you, not me."

Brent put his arm around her again and it was all she could do not to slap his handsome face. "Darling, I'm an attorney, remember? Good old Carnivorous can only make me state the facts. I was closest to you. I did see the diamonds."

His words extinguished the flicker of hope, but she gave it one last try. "Can't someone else testify? Does it have to be you?" If Mitch had taught her one thing, it was that the actual facts counted less than the jury's perception of those facts. Her fiancé testifying against her would be a serious liability.

"Caroline claims she wasn't close enough to see, and my parents think it's undignified to testify. Father insists I do it."

What was the point of staying? She slipped across the worn leather seat.

Brent caught her arm. "Look, if it's so important to you, I won't testify. They'll have to persuade my father to do it." His expression said this was about as likely as getting a search warrant for the Vatican. "Of course, Mother's health is too fragile for her to take the stand."

Royce suppressed a derisive snort. Eleanor had the constitution of a water buffalo. But Brent would never admit that. He always made excuses for his mother, she thought, reviewing their time together. Once she'd seen this as an admirable trait, but she realized it was a weakness, a crutch.

She waited while Brent paid the bill. He kept his hand on the back of her waist as he escorted her to the door.

"You're lonely, Royce. Let me come home with you."

She was thankful he was slightly behind her so he couldn't see her expression. If he came home with her, he'd want to make love to her. Oh, Mitch, how could she make love to anyone else again? "You can't. No one is to know where I am."

"That's so Durant can keep you to himself."

"No." She turned to face him, determined to dispel his suspicions, determined to keep this jerk on her side. "Paul Talbott insisted. The media is ruining my chance for a fair trial."

"You're right," he conceded. "Tobias Ingeblatt has done a number on me too. You know, he's always following me, angling for a story that isn't there."

Make the most of this, cautioned her inner voice. "You can call me. I'm home — by myself — every evening. Even if I move, the portable phone has the same number." Somehow she mustered a tear — undoubtedly Sarah Bernhardt was now turning over in her grave. "I'd be less lonely if I could talk to you." There! Now he wouldn't think she was involved with Mitch.

"Maybe we can meet again," Brent suggested.

"We'll see," she said as they stepped outside. By habit Royce scanned the street for anyone who might be following her. Nothing. "Goodbye."

He smiled at her, the intimate smile she'd seen so many times, and she knew he was going to

346

kiss her. She didn't want him to, but didn't move away. What was the harm? A kiss would bind him to her, making him believe she still loved him, but she didn't care. Keeping him off the stand was more important than one kiss.

And another thought hit her just as Brent's lips met hers. After so many passionate kisses with Mitch, what would she feel?

Mitch sped along the freeway into the city. In the distance the sun dipped below the Pacific. He'd been gone ten days, but it felt like ten years. Jesus, he needed to slow down, but he'd scheduled these cases months ago. Before Royce.

Aw, hell, what are you going to do about her? Damned if he knew. He hadn't called her once because he didn't know what to say. What the hell could he say: You're the only person in my life who hasn't disappointed me? You were better than my wildest dreams?

Christ, no. That sounded as if all he cared about was great sex. It couldn't get any better than what they'd had, but sex didn't begin to explain how he felt. He'd waited five years, five long, lonely years, to get a second chance with Royce. It hadn't been easy. He'd pressed harder than he liked to get her into bed. But once he had, he knew she wanted him just as much as he'd wanted her.

Trouble was, he didn't know how to express what he felt. Mitch laughed out loud. He was returning from L.A., where he'd been the penalty phase attorney for a man found guilty of murder. He'd persuaded a judge to sentence the man to life instead of the electric chair. The words had come easily — the usual dysfunctional-family/failure-of-the-system argument — but he couldn't think of a damn thing to say to Royce.

What could he say after that macho bit? *I want to get you out of my system.* "That won't get you far with Royce," he said out loud. "You have to say something to let her know what you feel goes beyond sex."

He thought about the two women who'd betrayed him. He'd almost forgotten the incident at Stanford, but almost twenty-five years later he still recalled the murderous look on his mother's face.

"Royce is different," he told himself, his voice echoing in the sports car. "You disappointed her. It's up to you to win her back.

"Okay, but how? How do you turn lust into love, into trust, into caring?"

Women are sentimental, he thought. That's why cards and flowers and all that crap sold so well. What would Brent have done? The morning after that wuss would have sent long-stemmed roses and a syrupy card. Well, hell, it was too late for that, but he had to make some move, a small gesture to change the balance of their relationship.

He drove to a newsstand that had a florist's cart stationed beside it. Mitch parked in the red, thinking a bouquet of wildflowers would be perfect. Roses were too formal, but a mixture of fragrant, colorful blossoms would say what he couldn't, what he didn't want to say just yet.

He handed the man the money for the flowers and spotted the newspaper rack. Suddenly, his mouth was as dry as the Sahara and he couldn't hear the sound of the traffic on the street — even with his good ear.

Somehow he managed to pay for the paper. He got in his car, shot out from the curb, and rounded the corner on two wheels. He threw the bouquet out the window and it landed blossoms down in the muddy gutter.

Royce threatened Oliver, waving a wooden spoon at the cat. "Get away from the prosciutto."

The cat retreated to the window box, but she had no doubt he'd jump up on the counter the first chance he got. She was too nervous about seeing Mitch to worry about that fatso. Last night after returning home from seeing Brent she'd carefully evaluated her feelings. She was only deceiving herself by not admitting Mitch meant more to her than one night of hot sex.

Being with Brent again had demonstrated how selfish he was. Until she'd bullied him into not testifying against her, he'd been willing to do it to avoid a confrontation with his father. What had she been thinking when she'd persuaded herself that she was in love with him? She'd been desperate — plain and simple. And with her biological clock grinding to a halt, she'd assessed the situation. Brent had been a charming and caring — not to mention rich — man in a city where heterosexual men were about as easy to find as the Holy Grail.

She'd given up on the kind of love her parents had enjoyed. She'd been willing to settle for less. Now she knew it was a mistake.

What about the surge of emotion that swelled within her every time she thought of Mitch? Was it love, or the lingering afterglow of a night of lust? She'd made up her mind to find out, but she was nervous about seeing him again. What if he had gotten her out of his system? What if she'd been just another roll in the sack?

"I thought you might be hungry," she rehearsed out loud, anticipating seeing Mitch for the first time in over a week. "This is Mama's carbonara recipe."

What would he say? "You're out of my system. Get out of my kitchen."

Not likely, she thought. All right, he hadn't called, but her sixth sense — which was usually accurate — told her he cared for her more than he was likely to admit. After he'd made love to her the first time, he'd become increasingly gentle. Almost loving. And when they'd finally fallen asleep, his leg was possessively curled across hers as if he didn't want to chance her getting away.

"Then why didn't he call?" she asked Jenny. But the retriever's answer was a happy swish of her tail and a hopeful look at the pasta drying on the rack. Royce tossed her a piece. "That's all. Do you want to become a porker like Oliver?"

Before Jenny could swallow the pasta, Royce heard Mitch coming in the back door. She reached for the wooden spoon and sucked in a calming breath. Mitch strode into the kitchen, a suitcase in each hand and a newspaper tucked under one arm. The look on his face could have frozen lava.

"What in hell are you doing here?"

"I thought you —"

"Get out." He dropped both suitcases. Jenny shied away, but Mitch gave her a reassuring pat.

But there wouldn't be any such welcome for her, Royce thought, miserable that she'd so drastically misjudged the situation. Not only had he gotten her out of his system, he seemed to hate her now.

He whipped out the paper still tucked under his arm and held it up for her to see. The front page was covered with a picture of her kissing Brent and the headline: FATAL ATTRACTION?

A suffocating sensation gripped her throat, stealing her voice. Oh, no. How had Ingeblatt discovered them? She'd been so careful. He must have followed Brent. "I can explain."

"Don't bother. Just get out."

His tone was shockingly vicious; words stalled in her throat. He threw the paper on the counter and she took a closer look. The grainy texture indicated it had been shot from a distance with a telephoto lens. She turned to explain Tobias Ingeblatt must have followed Brent, but Mitch

351

had left. She chased him and caught him on the stairs.

"Listen to me. I convinced Brent not to testify against me."

His very stance spelled danger and he wasn't going to be appeased easily. "You use that body any chance you get, don't you?"

The revulsion in his voice made her want to run and hide. Even Jenny was cowering beside Mitch. "He kissed me only once."

"You expect me to believe that?" He laughed, a bitter, derisive chuckle. "I know what a hot number you are."

She wanted to whack him, she honestly did, but another deeper part of her was profoundly hurt. Yes, she'd known Mitch would be furious about Brent, but she hadn't anticipated the depth of his anger. And it truly frightened her. There was a side to this man she didn't know.

"Mitch, I hadn't heard from you," she said, following him into his bedroom. "I would have told you —"

"Liar." His voice boomed and Jenny retreated to a corner, tail between her legs. "Paul could have found me. You wanted to see Brent."

"You're right," she conceded. "I wanted —"

He took one step toward her. Then another. He glared at her with burning, reproachful eyes. His look was so galvanizing, it sent a tremor through her. She didn't notice his hands on her shoulders until he pushed her down onto the bed, falling on top of her. For a second she thought he was going to strangle her. Hate glittered in his eyes, silently damning her.

Anchored between his torso and the bed, she struggled against his superior strength, determined to get away, but escaping his brutal hold was impossible. She twisted madly in an effort to free herself, fear building inside her. She read his intent and the flare of desire in his eyes just as the swelling hardness pressing against her thigh registered.

Before she could say a word, Mitch's lips smothered hers, his powerful body covering hers as if he wanted to keep her pinned to the mattress forever. He shifted his weight, his erection a hard wedge against the juncture of her thighs. Shock arced through her as she realized what he was going to do.

Usually when Mitch was rough, she found it exciting because she sensed an inner restraint, a playfulness. Not this time. Tonight he seemed balanced on some emotional cliff — one foot over the edge.

Surely he was overreacting to what she'd done. She didn't know this man — not at all. She refused to let him make love to her. Not like this, not in anger.

"Jenny!" she screamed.

The dog bounded across the room and leapt up on the bed, responding to the distress in Royce's voice. Jenny hovered over them, whining. Mitch raised his head, his expression still venomous.

"I had to go to Brent," Royce said, her voice as taut as her emotions. "From the moment I opened my purse and found those diamonds, my fate has been in someone else's hands. Despite everyone's hard work, this case is lost, isn't it?"

Mitch didn't deny it.

"This was my chance — for once — to do something to help myself. Do you think you could have persuaded Brent not to take the stand? Of course not. But I did." She levered herself up on her elbows. "I didn't sleep with him to convince him, but I might have been tempted had I thought that was the only way to convince him. I have to do something to save myself."

Why couldn't Mitch understand? He'd lived through hell. "Haven't you ever done anything wrong because it would save you?"

Mitch rolled onto his back and closed his eyes. Jenny nuzzled him several times, but he didn't respond. Finally, he said, "Get out."

20

Getting to see Ward Farenholt was surprisingly easy for Paul. Ward's vanity got the better of him. He agreed to an interview with a reporter from *The Lawyer*. The prestigious ABA magazine was sent each month to members of the bar.

Paul had a professional makeup artist disguise him so he could pretend to be a reporter without Ward's recognizing him. He'd never actually been introduced to Ward, but Paul had been seen around enough to be concerned. Ward didn't seem to recognize him as his secretary led Paul into the office that looked like an antique showroom with a mahogany desk and an armoire that dated back to the turn of the century. Just which century Paul couldn't say, but the thing was old. And damned impressive.

Everything about the office was designed to impress. Antiques. Original oils worth a fortune. Paul couldn't help comparing it to Mitch's office. Mitch's office was three times as large as Ward's. Mitch had had several walls removed to make one gigantic office, but it wasn't filled with expensive furnishings. In fact it had an empty feeling to it, as if it weren't quite finished.

Until Mitch walked in. Unquestionably, Mitch was so impressive that he didn't need a backdrop of priceless antiques to impress his clients.

"My article is on multigeneration law firms," Paul explained.

"I see." Ward didn't bother hiding his disappointment. Obviously, he'd expected to be the focus of the article.

"Your father founded this firm, didn't he?"

"Yes, but I built it into the powerhouse it is today." His tone stated plainly that he considered himself — and no one else — responsible for the firm's success.

Paul asked a series of questions suggested by an attorney in Mitch's office so that Ward would relax and assume the interview was legitimate. Ward exuded an arrogance that bordered on outright disdain. Paul knew, without a doubt, Ward Farenholt would never have spoken to him unless he believed he was a reporter from *The Lawyer*.

What type of woman would be attracted to such a man? Paul asked himself. Black hair brushed with silver and a sportsman's tan acquired on the Olympic Club's golf course. While Brent resembled his mother, with pretty-boy appeal, Ward was intensely masculine. Totally domineering.

He was the kind of man who demanded a showpiece mistress. Young. In awe of a powerful older man.

But Ward had carefully guarded the secret mistress with almost an animal cunning that Paul thought had been bred out of the very wealthy. Obviously, as much as he dominated his wife, she had the money. Ward was far too clever to let a mistress break up his marriage.

"Is your son helping build the firm, the way you did?" Paul asked, edging into the territory he wished to discuss.

"Yes." The single word sounded as if a mule team had dragged it out of Ward's mouth. "His mother spoiled him, but he's on track now."

"I guess that Winston woman distracted him."

For a moment Paul thought Ward wasn't going to take the bait, then he spoke. "Royce Winston is a cheap slut. You watch, she's going to spend the best years of her life in prison."

There was almost as much hatred in Ward's voice as there had been in his wife's at the mention of Royce's name. Paul decided that it was entirely possible either or both of them had framed Royce. But why? Why hadn't Ward bullied Brent into giving up Royce? His sources confirmed Ward had no trouble manipulating his son.

"Caroline Rambeau is a much more suitable wife for your son, don't you think?"

"No." The word thundered through the room, catching Paul off-guard — just the way Caroline's defending Royce had blindsided him. What was going on here?

"My son," Ward continued, his tone now softer, apparently realizing he'd come on too strong, "and Caroline have known each other for years. If they loved each other, they'd be married by now."

"Jesus, I've never had a case like this," Paul complained to Mitch. "I can't find a trace of Ward Farenholt's mistress. I'll bet she knows all the Farenholt business. Mistresses usually do, you know. Statistics prove that men tell their lovers more than their wives."

He waited for Mitch's response, but he kept looking out his office window at the moon rising over the bay. In the week since Mitch had returned, he'd been unusually silent and withdrawn. Even when Paul had told Mitch about his interviews with the Farenholts and Caroline, he hadn't seemed interested.

No one needed to tell Paul that Mitch was having problems with Royce. Tobias Ingeblatt's picture of her with Brent had rocked the legal community. Abigail Carnivali had withdrawn Brent Farenholt's name from the witness list. A small triumph, Paul thought, but one that had cost Mitch. For reasons Paul never fully understood, Mitch hated Brent.

Seeing Royce in Brent's arms after all Mitch had done for her must have pissed Mitch off — big time. Paul was certain they'd been having an affair, but now . . . who knew? The team was still working on Royce's defense, but Mitch hadn't even stepped into the suite where they were conducting the mock trial.

Mitch broke the silence, turning his back on the panoramic view. "What do the polls say?"

"Interestingly enough, the latest poll is quite favorable to Royce. At least Brent was honest enough to say that he called Royce and asked to see her. The public loved that. The fatal-attraction syndrome."

Mitch shuffled through some papers on his desk, but Paul wasn't fooled. He'd straightened those papers just moments ago.

"Look," Paul said, "I'm sorry I haven't been able to find out who's behind this. I may never solve this case."

"You're kidding," Mitch said, looking up.

Paul gazed into his friend's turbulent eyes. So that's the problem, Paul thought. Mitch doesn't have a way to save Royce either. He'd been counting on Paul.

"I'll keep looking for Ward's mistress," Paul attempted to assure Mitch. "I'm positive she's the key to this case."

Mitch didn't respond, and Paul glanced at his watch. Val was waiting; she was upset enough without him being late. "Mitch, I've got to run."

Paul hustled up the back stairs to his office to meet Val. Now he understood why it was wrong for an attorney to represent someone he was involved with. You became so emotionally entangled that it was difficult to know how best to handle the case. If Royce was found guilty, Mitch would never forgive himself.

"All set?" Paul asked Val as he came into his office.

She rose, adjusting her summer suit, a soft lemon-colored creation that accentuated the copper highlights in her auburn hair. "I'm ready."

Paul held the door for her, thinking it had been days since she'd learned of her brother's terminal illness, agonizing days spent in an emotional tug-of-war. When she'd finally decided to face her whole family again, she'd insisted Paul accompany her. He was relieved she wanted him. Surely it was a sign that she loved him — even though she'd never said the words.

David Thompson's house on Lafayette Square was like many others in the affluent neighborhood. It was a three-story townhouse with a garden in the rear. Like the rest of San Francisco parking was at a premium, and Paul had to double-park behind a Porsche in David's driveway.

Inside Val's parents greeted them, and then scuttled away. Obviously they didn't want to be around when Val talked to her brother. Paul wondered if he should be there either. Wasn't this too personal? But Val's courageous smile never left her face, nor did she relax her grip on his arm.

Upstairs, they met Trevor, Val's former husband. The boy next door, Paul thought, noting his sandy-blond hair and square-cut jaw. He sure as hell didn't look like a guy who'd deceive his wife — for years. And he didn't look gay, but who could tell? Living in San Francisco had shown Paul the absurdity of stereotypes.

"Val," Trevor said, his voice breaking. "David's so ill . . . I don't know what I'm going to do."

Val didn't answer; Paul knew she couldn't. Even though Trevor was too distraught to notice, she was still angry with him.

"Don't upset David," Trevor insisted. "He's weak from all the tests."

Val nodded and walked into the bedroom. She stopped at the door and Paul felt her tense. Propped up in the four-poster bed was a man who so closely resembled Val that he had to be her twin. Auburn hair, intriguing hazel eyes, softly sculpted lips.

"Y-you came," David said, his voice slightly slurred by the brain tumor that would soon claim his life. "I — I didn't think you would." His eyes misted over. "I wouldn't have blamed you if you never spoke to . . . me again."

Paul nudged Val forward. He had no idea what she was thinking, what she might say. She sat on the edge of the bed and Paul positioned himself behind her, waiting for her to introduce him, as she had to the others, as her "friend."

Val took her brother's hand. The skin was a livid purple from an IV shunt. "The other night I was thinking about the time we went to that dude ranch in Montana, remember?"

David smiled, a slow, tentative smile that was exactly like Val's when she was unsure of herself. "You fell off the horse onto a cactus, and I had to pull two dozen quills out of your jeans."

Val laughed, or tried to, but the sound was low, bordering on a sob. "Yep. You saved my butt — more than once. We had plenty of good times, didn't we? A lifetime of happy memories."

David brushed back a tear with his forearm. Paul felt like an intruder and started to move away, but Val caught his hand and gave it a desperate squeeze.

"Val, I want to explain about Trevor."

"Don't. It doesn't matter anymore. We have now what we had when we were kids — each other. Mother and Father never cared. They never wanted children, you know. But we loved each other. Everything I did, I did to please you. You were everything to me. A father. A brother. A friend."

David didn't try to stop the tear that dribbled down his cheek. "And you were everything to me. That's why it was so hard . . . impossible for me to tell you that Trevor and I had fallen in love. I couldn't bring myself to hurt you. In the end I hurt you even more, didn't I?"

"It doesn't matter," Val said, although Paul knew it mattered very much. As a child Val had given up on her parents' love, but she'd never expected to lose David's. "I understand what happened."

"Forgive me. I'm being punished now. Can you imagine what it's like knowing you're going to die? I'd thought, I'd hoped, that time would heal your wounds and we could somehow be close again. I'd counted on you finding someone special." For a moment his gaze met Paul's and Paul saw the suffering in the eyes that were a mirror image of those of the woman he'd always love. "I'd counted on your children, Val. My nieces and nephews. On baptisms and birthday parties and school plays. Piano recitals."

"Oh, David," Val said, the threat of tears in her voice. "Don't think of what you'll miss; think of what we had. Sunsets at the cabin on the Russian River, the rose trees we planted in your garden out back, the way we'd sit in the window seat, talking and watching the fog creep across the bay, the sound of thunder rumbling over Golden Gate Bridge that sent us under the covers, hugging each other until the storm passed."

David offered her the suggestion of a smile.

"I doubt two siblings have ever been closer."

"Never," Val assured him. "I love you, darling. I'll always love you."

"I love you too." His sharp intake of breath sounded unusually loud in the quiet room. "I don't have long, you know. I'm already paralyzed on one side. Soon I won't be able to talk. I don't know what I'll do then."

Val leaned forward and kissed his forehead. "Don't worry. I'll be here."

"Promise me you won't leave me. Promise me you'll hold me the way you did when we were afraid of the thunder. I'm afraid, so terribly afraid of dying."

"I won't leave you, I swear. And when it's over, when you're with the angels looking down on us, I'll take care of Trevor."

"Oh, Val, could you? He's not strong, you know. This will be horrible for him. Mother and Father won't be any help. I need you to do this for me . . . in spite of what I've done and how I hurt you."

Val threw her arms around David and cradled him, rocking gently. "Don't worry about me. Losing Trevor wasn't so hard. Some part of me always knew it wasn't real love. It was losing you that nearly killed me. But things worked out for the best."

She turned to Paul. "I found the love of my life. And I promise you, David, as surely as the sun sets over the bay and your rose trees bloom each spring, we'll name our first son after you."

363

She gently laid her brother against the bank of pillows. Obviously, he was very weak now, his eyes half closed, but Paul thought he looked more at peace than he had when they'd arrived. Val pulled his hand to her breast.

"David, from now until eternity, you'll always be right here — forever in my heart."

Royce could barely concentrate on the videotape of her interrogation that the defense team reviewed at the end of each session. A secretary had whispered Royce was to report to Mitch's office as soon as she finished. What did he want after almost two weeks of ignoring her? Surely, if he was going to drop the case, he would have done it by now.

"Two minutes," Mitch's secretary warned when Royce came into his office. "He's scheduled a conference call at four — sharp."

Royce walked in, crossing the carpeted office that was as large as a football field and stopping in front of his desk. The highly polished walnut stretched out like the deck of an aircraft carrier. Only one pile of papers was on top, along with a telephone and a computer modem, but she knew the drawers must be a mess, the way they were at home.

Mitch didn't look up until she'd been standing there a full minute gazing down at his dark head, noticing how the hair was a shade too long, dusting his collar in back. Had she'd actually made love to this man?

Was that what made him so possessive, so irrational? If she hadn't known better she would have thought he was insanely jealous. The depth of his fury went beyond any normal reaction.

She'd achieved her goal. Brent wouldn't testify. But had she created an insurmountable chasm between herself and Mitch, a chasm that would be impossible to cross? What could she do?

Mitch stood and tossed his pen aside. "I suppose you expect me to represent you at the trial?"

"Yes." The word came out like a croak. So, this interview was going to be about the trial — not their personal relationship. Well, what had she expected? An apology? A declaration of undying love?

He rounded the desk and sat with one leg hitched up on the polished wood, his eyes scouring her body. "Let's get a few things straight." He touched her cheek, running his knuckles up the gentle curve.

She held herself completely still, not knowing what to expect, but knowing how she reacted — her entire future — depended on getting him to forgive her for kissing Brent. She managed to ask, "What things?"

His hand was on her shoulder now, warm, firm, thoroughly disturbing. She didn't like the look in his intense eyes. She'd seen it before and knew exactly what he was doing. He was the master of sexual intimidation. Despite all that had happened, and all that was at stake, he somehow knew she still wanted him, that she still lay awake at night dreaming about him, that she'd blocked out the memory of her father for him.

"You're taking my case seriously, aren't you, Mitch?" she asked, striving to keep this conversation on a professional level.

"Sure — if we can come to terms."

"What terms?"

"I've got what you want. And you've got what I want, right?" His hand cupped her chin, the thumb resting on the full curve of her lower lip. His strong fingers tilted her head upward, so she had no choice but to look directly into his eyes.

He was staring at her lips. When his gaze met hers, his eyes were so intense, so compelling that she was powerless to do anything but stare back.

He grinned, playing on the charge of sexual tension between them. Before she could speak, his mouth overpowered hers. There was absolutely no artistry to the kiss. It was hot, hard, wholly carnal.

It suffocated her cry of protest as the heat of passion seared through her defenses with alarming speed. His tongue probed at the soft interior of her mouth while his hands delved into her hair, holding her head in place for his assertive kiss.

After the lonely days — and even more lonely nights — without him, she savored the kiss, allowing a tiny flame of response, unwanted and thoroughly aggravating, to ignite. Mitch must have sensed her acquiescence, for he lifted his head, his lips achingly close to hers.

"Move all your things into my place — tonight

— before I get home. You can get domestic if you like and make dinner. But plan on serving it in bed."

The intercom on his desk buzzed and he turned away from her, not bothering to see if she agreed — just expecting it.

So that's how it is. Her muddled thoughts cleared as she walked out of his office. Sex. That's what it always came down to with Mitch. She couldn't bank the surge of anger that welled up inside her. She struggled to calm herself, but couldn't. She wasn't just hopping into bed with Mitch. Not this time.

The ruckus at the door interrupted Mitch's conference call, and he looked up. Royce was storming in, his secretary trying to keep her out. What was going on? He thought everything was settled, but the mutinous expression on Royce's face reminded him of the way she'd attacked him at her father's funeral.

He motioned to his secretary to let Royce stay and hoped she'd cool down by the time he finished his call. She hustled around behind his desk, her long hair fluttering against her cheek. She jammed her thumb down on the button, disconnecting him.

"You've just pissed off four of the most important attorneys in the state." He tried for a joking tone. What the hell was the matter?

"Tell me you understand why I went to see Brent."

Christ! He didn't want to discuss this. That photo of Royce kissing Brent had surprised him. Okay, okay, he'd been blown away. Against his better judgment he'd forgiven her. "Yeah, I understand," he stated in a smart-ass tone that clearly said he was clueless and always would be.

"Don't joke, Mitch. Explain why you were so angry about it."

He sensed there was a lot at stake here. Don't screw up by being a wiseguy. "We agreed that I was in charge of the case, right? But the first chance you got, you went off half cocked. You're damn lucky it turned out so good. Ingeblatt's photo could have ruined all the work we've done to improve the public's image of you."

"I had to take the chance. I had to keep Brent off the stand. You were the one who told me how negatively the jury would view me if he testified."

He studied her, recalling with aching clarity his own bout with being helpless, feeling trapped. Of course, that had been years ago, but sometimes it felt like yesterday.

"I don't blame you for doing it," he said, not because he'd totally forgiven her, but because he realized he had no choice. She was asking for understanding, trying to make a connection. He had to give in even though the thought of her kissing Brent made him want to put both hands around her slim neck and squeeze.

"You're saying I did the right thing?"

"Yeah." He choked out the word.

She actually smiled, a satisfied, sincere smile. "You understand that Brent calls me every night and I'm going to talk to him. Since the Farenholts refuse to discuss the case with anyone, I might learn something from Brent."

Now she was pressing her luck. Why did she need to talk to Brent? Mitch knew only too well that the cocky little prick had a talent for charming women.

"Brent's convinced you and I aren't involved. I don't want him to be suspicious, do you?"

"No," he reluctantly conceded. "Did he ask about me?"

She hesitated a fraction of a second; Mitch had cross-examined enough witnesses to know when someone was withholding information.

"Brent thinks you might be the one framing me."

That shit! He was at it again. "What do you think?"

This time Royce didn't hesitate. She leveled those smoldering green eyes on him. "I think you're the only person I can count on."

He wanted to kiss her, but he didn't. He'd relied on sex too long already. He needed to communicate with her on an intellectual level. It was hard as hell because he didn't have much experience at it. And he'd missed her so damned much that he welcomed any excuse to take her into his arms.

"Why did you kiss him?" Jesus! Had he really asked that?

Though the question was spoken softly, it was deadly. She sensed her answer would alter the course of their relationship. "If I didn't kiss Brent, I thought he'd be suspicious about my relationship with you." She hesitated and he knew she was again withholding something. "And I wanted to find out if I felt the same way I did when I kissed you."

He stifled a gasp with the adroitness of a man accustomed to concealing his deepest feelings. Sure as hell, she'd cold-cocked him with that one. What was she trying to tell him? "Well, what happened?"

Now her expression was mischievous. "When you come home tonight, I'll tell you." She adjusted the knot in his tie, then lightly kissed his cheek. "And be ready to tell me the whole truth about you and Brent Farenholt."

21

Royce sipped a glass of the Chardonnay that Mitch had brought home for dinner and waited for him to explain about Brent. Was she going to have to bring it up herself? Probably. So far he seemed content to make small talk while they waited for dinner to cook. She smelled the osso bucco and hoped it wasn't burning.

"Brent called just before you came home."
Home? Had she really said that? She'd done what
Mitch had asked and moved her things into his
house. But living in his house, cooking him dinner
implied a level of intimacy that merely sleeping
with him did not.

She wasn't quite comfortable with the idea.
What would her father have said? How would
Wally feel if he found out? She'd reconciled her
own feelings, deciding there was little difference
if she lived in Mitch's apartment or in his house.
Once they'd begun the affair there was no turning
back, and she didn't mind. The week Mitch had
been angry with her had been longer and lonelier
than any other time in her life. With the trial
looming over her like a guillotine she needed
Mitch's strength, his confidence.

Mitch's expression was dead serious. "You're
positive Brent doesn't know anything about us?"

"Positive, so don't be surprised if he calls —
at all hours. He often phones late at night, assuming I'm alone."

"Be sure he doesn't suspect anything. The last
thing you need is to have Ingeblatt smear you
again."

"It wouldn't do your career any good either."
She knew Mitch valued his reputation. He was
a maverick in a lot of ways, an attorney who
often used unorthodox methods, but he went
overboard to keep his image pristine. Was he
planning a political career? She couldn't help wondering.

"I don't trust Brent." Mitch put his glass down on the black onyx coffee table with a bang. "I never have."

"Do you think he's behind this?"

"No. What possible motive could he have? Besides, I watched him as they arrested you. The wimp was embarrassed as hell. Ward let him have it." He hesitated, measuring her for a moment. "We agreed my past was off-limits, remember?"

"I'm not asking about your childhood. I'm asking if something happened with Brent that might have bearing on my situation."

"You have a right to know," he conceded, but he didn't look thrilled about it. "Brent hated me from the moment he found out I was getting better grades than he was. He never lost the opportunity to let me know I was a hick and would never be part of his circle of friends. I didn't give a damn. I'd been through too much to care what some rich prick thought of me. I just wanted to get a good education.

"I met a girl who was a lot like me. Poor. Working to put herself through school. I didn't mean to fall in love with Maria. My timing couldn't have been worse — I couldn't even afford to buy her a Coke — but it happened."

So he'd been in love. Royce experienced a twist of her heart that she hesitated to label as jealousy, but she was stunned at how much his words hurt. Even after all these years there was still a hint of fondness in his voice, a softening of his expression that said Maria had meant a lot to him.

Perhaps she'd been the first person to love Mitch. Suddenly Royce was glad Wally was investigating Mitch; she needed to know more about him. Without learning about his past would she ever understand him?

"We planned to get married and live in Salinas near her family. Maria's parents were Chicano farm workers, and she was determined to join the California Rural Legal Assistance so she could help her people. I loved her and trusted her completely. When she and Brent were assigned to the same contracts class, I wasn't concerned."

Royce knew, without being told, exactly what happened. Maria had fallen for Brent. His charm, his money, his sophistication, would be a powerful aphrodisiac to a poor girl. All Mitch had to offer was his love.

"I didn't suspect a thing until Maria told me she had gone home for the weekend and I found out she'd been with Brent. I confronted her and she admitted she loved Brent."

Royce tried to imagine how hurt Mitch must have been. He was an insular man; even now he wasn't close to many people. Maria had been his friend and his lover. Since her arrest Royce had experienced a sense of loneliness that almost reduced her to tears at times. Life was meant to be shared. When you were isolated it was like living in an emotional straitjacket.

"Things got worse. Maria was pregnant. I knew the baby wasn't mine. I'm always very careful, I'd never desert my child and let him live a life of hell. A child needs his father. You can't always count on your mother."

The conviction in his tone and his intense expression stunned her. Obviously, Mitch's father had deserted him and something bad had happened with his mother. She was even more anxious now to hear what Wally learned.

"Brent insisted it wasn't his baby — that it was mine."

"Wouldn't a blood test have proved —"

"Back then blood tests were expensive. I didn't have the money. Naturally, Brent didn't volunteer to take a test. The dean called us into his office. Ward Farenholt was there, reminding everyone how much the Farenholts donated each year to the school. Of course, he insisted Maria was a fortune hunter who'd do anything to force his son to marry her."

Royce easily imagined Ward intimidating everyone. How devastated Maria must have been. Had Brent really cared for her, or had he pretended to in order to get even with Mitch? Royce would have sworn she knew Brent, and that he would never have done anything like this. But then, she wouldn't have believed he'd desert her when she'd needed him the most.

She decided Brent was a weak man, a man who wanted to be liked, a man who wanted to please a father who could never be pleased. But was Brent so spiteful that he would deliberately have made a play for Maria? Probably not. More likely, he'd fallen for her only to have his parents condemn him for loving a woman whose social and racial background they felt was inferior to theirs.

"I got lucky," Mitch continued, refilling his wine glass. "One of the professors on the review committee volunteered to give me the money for a paternity test. When Ward saw I couldn't be bullied into marrying Maria, he agreed to give her a cash settlement rather than put everyone through the public embarrassment of a test."

"How gallant of him," Royce said, but her thoughts were on Maria. Had she regretted losing Mitch, or had she gone through this ordeal still loving Brent? "Did you forgive Maria?"

He looked at her as if she'd just suggested Hilter was a saint. "No way. Everyone gets one chance with me. That's it. If you keep forgiving people, they never stop letting you down. Maria had her chance. She chose Brent."

Royce heard a silent message in Mitch's response. She'd let him down once with Brent. There would be no second chance. She had no illusions about what would happen if he discovered Wally was investigating him.

"What happened to Maria?"

"She dropped out of law school. She's married and running a day care facility for migrant workers. Her son looks just like Brent."

A tide of emotion rose in Royce. How sad, she thought. Maria had found a man willing to share her dream, but hadn't been able to appreciate what she had until she lost it. How disappointing for Mitch too. He'd found someone to love after what must have been a hellish youth, but she'd been taken away from him by a man who had so many people who loved him that he never understood what a gift love is.

Had Brent ever truly loved a woman? Why should she care if he'd ever really loved anyone? It was Mitch who was important to her. He had the capacity to love with depth and passion.

"Ward had his revenge, though," Mitch said. "I'd worked hard to graduate first in my class so I'd be hired by a top legal firm in San Francisco. The best ones interviewed me and seemed enthusiastic, but I didn't get a single offer. Later I found out Ward had pressured them not to hire me."

"I'm not surprised. Ward is the most despicable, arrogant man I've ever met. It's a wonder he even thinks Caroline is good enough for his son."

"I can't help wondering if Ward's behind your troubles. You interfered with the grand scheme he had for his son."

"True, he didn't approve of me, but would he resort to such drastic action? If we could find Ward's mistress, she might answer a lot of questions." Royce noted how deftly Mitch had steered the subject from his personal life to her case. All this was old news to her. How many nights had she lain awake speculating about the possibilities? Until they had proof, that's all they were — possibilities.

"The night of the auction you implied you

planned to get even with me on the next interview," she asked wanting to draw Mitch out more. "Just what were you planning?"

He set his glass aside and combed his fingers through her hair, testing its weight, its softness. His gaze locked with hers, he lowered his head and kissed her. The touch of his lips elicited reactions she'd come to expect and anticipate: nipples contracting, a sensation of heat and fullness between her thighs. She couldn't keep her arms from going around his neck, her breasts from seeking the solid wall of his chest.

"I knew you couldn't really love that wuss or you wouldn't let me kiss you and put my hand down the back of your dress. After the interview I was going to kiss you again and make certain Brent found out."

"Revenge." She had the sickening feeling she was just a pawn. "Retaliating for a lost love and thwarted career ambitions?"

"Hell, no. I had my revenge. I proved I'm a better lawyer by building my own firm. I got over Maria." His tone was firm, final, reflecting the determination she always sensed in Mitch. "I was prepared to do anything to get you away from Brent."

She should have wondered if he'd resorted to framing her as Brent suggested, but she remembered the night the narcs searched her house. He hadn't been acting, he was as shocked as she was. Even if she hadn't seen his expression, every instinct she possessed told her Mitch would never do anything like this.

"Admit it. There's been something between us that's survived five long years." His fingers scaled down the bare skin of her throat to her shoulders and lingered at the crest of her bosom, hot and tantalizing. "Ask yourself why you like me to get rough with you and force myself on you. It gives you an excuse to make love to me."

She couldn't answer. Of course she'd asked herself why she felt so physically attracted to a man she once hated. After that first kiss in the dark, guilt and shame had overwhelmed her. Still, she'd let Mitch touch her again. Even now she felt the heady sense of excitement that had swept through her when he'd slid his hand down her back.

And when they'd finally made love, it was everything she anticipated. No. It was better. Obviously, her body knew what her mind couldn't quite accept: Mitch was perfect — for her.

22

Mitch studied the shadows flickering across the ceiling above his bed. Jesus, he couldn't sleep. How many nights now? Five? Six? He'd be worthless in court tomorrow, but he didn't give a damn. He knew exactly what was keeping him awake. Royce.

He moved a little and she unconsciously snuggled against him, her breasts nestled against his rib cage, her heart beating against his own. A sliver of moonlight played across her face. She looked peaceful, happy, and he should be too.

Since their talk three weeks ago they'd settled into a comfortable routine. During the day they both worked at the office, he on his cases and she on the upcoming trial. They seldom saw each other until evening, when he'd return home to find Royce busy in the kitchen with Oliver perched on the counter, set to steal anything, and Jenny at her heels.

Some men might have been threatened by the sudden domesticity of their relationship, particularly after years of living alone, but Mitch wasn't. Okay, Royce got on his nerves at times. She insisted on organizing his drawers, claiming she couldn't find anything. And she kept getting those damn Oreo cookie crumbs in his computer keyboard as she worked on the homeless files. A tragedy, sure, but nothing compared to not letting him eat pizza every night. Still, living with her was like making love to her — better than he'd imagined.

She shifted positions, her body still touching his, and her hand brushed his cock, coming to rest on the flat plane of his stomach. He ignored the upsurge in his groin.

Royce never initiated sex. Hell, she loved it and probably expected it just the way she got it — twice a night. But she expected him to initiate it, and she responded much more passionately if he was rough with her.

Well, could he blame her? She had to justify their relationship with the memory of her father. Long dead, but never, no never, forgotten.

If Mitch forced her to make love, she could tell herself it wasn't her idea. At least by deceiving herself she was able to keep up a front. Every night Brent called and she chatted with him, saying how lonely she was.

She used the same routine when her friends called each night and with Wally, who was still down South. Of course, during all these calls, Mitch wasn't far away. It was a hoot to know Brent was talking to Royce, believing she was alone, when Mitch was actually in bed beside her.

He ran his hand over her golden hair where it fell alluringly across her bare shoulder. What in hell was he going to do? No wonder he couldn't get any sleep. Her trial was a month away and he had no idea how he was going to defend her. Night after night he'd make love to her, then fall into a blissful sleep only to awaken later sheathed in sweat, tortured by the image of Royce in jail.

He realized Royce expected one of his miraculous defenses. But this time he couldn't conceive of an argument that would convince a jury to acquit her — not with her getting caught red-handed. Twice.

Jee-sus! A diabolical mind was behind this. His

money was on Ward Farenholt, but so far Paul hadn't been able to implicate him.

Mitch gazed down at Royce, her face soft and sweet in the dim light of the moon. Trusting. He imagined the look she'd have for him if the jury returned a guilty verdict.

Unbidden, the past intruded on the present. He was a grown man, holding Royce, but in his mind's eye he saw a haunting vision from his youth. He was a young boy again, calling to his mother as she worked in the garden.

His mother rose to her knees, the three-pronged trowel in her hand as she turned to him. The smile on her face was like Royce's, soft and sweet. Trusting.

Until she saw him.

Up to then his young life had been miserable, but from the moment his mother turned on him, it became pure hell. Of course, his father was responsible. He was never going to find him, but if fate ever changed its mind, he'd kill the bastard.

On Saturday morning Mitch was in the shower when Wally called Royce.

"I found that school where the nun worked," he said after a brief greeting.

"Oh," she responded cautiously, hearing the shower turn off. She headed downstairs, the portable phone to her ear. "What did she say?"

"She isn't there. The school's gone too. It's a strip mall now."

In the kitchen out of Mitch's hearing range,

she stopped. "A dead end."

"Not at all. I know where Mitch got the name on his phony birth certificate. That Catholic school was on the corner of Mitchell and Durant streets."

"No." The word came out somewhere between a moan and a whisper. A cold knot formed in her chest, her heart refusing to accept what he'd just told her. She'd imagined Mitch's mother lovingly choosing Mitchell from a list of names she'd considered for months, but it hadn't been that way at all.

Mitch wasn't even his real name. She could understand him changing his last name, but why hadn't he used his real first name? Wouldn't that have been the logical thing to do? "His given name must have had terrible memories."

The words were hardly out of her mouth when Mitch walked into the kitchen, still damp from the shower. A tuft of wet hair kicked upward like a rooster's comb, and a towel hung from his hips, barely covering his strong thighs. She flashed him a smile that she hoped didn't look too guilty and mouthed, "Wally."

"It's more likely he changed his name because he had a police record," Wally informed her. "That would have kept him out of the Navy."

"H-mm." She watched Mitch brush Jenny, the way he did each Saturday morning. Just like the Italian count Mitch had become a new person. Why? What had he done?

Mitch cocked his head, favoring his good ear

382

as his private line rang upstairs in the office. He walked out of the kitchen and Royce relaxed.

"I've got a line on the nun, though." Wally sounded so clear, he could have been in the room with her. "She must be retired by now. There's only one retirement convent down here. It's in Bascom Springs, not far from Woodville."

"Woodville. Mitch is supporting someone in a clinic there," Royce blurted out, then cursed herself. He might return any second. Things were going so well between them that she couldn't afford for him to find out what Wally was doing.

"They're seven miles apart. I can visit them both in a day."

"Please, don't —" Royce halted midsentence. Mitch walked into the kitchen.

"Don't worry. I'm a pro, remember? Mitch isn't going to find out a thing."

Mitch studied her like a wolf picking up a scent.

"Come home, Uncle Wally. I need you."

"I'll be back soon," Wally assured her. "My reports are being used by UPI. I can't leave now, honey."

For the first time she questioned Wally's motives. Was another Pulitzer more important than she was? What if she didn't have Mitch? She'd be all alone. She barely heard Wally's parting remarks.

"What didn't you want Wally to do?" Mitch asked as she hung up.

"To stay there." The lie sounded as flat as week old beer. "The trial's so close. I — I need

383

—" The look on Mitch's face told her that he suspected something.

"I need to get out. I feel like Rabbit E. Lee trapped in a cage. Can't we go to the park and picnic with Jenny? Please?" she pleaded, unnervingly aware of the strange look on his face. "Unless you have to work. Was that call —"

"Jason," he said, stepping closer and she realized she was shaking. "He's back from camp." Mitch locked both arms around her, his eyes brimming with tenderness and understanding. "Don't be afraid."

She wasn't trembling with fear for herself. Heartfelt anguish ripped through her. For God's sakes, why had he named himself for an intersection? Tears dampened her lashes, making it hard to see the muscular curve of his shoulder as he held her.

What a story! A tale of courage and eventual triumph. A story that could win a Pulitzer. A fresh rush of tears blurred her vision even more.

Wally. He was absolutely fascinated with this story, and in his own way he was every bit as ambitious as Mitch. Once she would have sworn his word as a premier reporter would have guaranteed he'd never break his promise.

But now she was worried. So much had happened — all of it bad — that she wondered. She had to stop Wally.

Mitch framed her head with his palms and looked into her eyes. "Angel, it's going to be all right."

"Please, let's go to Golden Gate Park for a picnic. Let's rent bikes and —" Oh, Lordy, why had she suggested that?

"It's okay, Royce. I know you pumped Jason for information about me. So, I can't ride a bike." He shrugged and shot her a who-gives-a-damn grin, but she thought she detected a flicker of pain — or perhaps anger — in his eyes. A childhood lost; a past that couldn't be regained. "Every kid in America isn't given a bike, you know."

"I could teach you to ride." She pointed to the warm sunlight trumpeting a summer song through the window. "Please, it'll be fun."

"I look like an ass," Mitch cussed as he wobbled along a trail on a bike, Royce running beside him, keeping him upright. Jenny scampered with him, too, but she had the sense to give him a wide berth. He'd tipped and almost fallen a dozen times or more. What the hell was he doing?

Making Royce happy. When she looked up at you with tear-filled green eyes, you couldn't say no. She was more vulnerable now with the trial so close. She needed him, not just physically, but emotionally as well. That knowledge frightened him in a way that he hadn't been truly frightened since he was a kid. What if he couldn't save her?

"Way to go," Royce cheered, and he realized he'd traveled quite a distance without her guiding hand. "That's it!"

Jenny barreled ahead of him, her tail held high.

Over the top of the hill he sailed, going faster, then shot down the other side. Without warning the bike teetered, but he obeyed Royce's earlier instructions and concentrated on keeping his balance.

He hit the hairpin turn — out of control. Shazammm!! He skidded onto the grass beside the trail and landed on his hip, the bike between his legs.

Jenny bounded up to him and licked his sweaty face. He groaned and lay back on the grass. Royce trotted up, laughing.

"That'll teach you to go too fast. Can't you keep a normal pace?"

"Nah, I love speed. Give me fast cars and faster women."

She dropped to the ground beside him. "If you rode slower, I could rent a bike and ride with you. You're ready to ride on your own."

He lay on his back and stared up at the cloudless blue sky as if he couldn't tolerate the thought of an afternoon riding bikes, but the hell of it was, he was having an unexpectedly good time.

"Ride all the way back to the stand?" He stroked Jenny's head, moaning. "Tell her to have mercy."

"Come on, crybaby."

"Meanie," he teased, giving her a thorough, intimate appraisal. She looked so damn cute in those shorts. Even the bandanna tied babushka style to disguise her and sunglasses the size of hubcaps added to her appeal. Aw, hell. He liked her in anything. Or nothing. Preferably nothing.

Mitch leaned across the fragrant grass, warm and moist in the summer sun, intent on kissing her, but he stopped when he looked into her eyes. And saw the future. Other summer days — and summer nights. Cool winter evenings by the fire. Colder winter nights making love in his bed.

Most of all he saw two images of Royce he knew he'd never forget even if he lived long enough to go to hell. Royce in the morning. Waking slowly, snuggling into his pillow, determined to go back to sleep. And Royce in the evening when he opened the back door and found her in his kitchen.

He slumped back on the grass and gazed at the blazing ball in the sky until he was forced to close his eyes. Why in hell had he fought for mandatory drug sentences? If they weren't in effect, he'd stand a chance of getting her off with a suspended sentence, a steep fine, and a whopping number of community-service hours. But as things stood, he was scared pissless she'd get the max.

Jenny licked his nose and Royce said, "We can quit if you want."

It took him a second to muster a playful tone. "I'm no quitter. Let's get you a bike. After the picnic we'll race."

They rented a bike for Royce, then rode through the park. The trails were skateboarders' turf. They whipped up and down the hills, nearly colliding with yuppie cyclists on Italian bikes that were as expensive as cars.

Around the windmill, like a garland of bright flowers, were the homeboys in their gang colors. In the park's neutral zone by the teahouse were groups of preteens, their boom-boxes blasting rap or salsa.

The benches along the walks were off-limits to anyone under seventy-five. Clusters of stoop-shouldered men sat there playing cards. Nearby sat the gossiping old women, swathed in black despite the heat.

But the grass — the rolling meadows of blue-green grass — was for the dogs. And lovers. On the far side of the park Royce and Mitch found a shady patch of grass in a deserted area. Jenny charged into the brush after a squirrel.

"Did you have a dog when you were a kid?" Royce asked as she offered him a sandwich she'd made at home.

"Yeah," Mitch said, hoping she wasn't going to ask a lot of personal questions. "I had a dog . . . once." Naturally there was no stopping Royce.

"What kind?"

He swallowed the bite of chicken salad. "My past is a closed book. Remember?"

"I was just thinking how well you trained Jenny and wondered if you had a lot of experience."

"I had just the one dog." It had suffered such a painful death that it had taken him twenty-five years to get another.

"Jenny," Royce called and the retriever darted out of the bushes, her tail wagging. "Here's a Bonz for you."

Jenny obediently sat, paw raised, to shake for her treat. Mitch couldn't help smiling. Like people some dogs have it so good, while others have nothing but misery. Even all these years later he could still hear his old coon dog's soulful whimpering.

If he told Royce about it, she'd cry. He wasn't ready to trust her with his secrets quite yet. When the trial was behind them and the future decided one way or the other, then he'd have a better idea of how she felt about him. If she admitted she cared for him, he'd be damn tempted to tell her, but she held back. Would she always hold her father's death against him?

Royce waited several minutes, but Mitch didn't speak. Well, he certainly wasn't going to reveal anything about his past. She sucked in a calming breath and cursed herself for leaving her portable phone at home. If she had it, she could slip off to the restroom and try to reach Wally. She had to convince him to stop investigating Mitch. A man who guarded his privacy so much that he couldn't talk about his dog would be furious if he found out about Wally.

"Come on," Mitch said. "Let's race."

She watched his powerful thighs pedaling the bike and recalled those same thighs, slightly rough with hair, covering hers. Since when had desire replaced hate? Why did she want to get closer rather than run away?

Day by day her feelings about Mitch had been changing. Surely she wasn't falling in love with him, was she?

By late that afternoon when they returned the bicycles to the stand, Mitch wasn't doing wheelies yet, but he was riding quite well. Best of all, he seemed to love it. Maybe next weekend she'd teach him how to roller-skate.

"Where to?" he asked as they left the rental stand.

"Let's make our own pizza for dinner. There's a great Italian market nearby. We can get everything there."

Mitch draped one arm over her shoulders and they walked out of Golden Gate Park, Jenny leading the way. They hadn't brought his car. Attempting to park near the popular recreation area was impossible, so they'd walked.

Once Royce would have caught a bus, too much in a hurry. Now, with this weekend disappearing and with only three weekends left until the trial, she cherished the opportunity to be outside. Free.

"I'm leaving tomorrow for Chicago," Mitch announced. "I'll be back at the end of the week."

She wanted to beg him not to leave. Just knowing he was in town — even if she wasn't with him — was comforting. More comforting than she had realized until now. But she couldn't beg him. He had his job, his own life that didn't include her.

Instead of commenting on yet another absence, she called to the dog. "Jenny, be careful. Wait for us."

"I wouldn't go if I didn't have to. This has been scheduled for months."

What could she say? It was immature to dread the lonely nights. And tomorrow, Sunday, she'd mentally made plans, but now she'd be alone with Jenny. She spotted the retriever ahead of them, one paw in the crosswalk.

She yelled, "Jenny, wait."

A car careened around the corner and caught Jenny stepping off the curb. The dog bounced off the fender and for one heart-stopping moment was suspended midair. She landed headfirst in the middle of the street — limp.

Mitch charged down the sidewalk with Royce at his heels. His frantic cry — "Jen-n-ny" — was butchered by the squeal of brakes. A van skidded to a halt just inches from Jenny's head.

Mitch leapt off the curb — nearly being struck by a taxi — and bounded to the center of the street. He dropped to his knees beside Jenny.

Royce followed him, cutting through traffic and crouching next to him. Jenny whimpered, her head lolling from side to side in pain, blood seeping from her golden fur.

"Hang on, old girl," Mitch pleaded, his voice rife with anguish.

Jenny gazed up at him, her doe-brown eyes glazed with fear, her breathing labored. Foam coated her muzzle and blood now gushed from

391

a wound on her leg. Royce whipped off her scarf and made a tourniquet.

"Please call Pet Alert," Royce yelled, certain someone in the traffic jam they'd created had a car phone and would call the pet ambulance.

Mitch drew Jenny's head onto his lap and caressed the fur on her noble head. In that unguarded moment his expression revealed all the pain she'd only suspected he'd been hiding, an emotional wound so deep that it had become a part of him, never to be healed. Tears burning her eyes in a scalding rush, she longed to hold him, to ease his suffering, but sensed she'd be intruding on a very private moment.

"Please, Jenny," he whispered brokenly, raw grief flickering in his eyes. "Don't leave me."

But Jenny didn't respond. Her soulful eyes drooped shut and a spasm shook her, bringing a rattling sound from her chest.

"O-h-h-h, Jenny," Mitch's tone implied this might be the last chance he had to speak with his beloved pet. "No-o-o. You can't die."

Tears blurred Royce's vision as she searched the crowd for any sign of the pet ambulance. *Don't let Jenny die. Please. She's my friend.*

How many nights had she been alone except for Jenny? Too many to remember them all. But Jenny was always at her side, always wagging her tail. Without question Royce knew Mitch had experienced the same overpowering loneliness. But he'd lived with it all his life.

Mitch was staring down at Jenny, her broken

body cradled in his arms, her blood covering his thighs. "So loving, so loyal," he whispered to the dog who no longer knew he was there.

At the veterinarian's office Mitch went into the examining room with Jenny while Royce gave the receptionist his Visa card. The young woman looked at Royce closely, and Royce realized she'd been recognized. No doubt, motorists at the intersection had recognized her as well.

What could she do? Nothing. Fate seemed to have her in the palm of its hand, determined to squeeze the life out of her. But don't take an innocent dog, Royce prayed. She was still praying when Mitch returned to the waiting room.

"She's in surgery." He collapsed onto the sofa beside Royce.

He looked so — so defeated that it actually hurt to look at him. Usually he was tough and cynical, making no allowances for weakness in himself. He would never have survived if he hadn't. Along the way he'd abandoned the comfort of a close personal relationship. Except for a dog.

She recalled his cautious admission that he'd "once" had another dog. Amid the horrors of modern society animals represented a precious link — someone you could trust. Pets have a special place in our hearts, she realized, thinking of Rabbit E. Lee. Unlike people they loved you without question.

"Jus' like my ole coon dog. Jenny's suffering."

Mitch's voice was soft, his slight southern accent

393

now more pronounced, the way he sounded when he was really angry — or upset. He stared straight ahead, almost as if he didn't know she was there, in his voice a low yet ominous quality that instantly alerted her. Without knowing what he was going to say, she hurt for him.

"I bought Jenny for myself . . . for a birthday present. Twenty-five years after Harley died." Mitch kept looking forward at the deserted waiting room now cloaked in the shadows of early evening.

"I can still remember the first time I saw Harley. It was my eighth birthday, but I wasn't counting on getting a present. Hell, I was six before I found out when I'd been born. I'd never gotten a present and knew better than to expect one."

Her breath seemed to have solidified in her throat. The rare and totally unexpected glimpse of his early years left her speechless. And angry. Who could be so cruel to a child?

Her own youth had been a succession of joyful birthday parties — so many that they now were a blur in her mind. But overriding those fuzzy images was the impression of happiness — and love.

But then another bit of information fell into place. Jenny was just two. That meant it had been twenty-seven years since Mitch first saw Harley. That would make him thirty-five, not thirty-seven the way his birth certificate read.

Why had he lied about his name — and his age?

"Harley wasn't a pup," Mitch went on, totally unaware of what he'd revealed. "He was an old coon hound, white around the muzzle, with long, droopy ears. He came trottin' up the dirt lane, and I figured God had sent me a present.

"He had no collar, so they thought he'd fallen out of a truck and wandered in from the highway. I begged for days and they finally let me keep him."

Look at me, Royce silently pleaded. Tell me this — not an empty waiting room. Mitch had a fundamental distrust of people so ingrained that it had become an integral part of his personality. But the shock of Jenny's accident had prompted him to talk. She was afraid to touch him, afraid to break the spell.

"For the next three months Harley and I were always together. Finally, I had someone to play with. The only time he left me was just before dawn when I let him out to go to the bathroom. He'd come back after sunup. Then one day they served breakfast and Harley still wasn't back."

He didn't have to look at her — although she wished he would — for his tone to betray his inner turmoil. She longed to touch him, to close the chasm between them, a distance he carefully maintained with everyone. Somehow, even with her silence, she wanted him to know he could count on her.

"By noon Harley still hadn't appeared. I started checking the woods, the hollows. I even went up to the fishing hole, but he wasn't there.

Nuthin'. Everyone said Harley had wandered off jus' like he'd wandered in.

"But I knew better. He loved me; he'd never leave me. I spent the whole night searching. I hollered his name so loud, they must have heard me in the next county." Now, Mitch's tone was flat, but it didn't disguise his anguish. "I knew Harley was somewhere hurt, waitin' for me to rescue him."

Royce kept her eyes open wide to hold back the tears. Where were his parents, for God's sakes? She ached with a pain more intense than anything she'd ever known, experiencing the heart-wrenching torment of a lonely little boy as he traipsed through the dark woods desperately searching for the dog he cherished. Crying. Brokenhearted.

"On the second day I went by myself to the nearby farms. I came to Slocum's Chicken Farm last. The farmer came out — a big burly guy with a long beard like they wore in the Old Testament. 'That yore dog, boy? That ole coon hound with the long ears?'

" 'Yessir,' I said, proudly. 'Harley's my dog.'

" 'Hoo-ee,' the farmer said, grabbin' me by the arm. 'Lemme show you what happens to egg-suck dogs.' He dragged me behind the barn."

Mitch hesitated and Royce closed her eyes, knowing whatever Mitch had seen behind that barn was a sight so terrible, no child should ever have seen it. Harley wasn't just any dog. He'd

396

loved Mitch. Quite possibly the only love Mitch had as a child.

"The farmer had nailed his four paws to the barn, and his ears were high above his head, pinned to the wood with a single nail. That bastard had crucified him. Harley was alive — but barely.

"I called to him and he finally managed to open one eye. He looked at me, pleading for help and whimpering . . . just like Jenny. He was begging me to save him, but I couldn't reach him."

Royce's stomach roiled spasmodically. She'd never heard of anything so barbaric. She could actually feel the heart of an eight-year-old beating in double-time, desperate to rescue his beloved pet. But helpless.

" 'Where you been, boy?' the farmer yelled. 'Don't you know that's what happens to egg-suck dogs in these parts? He's stayin' nailed to the barn until he dies.' The old goat tucked his thumbs in the pockets of his bib overalls. 'If'n you want to save him, you'll have to shoot him, boy.'

"I couldn't bear to leave Harley nailed to the barn to die in the hot sun. Already flies were all over his wounds and his tongue was black and swollen from lack of water. I said, 'Git me a gun.' "

Tears rolled down her cheeks in a silent parade, Mitch's story shattering her composure. Dear God, what had that farmer done to an innocent child?

"He brought me a shotgun. I'd never fired a

gun. I didn't know I was standing way too close. I didn't know the kick would knock me on my ass.

" 'Good-bye, Harley,' I said. 'I'll never forget you.'

"Harley whimpered. It was the most pitiful sound I've ever heard. Even now, all these years later, I can still hear his tortured cry, and see him hanging there, helpless. Suffering the way no living being should ever be made to suffer.

" 'I love you, Harley. I'll always love you.' I closed my eyes and fired. When I opened them, I was on the ground — covered with Harley's blood and bits of his fur. All that was left of him was his four paws hammered to the barn." Mitch's voice kept dropping with each word. "And his long ears — coated in blood — swinging from the single nail."

An explosive gasp echoed through the room, but Royce hardly realized the sound came from her own lips. Instead, as if she'd been transported back in time, she suffered the heartfelt torment and pure horror of an innocent young boy, knocked flat by the force of the shot, having killed the dog he loved so dearly.

His only birthday present. A gift from God.

23

"Oh, Mitch," she cried, throwing her arms around him just as she'd longed to do. "I would have killed that farmer."

Unexpectedly, the veterinarian emerged, his greens splattered with Jenny's blood. Royce held her breath, her arm circling Mitch. He had a much bigger emotional investment in Jenny than she'd realized until now. Somehow the dog represented a link with his past, a time in his life when he'd found something to love, only to lose it so tragically.

"How's Jenny?" Mitch asked the doctor, his tone level, but Royce detected subtle clues others might have missed. Mitch was mentally bracing himself, dead certain he'd lost Jenny the way he'd lost Harley.

"She's going to make it," the vet announced with a satisfied smile.

"Wonderful!" Royce hugged Mitch and he squeezed her so hard, her breath was trapped in her lungs.

"Finally" — he smiled, a rare, unguarded smile — "*we* get a break."

We. He'd said "we" as if they were truly a couple. Now wasn't the time to tell him that she'd been recognized. With luck no one would call Tobias Ingeblatt. Anyway, was it a crime to be walking with your attorney on a summer day?

"Jenny's going to have to stay here a few days. She has several broken ribs and her leg is fractured in two places."

"But she'll recover fully, won't she?" Mitch asked.

"Yes, but she's going to need lots of care after I release her."

"She'll get it," Royce spoke up, letting Mitch know he could count on her to take care of Jenny while he was out of town.

They left the clinic, but Mitch didn't say anything all the way home. Royce couldn't talk either. She couldn't shake the image of a young boy lying in the dirt staring up at those two ears.

Having killed the thing he loved most.

At home they showered in silence, then Royce tossed their bloodstained clothes into the washer while Mitch settled himself on the sofa in the living room without bothering to turn on the light. Why was he so moody? she asked herself. His initial euphoria at hearing Jenny would live had evaporated. Was he upset that he'd told her about his past?

Perhaps. But it seemed even more likely that he was somehow reliving that past. After talking about it, the horrible incident had brought back a wealth of unhappy memories. Maybe he was thinking about his parents — not just Harley.

Royce had no idea what to say and since Mitch seemed to want to be alone, she went into the kitchen. She peered into the refrigerator.

"Not much here," she said out loud, then realized she was automatically talking to Jenny even though she wasn't there.

She took out tomatoes and celery. Tomato soup was going to be the best she could do tonight. Her telephone rang. It was Talia, but Royce didn't have the energy to talk.

She should be grateful that Val and Talia called faithfully every evening to give her moral support, but lately the strain of not being able to discuss the case was eroding their friendship. How much small talk could she make?

Her friends seemed to sense the change in her too. They'd pulled inward; neither of them shared her private life with Royce the way she once had.

Later when she called Mitch to dinner, he gazed at the bowl of homemade tomato soup as if it had ants swimming in it.

"You should eat something." Had she really said that? She sounded like his mother, for God's sakes.

"I hate tomato soup," he said softly. Too softly. He didn't sound anything like himself.

"No wonder you pick the tomatoes out of the salad," she said, trying to keep her tone upbeat. "Aren't you hungry?"

"Let's order pizza." He called Godfather's for his usual order, then left the kitchen.

Her phone rang again, keeping her from following him, which was just as well because she didn't know how to comfort him. This time it was Val. There was nothing she could say to console her either. Talia had told Royce that David was dying, but how could Royce ease Val's pain? She tried a few platitudes and hung up, feeling shamefully inadequate.

When the phone rang for the third time, she almost screamed. She didn't want to talk to anyone, but she answered it, hoping it was Wally. She didn't know how to reach him and planned to call the paper to see if they knew his number, but she wanted to wait until Mitch wasn't around.

"I tried to get you all day." This from Brent.

Royce resisted the urge to hang up. "I was over at my place all day packing." Heavens, she was getting to be a proficient liar. "I'm going to have to sell my house to pay for my legal fees."

"If I'd known you were there, I'd have come and helped."

Why had she opened her mouth, she asked, knowing tomorrow she would be there, sorting and packing. She didn't need Brent to show up. "Where are you?" She changed the subject. "I hear music."

"Mother's having a dinner party. I had to come. I just wanted to check in and be sure you're not too lonely. Are you all by yourself?"

"Of course. I'm in a new safe house, you know." Amazing, how good she was getting at lying. "In the Haight-Ashbury area."

"The Haight's being rehabbed a lot. Some of the places are nice," Brent said. There was a noise in the background. "Darling, I've got to go. Mother's about to serve dinner. Should I call you later?"

"No." Had she said that too quickly? "I'm exhausted from all that packing. I'm going to bed soon."

He promised to call tomorrow and they hung up. She gave Mitch space and stayed in the kitchen cleaning. When she couldn't think of another thing to do, she took the trash and headed for the Dumpster in the alley. As she lifted the heavy lid and tossed in the sack, headlights hit her in the face and she quickly turned away. Why hadn't she remembered Godfather's Pizza always delivered to Mitch's back door? There was never any place to park on the street.

She had no choice but to march ahead of the young man delivering the pizza and hope he hadn't recognized her. He didn't look like the type who'd read a paper — even the *Evening Outrage*.

"Mitch," she called, opening the back door. Oliver lunged toward the opening; she pounced on the tubby tabby before he escaped. But not before she'd stood nose to nose with the delivery boy.

"I know you. You're —"

"We're working," she said with as much authority as she could muster, considering she was standing barefoot in shorts holding a fat cat bent on scratching her eyes out. She spun around and saw Mitch coming toward them.

What else could go wrong today? she asked herself as Mitch paid the delivery boy. Mitch didn't mention the incident but he had to have heard what the delivery boy said. She didn't have the heart to tell him that several people had recognized her today. Undoubtedly Tobias Ingeblatt would get wind of this and do his best to smear Mitch's reputation.

Mitch ate part of one slice of pizza before returning to the dark living room. She put the pizza away before Oliver could help himself and joined Mitch on the sofa. She scooted close and lifted his arm, draping it across her shoulders.

More than anything she wanted him to tell her all about his past. She wanted him to trust her enough to share things with her. "Mitch," she said and he turned to her. "You did the right thing. You had to kill Harley."

There was a long silence. Finally, he said, "When you love something enough, you'll destroy it before you let it suffer."

She wanted to say more, but couldn't find the words. Snuggling closer, she tried to physically telegraph her support; Mitch didn't seem to notice. His eyes were on the twinkling lights of the bay, but she'd bet anything his mind was preoccupied with memories of his youth.

And the dog for whom there had been no happy ending.

She looked up at him, his distinct profile shadowed by the dim light, and she realized, she'd never met anyone remotely like him. His lone-wolf mentality concealed layer after layer of his personality, aspects of him she'd yet to uncover. But she had to wait. No matter how much she longed to ask him about his past, he'd tell her when the time was right.

It was almost one o'clock and they were still in the dark living room watching the lights on the bay, when Royce heard pounding on the back door. The police, she thought with a surge of panic. Couldn't be. She hadn't done anything wrong.

Mitch expelled a sharp breath, ruffling the dark hair across his forehead. "It's Jason."

"How do you know?"

He rose. "The kid got home today. His mother has a new baby. That'll mean a hyper daddy and more rules."

"I'll go upstairs."

"What's the point? Jason already knows about you."

A minute later Mitch escorted a very sullen Jason into the living room. Despite his own problems Mitch was listening intently as Jason complained. It took Mitch almost an hour to explain why heavy metal music wasn't good for babies.

Did she really want kids? she asked herself. Would she be this patient with a selfish teenager?

She wasn't certain, but she wanted the chance to try. And she wasn't going to get it in prison.

"You'd better spend the night here," Mitch said, his exhaustion now showing in his voice. "I'll call your mother and explain."

"No!" Jason shouted as Mitch stood.

Royce spoke up. "Your mother will worry, won't she?"

"Yeah," Jason sullenly conceded.

Royce encouraged him with a smile. "Let's call her."

"The man won't let me spend the night."

"Who? Your stepfather?"

"Yeah, he's got shit for brains." There was something in his voice that told Royce there was more to this than Jason was telling. "He's always dissin' everyone."

She leaned closer. "What do you mean?"

"He hates Mitch." Jason directed this bombshell to his half-laced tennis shoes.

Royce glanced at Mitch but couldn't tell what he was thinking. She almost screamed that Mitch had done so damn much for Jason that his stepfather should be grateful, but somehow she kept her voice level. "Why?"

For a moment she didn't think he was going to answer, but he finally whispered, "He thinks — he says Mitch must be a fag" — now his confession was coming out in a breathless rush — "to want to spend time with me."

"That's ridiculous." She ventured a glance at Mitch; as usual his face was expressionless. "He's trying to give you the help he never got at your age."

"I know," Jason sheepishly acknowledged. "Try'n tell that to the man."

Royce stood up. "I'm going to fix your stepfather. I'm calling your mother and telling her that I'm Mitch's girlfriend." Mitch started to interrupt, but Royce raised her hand to silence him. "I'm not giving my name, but I'll say that I'm spending the night here and we're putting Jason on the sofa. That way she won't worry — and your stepfather can eat his words."

While Mitch went upstairs for linens, she called Jason's mother, then hung up, satisfied she'd done the right thing. The telephone rang and she reached for the wall phone she'd just used before she realized it was her portable telephone ringing.

She checked the kitchen clock. Two thirty-three. Not even Brent called this late.

"Hello?" She hoped she sounded groggy, as if the call had awakened her.

There was a strange noise that might have been a cough or someone placing his hand over his mouth to cover a laugh.

Obviously a prank. Obviously a wrong number.

III

Justice in America

24

Royce hesitated, standing in the entrance of the Starlight Bistro and seeing Val and Talia had already arrived and were waiting for her at a table on the terrace overlooking the bay. Their favorite café — scene of countless happy lunches to celebrate birthdays or just to get together — was sheltered from the summer sun by a leafy canopy of English ivy. Multihued impatiens grew in huge clay pots around the perimeter of the terrace.

How would this reunion go? It was the first time she'd seen them since the day of her hearing when they'd come to the courthouse. They'd been friends for years but doubts had subtly edged their way into Royce's mind.

Had their friendship merely been an illusion? Did one of them really hate her enough to ruin her life?

When it came right down to it, she trusted Mitch more than anyone else, but occasionally she even had suspicions about him. Was there something in his mysterious past that affected her? With the trial coming closer each day a rising sensation of panic engulfed her like a swimmer who sees the shore but knows he's going to drown before reaching it.

"Royce." Talia raced up and gave Royce a bear hug.

Several heads turned and Royce realized she'd been recognized. It didn't matter, she reminded herself. Mitch had allowed her to join her friends for lunch before going to his office for an afternoon session of trial preparations.

She was dressed in a beige suit and black silk blouse — very sedate, slimming, professional. If Ingeblatt spotted her, he could hardly tack a sexy label on this image.

"Talia," Royce said, shocked by the tears limning her friend's eyes. "It's great to see you."

She'd genuinely missed Talia. They'd been friends who often competed for the same boy, but they'd shared so much over the years — the good times and the bad — that it was hard for Royce to imagine Talia doing anything to hurt her. Inwardly, Royce sighed, profoundly depressed. Did she want to live in a world where you couldn't trust your family or friends?

Talia hooked one long strand of hair behind her ear in her so-familiar gesture of self-consciousness. "I've missed you."

The emotion in Talia's voice brought a hot sting of tears behind Royce's eyes. In spite of her suspicions she was truly glad to see Talia. "I missed you too." Arm in arm they walked to the table where Val waited.

Val looked tired, Royce decided, but somehow she appeared happier, more at peace, than ever before. Val rose and embraced Royce in her usual restrained way, not quite the full-fledged hug that Talia had given her.

Once Royce would have attributed Val's reserve to her relationship with her parents, who never showed their emotions, but now she wondered. Was Wally right? Did Val secretly hate her?

"You look terrific," Val said as they sat down. "You've lost a lot of weight."

"Close to twenty pounds," Royce answered. She'd stopped dieting weeks ago, but she continued to lose weight despite eating the Oreo cookies that Mitch never failed to tease her about.

"Not another pound," Val cautioned. "You're far too thin."

A silence followed that none of them seemed to know how to fill. Mercifully the waiter, who introduced himself as Toby and acted as if he were going to become their best friend, gave them menus and explained in excruciating detail how the specials of the day were prepared.

"How's it going?" Val asked, her amber hair gleaming in the summer sunshine filtering through the leafy ivy covering the lattice roof.

Royce shrugged; Mitch had allowed her to come today, but he'd emphasized the importance of not talking about the trial. No one knew about the informant having Royce's key or the Italian count's true identity. Nor did they know Mitch

413

was counting on finding Ward's mistress.

"I spent yesterday packing so I can sell the house," Royce said, thankful she'd found a subject she was free to discuss.

It had been a long, lonely Sunday. Mitch had taken Jason home at dawn, then caught a flight to Chicago. With Jenny still recuperating at the vet's, Royce had slipped into her house unnoticed and continued the packing she'd begun earlier. After spending the day alone it had been almost midnight when she'd returned to Mitch's.

"It's terrible that you have to sell," Talia sympathized.

"Do you think you'll get much for it?" Val asked, always more practical than Talia. "The market's so depressed right now."

"I don't have a choice." She was even selling what little jewelry she had. Her thorough search of the house hadn't uncovered her mother's missing charm bracelet. Luckily, Mitch had filed an insurance claim. She should receive the money soon.

The settlement wasn't much but she needed every cent. Mitch and Paul weren't charging her, but outside expenses were mounting at an alarming rate.

"I see your front door is still boarded up," Val said.

"I'm going to order a new one. I've put it off because Papa's stained glass panel is in the old one. It wasn't a work of art, but we'd made it together. Another door won't be the same, but the panel can't be repaired."

Royce's despondency must have shown in her voice; another uncomfortable silence followed. Royce steered the subject away from herself to a topic no more upbeat. "How's your brother?"

"David doesn't have long to live now," Val said. "I'm taking a leave from work to be with him until the end."

Talia unlooped the strand of hair from behind her ear, then looped it back over her ear again, a sure sign she was terribly nervous. Why? Royce wondered. Was it because she'd been the one to tell Royce about Val's reconciliation with her brother?

Once Val would have told Royce herself. Royce had been a little hurt, but decided Val was closer to her mysterious new boyfriend than she was to Royce. Another casualty of her situation, Royce thought with a renewed sense that her life — even if she were acquitted — would never be the same.

"This must be very difficult for you," Royce said to Val, ignoring the warning look from Talia, who was far too nervous to ask Val about Trevor and David, "— after all that's happened."

"You mean facing everyone again?" Val asked, the picture of composure.

Royce realized Val had changed. The emotional tide pool of anger had vanished, replaced by an inner strength Royce envied. In many ways Val was facing a situation as devastating as her own. And handling it much better.

Royce opted for a more direct approach. "Is seeing your ex-husband difficult?"

"At first seeing Trevor was painful, but seeing my brother was even worse. I had to let go of my negative feelings. I came to realize that everyone makes mistakes. Everyone."

For some reason Val glanced at Talia, but Talia quickly looked away. "David loves me. He never did it to deliberately hurt me. In fact, wanting to spare me pain only made things worse."

Royce thought about Mitch. Little by little she'd let go of her negative feelings about him like grains of sand slipping through her fingers. But in her tightly clutched palm she still held a few remaining granules of bitterness.

Buoyed by guilt, that bitterness was hard to dismiss. David had deceived his sister out of love. What Mitch had done to her father had been spawned by pure ambition.

Still, she realized she should forgive him. Who knew how terrible his past was? It had molded him into an iron-willed individual who didn't live by the rules. He made his own rules.

At her father's funeral Mitch had apologized for what he'd done. Why couldn't she accept his apology?

"Well" — Talia paused to clear her throat — "guess what?" She didn't wait for them to attempt a response. She tossed her hair over her shoulder with one hand and toyed with her spoon with the other. "Caroline Rambeau dumped the count."

"Really?" Royce wondered if Caroline had discovered his claim to royalty was more bogus than Anastasia's had been.

"Caroline and Brent are an item again," Talia informed them.

"Are you surprised?"

Royce waited for Talia's answer to Val's incisive question. A large part of Royce's suspicions about Talia centered on how her friend really felt about Brent. When Brent had asked Royce out, Talia had encouraged her to go, but since she'd been arrested Talia had spent a lot of time with Brent. Was she really trying to help Royce as Talia claimed, or did she have another motive entirely?

"No," Talia said emphatically. "I wasn't surprised that Brent is seeing Caroline. The Farenholts have always wanted Brent to marry her."

Royce listened to detect a note of jealousy in Talia's voice, but heard nothing but a factual statement without any emotional overtones. She turned her thoughts to Brent. He hadn't called last night, but he had called the previous night, Saturday, from his parents' home.

Obviously, Caroline had been there. Had that been the night they'd resumed their relationship? Was that why he hadn't called Sunday evening as he'd promised?

Not that she gave a damn about Brent getting back together with Caroline, but she didn't want him to testify. And while he was still calling her, insisting he cared about her, she could influence him not to take the stand. But now, who knew what would happen?

"Does that mean they're engaged?" Val inquired.

"No," Talia replied as Royce noticed a flash of blue at the door of the restaurant. The police. A ripple of fear shimmied up her spine.

"Caroline is upset about breaking up with the count. Brent's helping her get through this crisis."

"Some crisis," Royce said, her eye on the cops who were speaking with the maître d'. The jolt of panic escalated; she struggled to remain calm, rational.

Had her experience left her permanently damaged? Why was she afraid? She hadn't done anything to worry about. There could be a thousand reasons why the police were here.

"Of course, Brent's just being kind to Caroline," Talia replied, raking her fingers through her hair. "You know how compassionate he is."

"Where was he when Royce needed him?" snapped Val.

For once Talia didn't hedge. "It surprised him. He was embarrassed. When he realized —"

"It took him long enough," Val cut in. "We had to hire an attorney, remember?"

"Brent didn't mean —"

Royce refused to let a jerk like Brent cause an argument and spoil her first outing in weeks. "It doesn't matter. I don't care about Brent. I don't think I ever really did. I wanted a home, my own family."

Talia quickly agreed. "He's not your type. Not at all."

Royce's eyes were still on the policemen. Now they were angling their way through the tables. She looked directly into Talia's deep brown eyes, striving to concentrate on their conversation and ignore the police.

"But I have to admit Brent was wonderful when Tobias Ingeblatt published that photo of us. He took the blame for arranging our meeting. He could have dodged the press and let them call me a femme fatale, but he didn't. I'm sure his parents weren't thrilled about it either."

Royce looked up and saw the policemen were coming closer to their table. Fear, raw and primitive, overwhelmed her. Why were they here?

Talia smiled, her expression affectionate. "Brent's always so supportive. That's why I —"

The policemen stopped beside their table. There was an unnatural silence in the café, like the eerie stillness between a jagged bolt of lightning and the inevitable crash of thunder. Every eye in the café was on them.

The taller policeman spoke first. "Royce Anne Winston?"

No one at the table answered. The silence echoed throughout the restaurant. Not even a tinkle of an ice cube could be heard. Finally Royce raised her head and faced the officers with a bravado she certainly didn't feel.

"I'm Royce Anne Winston."

"You're under arrest for the murder of Caroline Rambeau."

Royce stretched out on the cot and stared at the cockroach creeping across the ceiling above her prison bunk. An overwhelming sense of hopelessness engulfed her. Why me? Who would want to do this to me? As usual there wasn't any answer.

What evidence could they possibly have? She'd never been to Caroline's home. She'd barely known the woman. Still, they wouldn't have arrested her for murder without some damning evidence.

Why hadn't she heard from Mitch? Royce wondered. It had been almost twelve hours since her arrest. So far only an associate from Mitch's office had come by, and he'd been confused, uncertain what they were going to do.

With Mitch in Chicago the defense team didn't seem to know how to handle the situation. Or maybe they didn't care, she thought. They knew a lost cause when they saw one.

And she was a lost cause. How could she beat a murder charge when she didn't have an alibi for the last thirty-two hours?

Since Mitch and Jason had left the house Sunday morning, Royce had been alone. Not even Jenny had been with her as she'd packed up the contents of her parents' home. She'd been so careful — coming and going — no one had seen her.

Buck up, Royce. Remember, you'll never walk alone. But now her father's comforting words did little to console her. Anger welled up inside her, intensifying with each thought. If only she understood why she'd been targeted.

And why Caroline Rambeau had been murdered.

Her money, she reasoned. Caroline was just a few months from inheriting a trust that would make her one of the richest women in the country. Ward Farenholt had been executor of that trust for years.

The money had to be the key. What had Paul Talbott told her? Most crimes fell into two categories: crimes of passion and crimes of greed.

If only she could talk to Mitch, she'd have a better idea of what to do. He hadn't deserted her, had he? True, he liked to be on the winning side, but surely he'd stick with her. Or had she become a political liability?

Some inner sensitivity that she didn't quite comprehend told her Mitch had suffered loss and betrayal. He understood what she was going through and would never desert her. Still, so many terrible things had happened that she couldn't help worrying he might toss her aside.

This seemed out of character — but then did she really know Mitch? Once she would have sworn Talia and Val were above reproach, but now she questioned their motives. God help her, she even wondered about Wally. When it came right down to it, she could rely only on herself.

"That's my bunk." A short Vietnamese woman interrupted Royce's thoughts, speaking with a heavy accent.

Royce looked down from the top bunk at the three Vietnamese women who'd come into the cell just after she had. Small but wiry, they stood shoulder to shoulder, itching to take her on. The Vietnamese gangs were notorious for their brutality.

But beneath Royce's debilitating sense of hopelessness rage simmered raw and primitive. She was sick of everyone ganging up on her. She'd had enough. Now was the time to fight back and she didn't give a damn if they beat her senseless.

No one — but no one — was going to take advantage of her. The spark of anger — in an instant — became full-blown fury.

She swung down from the top bunk as if she were capitulating to their demands. At the last second she kicked up one foot and rammed it into the gut of the woman Royce instinctively knew was the leader. The woman collapsed, doubled over in pain. Royce grabbed another woman and dragged her over to the toilet in the corner. She shoved her head into the bowl.

The third woman jumped on Royce's back, her fingers clawing at Royce's eyes. But Royce refused to let go, banging the woman's head against the rim of the toilet bowl. For an instant Royce was surprised at her own strength and the depth of her fury, barely recognizing the primal urge to survive.

Finally, the woman screamed, "Stop."

Royce let go and the woman slumped to the floor. Whirling around, hardly conscious of the blood dripping from the scratch on her cheek, Royce charged the woman who'd been on her back, knocking her against the cell's metal bars.

A surge of adrenaline gave her unusual strength; a riptide of past injustices spurred her to fight until her tormentors were vanquished. Or she died. At this point Royce didn't care which.

"Hey! What's going on in there?" called a guard from the cell door.

Royce let go of the woman and drew back, the sudden interruption stunning her. What was she doing? She'd never attacked anyone like this, but her animal instincts cautioned her. Inside the gray-bar Hilton — as the prisoners called jail — only the strong survived.

She kept the side of her face with the scratch away from the guard. "Nothing's happening."

The guard looked at them suspiciously, but the Vietnamese women didn't contradict Royce. They all knew the rules of the jungle. Snitches were as good as dead.

The guard walked away and Royce turned to the three women, who were now huddled together on one bunk, looking at her as if she were crazy. "Leave me alone or I'll beat the hell out of you."

Mitch checked his watch. Almost six. Jesus H. Christ. This was unbelievably late. Most judges knocked off at four. The expert witness the pros-

423

ecution had called was boring as hell. Even the jury foreman was nodding off. It was a dead cinch that Mitch would win this case — after they waded through days of tedious testimony and a parade of experts about as interesting as tapioca.

Toying with his pencil Mitch detected someone staring at him. He eased his chair sideways and gazed across the courtroom. Paul.

What the hell was he doing here? Jenny, Mitch thought, then quickly changed his mind. No. Royce. Something had happened to Royce. Something terrible.

It was the longest twenty minutes of his life until the witness completed his testimony, and the judge adjourned the court. Mitch rushed to the back of the courtroom. Paul put his hand on Mitch's shoulder, and he was positive Royce was dead. What else could bring Paul halfway across the country and make him look this grim?

"Royce has been arrested for Caroline Rambeau's murder."

It took a second for the words to register. "Caroline Rambeau? Who'd want to kill her and try to pin it on Royce?"

"Beats me." Paul jammed his fists in his trouser pockets. "I've always felt there was something strange about this case."

Mitch refused to believe this was happening. "They can't have any proof."

"I haven't talked to the detective in charge, but I hear they have physical evidence implicating Royce."

Mitch turned away, damning his own arrogance. Early on he'd been dead certain he could beat the charges and save Royce. But day by day he'd discovered his pride had been assaulted by an unknown enemy — one bent on destroying Royce. He'd saved numerous felons, a few murderers, and even a starving cougar. Hell, he'd pioneered the challenge to DNA.

But he couldn't save an innocent woman. He'd isolated her, setting her up, making sure no one knew where she was and no one saw her. No alibi.

"Paul," Mitch said, realizing his voice was barely above a whisper, "see what you can find out."

"I will . . . but —"

Paul didn't have to spell it out to Mitch. He knew the truth. He'd gambled and lost.

25

Paul ducked under the yellow and black crime scene tape at Caroline Rambeau's Nob Hill home and yelled, "Yo, Wilson, you there?"

"Yeah, in the living room. Come in."

After Paul had told Mitch about Royce's arrest, he'd returned to the airport, where the jet he'd chartered flew him back to San Francisco in record time. Shit! He'd never seen Mitch as traumatized as he was when he heard the news.

That's why Paul had flown halfway across the country to tell him personally. It didn't take a rocket scientist to realize Mitch was nuts about Royce. And Paul had known exactly what Mitch would tell him to do: Throw everything you've got into this case.

Paul had to confess he hadn't seen this one coming. Was he losing his touch? Who would have thought Caroline Rambeau would be murdered? Or that the police would find Royce's prints at the scene as well as other evidence she'd been there?

The perp was clever, Paul granted, but somewhere he'd made a mistake. And Paul wouldn't give up until he found it. There was no perfect crime.

Inside the marble foyer that spoke of money — lots of old money — Paul whisked out a book of matches. Christ, nothing, but nothing, smelled like death. The sulfur from matches helped mask the odor of decaying flesh, but not much.

He couldn't help remembering the last time he'd been here. There hadn't been any hint of trouble. How wrong he'd been.

He walked into the living room where evidence technicians were combing the carpet, using hand-held mini-vacs that sucked everything loose into special filters. Later the bits of hair and fibers would be analyzed as possible evidence.

The outline of Caroline Rambeau's body had

been drawn in red chalk on the arctic white carpet, but a bloodstain covered an area two feet on either side of where her body had been.

Whoa! That's a lot of blood.

A charge of excitement jolted Paul. He hated to admit it, but he found murder stimulating. The ultimate crime. Was there anything more precious than life? No. And for a detective nothing was more satisfying than finding a killer. It was a challenge he missed.

Tom Wilson was the homicide detective in charge of the investigation. When Paul had called him and told him to meet him at the scene, Tom had readily agreed. He didn't have to be reminded he'd be in jail if Paul had rolled over on him.

But Paul hadn't told anyone that Tom had taken the money during the drug bust that had cost Paul his job. He figured Tom had more than paid for his crime. He'd taken the money to help his kid, but the boy had died of leukemia anyway.

"Over here," Tom called to Paul.

He crossed the plush carpet, his feet sinking in as if he were walking on a sponge. He came up to Tom, who had the murder book spread out on a card table marked SFPD. The blue binder contained the chronological record of the investigation and the various reports from the coroner and the crime techs.

"Who discovered the body?" Paul inquired.

"Brent and Wade Farenholt. Caroline was supposed to come to dinner. When she didn't show or answer the phone, Eleanor sent them over."

"And the last person to see her alive?"

"The Farenholts. She'd been at their home."

Paul mulled over the information. The statistics were overwhelming that the last person to see the victim alive or the person who discovered the body was the perp. But there were exceptions. So far, nothing about this case followed the rules.

"What happens to the fortune Caroline was about to inherit?" Paul asked.

"Some distant cousin living in Rome is about to become a very rich lady."

"Rome, huh?" Paul decided to take another look at the phony Italian count. "May I see the photos?"

Tom took a stack of crime scene photos out of the special pouch in the back of the murder book. Even in death Caroline was exceptionally beautiful. She wore an ivory peignoir set trimmed in marabou fur with matching mules. She'd been shot in the abdomen and the blood showed up in the photos with astonishing clarity. He could just imagine the jury gagging.

"Here's how we figure it," Tom said, obviously anxious to show off his skills. "The victim let in the perp. No sign of forced entry."

Paul had already noted that, but didn't point it out. He also noticed Wilson's years of training kept him professional, referring to the killer as "the perp." The papers had trumpeted Royce's arrest, but to the police she was innocent until proven guilty.

Paul intended to be the one to clear her name.

"Caroline was comfortable enough to have a Coke with the perp," Wilson continued, pointing to one photo showing two Coke cans on a small round table. "They sat in those wing chairs, chatting."

Paul glanced across the room at the two white brocade wing chairs and the antique table between them. It was exactly where he'd sat when he'd interviewed Caroline, pretending to be a reporter from *Town and Country*. He examined the photo more closely. "No glasses? They were drinking out of cans?"

"Yep. We got the perp's prints on one can."

"Rich, classy women like Caroline don't serve guests drinks in cans."

Wilson shrugged off the observation. "They must have argued. Caroline Rambeau stood up and the perp shot her here." Wilson pointed to his gut, which slopped over a belt that was already on the last hole.

Paul nodded, not because he agreed with Wilson's scenario, but because he knew Abigail Carnivali, like the media, would build her case on the jealousy theory. The women had fought over Brent Farenholt.

"Were Royce Winston's prints found on anything but the Coke can?"

"Nah." Tom shook his head. "We cut the pearl buttons off the victim's gown. We're cookin' them."

Paul doubted that the heat chamber filled with

Super Glue would reveal any latent prints. The killer was too careful to make an obvious slip.

"Now, this is the good part." Wilson chuckled and Paul winced. He'd almost forgotten the gallows humor that was a cop's way of dealing with all the shit they saw every day.

"The shot wasn't fatal. But the perp sat in that chair" — Tom pointed to one of the wing chairs — "drank a Coke, and waited for Caroline to die."

"Jeee-sus." Paul whistled. "A wacko."

"Wait. It gets better." Wilson pulled out another photo. "The perp moved this phone close to Caroline. See, it's on the floor not far from her head."

Paul looked at the photo and saw the phone had been moved from the sofa table, its cord stretched taut to position it close to Caroline.

"You see, the perp wanted her to suffer, to know she was going to die." Wilson shook his head, disgusted. "The phone was so close that if only she'd dialed 9-1-1, she would have lived."

Paul turned away. For some reason he imagined Val sprawled on the floor at the mercy of some psycho. He managed to keep his voice steady. "How long did it take for her to die?"

"Coroner figures she lived close to three hours."

"What kind of a person does something like this?" Paul directed the question to himself. Serial killers were charmers. Mass murderers were sullen, antisocial. But what about this killer? What kind of a person was he looking for?

"Unfuckingbelievable." Paul leafed through the photos once more. "What about the bruise on Caroline's wrist?"

Beside each subject a ruler had been placed to compare size and scale. This bruise was very large and had unusual curved edges. The vibrant purple color meant the victim had been alive when the injury had occurred.

"No sign of a fight. The bruise doesn't have anything to do with the crime."

Paul walked across the room and borrowed a magnifying glass from one of the evidence techs. He took a close look at the bruise, taking his time to examine it from several angles.

"Check that bruise again, Wilson. I think you'll find Caroline tried to trick her killer. She pretended to be dead — then made a grab for the phone. The perp stepped on her wrist. I'm willing to bet the perp stood on it until she died."

Paul took the elevator to the fifth floor condominium Gian Viscotti was leasing. The building wasn't far from Caroline's home. And like the murdered woman's building Gian's building was tasteful, a reminder of generations of inherited wealth, an echelon of society that welcomed only their brethren.

Before he knocked on the double doors of Gian's condo, Paul checked his watch. Seven minutes flat. He hadn't been walking fast, but that's how long it had taken him to get here from Caroline's. Late at night Gian could easily have made it between the two buildings without being noticed.

The tall man who answered Paul's knock was even more handsome than the photographs Paul had seen. Dark hair, dark brooding eyes. Italian-looking, all right, especially for a guy from Dalhart, Texas.

"Yes?" Gian said with the merest hint of an Italian accent.

Paul flashed his ID card that identified him as a private detective. He closed it with a snap before Gian could look closely, a trick that often deceived people into thinking he was a policeman. "I need to ask you a few questions about Caroline Rambeau."

"I already gave a statement," Gian said, but he stepped aside, allowing Paul to enter and quickly note the expensive furniture, the clusters of family photographs in sterling silver frames, and the crystal ashtray overflowing with ground-out half-smoked cigarettes.

"I'm just here to clarify a few details." Paul took out a small notebook he kept in his jacket pocket for occasions such as this. People expected you to take notes — it made them more comfortable. "You and the deceased had just terminated your relationship, correct?"

"Yes," Gian admitted, gesturing for Paul to take a seat.

Paul sat and studied Gian's clothes. Where would you buy white lizard loafers? And why would you? Well, they did complete his Continental look: navy blazer with a red scarf flamboyantly tucked in the pocket and white linen slacks with creases as sharp as a stiletto.

Gian whisked a gold cigarette case out of his pocket and lit a cigarette. He took a deep draw and blew the smoke over his shoulder away from Paul before responding. "Caroline and I decided to date other people."

"Whose idea was that?"

"Hers," Gian reluctantly admitted.

"When was that?"

"Friday afternoon."

Paul scribbled a note to remind himself to buy some flowers to cheer up Val. "Did you see her after that?"

"No." Gian ground out the half-smoked cigarette and tossed it into the mound of cigarettes in the crystal ashtray.

The guy was polished, Paul granted. Just a touch of an Italian accent, not overdone. Outrageously handsome, but still masculine. The kind of guy likely to land himself an heiress. But why was he so nervous that he was chain-smoking?

"Did Caroline call it quits because she found out your real name is Billy Joe Williams and you haven't got a pot to piss in?"

There were several seconds of total, astonished silence. This was information the police didn't yet have, so whoever had done the initial interview couldn't have hit Gian with this.

"No," Gian said quietly, defeat in his voice. "I'd been pressing Caroline to marry me. She kept putting me off . . . like she did every other man who was interested in her."

Paul mentally rolled the dice, knowing there was something more. He wanted to get it out of Gian before the police did. It was a point of pride now; he wanted to nail the perp himself. After all, he'd been working on this case long before Caroline's murder.

"Look, I don't care who you really are. If you didn't kill Caroline, it doesn't matter, but I have to know exactly what your relationship with her was like."

Gian took his time, lighting yet another cigarette and blowing a stream of smoke toward the ceiling. "We dated two, three times a week for months, but Caroline was always very cool, very distant. That's not the reaction I usually get from women, so I was captivated — for a while. Then I stopped calling her. Why bother with a woman who won't even sleep with you?"

Paul had to admit it must have come as a shock to this phony Italian stallion. How many women could resist a chance to hop in the sack with him?

"Then she called and invited me to the auction. She said she missed me. We were having a good time until the robbery. Then everyone was upset and Caroline insisted on going home."

"Did you put the earrings in Royce Winston's purse?"

"Of course not. Why would I?"

"I thought maybe one of the Farenholts asked you to."

Gian shook his head. "No. I liked them, though. They treated me like gold. Ward even called after Caroline and I broke up and said how sorry he was."

Paul studied the cigarette burning between Gian's fingers, his nails manicured and buffed to a high gloss. Could he have been so angry with Caroline that he'd wanted her to die a slow, excruciatingly painful death?

"Was sex a problem after you and Caroline got together again?"

Gian lifted both shoulders in an angry shrug. "We slept together — a few times — but that's it."

"You were willing to put up with that?"

"When a lady has a lot of money, you're willing to put up with crap. Anyway, I thought she was frigid. It wasn't until I got the big kiss-off that I found out the truth. She was in love with someone else."

"Who?"

"She didn't say, but I knew." Gian stood and jammed his clenched fists into his trouser pockets. "I was a fool. She always had this thing about Brent Farenholt. She always wanted to hang around the Farenholts so she could be with him."

Forty-six hours. Royce had waited the long hours without sleeping, her eyes constantly drawn to the hall clock. In two hours they'd have to charge her or let her go. What evidence could they possibly have? She didn't have an answer just as she didn't have an explanation for why Mitch hadn't at least called. Surely he hadn't deserted her.

Once she'd trusted her friends, her uncle. Mitch. Now she was alone, truly alone. The past months had reduced her to a bewildered shadow of the person who'd been Royce Anne Winston, but now, thanks to a wellspring of rage, she'd metamorphosed into a new person.

She wasn't positive she liked her new persona — someone who'd ruthlessly hold a woman's head in a toilet bowl — but she sensed she'd need her newfound strength to get through this ordeal.

A guard shuffled up to her cell. "Come on, Winston."

Oh, boy, judgment day. Would there even be an attorney to stand by her side when the charges were filed? she wondered as she followed the guard. Where was Mitch? It didn't matter. She could go through this alone.

But she wasn't led to the elevator that would have taken her to the van used to transport prisoners to court. Instead, she found herself in the booking room. Stunned, Royce stared in disbelief as the property clerk handed her a wire mesh basket with her clothes in it.

"Omigod, they're not charging me."

The clerk shoved a receipt across the scarred wood counter and Royce signed for her things. Inside the changing room she ripped off the prison jumpsuit, nearly bouncing off the walls with joy.

Hold everything! They could let her go now

because they didn't have sufficient evidence. But they could rearrest her later.

"The dicks in charge of the Rambeau case want to talk to you," the guard said when Royce emerged dressed in her own clothes.

"Without an attorney? No way. They can go to hell."

The guard shrugged indifferently and led her through a door and down a hallway. It was a route Royce had never taken before. The guard left her outside a door marked private.

"They're waiting for you in here."

Royce yanked the door open. "You have no right to detain me."

Mitch! She barely stifled a gasp of relief. He hadn't deserted her. How could she ever have thought that he had? Her gut instinct had always told her she could trust him.

She noticed two men she instantly identified as policemen, even though they were dressed in suits. What was going on here? Mitch was sitting at the table, the two detectives opposite him.

He flashed her an encouraging smile and pulled out the chair next to him. "The detectives would like to ask you a few questions."

"Am I being charged with a crime?" She directed her question to the cops.

"No. Not . . . yet."

"Then what do you want?" She knew she sounded positively bitchy, but she was beyond caring. She'd been arrested three times, for God's sakes. Once she'd thought of the police as her

437

friends. Now all she could think about was the agonizing days she'd spent in jail.

Mitch said, "Royce, I know you're upset, but if you'll just cooperate we can clear your name."

Wary, her anger threatening to erupt, Royce plopped down into the chair.

The beefy detective, with jowls like bowling pins, punched a button on a tape recorder. "Tape's on. For the record, state your name."

She bit out her name, conscious of the concerned expression Mitch wore.

"Miss Winston, you're not being charged with a crime and you are giving this statement of your own free will in the presence of your attorney, correct?"

"I've been advised to cooperate."

"Let's go back to last Saturday. Tell us exactly what you did that day."

She turned to Mitch and he nodded. "I got up at about eight o'clock."

"Where were you?"

Uh-oh. This was top secret. "I don't give out my address."

The younger detective, who hadn't spoken, now said to Mitch, "I thought she was going to cooperate."

Mitch turned to Royce. "Tell the truth. The whole truth."

"I was at Mitch's home," she hedged. "I've been living in the apartment over his garage."

"Is that where you woke up?"

"I don't remember." Her thoughts spun angrily. What did this have to do with Caroline's murder?

"Royce, they know you spent Friday night in my bed," Mitch said.

Why would he tell them? She looked the beefy detective in the eye, feeling defensive and hostile. "Is that a crime?"

Evidently, he'd interrogated his share of hard cases. Her surly response didn't bother him. "I'm asking the questions. Tell us how you spent Saturday."

She gave them a very factual, bland, and annoyingly brief summation of the day's events right up to Jason's arrival. She paused, uncertain. "Some boy Mitch befriended came by about midnight."

"How long did he stay?"

"All night. He slept on the sofa. I called his mother to let her know."

"What time did you make that call?"

"Around two-thirty."

"Did you identify yourself?"

"No, I just said I was Mitch's girlfriend."

"Then you returned to the apartment."

She was half tempted to say yes to protect Mitch, but she felt his thigh pressing against hers and thought he was prompting her to tell the truth. "No. I spent the night in the house."

"Where?"

She hesitated, but he nudged her again with his knee. "In Mitch's bed."

"Where was he?"

"I don't see what this has —"

"Answer the question." The detective loosened his tie.

"Mitch was in bed with me."

"You're certain he didn't get up all night?"

What was going on here? Did they suspect Mitch? "I didn't fall asleep until dawn. Mitch never got up once."

The two detectives looked at each other. The younger one shook his head.

"Your story corroborates the statement given to us by Mr. Durant."

"I have sworn statements from the pizza delivery man and Jason Riley," Mitch said. "A check of my telephone records will show the exact time Royce called Jason's number."

"An airtight alibi," the young detective said grimly.

"Alibi." Royce gasped. "You mean Caroline was killed on Saturday, not Sunday?"

They nodded glumly. An hysterical laugh burbled past her lips. Suddenly she was giggling uncontrollably. Mitch put his arm around her, giving her a reassuring hug.

"The coroner says Miss Rambeau was killed between midnight and five-thirty," the younger man informed her.

Royce blurted out, "She was alive at two thirty-four."

26

All three men stared at Royce as if she'd just confessed to the murder.

"I — I mean I *think* Caroline was alive at two thirty-four."

She directed her response to Mitch. "You see, my portable phone rang just after I spoke to Jason's mother. When the caller hung up, I believed it was a wrong number. I'd spoken with Val and Talia and Brent earlier, so people knew I was home, but no one knew I was with you. Now I think that someone called to make certain I was home — alone."

The detectives looked baffled, but Mitch said, "You're right. The drugs were planted in your home to cover what the killer really wanted. Someone took a Coke from your refrigerator that had your prints on it." He turned to the detectives, who were listening intently. "That's why the Cokes were still in the cans. The killer couldn't use a glass. Royce's prints wouldn't have been on it."

"Is that the only place you found my prints?" Royce asked.

"Yeah," the brawny detective glumly conceded.

Obviously, he resented giving up his prime suspect. No doubt he'd thought her story would become a TV movie with him as the hero.

Mitch smiled at Royce. "They discovered your charm bracelet between the cushions of the chair where the perp sat."

"Is that all the evidence against me?"

The younger detective's eyes cut to the beefy man, who was toying with his pencil. Clearly, they had more evidence. The bubble of hope floating inside her turned to lead.

Mitch grinned. "I understand you found a few blond hairs that you'd like to compare to Royce's."

"Yup," the younger detective responded, annoyed at the question. Obviously, he didn't like Mitch having confidential information.

"Wanna bet the killer took that hair from a brush or comb in Royce's home the night the drugs were planted?" Underneath the table Mitch squeezed Royce's hand. "Since then an image consultant straightened her hair. They'll never match."

Royce dug her nails into Mitch's palm to keep from crying out. Please, let it be this easy. Let this psycho screw up.

"I guess we don't have a case," the chief detective conceded, jabbing the off button on the tape recorder with a pudgy finger.

They were so clearly disappointed she wasn't the killer that the anger she'd been suppressing refused to stay locked inside her. "I reported that bracelet missing after your cronies in Narcotics kicked in the stained glass door my father made and ransacked my home."

Mitch put a hand on her shoulder. "Calm down, Royce."

She swallowed hard, but there was so much pent-up anger, she could barely think clearly. She answered a few more questions, then left with Mitch. As soon as the elevator doors had closed, she sagged against the wall. "God, Mitch, I was so worried. I thought you'd deserted me."

He stared at her, utter disbelief written across his face. "What?"

"Why didn't you at least visit me?"

He hit the off button, bringing the elevator to a jarring halt between floors. "I thought you were smart enough to realize I was busting my ass to free you. Shit! I just got back from Chicago twelve hours ago. I had to track down the pizza guy, who got himself fired.

"Then I had to find Jason. I'd promised him a new leather jacket if he never mentioned your name. Well, guess what? 'The man' had taken him fishing. It took me hours to locate Jason's stepfather and get Jason's sworn statement."

He glared at her with smoldering, reproachful eyes, and she really couldn't blame him for being angry. Deep down she trusted him, but she had been so vulnerable, weighted down by everything happening to her. She put both arms around him, even though he felt as cold and unresponsive as a tombstone.

443

"I'm sorry, darling, but it's gotten to the point where I don't know what to think — or who to trust." She rested her head against the solid wall of his chest, his heartbeat as steady and re-assuring as it was when she'd awaken late at night, terrified. "I knew I could count on you, but I was frightened. So much has happened — all of it bad — until now. Thank you for helping me. I'm sorry I doubted you."

He put both arms around her waist and whispered, his lips brushing the top of her head. "If you don't know by now I love you, when are you going to figure it out? Hell, I persuaded Arnold Dillingham to give you a shot at that TV anchor position just so I could see you again."

"Really?" She looked up into his intense eyes. "You went to all that trouble?"

He framed her face with both hands. "I've loved you from the moment I sat beside you on that rock with the surf pounding at our feet."

Dumbfounded, Royce remembered the exact moment when she'd met his eyes, his face just inches from hers. Even now, years later, she could hear the surf crashing on the rocks almost as loudly as the beating of her heart. She'd tried to forget him, she truly had. She'd run away to Italy and stayed for five years.

Mitch drew back, evidently mistaking her reminiscing for rejection. "Your father's always going to be between us, isn't he? What can I do? Five years ago, I said I was sorry. I admitted the evidence was weak and I'd pushed to prosecute him out of blind ambition. But I can't change what happened. I can't bring back the dead."

Royce didn't know what to say. She'd been forgiving him — by degrees — for weeks now. Maybe she'd subsconsciously forgiven him after he'd apologized at her father's funeral. That would certainly account for the way she'd physically reacted to that kiss in the dark. To be honest, she wasn't certain exactly when — or what — had made her forgive him. But she had.

She recalled what Val had said about forgiving her brother. Everyone makes mistakes. If you love someone, you can forgive them. And set yourself free. Her father would understand. He knew what it was to love someone passionately.

What more could any woman ask of a man? Mitch loved her. He'd waited five years for her to forgive him. And when the legal system nailed her to the cross of justice, he'd come to her rescue.

He punched the start button and the elevator began to move. She knew that hordes of reporters would be waiting on the street level. She had to talk to him now. She pressed the stop button and turned to Mitch as the elevator again jerked to a halt. He gazed at her speculatively.

"My father isn't between us, Mitch. Not anymore." She wound her arms inside his jacket and around his back, pulling herself against his muscular torso, her eyes never leaving his.

"I *do* love you. I hesitated because you shocked me. That day on the rock, I looked into your eyes the way I am now. I said to myself: Oh, no. Not him. Mitchell Durant is everything you despise — a cocky lawyer. But in my heart I knew you were the man I'd been waiting for."

He brushed her lower lip with the pad of his thumb. "Say it again."

"I knew you were the man I'd been waiting for." She gazed into his captivating eyes. "I'll always love you."

"Not as much as I love you." His lips met hers in a suggestion of a kiss, a sweet, gentle caress that was so unlike the aggressiveness she'd come to expect from Mitch.

"I can't believe we're having this conversation in an elevator covered with gang graffiti," she said. "Not too romantic."

Mitch turned on the elevator, but kept his arm around Royce. "Tomorrow night we'll go out and celebrate with a romantic dinner."

She rested her head against Mitch's shoulder, at peace for the first time in months. Even the anger she'd vented on the detectives had disappeared. Mitch loved her. And the killer had made a mistake that would surely expose him.

"Will all the publicity about our living together cause you a problem?" she asked. She loved him so much. The last thing she wanted was for their relationship to become an albatross. Politicians were expected to be saints.

"Don't worry about it. If I'm not appointed to the bench this time, there'll be other vacancies."

"A judge! You aren't going into politics?"

"No. That's the last thing I'd do." He laughed and ruffled her hair. "See, angel, you outsmarted yourself. My name's up for a superior-court appointment."

The elevator doors slid open and they stepped into a dark lobby. She'd been cruel, needlessly vindictive, when she'd interviewed him on television. But he loved her anyway. Was she worthy of his love? Had she ever done anything for him?

He'd spent untold hours and a small fortune defending her. Even more importantly, he'd given her courage and moral support when she'd needed it the most. And how had she responded? Like a miser with a gold nugget, she'd clung to her anger.

Outside the station she saw a phalanx of reporters and she braced herself. She had no doubt that the reporters, with their myriad sources, already knew about her alibi. They'd turn her relationship with Mitch into an ugly scandal. He wouldn't be appointed to the bench this time. Maybe his name wouldn't even be proposed again.

"Ignore them," Mitch said. "My car's right over there."

A blast of klieg lights hit them. "There they are."

Mitch cussed under his breath as the reporters charged up and dozens of microphones were shoved in their faces.

"Hey, Durant, is it true you're sleeping with your client?" yelled Tobias Ingeblatt.

"Miss Winston," called a female reporter, "when did he seduce you?"

Royce felt Mitch's arm go rigid, but he kept his face expressionless as he shouldered his way through the crowd.

"Mitch, I'm going to talk to them." She stepped away from him and turned toward the cameras. "I have a short statement. Then we're leaving. I haven't slept in three days."

The crowd stilled, all eyes trained on Royce. What the hell was she doing? Mitch asked himself. He watched her take a calming breath. She loved him, Mitch thought, amazed. He'd done the impossible. He'd made her fall in love with him.

"The murder charge against me was dropped because I have an irrefutable alibi. I spent the entire night with Mitchell Durant."

Mitch wasn't surprised at the knowing looks and the eyeballs that rolled heavenward. He could kiss the appointment good-bye. Hell, he might even get a reprimand from the bar. Not that he gave a damn. He'd trade everything he had, or ever hoped to have, to save Royce.

"This is not a case of an unscrupulous attorney seducing a client." Her voice rose above the twitter, silencing everyone. "We fell in love five years ago. It didn't work out. But when we met again — before I was ever arrested — we discovered we were still in love."

She paused for dramatic effect. "Make no mistake about this, I wouldn't trust my life to anyone else except the man I love. And I'm certainly glad I did. Our relationship foiled a perfect crime."

She pointed her finger at the pack of astonished reporters. "Do you know why the public no longer trusts the media? Because you're here to-night for the wrong reason. You're here to destroy Mitch's reputation and make our love into an ugly scandal. If you're investigative reporters, your job should be finding the maniac who so brutally murdered Caroline Rambeau."

"This will only take a minute," Mitch told Royce as they walked toward Paul's office after she'd given her statement. "Paul's been working nonstop on your case since you were arrested."

"Couldn't you have talked to him on your car phone?"

"Nope. It's on the fritz. It keeps cutting out. Besides, one of the homeless guys living behind the office told me Ingeblatt's roaming around using a scanner that picks up portable phone signals as well as cellular conversations. Paul's cautioned us all to use only land lines when discussing the case. Watch what you say on your portable phone."

"Yes, sir." She gave him a sharp military salute, but she looked exhausted. He doubted she'd slept in jail.

Was there something deeper than love? Surely, what he felt was more powerful than "love" — the word everyone tossed around. He was still stunned by what she'd said to the reporters.

Obviously, she'd been trying to salvage that

judicial appointment — not that he cared. But she loved him enough to face down the carrion eaters of modern society and tell them that their stories had become gossip mongering — not investigative reporting. That struck a raw nerve, for damn sure.

Where did she get her courage? Hell, he'd seen more than his share of hardened criminals facing a trial. They all became weaker, relying on him more and more as the court date drew nearer. Not Royce. If anything, she was stronger now than she had been at first.

Mitch opened the door to Paul's office and let Royce walk in ahead of him. He stopped in his tracks as he spotted Valerie Thompson beside Paul. What the hell was she doing here when Paul was working on Royce's case? Before Mitch could protest, Paul spoke.

"Val has an airtight alibi for the night Caroline was killed." Paul turned to the attractive woman beside him. "She was with me — in my bed — the way she is every night."

For a moment Royce appeared startled, then she bounded across the room and hugged Val. "Paul's the man you've been hiding from everyone? Wonderful!"

"We're getting married," Val said, unmistakable love in her eyes.

Mitch shook his head. How was it his best friend was getting married, and he hadn't even known Paul was in love? Come on, you should have suspected. Why in hell do you think he hired Val?

"Fabulous." Royce sighed. "Married."

"Royce is going to have to marry me," Mitch said before he could stop himself.

Royce turned to him, one arm still around Val. "Why? Are you pregnant?"

They all laughed, the giddy, relieved laughter that comes after you've weathered a crisis. When they'd regained their composure, Royce was in Mitch's arms and Val was nestled against Paul.

"Look," Mitch said, "I need to get Royce home. She hasn't slept in days. Is there anything new on the case?"

"They're in a tailspin at the police station," Paul said, more than a hint of satisfaction in his voice. "The coroner says the bruise on Caroline's arm definitely came from intense pressure — probably from a shoe."

It took a minute to explain the details to Royce. She closed her eyes for a moment. "That poor woman knew she was going to die. How terrifying."

"We've got a psycho on our hands," Paul admitted. "My guess is the perp also killed Linda Allen. I've prodded ballistics into comparing the bullets that killed the informant and Caroline. We should have an answer in a day or so."

Mitch raked his fingers through his hair. "So what the hell do we do until the killer is found? Royce could be his next target."

"True," Paul conceded, "but if he — or she — wanted to kill her, Royce would be dead by now. I believe Royce was merely someone to frame. Still, you've protected her, Mitch, by keeping her hidden and being with her."

"She sure as hell won't be hidden now. The world knows we're living together."

"Exactly," Paul said, "so I've hired security to patrol your grounds. If nothing else, they'll keep Ingeblatt and the other reporters from bothering you. And when you're not with Royce, I've arranged to have Gerte be with her. I don't want her alone for a moment — until the killer is arrested."

"Good thinking," Mitch said. "I have to be in court tomorrow. I won't be able to stay with her all day."

"Remember" — Paul looked at them each in turn — "don't use the car phones or portable phones to discuss the case. Use regular land lines that require a wiretap to monitor our conversations. We don't want the perp to know what we're doing. He won't use a wiretap. They're impossible to get."

"Speaking of phones," Mitch said, "won't the list of people who have Royce's portable phone number help narrow down the suspects?"

Paul shook his head. "Val and I went over the list. Wally, Val, and Talia called Royce every evening."

"Don't forget Brent," Val cut in.

"But they gave out her number to others, and the word was out she was living alone in a safe house."

"It's true," Royce added. "I did speak to several old friends, people who knew my father, people who worked on the paper. I always gave the impression that I was living alone and moving constantly from safe house to safe house."

"I know you were counting on the perp being one of the people who called Royce the evening of the murder," Paul told Mitch, "but it doesn't wash. Too many people could have thought she was alone that evening."

"What about that call just after two-thirty?" Royce asked.

Paul shrugged. "So far we can't tie it into the crime. Could be a wrong number or a prank. Who knows?"

"We're back to where we started," Val said. "What was the motive for killing Caroline? Money?"

"No," Paul said, emphatically. "This was a crime of passion. Someone hated Caroline Rambeau and wanted her to suffer. I haven't ruled out the Italian count. He's a strange one."

"The house seems quiet without Jenny," Royce observed as they came through Mitch's back door. "How's she doing?"

"She's better. We'll stop by and see her tomorrow on our way out to that romantic dinner I promised you."

Mitch's arm around her, they crept upstairs without turning on any lights that would alert the herd of reporters hovering out front.

"Why's Wally been in the South so long?" Mitch asked.

Oh, no, Royce thought. Don't let Mitch suspect. Tonight marked a new beginning. She needed to solidify their relationship before confessing what she'd done.

"Wally's doing a series of articles on how southern states are stealing California's businesses by luring them away with tax incentives and cheap labor." She blessed the darkness; she couldn't have looked Mitch in the eye. "You saw the article on how chickens from the South are so much cheaper than chickens raised here, didn't you?"

"Yeah. Are you sure that's where he is? Have you actually called him down there?"

Royce stopped, shocked at what Mitch's words implied. He suspected, all right, but he didn't think Wally was investigating his past. He suspected Wally had something to do with the murder. "What are you saying?"

He hesitated a moment. "Nothing, angel. Just thinking out loud."

"No, you're not. You think Wally framed me, don't you? Well, you're wrong. Why would he kill Caroline Rambeau?"

"He doesn't have a motive," Mitch conceded, gently urging her up the stairs. "But there's something about him that bothers me. My imagination, I guess."

Again Royce blessed the darkness. Mitch was extremely intelligent — and intuitive. He'd sensed Wally was up to something. Don't let Mitch find out, she silently prayed.

"Do something for me."

"Anything," she whispered.

"When Wally returns, meet his plane. Be absolutely certain he gets off a flight from — where did you say he is?"

She could barely get the words out. "I didn't. Last I heard, he was in Arkansas . . . I think."

Oh, Lord, she hated lying. Should she tell Mitch the truth? He loved her, didn't he? Yes, but what would he think of her so cavalierly breaking her promise?

Like the dark side of the moon, there was a hidden element to Mitch's personality. She trusted him with her life, but she didn't quite trust him to understand why she'd allowed Wally to delve into Mitch's past.

"Humor me," he said. "Make sure your uncle was down South."

"I will," she promised.

"The killer made a mistake — but a crucial one," Mitch assured her. "I can prove incriminating evidence was planted at the murder scene. What jury won't believe the other crimes were committed to frame you? Carnivorous knows this. She's going to drop the charges rather than face a not guilty verdict that will tarnish her conviction record."

"The charges will be dropped. Thank God." Royce sighed. "It's finally over." She should have screamed with joy, but a bone-deep numbness had taken over her body, her mind. Free at last. Somehow the thought didn't quite register.

Royce tossed her clothes in the hamper and

headed for the shower, aware that she was totally comfortable with Mitch. Being nude in front of him didn't bother her. They loved each other; they belonged together.

She should be able to tell him about Wally, but the words wouldn't come. When she was rested and could think clearly, she'd find a way to explain what she'd done.

She climbed into the shower and let the water sluice over her head, intending to wash her hair, but unexpected tears blurred her vision. Free at last — the reality finally hit her. Hot tears flowed down her face, mingling with the warm water. For months she'd looked ahead and seen nothing but a black hole for the future. Now — horrible as it was — thanks to Caroline's death Royce had her life back.

Mitch stepped into the shower beside her and gathered her into his arms. He didn't say a word, but she sensed he was every bit as relieved as she was. He'd been frightened for her, she realized, maybe even more frightened than she. He cuddled her, letting the water wash over them until her tears stopped.

Now her future was again bright with promise, the bleak, dark world banished by a thousand shimmering possibilities for a new, better life. She loved Mitch — more than she'd thought it was possible to love another person. She needed to show him, little by little, day by day, how much she loved him.

Mitch helped her wash, lathering soap and

gently running the washcloth over her. His movements were quick, businesslike. There was nothing sexual about what he was doing, and she knew he understood how exhausted she was. She helped him shampoo her hair and rinse out the suds. Then he sent her out of the shower.

She dried herself with a terry towel, listening to the thoroughly domestic sound of Mitch singing off-key as he showered. She flipped her head upside down and grabbed the blow-dryer from its wall bracket. She combed her thick hair with her fingers, letting the hot air dry it.

Mitch stepped out of the shower and treated her to an inverted view of his body. Tall and lean but sculpted with muscles across his impressive chest. Glistening with water droplets, his sex hung heavily between powerful thighs.

He was so superbly, utterly male that a familiar thrill spread out in ever widening circles from her lower body. She stood upright and tossed her hair back away from her face. Catching her reflection in the mirror, her unruly hair framing her face, she looked wild, wanton. She turned, ready to share some flip remark about her appearance with Mitch.

He'd dried his tousled hair — or at least attempted to — but his hand was now resting on the towel bar and he was staring at her. They'd seen each other without clothes many times. Why on earth was he giving her that odd look?

Her gaze traveled the length of his magnificent body, and she noticed his shaft was hardening as she watched, growing longer and thicker and rising slightly. The reaction of his body to just looking at her filled Royce with a heady sense of power. Until she realized merely gazing at him elicited a purely feminine response from her own body.

She forgot about her wild hair; in two strides she was across the spacious bathroom and standing before him. Sinking to her knees, she kissed the sensitive spot just below his belly button where no hair grew. Leaving a trail of moist kisses she moved lower and lower over his flat belly that was slightly damp and had the fresh, clean smell of soap. She stopped, his erection brushing her nose. She eased her hand between his thighs and cupped the full weight of his sex in her hand.

Heat swirled through her body, a brazen indicator of how easily Mitch aroused her. She ran one finger up the ridge of his cock, then circled the tip and was rewarded with a low moan. Mitch's fingers were in her hair now, gently massaging her scalp. She playfully licked him, her tongue retracing the route her finger had blazed. Another low moan. She smiled to herself, aware of the heavy, congested feeling between her thighs, as she stroked him with her tongue.

Mitch twined his hands in her hair and pulled her head back. "Dammit, Royce, if you don't stop, I'm going to —"

"I know. I want you to —"

"No, you don't." He drew her to her feet.

"I'm in charge tonight," she said with a flirtatious smile as she switched off the light. She pushed him backward, forcing him to sit on the edge of the Jacuzzi tub. Facing him, she looped one leg around his waist, then the other, and sat on his lap. Shifting her weight, she used one hand to guide him inside her.

They rocked back and forth, gathering momentum. Her mind reveled in the sensation, possessing him for a change, owning him the way he'd claimed her for so long. She'd made love to him enough times before to recognize the signs. Any second, he'd climax. She couldn't help smiling inwardly; tonight Mitch couldn't control himself the way he usually did. She felt her own body clenching, but she forced herself to tip Mitch's face upward.

A stray moonbeam played across his face, heightening the hollows beneath his cheeks, casting shadows from his eyelashes, and deepening the two scars that she'd wondered about so often.

"I love you, Mitch. I'll always love you. No matter what." She didn't give him a chance to answer, covering his lips with hers.

A shudder racked his body just as her body peaked, and his powerful arms clutched her tightly. She collapsed against him, spent. And satisfied with herself.

Before she realized what was happening, he had her in bed, between cool, clean sheets, and was smoothing her tangled hair away from her damp temples. He murmured words of love, of their future in a hushed, affectionate tone that was uncharacteristic for Mitch.

They were cradled in each other's arms, drifting off to sleep, when a noise came from downstairs.

"Oliver," Mitch whispered against her cheek. "I forgot to feed him. If I don't he'll keep us up all night."

"It wouldn't hurt the fat little beast to miss a meal," Royce insisted, but Mitch was already out of bed.

He'd been gone a few minutes when her portable phone rang. She quickly checked the luminous dial of the clock-radio. Ten-thirty. It seemed a lot later. Reluctantly, she trotted across the room and retrieved the phone from her purse.

"Royce?"

"Uncle Wally —"

"I don't want you involved with Mitchell Durant."

She sighed; obviously her arrest hadn't made national headlines. He didn't know what everyone in the Bay Area already knew. She'd better tell Wally and hope he would understand why she loved Mitch.

Before she could break the news, Wally rushed on. "This is an unbelievable story, Royce. Do you know where Mitch was before he came to St. Ignatius Academy?"

Mitch walked into the bedroom and whispered, "Land lines, Royce, if this has anything to do with the case."

She covered the receiver and whispered, "It's Wally."

"By God, Royce," Wally continued, oblivious to the side conversation, "Mitch came to St. Ignatius from the Fair Acres Home for the Criminally Insane."

27

Royce stood with Gerte at her side as a stream of passengers scurried down the tarmac until the crowd thinned to a trickle. Where was Wally? The vague sense of alarm she'd felt since Mitch asked her to meet her uncle's plane intensified.

She was positive Wally would never do anything to hurt her. But — there it was again, that shadow of a doubt. At least she could be certain now that Val wasn't involved. That was some comfort, but it was eclipsed by her concern about Wally. And Mitch.

Utter exhaustion had forced her to sleep last night. Still, she'd been haunted by dreams. What had Mitch done to be sent to an institution for the criminally insane?

"I don't want you involved with Mitchell Durant." Her uncle's warning had sounded dishearteningly ominous.

Dammit, she didn't know what to think. The only thing she was certain about was Mitch. She'd lived with him more intimately than she had with

461

any other person. She would have sensed a psychological quirk that would have indicated he was a dangerous man.

But she hadn't. Granted, he was cynical, totally disillusioned with the world. That didn't make him a menace to society.

How could she explain the scars on his face, and his being deaf in one ear? Why did she think he might have — with cause — hurt one of his parents? Then he would have been sent to an institution. If so, had they released him, or had he escaped?

There had to be an explanation. One that would clear Mitch. Despite all he was and what he'd done to her father, she knew — in her heart of hearts — he wasn't a bad person. There had to be a reasonable explanation for his having been in such an institution.

"Your uncle is not on this plane," Gerte stated as the pilot walked off.

Acute disappointment and a nagging sense of suspicion kept Royce silent. She turned to leave, catching something in her peripheral vision. She spun around. "Wally?" Thank God, it was her uncle walking with a flight attendant, his bag slung over his shoulder.

"Sorry," he apologized with a one-armed hug. "Haven't slept much. I got on the plane and I was gone. I'd still be asleep if this young lady hadn't woken me up."

Royce barely heard Wally say good-bye to the flight attendant. Weak with relief, all Royce could think was that Mitch was wrong. Wally had been down South.

"Wally, this is Gerte Strasser. Paul wants her to stay with me at all times. Increased security. Ingeblatt's hovering around, using a scanner to eavesdrop on phone conversations. That's why I couldn't talk last night."

Wally smiled good-naturedly at Gerte, who merely grunted and fell into step behind them as they left the airport. Naturally, Wally didn't mention Mitch. By the time they'd reached Gerte's BMW, Royce knew Wally had read about Caroline's murder, but he didn't discuss her alibi. When her uncle spoke, he concentrated on the question of who would possibly want to kill Caroline.

It was a question Royce had asked herself countless times. If they could determine the motive, they would find the killer. Right now, though, the murder wasn't Royce's top priority. Mitch was. The drive into the city seemed three times longer than usual. She couldn't question Wally until they were alone.

Inside Wally's apartment Gerte was content to plunk herself down on the sofa and watch soap operas while Royce and Wally went into the kitchen on the pretext of making coffee.

"What were you trying to tell me about Mitch last night?" Royce asked the second they were out of Gerte's range of hearing.

Wally pulled two cassette tapes out of his jacket pocket. "I swear, this is Pulitzer material."

He was smiling with such glee that she was tempted to whack him. "Remember, Wally, we promised. A reporter's word is his bond. You taught me that." He reluctantly nodded and she continued, "Tell me why Mitch was in that institution."

"Listen to these tapes and hear for yourself." He pulled his tape recorder out of his duffel bag. "The nun, Sister Mary Agnes, told me about Mitch, so I went to the Fair Acres Home." He inserted the first tape. "The home is cruder than most state run facilities. It's set up in a rural area surrounded by farms. The home is a farm too. The inmates who aren't dangerous work in the fields."

Royce waited, trying to picture Mitch hoeing a row of corn, as Wally turned on the tape. Did she really want to hear this? What if it destroyed her image of the man she loved?

"This is my interview with Emma Crowley, who worked at Fair Acres when Mitch was there." The whir of the tape became Wally's voice, which was slightly higher pitched than he sounded in person. "Do you remember a boy whose last name was Jenkins?"

"You a reporter?" The female accent was southern; the tone hostile.

"Yes. I'm with the *San Francisco Examiner*."

"I don't have nothin' to say."

"I swear none of this will appear in print."

"I ain't saying nothin' bad about the Jenkinses."

A long silence, then, "Is the boy in trouble?"

"Hardly, he's a very successful attorney. People come to him when they're in trouble. He's defending my niece. That's why I'm here. I'm worried about her."

"That so? A lawyer, huh? Always was a fast talker."

"Tell me about him." Wally's tone was soothing, and Royce could just imagine the other woman responding to his comforting smile.

"His ma, Lolly Jenkins, lived down yonder in the hollow with her cousins. Pert' near everybody knows everybody else in these parts. Lolly was two years older 'n me. She always was a little tetched. Not loony like the people in this joint, but dreamy-like. Everyone said it was cuz she was from New York City, but Pa claimed it was cuz she'd been in the car when her parents were killed in the accident.

"One night when Lolly was about sixteen, she up'n disappeared. Two days later the sheriff found her wandering on a back country road. Nearest anyone could tell — Lolly couldn't talk — a buncha college boys had raped her. They beat her up real bad, don'tcha know."

Royce put her hand over her eyes, blocking out the bright sunlight streaming in the kitchen window. The shock of this discovery hit her full force. Now she knew why Mitch refused to defend any man accused of rape.

"The sheriff took Lolly back to her cousins' farm. The minute the sheriff let her out of the car she hightailed it for the barn and hid. Poor

465

thang was terrified. 'Course, everyone thought she'd come out of it. But three days later she was still in the barn."

Royce stared at the recorder, imagining Lolly's terror with heartwrenching compassion. She'd had nowhere to turn; no one to understand. She'd done the only thing she could to protect herself. She'd hidden, taking refuge in the comforting darkness of a barn. She'd needed a doctor. Counseling. Someone who loved her.

"Lolly's cousin went in to get her. She upp'n killed him with a pitchfork. At the hearing it was plain enough why. They had to keep her in a straitjacket. If she saw a man 'bout college age, she'd try to kill him."

"Didn't the sheriff try to find the boys who'd gang raped her?" Wally interrupted.

"Tried, but don'tcha know they could have been from State or Tech. Someone saw a car of college kids the night Lolly disappeared. But Lolly was too far gone to help the sheriff."

"She didn't try to attack the sheriff?" This from Wally.

"Nah, T-Tommy Pickett was real old. Lolly wasn't afraid of young boys or old men. The judge said this was the saddest case he'd ever seen, but Lolly had murdered one man and was likely to kill again. So, insteada sentencing her to life in prison, he sent her here."

"My God," Royce cried out, then quickly lowered her voice, remembering Gerte was in the next room. "Mitch must have been the result of that rape."

The thought froze in her mind, numbing her. When had Mitch realized the horrible truth? For years Mitch had lived with the fact that he'd ruined his mother's life.

Emma continued, "When we found out Lolly was carrying a baby, it was way too late to do anything about it. We thought she'd try to kill it, but don'tcha know, when he was born, she loved him. She didn't seem to make the connection between the rape and the baby."

"I take it she got better," Wally commented.

"Nah, she was in the female wing, so she didn't see many men. Her plot in the garden was just outside the building. She spent most days out there tendin' her veggies. The attendants made sure no men strayed into the area. But Lolly never got better. Maybe her condition has improved now. 'Bout ten years back her boy had her transferred to some fancy private hospital."

That's it, Royce thought. His mother's in the home. But why would he funnel support money through the Caymans? It didn't matter. She blessed him for obtaining the best care he could for a mother whose life had been so tragic.

"Miz Raymond was director of Fair Acres back when the baby was born. She felt sorry for Lolly. She said, 'What's the harm?' and let her keep the baby for a little while. The years, you know how they go by, and Miz Raymond couldn't bring herself to break Lolly's heart by taking Bobby."

Bobby? Probably short for Robert. Mitch's real name was Robert Jenkins. It didn't seem to fit

467

him, she thought. Robert was too ordinary a name for a man as distinctive as Mitch.

"What about school?" Wally asked.

"Bobby went to the one-room school right here on the grounds. It's set up for the employees' children. 'T'ain't much — now or then. Everything might have worked out if it weren't for that ole coon dog that wandered in one hot afternoon in late August. Named him Harley after those motorcycles.

"More'n anything Bobby loved that old hound. Lolly spent most of her time in the garden. There weren't any kids Bobby's age."

Her heart went out to Mitch, experiencing the loneliness of a young child trapped in such a place. No wonder he'd treasured Harley. She barely heard Emma's account of how Mitch was forced to shoot the dog he loved. His only friend. A gift from God.

"If'n you're askin' me, I say the farmer got what he deserved. Bobby clobbered him with the butt of the shotgun. Whacked him a good one too. Took six stitches to close the wound. The farmer filed charges and Bobby was arrested."

"An eight-year-old?" Wally questioned.

"T-Tommy had retired and we had a hotshot young sheriff who thought Lolly was crazy and so was her kid. They put Bobby in jail until a judge could come down from Tylerville."

"That's positively barbaric," Royce cried with a shuddering breath, putting herself in Mitch's place.

Something inside her died. Innocence. A child's trusting view of the world. Shattered. She experienced the shock of innocence being ripped away from Mitch just as if it were happening to her. How well she remembered her own fear at spending time in jail. How would a young boy have felt? Especially after he'd just destroyed the dog he adored.

"Well, don'tcha know, Bobby did go crazy. Least'n, that's what they said when he began screaming and banging his head against the wall. I went to see him myself to see if I could help. I can tell you it's a sight I won't forget.

"They had him in a straitjacket. He was babbling something fierce, saying someone was in his head talking to him. Poor little thang. He was just a mite of a boy. Who knew he'd grow to be so big?

"Anyways, I was the only one with a peck of sense. Right quick I ran and got the young doctor who was doing a summer internship at Fair Acres. He gave Bobby a shot that put him to sleep.

"Don'tcha know what that young doc found? A chigger had crawled in Bobby's ear. Doc got it out, but they'd waited too long — sayin' he was crazy like his ma — he couldn't hear outta that ear no more."

Something in Royce went cold. What had happened to Mitch went so far beyond barbaric that it was difficult to imagine it happening in this country. A wave of anger swept over her, leaving utter frustration in its wake.

She wanted to strangle those people, but it was too late. It was over. The damage done. And nothing Royce did could change that fact.

"Well, the judge came and Miz Raymond hired old Buster Tatum, the only lawyer in these parts, to represent Bobby at the hearing. Buster was a real jawboner. He convinced the judge to let Bobby go, but the judge decided he had to be taken away from Fair Acres. Said it wasn't a suitable place for a young boy.

"Bobby had been sittin' beside Buster real brave-like, but when he heard he was being taken from his mama, he started to cry. I mean bawl. I can still hear him sobbin' — 'I want my Mama. Please don't take me from my Mama.' It took the sheriff and his deputy to haul Bobby into the squad car. I can still see him, his little nose pressed against the window, his fist poundin' on the glass. 'Mama, Mama, Mama.'

"My poor heart like'ta broke. If'n that wasn't bad enough, we had to tell Lolly."

" 'My baby,' Lolly sobbed when we told her. 'Don't let them take my baby. What am I going to do here all alone without my baby? I can't stand it here all alone. I can't. Somebody please help me.'

"I'm tellin' ya, Lolly stopped eating. She even stopped working in the garden, which she loved. All she'd say was, 'Don't leave me here alone. I'll die without my baby. I'll die.' "

Deep in Royce's chest an ache of sadness coiled so tightly that she actually felt pain. As if spring loaded that raw emotion erupted in a sob she couldn't have suppressed if she'd tried. She loved children; she'd always wanted a child of her own. How would it feel to have your child taken from you when you were trapped, helpless?

Wally turned off the recorder and patted her hand, his eyes filled with sympathy. "There's more, but let's listen to what Sister Mary Agnes has to say first. That way you'll hear the story in order, the way it happened to Mitch."

Royce could barely nod. She supposed she should be grateful that Mitch hadn't been in Fair Acres for committing a crime, but all she could think of was a lonely little boy who'd lost his beloved pet and his mother all at once.

Wally studied her closely. He drew a photograph from his pocket. "Emma had a picture of Lolly and Mitch. It was taken when he was five."

Royce held the faded photograph, her fingers trembling. "He's adorable. Oh, my, look at those freckles. And Lolly's beautiful."

Like Mitch she had midnight black hair and striking blue eyes. A touching picture, she decided. Mother and son. They could easily have been smiling into the camera for some slick Madison Avenue advertisement. Who could have guessed the heartbreak they would suffer?

"I want my Mama."

"What am I going to do here all alone without my baby?"

Royce blinked back tears. All her maternal instincts fired at once. Oh, how she loved Mitch.

She longed to hold him and make up for the years of love he'd missed.

"Are you ready to listen to my interview with the nun?" Wally asked.

She wondered if he'd guessed how she felt about Mitch. But she didn't care. Wally would have to accept that she loved Mitch. "I'm ready."

Sister Mary Agnes had a cultured voice. "Of course I remember Mitch. I'd been teaching at St. Ignatius just one year when the judge sent him. Sister Elizabeth was in charge and she told us to expect a mentally unbalanced child who would have to be straightened out.

"Instead we received an adorable little boy who kept begging to see his mother. My stars, you would have expected Sister Elizabeth to be compassionate. But her sense of duty — as she called it — compelled her to make certain the little boy never made another mistake. She legally changed his name so he wouldn't have to face the stigma of a 'half-baked' mother.

"She used the name of the intersection where the school was located. She claimed he'd always remember what he'd learned here. Personally, I thought it was sadistic. Everything she did to that child was cruel. His room had to be neater than ours. He had to pray even longer. If he did one thing wrong he had to eat tomato soup for a week. And, believe me, she always found something wrong."

How much could one child bear, Royce wondered.

"I truly believe Sister Elizabeth hated all men. Unfortunately, she had total control over the child and no one to challenge her. He went from being a rather happy child to a sullen, defiant adolescent.

"I never had a moment's trouble with him, though. He loved English and I gave him as much extra attention as I could. But of course, it wasn't enough. He confided in me several times that he missed his mother.

"He was with us for six years. By that time he had grown quite tall, but Sister Elizabeth still hadn't put him with children his own age. He'd been behind in his studies when he came but he'd caught up and shouldn't have been with such young children. Was it any wonder he didn't have friends?"

No friends. Royce had always had close friends like Talia and Val as well as a slew of others. No wonder Mitch was such an insular man. He'd been alone his entire youth while she'd had the comfort of friends and family.

"One day Mitch demanded to be placed with the other children his age, but once again Sister refused. The next morning Mitch was gone. We reported him missing, but no one found him. Two years later a Navy recruiter called me.

"I truly believe God understands why I lied. I knew Mitch wasn't eighteen, but I verified the information on the birth certificate. I didn't know where he'd been or how he'd survived those two years, but I thought he'd be better off in the

Navy. I couldn't help remembering a pathetic little boy crying over his dog and calling night after night for his mama."

Royce had never expected a story like this. The judge may have been right that Mitch didn't belong in an institution, but he had been with his mother eight years. Despite the sordid events that caused his birth, they'd forged a strong bond. And Lolly had been lucid enough to realize her son was being taken from her.

Once they'd had each other, then they had no one. She imagined them each in their separate beds — night after lonely night — crying. For each other; for what might have been; for what was never to be.

Why did Mitch have to encounter such an unsympathetic nun? It was a miracle he'd survived and become such a strong individual. But the psychological wounds were there — well concealed, but there. He'd reached out to Maria for love, then she'd betrayed him by choosing Brent. Royce realized the importance of not betraying Mitch. Too often, at crucial times in his life, the bond of trust had been severed.

"Royce," Wally said, "I asked if you're up to hearing the end of the story."

She managed a nod and he inserted Emma's tape once more.

"Don'tcha know, I was stunned when Bobby walked into Fair Acres one Sunday six years after they'd taken him away. Tall. No freckles. But the minute he said my name, I knew it was him.

Claimed he'd been allowed to take the bus from the convent to visit his mother. 'Course I knew better.

"His clothes looked like he'd slept in a hayloft. But I figured, what's the harm? Lolly grieved somethin' fierce when Bobby was sent away. It would do her broken heart good to see her boy again."

How brave of Mitch, Royce thought. Somehow he'd made it halfway across the state to see his mother, probably without a cent. That cruel nun, Sister Elizabeth, didn't sound like the type to give a child an allowance.

"I took him back to the garden where his ma was working. I knew they'd want to be alone. I watched from the door as he walked up behind her and called, 'Mama, it's me. I'm home.' "

Home? Royce thought of the quaint Victorian she'd lived in her entire life. Now, that's a home. Yet Mitch would go through life thinking of an asylum as his first home.

"Don'tcha know, the look on Lolly's face brought tears to my eyes. She hadn't smiled like that since they took Bobby away. She got up slowly, a garden trowel in her hand like she was scared to turn, afeard she was just dreaming. Bobby touched her shoulder. 'Ma, I love you. I'm back.'

"Lolly turned. Lord a'mighty, you'da thought she'd seen the devil. 'Not you,' she hollered. 'I'll kill you. I swear I'll kill you.' Before I could open the door she lit into him with the three-pronged trowel in her hand. If he hadn't been raising his arms to hug her, Lolly would have put his eye out with that darn thing.

" 'Run, Bobby,' I screamed. 'Git away from her.'

"He hightailed it, blood streaming down his face. Tears were pouring from his eyes. It like ta broke my poor heart.

"Lolly kept yelling. 'I hate you. Touch me again and I'll kill you.' "

28

"Omigod," Royce cried. "Lolly didn't recognize Mitch. She mistook him for the man who'd brutally raped her — Mitch's father. He must look just like him."

"Exactly." Wally switched off the machine. "Emma tried to explain this to Lolly, but she was so upset that they had to sedate her. Emma gave Mitch twenty dollars and made him leave before Lolly got worse."

What would it be like to go through life knowing your own mother had tried to kill you? Or would knowing what your father had done be worse? A heavy burden for a child.

After his mother attacked him, Mitch was truly alone in the world. And to think she'd crybabied about feeling alone during her ordeal. She'd always had Mitch. He'd never had anyone. Things would change, she assured herself. She'd show him how much she loved him, how he could count on her.

"Who knows how he spent the next two years?" Wally commented. "He probably lived on the streets until he somehow managed to forge a birth certificate and join the Navy."

"He was too young, not much more than sixteen."

"But he was big for his age and by the time he joined the Navy, Mitch probably had more street smarts than boys twice his age."

"No wonder he's so tough and self-reliant." A fierce need to protect Mitch gathered force inside her. "I don't want anyone to find out about these tapes. Obviously Mitch funneled his money to the Caymans so no one would bother his mother."

"I agree. Mitch moved Lolly the first year he was out of law school, when he finally had enough money. He had a job then with the DA, and he was ambitious. And smart enough to know that a high profile attorney attracts attention. Some reporter was bound to harass his mother."

"It's just the kind of sensational story the tabloids would adore." Royce sighed. "No wonder I love him so much. He'd do anything to protect his mother even though she'd kill him if she got the chance."

She shook her head, disgusted with herself.

"Why did I think Brent Farenholt was so great? Sure, he loves his mother, but for him it was easy. Exist and be loved. Adored, actually."

"I know how you feel." Wally reached across the table and clasped her hands with his. "I feel sorry for Mitch, too, but I still don't want you to become involved with him."

"That's what you said on the phone. Why? I know you're thinking of Papa, but don't you think his horrible experiences explain his burning ambition? Isn't success often a substitute for love?" She gazed into the eyes that were so like her own. "Papa might have killed himself anyway. He'd been horribly depressed since Mother died. The note he left me said he couldn't face the trial — or life — without Mama."

"I forgave Mitch — years ago — but I don't want you involved with him. You remember what happened to Shaun as a boy."

Oh, no, not Shaun, Royce thought. Wasn't Wally over him yet? As a child Shaun had been a victim of child abuse. She'd tried to be understanding but to be totally honest, she'd found Shaun to be self-absorbed and shallow.

"When children suffer traumatic experiences and don't have anyone to love them, they're rarely capable of sustaining a relationship. They want one, but they don't know how to go about it. Mark my word, Mitchell Durant will only hurt you."

Royce realized many psychiatrists might agree, but she knew better. Mitch had been emotionally

cut off. That didn't mean he couldn't love someone. "I'm not giving up on him. Not now. Not
ever. I love him."

"You're so like your mother." Wally sighed.
"Loving but stubborn. I never thought you'd forgive Mitch. Even when I read about your alibi
in the paper, I was surprised."

"I guess I am like Mother. Papa certainly wasn't
stubborn. He was understanding, forgiving. If he
were alive he'd forgive Mitch."

Wally hesitated, then said quietly, "No, he
wouldn't. There isn't anything to forgive. Mitch
was right. Your father's friend wasn't behind the
wheel."

Alarm rippled up her spine. No! It couldn't
be. She gripped the seat of the chair with both
hands. "You're not telling me Papa —"

"No. I was driving that night, and I'd had too
much to drink. With mandatory sentencing for
repeat offenders I would have been sent to prison.
Your father insisted on saying he was driving.
We thought we could get away with it. Bruce
had been thrown from the car and it was in flames,
which was bound to destroy the evidence. It did.
The police had very little to go on, but it was
enough to interest Durant."

Her hands seemed molded to the chair, almost
lifeless now like the rest of her body. Why hadn't
Wally told her the truth before now?

"I would never have let Terry be tried for my
crime," Wally said, his eyes misted over. "Your
father was more than a brother. He was a father

479

and a friend all in one. After the arraignment we agreed that I'd go to the police — with Terry — the following afternoon. But he killed himself. I would have turned myself in except the note Terry left me begged me — for your sake — not to go to the police. He didn't want you to be alone in the world."

It sounded just like Papa, she decided. He'd always been fiercely protective of those he loved — especially Wally. Papa had always done what he could to protect Wally because he knew how cruel the world was to him.

Prison — for a homosexual — would be hell on earth. No doubt Papa had done it to help her as well. Without Wally she would have been alone. Her mother's cousins in Italy were a world away.

"I haven't had a drink since that night," Wally said, "and I made myself a promise that I'd look after you just as your father would have. That's why I was driven to discover the truth about Mitch. That's why I'm concerned that he'll hurt you."

He took a deep breath and then exhaled slowly. "I only did what your father asked. I wouldn't have told you now except that I can see you love Mitch. He was arrogant and ambitious, but he was right. Please, forgive me for not having told you sooner."

Once Royce might have been bitter and blamed Wally as well as Mitch for her father's death, but no longer. Too much had happened, too many people had suffered, to cause any more heartache by holding a grudge. She scooted her chair close to his and gave him a loving hug. "Of course I forgive you. You know I love you. I understand why you did it. Our family always knew the importance of love. Please help me show Mitch what it means to have a loving family."

"Jenny," Mitch called softly, and her tail thumped against the wall of the enclosure as they stood in the recovery section of the animal clinic. Royce squeezed his hand. "I knew you had the heart to make it," he told the retriever.

"How soon can she come home with us?" Royce asked as she extended one hand to pat Jenny and the dog gave it an affectionate lick. The room seemed sterile, cold. Jenny would be far happier at home, where Royce could take care of her.

"The vet says it'll be a few more days." Mitch gazed at Royce, who was still petting Jenny. "Home with us," she'd said. Were there any sweeter words than those? For once things had worked out. Jenny and Royce were still his.

There was one last hurdle, though. Until the killer was apprehended Royce wouldn't be safe. The killer might not be stalking her, but who knew? The whole case was so damn crazy, unpredictable. He wasn't taking any chances with the woman he loved.

Mitch was uncomfortably aware that the seventy-two-hour rule had kicked in. Once that amount of time had passed without finding the perp, chances became slimmer and slimmer that the murderer would be caught.

The attendant told them their time was up, and Mitch guided Royce toward the exit. Behind them Jenny whined mournfully.

"I can see why the vet didn't want us to visit Jenny," Royce said. "Dogs aren't people, you can't explain that you're not deserting her. Jenny can't understand why you're not taking her home."

"Bye, Jenny," Mitch called, the retriever's mournful eyes haunting him. It was amazing how much she reminded him of Harley. It was her soulful eyes, windows to her loyal heart.

Royce was quiet as he drove to the restaurant and the waiter showed them to a table screened by lush ferns. Flickering candlelight revealed an intimate banquette upholstered in soft peach colored fabric and a table set with gleaming sterling and crystal.

Mitch had noticed that Royce hadn't been herself all day. She'd been surprisingly melancholy, considering her uncle had been on that plane. And she was unusually affectionate. She never lost the opportunity to touch him or kiss him. Hey, he wasn't complaining. He loved it.

For the last five years he'd tried to imagine what it would be like if Royce were in love with him. He'd thought she'd be more aloof. Uninhibited in bed, but distant during the day. Wrong. Royce was a snuggler, and he had to admit he liked her this way.

Mitch ordered a bottle of Cristal. Just as the wine steward popped the cork, Mitch's beeper went off. "It's Paul. Hold the champagne until I call him."

When he returned to the table, he knew he had a shit-eating grin on his face, but he was so damn happy that he couldn't help it. Royce responded with the first uninhibited smile he'd seen all day. He lifted his champagne glass to hers. "To victory."

Her matchless green eyes were wide with surprise. "You mean —"

"That was Paul. He called to say Abigail Carnivali went on TV — during prime time, of course — and said they're dropping the charges against you."

She closed her eyes, leaving a fringe of golden lashes that cast shadows across her cheeks. "Thank God." She opened her eyes, her expression earnest. "Is it over? Really over?"

Damn. He longed to say yes, but he had to be honest. "Your legal problems are over, but we can't forget there's a killer out there. Paul's sources say the police are about to make an arrest."

"Who?"

"Paul will call us the minute he finds out." He picked up his champagne glass and waited until Royce picked up hers. "Victory."

They sat quietly sipping champagne. He'd expected Royce to be more excited, but she seemed unusually introspective. She kept gazing at him, her expression difficult to read.

"Mitch, about what happened to Harley — did you —"

"Aw, hell. I'm sorry I told you about him. I don't want to dredge up the past tonight." He wanted to tell Royce everything about himself so she'd understand him the way no one had ever understood him, but not tonight. The past was too damn depressing to talk about on a night when he wanted to plan their future. "I promised you a romantic evening, remember?"

She smiled, a warm, loving smile and kissed his cheek. "Candlelight and champagne is a big improvement over the elevator in the police station."

"I love you, Royce," he said, his voice husky. "I've never felt this way about anyone."

"You know I love you too."

"No reservations about your father?" Aw, hell, why'd he asked that?

She didn't hesitate. "None. As a matter of fact, this morning Wally told me you were right. My father's friend wasn't driving." She took a deep breath. "Wally was."

"Wally?" For an instant Mitch was dumbfounded. "That possibility never occurred to me. The police thought he'd run down from his house when he heard the crash." He studied her a moment. "He just told you? Now? After all this time?"

"Yes. My father didn't want Wally to tell me."

Mitch listened to the rest of her explanation,

asking himself for the hundredth time if there was any way Wally could be involved in the aborted attempt to frame Royce. It seemed odd that he'd waited years to tell Royce the truth. Then again, maybe Wally couldn't risk losing her love. Mitch understood that perfectly.

"No matter who was driving, I prosecuted out of blind ambition. I wanted to make a name for myself. Of all the lessons I learned in the school of hard knocks — and some of them were killers — this was the worst. It cost me five years without the woman I love."

"Let's put the past where it belongs — behind us." She raised her glass. "To us. To the future — our future."

"To us." Mitch clinked his glass against hers, then took a sip. "I have to go into the office for a minute tomorrow morning. Afterward, let's go pick out a ring."

She almost gasped at his matter-of-fact declaration accompanied by his comment about business. Never mind, she chided herself. Interpersonal relationships weren't Mitch's forte. How could they be, considering the past?

"I don't remember you asking me to marry you."

He pulled her close, sliding her across the banquette and into his arms. "Royce, I love you. I want you to marry me."

His expression was more serious than she'd ever seen it, but there was a tenderness there as well that made him look vulnerable for the first time since she'd met him. A glimpse of a little boy looking for love, she thought, recalling the tragedy of his youth. She forced a joking tone into her voice, half afraid that if she didn't she'd cry. "That's better."

They both chuckled, not the uncomfortable laughter that they once would have shared, but the natural laughter of lovers. For a moment they sat, arms entwined, bodies pressed together, silently acknowledging their love.

"You realize this house has only one bedroom," Royce informed him after they'd eaten dinner and returned home.

Mitch tossed his shirt on the closet floor, more interested in watching Royce undress than anything else, but her disapproving glance reminded him to put his dirty clothes in the hamper instead of dumping them on the closet floor the way he usually did. Aw, hell, marriage was going to take some adjusting. Still, it was fun teasing Royce with his bad habits and letting her reform him.

"You're right. This place is too small. Maybe we should move to Marin where our kids can have a big yard."

Royce raised her arms, giving him a helluva provocative view of the length of her sexy body, as she slithered into a black silk nightgown he'd never seen before.

"Marin." Royce's lip curled, as if she'd spotted a disgusting bug. "I suppose you'll want a BMW — basic Marin wheels. No way. I'm a city girl."

He couldn't help smiling — not just at the adorable picture she made in that nightgown, but at her emphatic opinions. Now, this was Royce, the woman he remembered. He was going to have a lot of fun baiting her. He loved playing the devil's advocate just to hear another of Royce's offbeat ideas.

Royce slowly twirled around, the black silk sculpting every luscious curve. "What do you think?"

"Sexy." He ran his hands up the slender curve of her hips to her full breasts, the nipples barely visible through the lace inset bodice. "Don't plan on being in it long."

She shoved his hands aside. "It took me hours to find this negligee with that Nazi, Gerte watching." Her eyes were smoldering, seductive. "Besides, I'm in charge tonight."

"Again, tonight?" He almost laughed — she was so damn cute — but her hands were in his shorts, homing in on his cock. She gently stroked him, her head resting against his chest.

"I like having you make love to me," Mitch said.

She gazed up at him, her expression serious. "Remember what you said about me wanting you to force yourself on me? You claimed I used it as an excuse so I wouldn't feel guilty about my father."

"Didn't you?"

"No. I liked the excitement of not knowing how far you'd go."

Her tone told him this wasn't a prelude to making love, this was a serious discussion. "You're the only woman I've ever pushed like that, Royce. I wouldn't have done it if all your signals hadn't said you wanted me. Rape is an inexcusable crime. You can't imagine how much I hated myself that night you screamed for Jenny."

"You frightened me," Royce admitted.

"I wanted you to kiss me and say you loved me, not Brent, but I was so angry that I came on too strong."

"I understand," she murmured, then kissed the sensitive curve of his neck.

She didn't understand, but, aw, hell, he couldn't bring himself to tell her he'd come alarmingly close to forcing her. He'd told himself he would have stopped — that he was just teaching her a lesson — but the fact was Royce had found it necessary to scream.

For years now he'd looked in the mirror, not seeing what others saw. Instead he saw his father — a brutal man who'd sadistically raped a young girl.

Mitch had told himself that he was absolutely nothing like his father and he'd believed it — even though he avoided looking in mirrors. But that night with Royce proved the same aberrant genes that determined his physical appearance might also affect him psychologically.

He'd spent most of his life assuring himself that he only looked like his father. But now he wondered. What would Royce say when he told her about his father? Would she wonder too?

Damn, it was going to be harder than hell to tell her the truth. Even so, he would tell her everything. But not yet. Not when he finally had won her love.

Why not? If love didn't mean trust, it didn't mean anything at all. He trusted her the way he'd never quite trusted anyone else. So what was stopping him from telling her?

29

Royce followed Mitch into his office the next morning. The receptionist greeted them, then quickly looked down. They passed a cluster of young associates on the way to Mitch's office. More quick hellos, but they seemed almost . . . embarrassed.

Why hadn't anyone congratulated Mitch? Wouldn't that have been normal?

Mitch's secretary handed him a stack of messages and mumbled a brief good morning, sounding unusually nervous.

Mitch didn't seem to notice, saying, "Paul wants to talk to me. I'll see him, make a few calls, then we'll go pick out a ring."

Mitch was on the telephone when Paul and Val arrived a few minutes later. They both looked as if they'd just met the grim reaper.

"Is David . . ." Royce didn't know how to ask if her brother had died.

"He's doing a little better," Val said.

Why hadn't either of them congratulated her on having the charges dropped? With growing apprehension Royce noticed Val didn't look her in the eye.

Mitch hung up and asked Paul, "Did you find out who they're going to arrest for Caroline's murder?"

Paul nodded solemnly and Royce's scalp prickled. Not Wally, she prayed. What was wrong with her? Why would she even think that? What possible motive would he have?

Mitch looked expectantly at Paul, whose grave expression unnerved Royce. Why, he's upset, concerned about Mitch. Something's happened and it's going to cause trouble for Mitch.

Paul cleared his throat and shot a quick look at Val before responding. "They're going to arrest Gian Viscotti. They found the gun that killed Linda Allen in his possession. Ballistics says it's the same weapon that killed Caroline."

A wave of relief so intense it brought tears to her eyes swept through Royce. Not Wally. Not Talia. Not someone she loved. It dawned on her she wasn't in danger any longer.

Hallelujah! She had her life back. And the love of her life. She looked at Mitch, and he beamed at her, an intimate smile that said it was finally over. Now they could really begin their life together.

"A crime of passion," Paul stated flatly. "Caroline told the count to get lost."

"Aren't crimes of passion usually spur of the moment?" Royce asked.

"Usually, but not always. This was a complicated crime, and it was amazingly well planned."

"Great. Case closed." Mitch grinned, apparently missing Paul's disturbed expression. "The Italian count's going to need a good lawyer. Don't let him call me. We're going on a honeymoon."

She couldn't help smiling at the thought of becoming Mitch's wife, but she was going to have to train him to consult her before making decisions. Perhaps they could marry and postpone the honeymoon. She wanted to stay in the city to be with Val when her brother died. Val had been there when Royce needed her even though Royce had sold her short, questioning her loyalty.

"That's a good idea," Paul said quietly before Royce could protest. He opened his briefcase and pulled out a newspaper. "You may want to be out of town for a while."

A frisson of alarm exploded. The paper in Paul's hand was the *Evening Outrage*. What had Tobias Ingeblatt printed this time? She went up to the desk as Paul handed Mitch the paper.

Half the page was the close-up of an older woman, her face contorted so she appeared demented, crazy. The headline beneath the grotesque photo was typeset in a size usually reserved for serial killers: DURANT'S LOONY MOTHER.

Her pulse beat erratically. No! Please, no! How

had Ingeblatt found out about Lolly? It dawned on Royce that the photographer — a man — had caught Lolly off-guard. Perhaps he'd deliberately frightened her. And she'd gone after him, believing she was going to be raped. The poor woman.

The article that followed was full of half-truths and outright lies. Ingeblatt claimed Lolly had killed her cousin in cold blood. No mention of the gang rape. He suggested Mitch had violent tendencies because he'd been arrested for an unprovoked attack on a helpless farmer. The article concluded that Mitch had changed his name to hide his arrest record and the fact that his mother had been institutionalized.

Royce was so angry that if Ingeblatt had been in the room, she would have killed him. Now there was no chance that Mitch would be appointed judge. This could be so damaging to his reputation, he might never receive a judicial appointment.

And Lolly. Oh, God, what would happen to that tormented woman now?

Royce ventured a look at Mitch. He was squinting at the page like a scientist examining something under a magnifying glass. He lifted his eyes to meet her gaze and in them she saw profound anguish.

"Can't they leave her alone?" he said, as if he thought she knew the whole story. "Hasn't she suffered enough?"

"Mitch, no one will believe —"

"Bullshit. This is exactly the type of story that make rags like the *Outrage* millions." He turned to Paul. "You've got sources at the *Outrage*. Find out where Ingeblatt got his information."

Paul cracked his knuckles, his mouth crimped into a taut line. Finally he answered, "I already have."

Val looked as if she might cry any second. Suddenly Royce felt as if she'd fallen off a cliff and was about to land. Headfirst. No, she silently pleaded, but Paul spoke anyway.

"Ingeblatt got the story from Wallace Winston."

Mitch wheeled on Royce, his expression not one of an adult but that of a young boy whose trust has just been betrayed for the first time. In that instant she understood the depth of his love. And the trust that's the bedrock of love. She had no right to that love. Not now. Not after this.

"Mitch, I swear Wally would never . . ." Her voice trailed off; she couldn't lie to Mitch. She couldn't honestly say Wally hadn't investigated him, but she was positive he'd never tell Ingeblatt anything. "Ingeblatt's lying. Wally would never have a thing to do with him."

Mitch was studying her intently now, his expression guarded. "Did Wally go to the South to check into my past?"

Of all the terrible things that had happened to her lately, nothing compared with having to look Mitch in the eye and tell him the truth.

"Yes. But he was only trying to help me. He thought there might be something in your past that affected me."

"All along you knew what he was doing." Mitch's voice was low, devoid of emotion, but his southern accent was more apparent than usual, betraying his inner turmoil.

"Yes," she admitted, her voice was barely above a whisper. "I was desperate. I didn't know who was framing me or why. I know it was wrong, but I was willing to try anything."

"Even though you'd promised, you went behind my back. You were sleeping with me, but you couldn't trust me." He didn't raise his voice, but the anguish in his tone expressed feelings he once would have kept hidden. "It wasn't enough that I was willing to do anything — spend any amount of money — to help you, and all I asked was for you to respect my privacy."

He gazed solemnly at the picture of his mother, shaking his head; his voice dropped the way it had that night when he'd told her about Harley. When he'd been so upset he couldn't look at her.

"Now my mother will be hounded by reporters. She's never had a life. That was stolen from her years ago. She's been making progress these last few years. I thought — I hoped — one day I'd be able to see her again. But now . . ."

What could Royce say? She'd never anticipated the horrible impact this story would have on Lolly Jenkins. Mitch was right. Reporters were ruthless.

494

They'd be crawling all over that clinic, cameras in hand.

"Mitch, I'm sorry. I —"

"Get out." He turned around and stared out the window at the bay.

"Mitch, I" — she touched his arm — "I'm sorry. I never intended to —"

He spun around to face her. A wild flash of grief ripped through her, a pain so intense, it was almost physical. The minute she met his eyes, she realized what she'd done. His eyes. His expressive eyes were filled with profound agony — a glimpse of the young trusting boy he'd once been.

What could she say? She had encouraged Wally's investigation, hidden it even, and her actions had triggered this catastrophe. She tried to speak, not knowing what she could possibly say.

But Mitch spoke first. "Get out, Royce."

Paul followed Val and Royce up to his office after Mitch had stormed out, heading God-only-knew-where. Personally, Paul wanted to tell Royce to go to hell, but he loved Val too much. She didn't believe Royce could possibly be responsible for the derogatory article.

Royce slumped onto the sofa in Paul's office and Val sat beside her. Paul reluctantly took the chair nearby.

"What am I going to do?" Royce asked.

"You can go home as soon as Gian is arrested," Paul said, deliberately misinterpreting her question. Val shot him a scathing look. Paul couldn't help himself. Royce had gotten what she'd asked for. She'd ruined Mitch's career.

That was only part of the problem. He'd known Mitch was in love with her — but not how much. In those unguarded moments when Mitch discovered Royce had betrayed him, Paul had seen the depth of Mitch's love.

"When Mitch cools down, he'll understand why you were investigating him," Val told Royce. "He'll forgive you."

"No, he won't" — she turned to Paul — "will he?"

Val flashed Paul a cautioning look, but he couldn't bring himself to lie, so he merely shrugged.

"Wally didn't sell this story to Ingeblatt." Royce's voice had an edge of desperation. "If he had, he would have used more detail."

"My source said the information came from your uncle."

"I think Ingeblatt used a scanner and overheard part of my conversation with Wally. He must have called Fair Acres and gotten a few facts, then he had a stringer take Lolly's picture. If only he'd told the true story, Mitch would be a hero."

"Just what is the real story?" Paul's curiosity had been piqued by the article. With Ingeblatt you never knew how much was true. He claimed to get most of his info from extraterrestrials with a penchant for abducting women and seducing them aboard their spaceships.

"Mitch didn't change his name," Royce said, her voice charged with emotion.

Paul listened while Royce told a story about Mitch's life that was so unbelievable, it had to be true. Mitch. God damn. He'd known him over twenty years — and yet he'd never truly known him at all.

With every word Royce uttered, Paul's opinion of her changed another degree, and it had nothing to do with the tears streaming down Val's face. Royce spoke with so much love and compassion that Paul had to admit Val was right. Royce would never do anything to hurt Mitch.

Still, the damage had been done.

"Everything Mitch did was to help Lolly, not hide his past," Royce insisted. "Isn't there something we can do?"

"Believe me, Mitch will be on a plane to Alabama this morning," Paul said. "He'll take care of Lolly. The question is: What can we do to help Mitch?"

He wished he had an answer. He might not have known about Mitch's past, but the guy was the best damn friend anyone could want. Still, he couldn't think of any way to help him.

He gazed at Royce. Her eyes were brimming with unshed tears. A seed of an idea took root in his mind and grew in the silent room until he was certain that there was a way to salvage Mitch's reputation.

"You said you have a picture of Mitch," he

497

asked Royce, and she nodded. "Here's my idea. The *Outrage* is an evening paper, right? All the other papers are morning editions. Nothing was in any of them because they'd already gone to press by the time anyone saw the *Outrage*'s article, but by now everyone's investigating Mitch. It'll take time for reputable papers to investigate; meanwhile people will be discussing the *Outrage*'s story."

"And they'll believe it," Royce said with disgust. "I know. My family has been in the newspaper business my whole life. We know retractions never undo the harm of an erroneous article. Too often people want to believe the worst."

"That's why you have to act fast," Paul said. "Get over to the *Examiner*. Have your uncle help you convince the editor-in-chief to let you write the true story and use the picture."

"Me?" Royce vaulted to her feet. "I can't."

"Why not?" Val asked. "You're a fine writer."

"I promised Mitch I wouldn't."

Paul put a steadying hand on her shoulder. "Under the circumstances the promise is already broken, isn't it?"

Royce slowly nodded, looking confused and frustrated.

"If you beat the other papers with this story, you have a chance — just a chance — of clearing Mitch's name. Reputable papers will have to send reporters south to verify the facts. That'll take time. Meanwhile, you know people. Rumors will grow like a malignant cancer and the true story will get lost in the bullshit."

"I can't do the story justice, but Wally can," she said in a suffocated whisper, her anguish clearly written on her face.

"No, Royce. You have to do it. Tell the story just the way you told us — with love."

"I never told Tobias Ingeblatt anything." Wally paced the small cubicle that was his office at the *Examiner*. He raked one hand through his hair. "Why would he say such a thing? Believe me, I'm getting to the bottom of this or it'll destroy my reputation."

"I knew you'd never sell information to that jerk. I think he overheard our phone conversation using a scanner," she answered, but she found it hard to concentrate on Wally's reputation when the damage to Mitch's was so much worse.

"What did Mitch say about this?" Wally asked.

"He was furious with me." She slumped back in the chair and stared at the computer terminal on her uncle's desk. "I doubt if he'll ever speak to me again."

Wally stopped pacing. "He blamed you when I was the one who did the investigating?"

"I knew about it. I should have stopped you." She closed her eyes a moment, not believing that her life, which had seemed so wonderful just hours ago, now was as bleak as it had been when she'd been facing the trial. Worse, really. At least when she'd been facing a trial, she'd had Mitch with her.

"Oh, honey, I warned you." Wally expelled a martyred sigh. "Mitch is so like Shaun. A successful relationship is beyond their grasp."

"Mitch is nothing like Shaun." Really, she resented her uncle comparing the two. Why did Wally relate everything to Shaun? The answer came with startling clarity: You never get over losing the one great love of your life.

She should be more compassionate, she thought. Wally had been through so much. His battle with alcohol. A relationship that was nothing short of an albatross. But right now she didn't have the strength to discuss Shaun with Wally for the hundredth time.

"I didn't mean to upset you," Wally responded, obviously wounded by her waspish tone. "I love you. I'd do anything to help you."

"I know you love me. I didn't mean to snap, but I'm so upset about Mitch. And his poor mother. Can you imagine what she's going through? No doubt reporters are crawling all over that clinic, determined to get a picture of her."

"I'm sorry, honey. If there's anything I can do —"

"I have an idea. It's a long shot, but it just might help Mitch."

Wally listened intently as she told him that she wanted to write a feature article on Mitch. "I'll go to Sam Stuart myself and get him to agree to run your story."

"Thanks," Royce said, but she couldn't help wondering how the editor-in-chief would view

500

her writing such a serious article. When she'd been writing a humorous column, he'd rejected every serious proposal she'd given him. "He'll probably want you to write it instead."

Wally studied her solemnly and she wondered if he preferred to write this himself. After all, it was Pulitzer prize material. She glanced at the picture on the wall. A younger, trimmer uncle smiled out at her, thrilled with his Pulitzer.

"Royce, I'm going to tell Sam that only you have the information. I hate lying, but I don't want to give him any choice. He'll have to let you do it."

"Thanks," Royce said, hoping her smile hid her relief. Ever since Paul had proposed the idea, she'd been worried about how Wally would react. He'd done all the investigating; she had no right to ask him to give up his story.

But on a deeper level: This was her love. Her life. Her story.

"You realize this could backfire. Mitch might hate you for publishing this."

"I'm aware of the risk, but what can I do?" Royce conceded. "I have to do what I can to salvage his career. Do you know he's being considered for a judicial appointment?"

"I just found out this morning," Wally said. "I'm not surprised. He's one of the best legal minds in the country, but this scandal is bound to ruin his chances."

"Not if I can help it." Royce pulled the photo of Mitch as a child out of her purse. "I want this to run with the article."

"Great idea. It'll counter that sleazy photo Ingeblatt used. Let me dash up to Sam's office." Wally pointed to his computer. "You get started."

Royce stared at the blank screen. This was the most important article she'd ever write and she was terrified. She'd always wanted to do a serious article, but not now, not like this. Not with Mitch's love at stake.

Think of Lolly, she told herself. You've got this one chance to right a wrong. Lolly had suffered so much. There had to be a way to help her. But could Royce do this story justice?

You'll never walk alone. Her father's words came back to her and with them his spirit, his love. The type of love and support that Mitch had never had. This was the only way to show him how much she truly loved him — by letting the world know the truth.

"You're on." Wally grinned as he trotted back into his office. "Sam's giving you the upper front and moving the key article on Gian Viscotti's arrest to the lower half."

The top half of the front page. Lead position. These articles were supposed to increase sales, since they were the ones that caught the eye when someone glanced at the paper. Talk about pressure!

"And," Wally continued, "I promised Sam a doozy of a story. He's printing extra papers."

"Can I do this?" she asked Wally, her insecurity returning. "My last article was how to wash baseball caps and visors in the top rack of your dishwasher so they don't get ruined."

"Of course, you can," Wally said, using the same tone and bolstering enthusiasm that her father had always used to encourage her. "You never really wanted to be a television reporter, did you?"

"No," Royce admitted. "I wanted to write serious articles, but Sam always turned mine down."

"Your father cast a long shadow," Wally sympathized.

"You're right," Royce said, startled by her uncle's insight. "I never truly believed I could write as well as he could. Now I'll have to prove I can be as good."

Royce struggled, skipping lunch and then dinner, writing and rewriting. Wally read the numerous drafts and made suggestions. She was shaky from too much high-octane coffee when nine o'clock came and the article had to go to Sam's office for approval before the presses ran.

She wasn't satisfied with the article — how do you capture the feeling of trauma and desperation, then turn it into a lesson on the resilience of the human spirit? — but time had run out.

She might not be totally satisfied with her work; she could probably rewrite the story until she was dead and still not be really satisfied that she'd captured Mitch's anguish, his pain. His triumph over impossible odds. But her heart had been in every word. Her love in every line.

Forgive me, Mitch, darling. I love you. I never meant to hurt you.

Wally walked her upstairs to Sam's office, which was five times as big as Wally's but managed to look smaller because Sam kept stacks of old papers lined along the walls. He claimed he reread his favorite articles, but no one had ever seen him touch them. Pictures of Sam with every politician from Roosevelt to Clinton hung haphazardly on the pecky cypress paneling.

Royce stood in front of the massive desk, cluttered with computer printouts from the wire services, as Sam read her article. A hard-boiled editor, Sam was notorious for rejecting what he considered to be inferior articles. Wordlessly, he read the pages, his bald head tilted downward. After what seemed two lifetimes he looked up.

"No changes. Run it." His voice was terse, as it usually was, but Royce detected just the slightest sheen of tears in his eyes.

30

"The photograph of Mitch with his mother reproduced beautifully, didn't it?" Val asked Paul as they sat at his kitchen table reading the paper.

"Yes," Paul agreed, but his attention was on the article. It took several minutes to read what was on the first page and turn to the inside columns where the story continued.

"Royce is extraordinarily talented," Val commented, tears in her beautiful hazel eyes. " *'I want my mama. Don't take my baby. What am I going to do here all alone without my little boy?'* I swear, Paul, even though I know the story, it still makes me cry."

"I understand, darling. No one can read this article without seeing Mitch as a hero, not the scumbag Tobias Ingeblatt depicted. Thanks to Royce."

Val dabbed at her tears with the tip of a napkin. "Do you think Mitch will forgive Royce?"

Paul wanted to say yes, but he loved Val too much not to be honest with her. And, despite his earlier reservations, he sincerely liked Royce. He understood why she'd investigated Mitch. Still, he didn't want Val to give Royce false hope.

"I spoke with Mitch last night while you were at your brother's. He's moving his mother to a more secure facility. He asked me to change the locks on his house and the security code. He doesn't want to see Royce. I doubt he'll change his mind."

"That's not fair."

"He's been hurt, Val, deeply. Time is the only cure, and it may not make any difference. When Royce asks you, be truthful with her. Tell her to be prepared to wait."

"All right," Val reluctantly agreed. "Did Mitch say anything else?"

"He hardly talked. I told him I found out Caroline had a cleaning service clean her carpet and furniture the morning she was killed. Evidently, she was putting her home on the market and wanted it in top shape."

"Really? Where was she moving?"

"No one seems to have any idea. If the cleaning service hadn't come forward, we wouldn't have found out." Paul leafed through the pages of the newspaper, not reading, just glancing at articles. "I convinced the police to send the chair where the killer sat to the FBI. Remember that soft laser process I told you about?"

"The one that lifts prints off surfaces where it's usually impossible to get a print."

"Yes." Paul couldn't help smiling; he didn't think Val would recall that conversation. She had been terribly distracted the day he'd told her about soft lasers, but she always paid attention to everything he said. "The killer's prints will be on the brocade."

"Why bother? Gian Viscotti has already been arrested."

"True, but just in case . . ."

"In case what? Don't you believe Gian killed Caroline?"

Paul studied the photographs of Caroline's funeral that the *Examiner* had chosen to run on the back pages. Brent and Eleanor were clinging to each other while Ward stood alone. Clearly they were all grief stricken, but Ward's tortured expression mesmerized Paul. He looked as if he'd just lost his only daughter.

"Paul, answer me. Is Gian guilty? Or is the killer still at large?"

"I think they've got Gian nailed," Paul responded, although he wasn't entirely convinced. Something wasn't right. But what?

He pointed to the picture of the Farenholts. "Tell me what you see, Val."

She stared at the photograph for a long time, then she touched Ward Farenholt's face with a sculpted nail. Tears filled her eyes. "That's me when David dies."

Royce waited in the shadows of the building opposite the Golden Gate Pet Clinic. Val had told her that Paul would be driving Mitch in one of the security vans to pick up Jenny. Royce needed to see Mitch and try to convince him to forgive her. She knew he'd returned to the city last night, but he wouldn't answer his doorbell and he'd changed his telephone number.

In the days since her article appeared, the public's perception of Mitch had altered radically. Not only had her article cleared his name, it had made him a living legend. But had it done her any good? No. He didn't want to see her. He might never change his mind.

Dusk had fallen when the pizza delivery van Paul used for surveillance pulled up at the clinic's front door. Mitch got out, leaving Paul at the wheel, and Royce crossed the street where she could talk to Mitch as he helped Jenny into the van.

507

A few minutes later he came out the door with Jenny hobbling along beside him. Her leg was in a cast and her chest fur shaven and covered by a large bandage. Jenny noticed Royce before Mitch did. She whined and wagged her tail. Mitch halted, glaring at her.

"Is your mother all right?" Royce asked.

"Do you really care? If you'd given a damn, you wouldn't have —"

"Try to understand. *I was desperate.* I love you. I never meant to hurt you. And I certainly never meant to cause trouble for your mother."

Mitch led Jenny to the van and slid open the door. He gently lifted Jenny into the back and closed the door.

"Mitch, remember my father's funeral? You told me you'd made a mistake and you were sorry. I know how you felt. I shouldn't have allowed Wally to check into your past. I'm sorry."

He stared at her a moment, jaw clenched, eyes narrowed. "And what did you tell me at the funeral, Royce?"

She didn't want to remember how blindly furious she'd been, but she couldn't lie to Mitch. Not now. "I said if you didn't leave, I'd hack off your balls with a rusty machete."

"Then you know *exactly* how I feel." His voice was low, yet it held an undertone of contempt and the ring of finality. "I hurt someone you adored, and now you've destroyed the small start my mother had made on a normal life. How do you expect me to feel?"

508

Inside the van Paul looked at Mitch as he climbed into the passenger seat, leaving Royce standing on the curb, forlornly gazing at him.

"What are you waiting for?" Mitch snarled. "Let's get the hell out of here."

Paul gunned the engine and bullied his way into the early-evening traffic, noting the grim expression on Mitch's face. Once he would have kept silent, but Val, bless her, had taught him the value of communicating.

"Did you read Royce's article about you?"

It took Mitch a long time to say, "Yeah. I read it."

Paul didn't let Mitch's irritable tone stop him. "She saved your career, you know."

Mitch kept staring forward, one arm hung over the back of the seat to reassure Jenny, who was on the floor behind him. "What do you want to bet that Royce wins a Pulitzer for that story? That's all she's after — fame and money."

"Come on, Mitch. You don't really believe that. Can't you see how much Royce loves you? Forgive her, Mitch."

Mitch spun around in his seat. "You're supposed to be on my side."

"I am on your side. I want you to be as happy as I am, that's all."

"You don't understand a damn thing."

Paul wheeled the van into a red zone in front of a fire hydrant. He put the car in park, then turned to Mitch. "Explain it to me."

Mitch hesitated and Paul knew how he felt.

They had been friends for two decades, but they'd never shared their innermost feelings. Yes, Mitch had known how devastated Paul had been when he'd left the police force, but they hadn't discussed the emotional side of the crisis. Mitch had told him to get off his ass and get on with his life. A dose of macho bravado wasn't going to help Mitch — not now.

Finally Mitch sighed, staring straight ahead. "I expected Royce to trust me, to know I wasn't behind her problems. But even after I'd asked her to marry me, she never told me she'd broken her promise and had her uncle snooping around. If only she'd trusted me, my mother wouldn't be suffering."

"What would you have done, if she had told you? Would you have understood that she'd done it out of desperation?"

"I would have been pissed, but I could have taken steps to protect my mother." He shrugged. "I don't honestly know if I would have forgiven Royce. It's hard to say."

"Don't you think she knows how stubborn you can be? She loves you, Mitch. You don't know how much courage it took to write that article. She did it not only to restore your reputation, but to help you with what you want most — that judicial appointment."

Mitch turned to the back, where Jenny lay, and stroked her head. She thumped her tail, then licked his hand. When Mitch faced Paul, his expression was so profoundly sad that Paul was stunned.

"To hell with being a judge. Know what I wanted most? To be in the same room with my mother and talk to her without her going berserk. Royce ruined that for me.

"After years of therapy Mother was finally making progress. Then some half-assed reporter terrorizes her. Did you know he chased her through a garden the size of Golden Gate Park and into a potting shed to get that photograph?"

"Oh, God, Mitch, I'm sorry." The words didn't begin to express how he felt. One of the proudest moments of his life had taken place last weekend. His parents had flown out from Iowa and he'd introduced Val to his mother. What would it be like never to have had the love and support of your mother who was always there to cheer you even though you failed to touch third base and your home run was called an out?

"I have her at a private clinic out here now. She's getting excellent psychological care, but I doubt I'll ever be able to see her." Mitch broke off, frowning as if searching for the words to say something more; then he switched subjects. "Paul, I've got to get Jenny home. I have a night-court bail hearing for Gian Viscotti."

"*You're* defending Viscotti?"

"Sure. The best way to forget your troubles is to keep so damn busy, you don't have time for a private life."

"That's what we both had before this case — before Royce and Val — successful careers. Is that what you want now, a career, but no real life? That's not enough for me, not anymore."

Mitch's expression said he didn't give a damn; Paul knew better, but he also knew Mitch wasn't ready to admit how he truly felt.

"It doesn't matter what I want. I've agreed to defend Viscotti. That's my life right now."

"But, Mitch, Viscotti put us through hell. What about the money we spent trying to expose that bastard?"

Mitch chuckled with feigned humor. "Think of the head start we'll have on the case."

Paul edged the van into the tide of traffic. "You know the FBI is using a soft laser to lift fingerprints from the chair the killer sat in while Caroline bled to death, don't you?"

"Yeah, you told me. Interesting breakthrough. If the police can lift prints from anything, criminals are going to be a helluva lot easier to catch."

"Gian's prints weren't anywhere on the scene," Paul said. "I expect he wiped them off, so this chair could fry him. I should have gotten the results from the FBI today, but I didn't. I guess my contact will call tomorrow."

"Phone me the minute you hear. I want to know what I'm up against."

Paul pulled into the alley behind Mitch's house and stopped. He helped Mitch unload Jenny. "I'm taking Val over to visit with her brother tonight. Call me there if you need me."

Mitch put his hand on Paul's shoulder. "Thanks. You're a good friend. My only friend, actually. I guess I'm just one of those people who have trouble that way."

"Anyone would be proud to be your friend, but you don't give them a chance."

Mitch only lifted his eyebrows in response as if to say, *What can I do?*

"Royce is like Val — a lover and a best friend. If you have a heart, forgive Royce. Believe me, you won't be whole again until you do."

Paul sat with Val in the upstairs study at her brother's home. Trevor was in with David, who was no longer able to speak. Val kept his mind off his hopeless situation by telling him stories of things that had happened to them when they'd been children.

It wouldn't be long now, Paul thought. David would soon die, and Val would have to face the grim reality of death.

"Mr. Talbott," said one of the hospice volunteers from the hallway, "there's a call for you. Jim Wickson."

"Thanks," Paul said as he rose and crossed the room to the telephone on the antique desk. "Jim's my contact at the FBI lab in Quantico, Virginia," he explained to Val. "He's in charge of the soft laser program."

"I hope they found prints on that chair."

Paul picked up the telephone, thankful Jim had agreed to call him before he informed the police of their findings. "Hello, Jim. Were you able to lift any prints off that chair?"

Mentally he kept his fingers crossed. The technology was new. In the past police didn't have a method for lifting prints from fabric, Styrofoam, and other soft materials. The chair at Caroline's home was upholstered in brocade, a fabric whose texture was both smooth and rough, making it especially tricky. But the furniture had just been cleaned. If there were any prints on it, they would be the killer's.

"Bingo!" Jim said, and Paul could hear the broad grin in his voice. "Not only did we get prints, we got a positive ID by running the prints through the central computer in Sacramento."

The master computer in the state capital had files of prints for anyone who'd ever been fingerprinted in the state for drivers' licenses. Better yet, it had a new high-speed capability that could sort through thousands of prints in minutes, a task that once would have taken days or weeks.

Paul listened, sinking into the small desk chair. "Oh, shit!"

"What is it?" Val rushed up to the desk.

"Jim, call the police right way. Have them get out an all-points bulletin."

"What's happened?" Val cried.

Paul pressed down the button to end the call, but clutched the receiver in his hand. "What's Royce's number? I've got to warn her right away. You'll never believe whose prints are all over that chair."

Royce pulled her temperamental Toyota into the garage behind her house and turned off the

514

ignition. She sat, hands on the wheel, and stared into the darkness. What now? she asked herself, the memory of her meeting with Mitch still painful.

When he'd apologized for her father's death, it had taken five years for her to come to terms with her life. Mitch had waited. That's what she'd have to do. Wait. And hope.

No. Hoping and waiting were passive. She had to take action. But what? She wearily climbed out of the car. In the distance she heard her telephone ringing. She fumbled in the darkness for her house key and finally found it. She rushed up the path but the telephone had stopped ringing.

Inside, she turned on the light and scanned the kitchen. Stacks of unpacked boxes littered the floor and the counters. She'd decided not to sell the house now that she wasn't going to be marrying Mitch. That meant a lot of unpacking, but she supposed the physical activity would keep her occupied while she decided what to do about Mitch. Surely, she'd think of something.

The telephone rang again and it was Talia. "Don Alford is playing at the Jazz Circle tonight. Do you want to come with us?"

Talia had met a man in her encounter group and she'd been seeing him. Royce hadn't met him yet, but Talia seemed happier with him than she had with anyone else.

"No, thanks. Another time, maybe. I'm bushed."

In truth she felt guilty for having suspected Talia. Actually, she was uncomfortable with her friends and Wally. After living in a miasma of suspicion for so long, she was embarrassed, but everyone was trying hard to be understanding. With time her life might retain a semblance of normalcy. Except for Mitch.

"Okay," Talia responded, her tone unusually upbeat. "Brent called today. He's miserable. His parents really fell apart over Caroline's death. Eleanor's on Valium and Ward — well, Ward is comatose."

"Uh-huh," Royce muttered. What did she care about the Farenholts? Why had she allowed Brent's parents to treat her so shabbily? It was irrational to blame them for her problems, but she couldn't help being disgusted with herself.

And Brent. He had about as much backbone as a slug. What a mama's boy. She'd seen the photographs that the *Examiner* hadn't printed.

He'd clung to his mother — and she to him — during Caroline's funeral. Obviously, Ward was grief stricken, but at least he'd stood alone.

Where would Brent be without his mother? She couldn't help wondering if Brent had ever loved any woman except Eleanor Farenholt.

Talia said good-night and Royce hung up, still thinking about Brent and his mother. Mitch had been denied the comfort of his mother's love, but he'd emerged a strong, independent man. Who didn't need anyone.

That thought brought a rush of tears to her

eyes, but she resolutely blinked them away. Crying wouldn't solve a thing. A sharp knock at the front door brought her out of her thoughts. She edged her way around the unpacked boxes in the hall on her way to the front of her house.

Halfway there she remembered Wally saying he was going to replace the boarded-up front door with a new door today. He'd wanted her to come with him, but she didn't have the heart.

How could she choose another door to replace the beautiful stained-glass door her father had made? "You go, Wally," she had said. "Pick out whatever you think will look best."

Across the living room she saw the new door and halted. Some distant bell in her mind sounded a warning, triggering her sixth sense. The door. Something was wrong with the door.

But what? It looked lovely in the darkness: solid wood with a small hexagonal window of beveled glass. Still, something about the door disturbed her.

Another insistent knock. She stepped into the living room and a vision hit her with startling clarity. This was the door she'd seen in the nightmare she'd had when she'd come home with Mitch. Couldn't be. But it was. She steadied herself by leaning against the cool plaster of the wall, recalling with startling clarity that horrible dream.

Someone was trying to kill her.

Come on, Royce. You're overtired. Wally has come by, the way he has every night. Blaming himself for her split with Mitch, Wally had spent more time with her lately.

But hadn't Wally said he'd be attending a Press Club meeting tonight? Or was it tomorrow night? Her mind had been so obsessed with Mitch, she hadn't really listened.

With a sense of foreboding she approached the door and flicked on the porch light. Nothing. She'd momentarily forgotten that the light had been broken during the police raid. The memory of that blitz brought a groundswell of anger, and she yanked open the door.

"Hello, Royce."

First she saw the gun aimed directly at her heart, then she saw the knife — just like in her dream — the moonlight glinting off the silver blade.

31

Mitch looked at Gian Viscotti across the narrow table in the detention room where lawyers spoke with their clients, but his mind was on Royce. Since Paul had let him off a short time earlier, Mitch hadn't been able to think of anything else but Royce. Not long ago he'd sat in this very room — with Royce. Concentrate, he told himself. Hard work was the only way to forget her.

"I don't understand why they're denying me

bail," Gian said, all vestiges of his Italian accent gone, replaced by a Texas twang.

"There's no automatic bail for treason or murder," he said wearily. "Judges rarely set bail for anyone accused of murder. In your case it looks as if they're going to charge you with Linda Allen's murder too. That's two murder counts. You can forget bail entirely."

Gian ran his manicured fingers through his thick hair and Mitch saw they were trembling. No wonder. Jail was a real shocker — even for a killer. He almost felt sorry for the kid, then he remembered how brave Royce had been. She hadn't fallen apart, but Mitch had enough experience to know he'd have a basket case on his hands by the time Gian's trial rolled around.

"Since I got your cell changed," Mitch said, "are things better?"

"Yeah. Thanks." Gian shifted uncomfortably in his chair. "I don't shower every day. Sorry if I'm —"

"Good idea," Mitch said, but he wondered if the kid had any idea how tough things would be at a state prison. Being accosted in the shower would be the least of his problems. "Let's discuss the evidence, so I can start on your case."

"Evidence? Somebody planted that gun. I would never kill —"

"Wait," Mitch cut him off. "Just give me the facts. I don't want you tying my hands with some bullshit story."

By the time he'd listened to Gian's tale, a new

twist on the American gigolo, Mitch was exhausted. And he had the disturbing feeling that Gian — slick hustler that he was — hadn't murdered Caroline. He climbed in his Viper and headed toward his home, telling himself with Jenny there the house wouldn't be so lonely. He wouldn't miss Royce.

"To hell with her," he cursed out loud. Why had she insisted on investigating him? While he'd been busting his butt for her, she'd been sneaking around behind his back. Okay, okay, she had written a brilliant article that had saved his reputation. But it had been printed too late to do his mother one damn bit of good.

The car in front of him was going so slow that he slammed his palm down on the horn, his frustration with Royce getting the better of his temper. The telephone rang just as he floored the Viper and swerved around the poky car.

"Durant here," he said, and heard the familiar click of static. He'd been meaning to get the damn phone repaired, but hadn't had a spare second.

"It's Howard Schultz, Mitch. Can you hear me?"

"Yes, but this phone may cut out any second. If it does, I'll call you" — he paused for another volley of irritating static — "when I get home."

"I just wanted to tell you that you're going to be appointed to replace Judge Willner."

"Great." He tried to sound enthusiastic, but frankly, he didn't give a damn about being a judge any longer. Nothing seemed to matter. It was as if an alien being had taken over his body — most of it, anyway. Part of him still regretted what had happened with Royce, but he'd be damned if he'd let her become the focal point of his thoughts.

"It'll be —" Another burst of static, then nothing.

Mitch rattled the receiver. Silence. He dropped the phone back into the cradle as he came to a stop at a traffic light. Finally, he'd achieved his dream. He was going to be a judge.

Legal nirvana it wasn't, but he was sick of the parade of criminals he'd defended over the years. He was ready for a new challenge. Hey, he had no illusions. Same legal bullshit seen from the other side of the bench.

The phone rang again and Mitch picked it up, gunning his engine and shooting into the intersection just before the light turned green.

"Val?" It was Royce's voice. The hair across his neck bristled. He'd changed his home phone and left orders at the office not to accept Royce's calls, but he hadn't changed the car phone, expecting to replace it. What the hell was she up to? Don't tell me that she dialed this number by mistake.

"Royce, stop bothering me. Dammit —"

"I just wanted to tell you that I won't be able to go with you and David tonight to the late show. I'm really tired, but I'll call you tomorrow."

She said something else, but another round of

static butchered her words. "Royce what the hell are you talking about? You know David isn't —"

"When you see Mitch, tell him I loved him. I honestly loved him. I —"

Suddenly the line went dead, but the dial tone was clear. What the hell? The phone hadn't cut her off. She'd hung up without finishing her sentence. Son of a bitch.

The whole conversation was weird. Why would she call and make up such a half-assed story? Didn't make sense. So what else is new? Royce was always a little offbeat. Once he'd found that charming.

He sat at the stoplight for so long he could have read *War and Peace*, trying not to notice that with a left turn, he'd be at Royce's house in minutes. Why would he go there? She wasn't in trouble. Naaah. Royce was just trying to get his attention. Damn straight. That's all it was.

Kicking himself, he turned left, accelerating way past the speed limit. He was in front of Royce's house in minutes. The house was dark except for dim light leaking out from drawn blinds in the attic. He parked, telling himself he was a class A sucker. No one answered the bell, then he remembered it had been disconnected during the police search. He knocked but no one came.

He started to leave, but turned back to study the new door. It was remarkably like the one Royce had described after her nightmare. Why would she buy a door that was bound to trigger unpleasant memories? Didn't make sense. The ominous feeling he'd had since her telephone call intensified.

What if her call had been a plea for help?

Christ! Maybe he was imagining things. If he were dead honest with himself, he'd admit he loved her. No matter how he tried to convince himself, his feelings hadn't changed. And Paul's words kept nagging at him. Some part of him — okay, his weak side — wanted an excuse to forgive her.

He raced around to the back and was surprised to find the door unlocked. He quietly entered, some inner voice cautioning him not to call out her name.

Flicking on the light, he saw the stacks of boxes, but nothing to cause alarm. He tiptoed into the hall, where the telephone sat on a stand in the alcove. A drop of something dark marred the ivory-colored receiver. He touched it with his finger and brought it up to the light filtering in from the kitchen.

Blood.

Royce's blood.

The truth hit him with the impact of a blow to the solar plexus. His gut instinct hadn't been wrong.

The killer wasn't in jail.

Gian had been framed, just like Royce. Mitch didn't have to ask who. The answer didn't even startle him. He should have seen it all along.

Son of a bitch, he'd been an arrogant fool.

In a maelstrom of debilitating panic he realized

just how much he loved Royce. Hadn't the five years they'd been apart taught him anything? He'd missed her so much, but not the way he did now that he really knew her. How could he live with himself if something happened to Royce?

He grabbed the receiver, set to call the police, but the line was dead. A muffled noise drifted down from upstairs. Mitch's hand froze in midair as he identified the sound.

A man's laugh. Royce must still be alive. Thank you, God.

In an instant Mitch evaluated his options. If he went for help she might not be alive when he returned. He couldn't risk it.

He crept up the stairs as quickly and quietly as he could. As he neared the second floor, the voice became louder, the tone almost conversational. A husky masculine baritone and Royce's softer voice. Attagirl. Keep him talking.

The last flight of stairs to the attic was narrower than the main staircase. Mitch tiptoed up and halted at the top, hidden by the half-open door. Through the crack between the hinges and the doorjamb Mitch peered into the small room. Royce was lying on the daybed with her hands tied to the bedposts and sitting beside her, his back to Mitch, was Brent Farenholt.

Sonofabitch! Why didn't he have a gun? He wouldn't even feel guilty about shooting the bastard in the back. You're so stupid. You totally underestimated Brent.

While Mitch mentally accused himself of being an arrogant imbecile, he stuck one finger through the crack and wiggled it. His eye to the opening, he saw Royce catch the movement and quickly look away.

Tears filled Royce's eyes. Thank heaven, Mitch had understood her cryptic plea. She'd been surprised Brent had allowed her to make the phone call. She'd gambled on Brent believing her hastily concocted story about going out with Val and her brother. She'd dialed Mitch's car phone — for once luck was with her — and he'd answered, instantly suspicious when she'd pretended he was Val.

Royce quickly found out why Brent hadn't wanted Val to come looking for her. Sadistically, Brent wanted her to die slowly — like Caroline. To suffer over a number of hours while he enjoyed the sight.

Already he'd cut her — minor cuts — but in time she'd bleed to death. Even now she felt weak and her clothes were sticky with her own, still warm, blood. She knew she didn't have that long to live unless her wounds were treated.

"Caroline never cried, you know," Brent said, mistaking Royce's tears of relief at seeing Mitch for fear.

Royce was emboldened now. Having Mitch so close gave her hope, although she knew he didn't have a weapon or he would have charged into the room.

"She tried to trick me by playing dead, but

it didn't work." Brent chuckled, the disarming laugh she knew so well. The laugh that put everyone at ease. "She made a grab for the phone, but I stepped on her arm and held her down until God himself couldn't save her."

Why hadn't she detected the evil side to this man? Royce reminded herself that many psychopaths seemed amazingly sane. Even when he'd slit her veins, he'd had the detached manner of a surgeon performing a delicate operation. The only time he'd lost his temper and revealed his psychopathic side was when she'd said she loved Mitch. Brent had jammed down on the phone, cutting her off. In a second he'd slashed a small vein on her arm and she'd begun to bleed.

Royce blinked back the tears, thinking she needed to be able to see clearly if she were going to help Mitch. Brent had tied her, but carelessly. One wrist was very loose.

With a Glock semi-automatic in his hand he was cocky about her making hasty moves. She knew he didn't intend to shoot her, he'd keep using the knife, slowly opening more veins until her lifeblood drained into the mattress beneath her.

"A gun and a knife," Royce said, desperate to let Mitch know what he was up against. "If you want me to bleed to death, why the gun?"

Holding the flat blade of the knife under her chin Brent said, "I might change my mind and shoot you. You really pissed me off, you know. I liked you. I was searching for someone to frame, but you were so cute, I almost let you go."

"What changed your mind?"

"A kiss in the dark."

Royce remembered the kiss with startling clarity. *A kiss in the dark*. Brent had been outside the door when she'd kissed Mitch with such passion. That night her life had changed forever, but she didn't know it until now.

"I came upstairs looking for you. There you were — engaged to me — but in Mitchell Durant's arms, kissing him like a two-bit hooker on Mission Street. Did you know how many times my father threw Mitch in my face? Shit! Did you think I was going to let him walk off with my fiancée too?"

"Your father would have been glad to get rid of me," Royce said, conscious of the need to keep him talking while Mitch took action.

"True. He thought you were cheap with your flamboyant clothes and those big tits. Personally, I liked the tits." He chuckled and playfully lowered the knife, skimming across her chest to the shadowy valley between her breasts.

He turned the knife on its side and ran the cold blade down her cleavage. Then, with a flick of the razor-sharp knife point, he severed the thread on the top button of her blouse. One by one he cut the others free. The fabric parted, revealing the lacy cups of her demibra.

Outside the door Mitch groaned low in his throat, hardly able to contain the urge to catapult into the room and kill the son of a bitch. But with one shot Royce would be dead. He needed to distract Brent. But how?

Mitch remembered the condom he always kept in his wallet. It had been there for so long now, it was probably useless for its intended task, but it would suit his purpose. Slowly he inched his wallet out of his hip pocket, aware that any sound could alert Brent. But Brent wasn't on guard. He continued to talk.

"Caroline wasn't perfect, you know," Brent said. "She was a little flat chested, but I loved her."

"If you loved her, how could you kill her?"

There was a moment of silence. Mitch stopped peeling the foil off the condom in case the noise tipped Brent before he was ready to strike. He couldn't see what Brent was doing but he could see that Royce's blouse was hanging off one shoulder and her breasts were now bare.

Come on, Mitch said to himself, someone say something so I can unwrap this damn thing. Royce must have read his mind.

"I don't want to die until I know the whole story. Isn't it only fair that you tell me?"

"Ever since I can remember, I was in love with Caroline. Before they were killed in the accident, her parents were my parents' closest friends. They'd come over and Caroline and I would sneak away. Usually we'd play doctor." Brent shrugged, the one-shouldered gesture that she'd once found so charming.

He seems so normal. Even now. Royce's stomach clenched. He spoke logically, appearing for all the world to be a rational man, not a sadistic killer. But there had to have been signs. Her mind sifted through their months together for clues.

There had been some. His relationship with his family had been abnormal. With startling clarity she remembered how he'd behaved the night of the auction. He'd turned on her because he'd never really loved her. He'd been pretending. If she'd correctly analyzed the situation then, she would have understood that Brent's entire life centered on pretending. A charade.

"You know, the doctor game was Caroline's idea." Brent smirked. "Even when we were teenagers we'd still play. I'd touch her breasts like this." He put the knife in the same hand as the gun and palmed Royce's breast with his free hand, cradling its weight and brushing his thumb over the nipple.

Royce wanted to spit in his eye, but she didn't dare. Help was too close, life too precious.

"Caroline always took off her panties for me."

He used the ultrasharp knife on the cotton skirt she wore and sliced it off her before Royce could blink. It was a deadly hunting knife, she realized, the kind used to skin animals.

"I'd touch her here." Brent edged his fingers into the nest of curls between her thighs. "She couldn't get enough of it."

Royce vowed that if she got her hand on that knife, she'd go for his jugular. "So, why didn't you marry Caroline?"

Brent's hand froze. He studied her a moment, his eyes scanning her bare breasts, scouring her naked tummy and stopping where his hand rested so intimately against her.

"I wanted to marry Caroline, believe me. I asked her dozens of times."

Royce remembered what the phony count had told Paul. Caroline had been in love with someone else. Suddenly, everything made sense as she recalled little details she'd never put together before now. "But Caroline refused to marry you, didn't she? She was in love with your father."

Brent's skin turned an ugly mottled red and his eyes had the most wounded expression she'd ever seen. Honest to God, he thought of himself as the long-suffering victim. He took his hand off her crotch and grabbed the knife again.

For one terrifying second she thought she'd stepped over some invisible line and he was going to kill her. But he merely traced the tip of the blade along a blue vein on her breast.

Slowly, excruciatingly slowly, the deadly knife moved, seeking the perfect spot. Gently, as if she were a baby and exceedingly fragile, he pricked the vein. The cut was the size of a pinhead, but blood trickled down over her nipple.

Oh, Mitch, please hurry.

The crimson blood so stark against the white smoothness of Royce's breast almost sent Mitch barreling into the room to kill the bastard with his bare hands. But the logical part of his brain that had saved him countless times came to his rescue again. If he stormed in there, they'd both die.

No. Royce deserves to live. Trust me, Brent is the one who's going to die.

Mitch forced his fingers to slowly withdraw the fistful of change in his pocket. He shoved the coins into the condom, his fingers trembling with rage and fear. He wasn't afraid for his own life.

No. He'd conquered that kind of fear during the years of his youth when he'd lived on the streets at the mercy of anyone bigger and stronger. He'd survived. But now he was more afraid than he'd ever been back then when he didn't dare go to sleep at night for fear some one would slit his throat for a slice of stale bread. Or his holey tennis shoes.

"You know, Royce, you were always too smart for your own good." Brent's voice came from the other room. "You're right. Caroline loved my father . . . and he loved her. Know how I found out?"

It was a rhetorical question; Brent rushed on. "She came home from college one summer. For the first time she wouldn't sleep with me. She claimed she wanted us to date other people. I followed her and found out her new love was my own father.

"He couldn't be satisfied with making me feel like shit every day of my life. No, not the almighty Ward Farenholt. And he wasn't satisfied that he'd betrayed Mother by screwing the girl she loved like a daughter. He never gave a damn about anyone but himself. It probably thrilled him to know he'd seduced the one woman I could ever truly love."

Royce inhaled sharply, half thinking her light-headedness was from the cuts Brent had made on her hands and arms, but that wasn't the cause. The profound sadness in Brent's eyes solidified the air in her lungs. Of course, she'd known he was crazy from the first moment she'd opened the front door, but the depths of his insanity now shone clearly in his eyes.

"I waited, thinking Caroline would come to her senses and realize she loved me."

"Didn't you ever love anyone else?" she asked, thinking of Maria.

"Hell, no. You were the closest I came." He cupped one breast in his hand and squeezed slightly.

Royce couldn't help noticing the bulge in his pants was growing. Oh, Lord, he was sick. Heaven help her. She hadn't imagined that finger signaling to her, had she? Mitch really was out there, wasn't he?

Yes, of course he was. She sucked in a calming breath. Despite what she'd done, Mitch loved her. He'd come to save her.

"You were a hot number in bed," he continued, gripping the knife, but managing to stroke her with the same hand. "If you hadn't come on to Durant, I wouldn't have paid Linda Allen to plant that cocaine in your house."

"What about the jewels?" She turned her head to one side. Clearly, he was aroused, but she didn't want him to see how disgusted she was.

"Mother put them in your purse. She didn't think you were worthy of me. She was right, wasn't she? Mother loves me."

Royce mentally applauded her intuition. Eleanor Farenholt had been behind this — part of it anyway. She was as loony as her son. How was it people like this went free and women like Lolly Jenkins didn't get the psychological help they needed?

"Mother confessed to me right after you were arrested. She loves my father so much. She was terrified of what he might do if he found out." He continued fondling her breast, then moved to the other, dipping his thumb in her blood and smearing it over her nipple. There was no question about it; he found this sexually stimulating.

"I love Mother. She was always there for me. My father always made me feel like shit. Nothing pleased him. I told her to keep quiet. No one could prove she put the jewels in your purse."

There was a long pause. "I'm surprised Caroline satisfied your father," Royce said — just to keep him going.

"She was a younger, more malleable version of my mother. Ever notice how much they look alike? She's like a daughter to my mother. Can you imagine how devastated she would have been had she discovered Father was planning on leaving her for Caroline?"

"You mean, when Caroline inherited her trust your father —"

"Was moving to the south of France with Caroline. That's why she was selling her house." Brent shook his head, genuine pain etched his face. "The humiliation would have killed Mother. I spared her that by getting rid of Caroline.

"Never think it was a spur-of-the-moment crime. It took years of planning. I saved cash so there wouldn't be a paper trail. I kept up the good-ole-boy front, so no one suspected me. When the time was perfect, I took back what was rightfully mine — Caroline. Now Father knows how it feels to lose the one person you truly love. And I protected my mother."

"What makes you think Ward will stay with your mother now?"

"With Caroline gone my father won't divorce Mother. He likes her money too much. Remember, he wouldn't leave Mother until Caroline had her trust. You see, he loves money more than anything."

"Your father must have been humiliated by your mother. She kept her millions as separate property," Royce said, desperate to keep him talking. What was taking Mitch so long? "I understand she doled out money a quarter at a time."

"Not to me," he answered with unmistakable pride. "She gave me anything I wanted. Most of the money to buy those drugs I had Linda Allen plant at your place came from Mother."

"But the forensic accountant didn't find any unusual withdrawals or deposits in anyone's accounts."

Brent chuckled, obviously pleased with himself. "I saved the money, asking Mother for a little at a time. Who knows how much a wealthy woman spends in pocket money? Do you think I was stupid enough to deposit it in a bank where the IRS — or anyone — would find it and ask questions?"

"No," Royce conceded. "You're too clever for that."

He grinned. "That's right. I outsmarted everyone."

Royce searched for something else to say. What was keeping Mitch? The telltale erection in Brent's trousers gave her an idea. If he were really excited, he'd put down the gun.

Her hands were tied to the corners of the bed. Royce shifted positions seductively — she hoped — splaying her breasts from side to side without being too coy, too obvious.

"Please," she whimpered, even though ten minutes ago she would have died before she begged him, "don't kill me."

"Be real nice to me and I may let you live" — he smiled that intimate smile that she knew from experience was a prelude to sex — "awhile longer." He lowered his head and licked the blood off her nipple. Circling the nub with his avaricious tongue, he coaxed it upright, then he closed his mouth over it, his head bent low.

The knife was in one hand, the gun in the other, but neither had his attention. Where was Mitch? Royce desperately looked toward the door. Relief flooded her when it moved a fraction of an inch. Mitch's head edged around the frame, and she sighed, a low moan deep in her throat. Brent took it for a sound of pleasure, for he looked up at her, his chin between her breasts and a triumphant smile on his face.

"You're so hot, Royce. So hot." He dropped the gun and plunged his hand between her thighs.

Mitch saw the gun fall onto the bed and he threw the condom full of heavy coins, hurling with all his might, aiming for Brent's head. The condom hit, breaking on impact, coins hailing down on the bed. Brent yelped and jumped back, but not before Royce kicked, catching him squarely between the thighs. He rolled onto his back, landing on the floor doubled up, but the knife still clenched in his hand.

Mitch charged into the room and pounced on Brent. Royce struggled, desperately trying to free herself, but her hands were still bound to the bed. She wiggled her fingers, clenching them together while Mitch battled Brent. They were rolling across the floor, Mitch grabbing for the knife, attempting to disarm Brent.

The heinous expression on Brent's face — a vision from hell — terrified Royce. He'd appeared shockingly normal, but he was over the brink now, his face contorted in a hideous combination of jealousy and hate.

She yanked hard, finally freeing her right hand. Grabbing the gun, she tried to remember what she knew about Glock automatics from a humorous column she'd done on guns. Lightweight plastic, the Glock had a seventeen-round clip. But was the safety off?

She frantically looked at the men rolling around the floor. She'd never fired a gun. Unless she had a clear shot, she might kill Mitch. *Keep your wits, Royce. Bluff.*

"Stop," she screeched, her voice high pitched, panicky. "I've got the gun. I'm going to shoot."

Her words didn't even faze them. Either of them. Brent was on top of Mitch now, high on his chest so Mitch couldn't knee him. The knife hovered too near Mitch's jugular.

Still Royce was afraid to shoot, terrified she'd hit the wrong man. She aimed the gun at the ceiling and squeezed the trigger. A flash of light flared out of the muzzle and instantaneously a soniclike boom filled the attic. The kick of the gun knocked her back against the headboard, wrenching the one arm still tied to the bedpost.

The shot got their attention. Brent hesitated and Mitch looked at her. She scrambled to an upright position and aimed the gun at Brent. "Get away from Mitch."

For a moment the only sound in the room was their harsh, breathless gasps for air. Slowly Brent rose to his knees, the knife still in his hand. "You'll have to kill me, Royce."

Brent faced Royce, an unholy calm about him.

537

Anger gathered like a tornado deep inside her. He was an inhuman monster who'd put her through hell. He'd murdered two women and would have killed her too. And Mitch.

She wanted to kill Brent, she truly did, but something stopped her. Out of the recesses of her mind surged the memory of her father and all he'd taught her. Peace and love.

She paused, her finger on the trigger. Could she kill? Why couldn't she hold him at bay until the police arrived? Brent must have sensed her hesitation. He smirked, a knowing grin from hell.

"Come on, Farenholt," Mitch said from his position behind Brent. "It's all over. Give up."

Brent smiled again at Royce and everything inside her went on full alert. "Mitch, watch out!"

Too late. Brent was already whirling around and plunging the deadly knife into Mitch's chest. Mitch slumped to the floor, doubled over.

Brent charged toward her, the bloody knife still in his hand. It was no longer a question of could she kill. It was survival. He was inches from her, the knife aimed for her heart. She squeezed the trigger and the report of the powerful gun flung her backward.

For a second the world went black, then her vision cleared and she realized how close he'd been when she'd fired. She was covered with blood and hair and bits of skin. Brent had collapsed at the foot of the bed, a gaping hole where his chest should have been.

"Mitch," she screamed, struggling to free the

hand still tied to the bed. He was lying limp in a rapidly widening pool of blood. If she didn't get help fast, he'd die. Perhaps he was already dead.

She scanned the room for the knife and saw the force of the shot had sent it flying to the other side. To get to it and cut herself free, she'd have to drag the bed behind her over both men's bodies.

"The window, Royce," she cried out loud. "It's closer."

She tugged, dragging the heavy daybed behind her, and managed to get close enough to the window to kick out the lower pane.

"Help," she screamed, battling the sobs erupting in her chest, hoping to get the attention of a neighbor or a passerby. "Call an ambulance — quick."

32

Paul drove into Royce's driveway and heard frantic screaming. Neighbors were rushing out of their houses, alarmed by the panicked cries. He slammed the car into park and jumped out, the motor still running, and charged around to the back of the house. Royce's head hung out the attic window.

"Mitch. He's dying. D-dying. Am-ambulance."

Paul had never run faster. He was back at his car in a second, the car phone in his hand. He dialed the SWAT team's number, instructing them to send an ambulance and their elite force.

Who knew where Brent Farenholt was? He was one of the most dangerous men that Paul had ever met. Handsome and charming, not unlike the serial killer Ted Bundy.

Jesus! How stupid can you be? he berated himself as he raced around to the back of the house. Brent had been the obvious choice — once you really thought about it. Royce was still screaming, over the edge now, hysterical.

"Where's Brent?" Paul yelled as he ran toward the back door.

"D-dead. Get Mitch help. Please."

"An ambulance is coming," he shouted, his shoulder to the back door. Ajar, it instantly swung wide. He was up the stairs and in the attic office without even knowing he'd left the kitchen.

Mitch's crumpled body was on the floor, surrounded by so much blood that Paul's heart caught in his throat. Could Mitch possibly be alive? Paul dropped down beside him, his knees slipping in the warm blood. He rolled Mitch onto his back and pressed both hands on his chest to stem the flow of blood.

Royce's voice was now too calm, the voice of someone in debilitating shock. "You can save him, can't you?"

"You bet." Paul forced a positive note into

his voice. The knife had come damn close to severing Mitch's aorta. He was alive — barely — but losing blood at such a rapid rate that anything Paul could do would be like trying to put out a five-alarm fire with spit.

He gazed down at Mitch and began to pray. His friend's face was the parched white cops knew only too well. Oh, God, don't take Mitch. He hasn't really had much of a life. He has so much to live for. So much to give.

Paul had never had a brother, not a blood relative anyway. But Mitch had always been like a brother. As Paul looked down, his hands still pushing on Mitch's chest, the hot blood trickling through his fingers, Paul realized he loved Mitch. And if he lost him, his life wouldn't be the same.

Oh, he loved Val with a deep, abiding love that he had thought he'd never experience. But, in an entirely different way, he loved Mitch too. They understood and respected each other. If Mitch died, part of Paul would go with him. Maybe the best part.

Mitch always challenged him to try more difficult cases and to look into new technology. No question about it, Mitchell Durant was a special person — particularly to Paul. For some reason he thought of a Louis L'Amour quote: "Sometimes the most important things in a man's life are the ones he talks about least."

Mitch didn't have to tell Paul about his past. He was his friend. He understood.

In the distance Paul heard the forlorn wail of

an ambulance, but he wasn't certain he still felt Mitch's heart beating. With a groan of utter despair he recalled Lolly Jenkins's words:

What am I going to do here alone without my baby?

A wellspring of sorrow so deep, he hadn't even known it existed rose up inside him. Now he understood exactly how Mitch's mother had felt. There were some people in your life, your parents, your wife — a close, dear friend — who were so special. You might genuinely mourn the loss of others, but there were certain people who were forever in your heart.

Their death took part of you, part of your soul.

Without that special person — like Mitch — life would go on, but it wouldn't be the same. There would always be something — someone special — missing. And you'd find yourself looking, searching, for someone to fill the void. Forever.

Royce's cuts had been bandaged and someone had given her clothes. The skirt was too big, corkscrewing around her legs as she rushed into the waiting room, but she didn't notice. She'd refused painkillers.

Mitch, she prayed, please let him live. His condition had been critical when the trauma team wheeled him into surgery.

"Royce." Val rushed up to her and gathered her into her arms. "I came as soon as I heard."

Over Val's shoulder Royce saw Paul. "How's Mitch?"

Paul said, "He's still in surgery. I just checked."

"That's a good sign." Val guided Royce to the sofa.

Royce sat between Val and Paul. Royce tried to listen to Val's soothing words, but all she could see was Mitch's near-lifeless body being put on the stretcher in her attic. At that point she'd become hysterical and screamed over and over for the paramedics to hurry.

She was calm, now, but every bit as terrified. What if he didn't make it? What if she never had the chance to tell him how much she loved him?

Now she knew exactly how her father had felt, how difficult it would be to face life alone — without the person you loved so dearly. Had Mitch forgiven her? Was that why he'd come to her home? Or had he come just because he was so intelligent that he'd decoded her message?

She slumped back against the vinyl sofa and closed her eyes — not because she was tired, she was running on pure adrenaline now, but because she wanted to remember Mitch the way he'd been.

The night he'd kissed her in the dark. Yes, oh, yes, that was the night that had changed her life forever, bringing her a love she'd only imagined existed. And she'd gone through hell to find it. Still, she wouldn't take back a single second of it. Getting to know him, coming to love him, had been worth the sorrow and the pain.

Please, God, let him live.

With her eyes closed she could almost feel his strong arms around her, the way he'd held her so many times, willing his strength into her. Be brave, she told herself, for him. But when another two hours passed and still there was no word, she began to tremble.

Finally a weary surgeon, his greens splattered with Mitch's blood, shuffled into the waiting room. "He made it through surgery. He's in intensive care right now. We'll know more by morning." He shook his head sadly. "If he makes it through the night."

"May I stay with him?" Royce asked.

It was totally unrealistic, but she had the notion that if she stayed with him she could will her strength, her courage, into him. And where did that inner source of power come from? Mitch. He'd given her strength when she'd needed it. Now it was her turn.

The surgeon led her into the intensive care unit. Mitch looked so helpless, lying flat on his back, his powerful body covered by a white sheet. An IV dripped a clear solution into his veins. Hanging beside it was a bag of blood, replenishing what he'd lost in surgery. And from the knife wound she could have prevented, if only she'd had the guts to shoot Brent when she'd first had the chance.

If she had, Mitch wouldn't be lying here now, a jumble of wires and tubes connecting him to a bank of beeping, blinking machines. Guardian angels, she tried to reassure herself. Mitch had the best electronic care. And a cadre of nurses going about their duties in white uniforms and shoes so cushioned that their steps couldn't be heard above the machines.

"Darling, I'm here," she said softly, although she knew he couldn't possibly hear her. The surgeon had explained Mitch was so heavily sedated that he wouldn't regain consciousness until morning.

If he lived through the night.

She kissed his forehead, then sat in the chair beside his bed, cradling his cold hand between both of hers. She longed to gather him in her arms and cuddle him until he was out of danger, but she had to be content with holding his hand, gently caressing his long fingers and planting kisses in the center of his palm.

"Mitch," she said, convinced some corner of his mind sensed her presence, her support, her love. "Don't give up. You can make it. I'm sorry for what I did. Believe me, I never meant to hurt you . . . or your mother. I've had a lot of time to think about your mother, and I have an idea."

She held his hand, talking to him all through the long night. Occasionally, the nurses interrupted to check on him, but mostly it was just Royce sharing with Mitch her vision of their future.

At six the doctor made his rounds. He spoke

with the head nurse and consulted Mitch's chart. Finally, he told Royce, "The entire surgical team tried our damnedest to save him. Not that we don't do our best for everyone, but knowing how close to death Mitchell Durant was bothered everyone. After your article we knew someone very special was in our care."

"Is he going to make it?"

"Yes, if he keeps progressing the way he has," the doctor admitted with a shake of his head that indicated he was mystified by Mitch's progress. "By living through the night he beat the odds. His recovery is going to be slow. It'll take a long time."

"Don't worry. I'll take care of him. I have all the time in the world for Mitch." She gazed fondly at him. His eyes were still closed, his lashes casting a crescent-shaped shadow across his pale skin.

A short while later she heard, "Royce."

The sound was so faint, she thought she'd imagined it, because Mitch's eyes were still closed. She watched his lips closely. Nothing. Then his lips parted and her name came out like a whisper on the wind. The sweet sound brought tears to her eyes.

Thank you, God.

She clutched his hand tightly. "I'm right here, darling." She leaned close to his good ear. "I'm never going to leave you."

His fingers lifted, searching for her hand. She slipped her hand into his and interlocked their fingers. Slowly, as if weighed down by sandbags, his eyelids fluttered open. His pupils were dilated from the drugs and had a slightly unfocused appearance. But she didn't care. They were the same deep marine-blue that she'd fallen in love with that day on the rock years ago.

She had to lean close to him to catch what he was saying. "Are you . . . all . . . right?"

"I'm fine." She kissed his cheek, so thrilled to hear his voice that tears sprang to her eyes. "Don't talk. Save your strength."

For once in the entire time she'd known Mitch, he did as he was told. It wasn't until several hours later that he opened his eyes and spoke again.

"Tell me what happened."

"It's my fault. I should have shot Brent when I had the chance. Then he wouldn't have turned on you."

Mitch's eyes were glazed, his voice only a notch above a whisper. "I remember the look on his face. . . ."

"Now we know what the devil looks like." She tried to sound upbeat.

"Is Brent . . ."

"I killed him the second I realized he'd stabbed you."

"Good." Mitch tried to smile. "You saved the taxpayers a bundle. Do you know what a murder trial costs these days?"

Royce laughed — or tried to. "Same old Mitch — a wiseguy. Now I know you're getting better."

"No way. I'm a goner unless you tell me you love me."

"Don't joke, Mitch, not now, not after all we've been through." She kissed his cheek and touched his thick hair where it brushed the pillow. "You know I love you. I'll always love you."

"I love you too. I want you to marry me as soon as I get out of here."

She inhaled sharply, not wanting to break the spell, but needing to tell him. "I'm sorry about your mother. I —"

"There's nothing to be sorry for. When I thought Brent was going to kill you, I blamed myself. If I hadn't been so stubborn, you would have been with me — where you belonged — and Brent couldn't have caught you alone. If I'd lost you —"

"But you didn't. We have the rest of our lives to spend together."

"Royce, I'll love you forever." He tugged on her arm until she brought her head down to his lips. She kissed him, too aware of how cool his lips were, a chilling reminder of how close she'd come to losing him forever.

Their lips parted and he whispered, "Never underestimate the power of love."

Epilogue

Eighteen Months Later

Royce walked down the hallway of the old Victorian home nestled in the gently undulating hills of the Napa Valley outside San Francisco. At the end of a secluded country lane between vineyards, the Grayson Clinic appeared to be a large private home, not the residential care facility it actually was. Dr. Reynolds Grayson and his staff took pride in making the patients feel as if they were living in their own home.

Pausing outside the parlor where Lolly Jenkins was waiting, Royce recalled the first time she'd visited Mitch's mother more than a year ago. Royce had been accompanied by the psychiatrist on that visit, and she had been extremely nervous, unsure of what to expect or what to say, but she had to show Lolly someone cared about her. And loved her. Since Mitch couldn't do it, Royce was doing it for him.

During that initial visit Lolly had been quiet, wary. Gradually, with weekly visits, Royce had won Lolly's trust. But now it had been five weeks since Royce had last visited Lolly.

549

Royce had explained many times she was having a baby and wouldn't be able to visit for a few weeks. But had the message gotten through? Despite Lolly's psychological improvement she was often confused about the passage of time. How would Lolly feel about the weeks Royce hadn't been able to visit?

Royce cradled her son to her bosom and walked into the sunny room with a smile. Lolly looked up, her clear blue eyes complemented by white hair softly framing her face.

"Lolly, it's me, Royce. Remember?"

"Of course, but what —" She pointed to the blue blanket covering Matthew Jenkins Durant.

"I had the baby." She held up her month old son. "Lolly, this is Matthew."

Matthew chose that moment to have a gas attack and he smiled, his captivating blue eyes looking just like his daddy's.

"So-o-o cute. Your baby. My, my, how beautiful he is."

Royce sat on the sofa beside Lolly. The older woman gazed fondly at the baby and Royce struggled to maintain her smile. Her thoughts veered to all Lolly had missed — a lifetime of happy memories. A loving family — what Royce now held so dear. Royce forced herself to focus on the present: Lolly was slowly improving.

Royce and Mitch hadn't deluded themselves into believing Lolly would ever be completely normal. She'd probably needed psychological help from the night of the auto accident that claimed both her parents when she'd been a mere child. Most certainly, she'd been denied the necessary counseling after the gang rape.

But she had improved. The psychiatrist treating Lolly agreed with Royce that Lolly would continue to progress with the support of a loving family.

Never underestimate the power of love.

Today would be the test of the cornerstone of Royce's plan, and she was just as nervous as she had been the first time she'd visited Lolly. As Mitch's mother gazed at the infant she didn't realize was her grandson, Royce prayed her idea would work — not just for Lolly, but for Mitch. She loved him so much, it actually hurt sometimes. She'd do anything on earth to make him happy. Oh, he swore he was happy, but Royce knew how much he longed to see his mother.

Was there anything more powerful than a mother's love? No, Royce decided, as she cuddled Matthew. A mother's love was sacred.

"Would you like to hold him?" she asked Lolly.

"Oh, yes." Lolly held out her arms.

Now comes the hard part. Royce waited a few minutes to be certain Lolly and Matt were comfortable with each other. Lolly had the baby resting in her arms and was cooing to him. "Matthew's father is waiting outside. He'd like to meet you."

"Me?" Lolly asked in that faraway voice that meant she wasn't really concentrating. "Me? Someone wants to meet me?"

A spasm of doubt shook Royce. Was Lolly ready to see her son again? Was it too soon?

"Your husband, right?" Now Lolly's gaze was clear, totally lucid.

"Yes. He's just outside."

"Have him come in." Lolly smiled down at Matt. "I'm going to meet your daddy."

Royce stood, mentally crossing her fingers. This had to work. "Hold on tight to Matt. I'll be right back."

Mitch managed a smile when Royce came to the door and told him to come in. He loved her more than he could express, more than he'd thought possible. And together they'd created a miracle — a son.

He walked behind Royce into the parlor and saw his mother for the first time in over twenty years. The last time he'd seen her, she'd come after him with a garden trowel, nearly blinding him. She'd aged, her hair now white, but her face, a delicate oval with expressive eyes, remained the same. She didn't seem aware of them; she was too busy cooing to his son.

He whispered to Royce, "Thank you. This means the world to me — just seeing my mother with Matt."

Lolly kissed the baby's head where a single tuft of black hair grazed his forehead. Royce tugged on Mitch's hand, silently urging him forward.

"Lolly, this is Matthew's father, Mitchell Durant."

Mitch quickly sat in the chair the psychiatrist had positioned opposite the sofa, insisting tall men were less threatening when seated. Lolly clutched the baby, regarding Mitch without a flicker of recognition.

"Hello." Mitch suppressed a sigh of relief. Royce's plan had worked. With his phony mustache and his gray wig and thick glasses, he scarcely recognized himself. For damn sure he didn't look a thing like his father.

"Hullo," Lolly responded tentatively, eyeing him with suspicion and cradling the baby to her generous bosom as if she expected Mitch to snatch up the infant and toss him out the window. She turned to Royce, who'd sat beside her, and spoke as if Mitch weren't there. "Isn't he too old for you?"

Royce smiled at Mitch, silently telegraphing the first hurdle was over. "He's younger than he looks."

Mitch didn't say anything. The psychiatrist had cautioned them to take small steps. For today his mother's acceptance of him in the same room was enough to make him happy. Once he could never have conceived of having all the people he loved so much in the same room. Smiling. Happy.

Was it any wonder he'd fallen so deeply in love with Royce? This miracle had been her idea. She'd worked hard for over a year to make his dream come true.

"Mitch is a judge," Royce informed Lolly.

"That so?" Lolly gazed at him curiously. "Like Judge Wapner?"

"Something like that," Mitch answered, pleased his mother had directed the question to him. She'd spent so much of her life away from the world that her image of reality had been honed by television. No doubt her concept of a trial was the arguments that normally would have been settled in small claims courts but had been pumped up into soap-opera proportions for Judge Wapner on *The People's Court*.

"What was your most exciting case?" Lolly asked.

Mitch hesitated. In his short time on the bench he'd heard the usually depressing array of drug cases, a murder too gruesome to think about, and a child molestation case he couldn't possibly discuss.

Royce rescued him. "Mitch once saved a cougar."

"Really? What happened?"

As his son slept in his grandmother's arms, Mitch told Lolly about the cougar who'd attacked the turkey hunter. He slowly explained the case, keeping it exciting, but let his mother become accustomed to his face, his voice.

"That so?" Lolly cried, clapping her hands. "The cougar's still free. My, my."

Mitch had never viewed the cougar as one of his best cases, but what the hell? Justice was in the eye of the beholder.

Too soon a nurse dressed casually in jeans in

the noninstitutional attire all of the staff wore, called his mother in to lunch. The doctor had insisted Mitch's first visit be short, but this was too short. Still, he couldn't complain. They'd gotten much further with Lolly than any of them had thought possible.

"Good-bye," Mitch said.

Lolly clutched Royce's arm. "When are you coming back?"

"Would you like me to bring Mitch and the baby next week?"

Lolly looked shyly at Mitch. "Yes. I like those funny stories."

"We'll come next Saturday," Mitch promised. He stood, his arm around Royce, as his mother left, saying good-bye.

"Thanks," Mitch said quietly as Lolly disappeared.

"It's going to be all right," Royce said. "You'll see. This is only the beginning."

"I've waited so long for this day. I can't tell you how much I appreciate what you've done except to say, I love you." He kissed her lightly on the cheek, then patted his son's little bottom. "I love you both — more than I can say."

"I love —" Royce stopped.

Mitch turned, his arm still around Royce, and saw his mother rushing back into the room.

"Royce, wait," she said. "I forgot to tell you something."

Lolly stopped before them, her eyes on Matthew. He was fussing a little, reminding Royce it was time to nurse. The mewling cries side-tracked Lolly. She cooed to the baby and brushed a kiss across his plump cheek.

"Lolly," Royce prompted, "what did you want to tell me?"

Lolly looked first at Royce, then at Mitch, and finally back at the baby. "Once, a long, long time ago in a place far away, I had a baby." Tears pooled in Lolly's eyes. It was all Mitch could do not to take her into his arms and hug her.

"But they took my darling little boy away from me. Said I wasn't a fit mother. It wasn't true. Believe me, I loved Bobby. I've never forgotten him. He is the most precious thing in the world to me."

The employees of G.K. HALL hope you have enjoyed this Large Print book. All our Large Print titles are designed for easy reading, and all our books are made to last. Other G.K. Hall Large Print books are available at your library, through selected bookstores, or directly from us. For more information about current and up-coming titles, please call or mail your name and address to:

G.K. HALL
PO Box 159
Thorndike, Maine 04986
800/223-6121
207/948-2962